## PAID IN PASSION

"Now that I have returned your precious letter," said the Indian, "I would like a reward."

"But I've forgotten to bring any money," Erica answered.

"I don't want the white man's money," Viper replied. He paused, looking intently at the slender blonde's flawless features. "What I demand is a kiss."

The Sioux savage didn't wait for Erica to argue. He merely slipped his arms around her tiny waist and pulled her close, lowering his mouth to hers.

Taken by surprise, the lovely innocent couldn't think of what to do with her hands. First she placed them on his broad shoulders, then on his bronze chest, then, as his lips continued to caress hers, she wound her arms around his neck and lost herself in the magic of his affection.

Suddenly the sharp cry of a scolding crow brought the passionate beauty to her senses. Stepping back she whispered, "You must go!"

"Yes," he whispered fervently. "I must go where you go!" And deepening his kiss, he laid her on a bed of pine needles and swept them both up in a storm of desire neither had the power to control. . . .

# TENDER SAVAGE

## PHOEBE CONN

**ZEBRA BOOKS**
**KENSINGTON PUBLISHING CORP.**

ZEBRA BOOKS

are published by

Kensington Publishing Corp.
475 Park Avenue South
New York, NY 10016

First printing: February, 1989

Printed in the United States of America

## Dedication

*I would like to dedicate this book to the valiant spirit of the American Indian, and to all of us who proudly claim to share that magnificent heritage.*

## Acknowledgment

The excellent research materials available from the Minnesota Historical Society proved to be a valuable resource for this book. Their publications allowed me to create a work of fiction firmly based on fact, and for that wonderful assistance they have my sincere gratitude.

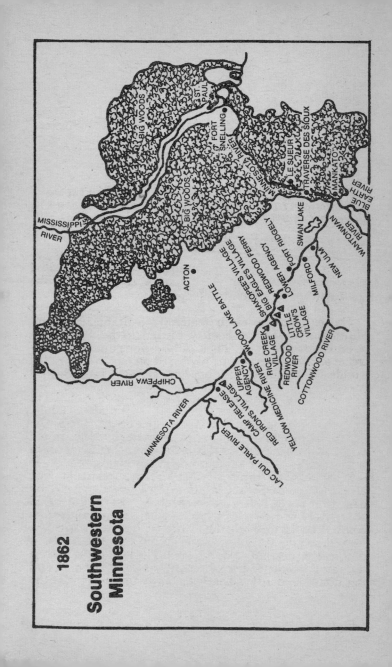

1862
Southwestern
Minnesota

# Prologue

## June 1862

Mark wound his fingers in Erica's glossy blond curls to hold her mouth fast to his as he deepened his kiss. He loved her with a passion that made his soul sing, and that she returned his enthusiastic affection with such unabashed delight was a source of endless joy and wonder. The lithe beauty lay in an enticing pose, reclining across his lap amid a heap of lavender silk and frilly sachet-scented lace. Although they were seated upon a velvet settee in her parlor, he had no fears her father would suddenly enter the room to spoil the beauty of the moment by angrily accusing him of leading his lovely daughter astray. The hour had grown quite late, but Lars Hanson trusted him completely with his beautiful daughter. Ashamed at how far he had led her this time, Mark pulled away. "Erica," he began, his deep voice hoarse with desire, but she simply pulled him back into her arms to claim his heart anew with another of her wild and delicious kisses.

Erica knew instinctively what Mark had wanted to say, and since it was the very last thing she wished to hear, she gave him no opportunity to speak it. Her tongue toyed seductively with his, insuring his silence as her fingertips combed lazily through the tawny curls at his nape. She longed to take their love for each other to the limits of physical expression, and that he still refused to do so both hurt and maddened her. She wanted him, all of him, and the desire that filled her heart gave her sweet kiss the

7

intoxicating flavor of fine wine. When he again drew away, she was disappointed her ploy had failed and began her argument in a breathless whisper before he could restate his.

"We still have a week before you have to report for duty, Mark. Why don't we wake the priest and get married tonight? When you insist you want me for your wife, how can you bear to wait another minute to make that dream come true?"

Mark Randall took a deep breath and let it out slowly, hoping to clear his mind, but the aching need Erica's lavish kisses had aroused within him still throbbed painfully in his loins, providing a terrible distraction to coherent thought. "More than anything in this world I want to make you my bride, Erica, but not yet, not until the war is over and won."

Thoroughly exasperated by Mark's continual refusal to see reason, Erica slid off his lap. Taking a step away from the small sofa, she began to pace restlessly, her gestures filled with the fury of her mood while her tone remained very much that of a lady: soft and sweet. "If we were married, then you'd have a home to which to return at the war's end, and possibly a family. We have a week, Mark, don't throw it away when there's the chance we can create a child we'd both love dearly."

Mark's admiration shone in his smile as the graceful blonde turned toward him, for he was certain she was the loveliest woman ever born. Even with her fair curls falling about her shoulders in casual disarray she had a more vibrant beauty than he had ever seen in another woman. Her eyes, the deep blue of plush velvet were framed by long, dark lashes, and her skin had the luscious pink blush of peaches and cream. Her features were delicate, and yet so wonderfully expressive he could not fail to see how badly she wanted him to agree to her request. Holding out his hands, he tried to coax her back into his arms, but she remained proudly aloof and he had to respond with words.

"Erica, you are barely seventeen, and while marrying so hurriedly might sound wonderfully romantic to you, I'll not risk leaving you alone and pregnant. It is precisely because I love you so much that our marriage will have to wait. I'll not take the chance of making you a widow, or

8

worse yet, seeing you tied to an invalid for the rest of your life. The conflict with the South can't last much longer. Truly it can't."

"It has gone on for more than a year already!" Erica reminded him with a defiant toss of her disheveled curls. He frequently called her too headstrong for her own good, but their marriage was too important an issue for her not to defend it as aggressively as she possibly could.

Mark nodded sadly. "That's true, and a lot of brave men won't be coming home no matter when it ends. I want only to spare you that grief."

Erica stared at her fiancé in angry disbelief. "How can you imagine my grief would be any the less deep if you were not my husband? If you were to suffer the slightest injury I would be heartbroken but I'd never stop loving you. If the war left you an invalid, I'd still want to be your wife. You aren't protecting me from sorrow by insisting we not marry until peace is declared. You are only causing me needless grief now!"

Since Erica hadn't returned to his embrace on her own, Mark rose and went to her. He slipped his arms around her narrow waist and drew her close. "Thank you for swearing to love me no matter what happens, but one day you will thank me for being so cautious, Erica, I'm sure of it."

"I'll never be grateful to you for denying us this chance at happiness, Mark, never!" Erica placed her hands upon his broad chest to shove him away, but he was far too strong a young man to be bothered by even her mightiest efforts to elude his grasp. When she looked up at him, ready to scream in frustration, he lowered his head and captured her mouth in a searing kiss that left her clinging to him when he finally drew away. But still she would not give in. "I'll not change my mind, Mark. I want to marry you now, or tomorrow morning if you'll not agree to having the ceremony tonight."

Mark stood with the slender beauty enfolded in his embrace. He could rest his chin quite comfortably upon the top of her head and did so as he talked to her in the most soothing tone he could manage. "Your father's plan is the best, my love. With both of us leaving Wilmington next week, you'll be far better off in Minnesota than here in Delaware. Your mother's people are already expecting you, and I'm certain you'll find New Ulm a charming community."

"It can't possibly have even an ounce of charm when you won't be there with me," Erica insisted darkly. "I am old enough to be married and run my own household instead of being shipped off to live with relatives as though I were some pathetic little orphan who is incapable of taking care of herself."

It took a long moment for Mark to think of an optimistic way to refute that sorry opinion, since he was convinced Lars Hanson's motives for joining the army were self-destructive rather than noble like his own. The man was a physician who had once been popular and widely respected, but since the death of his wife two winters past he had shown scant interest in his lovely daughter and even less in the other people who touched his life. Indeed, Mark had always feared the primary reason Erica loved him so desperately was because she had an extremely affectionate nature and craved the attention her mother could no longer provide and her father was too lost in his own sorrow to notice she needed. Emotionally abandoned by her only parent, she seemed already to feel like an orphan, and he was afraid she would soon actually be one, for more than one physician had lost his life while tending the wounded on the front lines.

"You mustn't fear the future, Erica. Someday soon we'll be able to make our life together, and I promise you it will be a happy one," he finally said.

He had relaxed sufficiently for the lively blonde to move back a step, and as she slipped from his arms she asked a probing question. "If you are positive our life together will be wonderfully happy, why won't you agree to begin it now?"

"Because I love you enough to want to wait," Mark reminded her softly, not taking the bait to begin their argument anew.

Erica smoothed out the folds of her full skirt so the whisper-soft fabric would fall in a graceful cascade over the hooped petticoat. But she knew it was wasted effort to be concerned about her appearance when her father wouldn't be awake to wish her a goodnight. He had gone up to his room right after supper with the bottle of brandy

10

that seldom left his side. Knowing no matter what they did her father would undoubtedly be too sound asleep to overhear, she suggested the only alternative she had left. "If you won't marry me, will you at least make love to me?"

Mark was so shocked by that provocative invitation that he simply stared at the persistent young woman until he finally realized she was serious. "Dear God in heaven, Erica. What are you trying to do to me, simply tear me apart?"

Feeling surprisingly calm, the lovely blonde explained what she wanted. "Since you won't give me your name, won't you at least give me your love? My father seldom awakens before noon, and our housekeeper left for her own home after supper. We can spend the night together in my room and no one need ever know. It will be our secret."

Mark swallowed hard, unable to catch his breath for a moment. Here was the beautiful young woman he adored asking politely if he would make love to her, and he knew the only honorable answer was a firm no. It took more willpower than he had thought he possessed to say it, though. "If you got pregnant it wouldn't be our secret for long, Erica and you would be in twice the trouble you would be in if we were married. I love you with all my heart, but we'll have to wait until after we're married to make love."

"And you'll not marry me until the war is over, no matter how many years it takes, will you?" Erica complained as her midnight-blue eyes filled with tears. She knew a lady should never ask a gentleman to make love to her, let alone beg for affection as she just had, but it was not her own boldness that appalled her but the fact that Mark had turned her down. She thought him incredibly handsome. He was tall and well-built, with curly light brown hair that the sun had kissed with golden highlights and warm brown eyes that were always filled with a loving glow. He was also so incredibly stubborn she didn't think she could bear to see him again before he left to become a lieutenant in the Union Army.

"I want you to go on home, and don't bother to come back until you're ready to bring the priest with you. I can't

11

face another night like this one where you've kissed me as though I'm your woman one minute and then treated me as though I'm still a child who must be shielded from all possible adversity in the next."

"Erica, please don't say that. Don't even think it," Mark begged. "I want to see you every chance I have. Tomorrow we can spend the whole day together if you like. We could go riding or go on a picnic, or—"

"What's the point, when the evening would end with this same pathetic scene? I want to enjoy every last moment of today and hope for the best from tomorrow, while you're determined the worst is going to happen to us both. You're making me feel as though I were already a widow, only I have no beautiful memories of a happy marriage. You know the way out," Erica sobbed as she raised her hand to muffle the sound of her tears. No longer able to argue, or to bear the confusion of his glance, she fled from the room and dashed up the stairs, hoping Mark would finally feel every bit as lost and alone as she did.

For the briefest of instants Mark considered pursuing her, but he knew he couldn't trust himself to keep his passions in check should they continue their argument in her bedroom since he could barely control his emotions in the parlor. "Damn it all, but you are still a child at times, Erica!" he muttered under his breath as he let himself out the front door. He knew he had made the right choice. As a man who prided himself upon being a gentleman, he was positive of that fact, but he had never imagined his decision to postpone their wedding would hurt Erica so terribly, and her sorrow touched him deeply.

When he returned to the Hanson home late the next morning, Mark held a large bouquet of colorful spring flowers. His sister, Sarah, had packed a scrumptious lunch in the picnic basket he had left in the buggy, and he was confident that with a wily combination of humor and charm he could coax Erica into spending the day with him no matter how furious her mood had been when they had parted. When her father opened the door, he greeted him warmly. "Good morning, Dr. Hanson. Will you please tell Erica I've come to see her?"

Lars was dismayed by that request, but nevertheless invited the young man to step inside. In preparation for his departure he had already closed the office he had had in his home and referred his patients to other physicians, so he had plenty of time to talk. Not yet forty, he was blond and blue-eyed like his daughter. They resembled each other only in coloring, however, for Erica had inherited her mother's sweet features rather than her father's handsome but decidedly masculine appearance. Embarrassed by what he would have to say, Lars nonetheless knew he had been cold sober that morning and that he could repeat his conversation with his daughter verbatim should Mark demand that he do so.

"Erica left for Minnesota on the morning train. She told me you two had said your good-byes last night, since she simply couldn't bear to wait until you and I had left town to begin her trip." When his visitor did no more than gawk at him in stunned silence, Lars continued, "She had her trunk all packed and woke me up in plenty of time to take her to the station. We stopped by the church to put some flowers on Eva's grave on our way. She seemed pretty upset, but I thought that was just because she was so worried about us. Well, worried about you mostly, I guess," Lars admitted with a faint trace of the grin his beloved wife had adored. 'I was surprised you didn't come down to the station to see her off, too."

Mark couldn't believe Erica had left him without even saying good-bye. They had had plenty of arguments of late, and all on the same subject, but he had never dreamed she would just up and leave town. She had always been high-spirited, but it wasn't like her to be so impulsive. Then he understood. She had obviously felt that by joining the army he was deserting her, so she had just beat him to it. She was a clever girl and her ploy had certainly worked. For the first time he felt the pain his coolly logical approach to the future had surely caused her. It hurt, and badly. He looked down at the bunch of bright blossoms he had wanted to give her and suddenly felt very foolish.

"Erica didn't even tell me goodnight, let alone good-bye, Dr. Hanson. Would you please give me her aunt and uncle's address so I can write to her?"

"What? I thought you two were engaged, or at least that was the impression you gave me last night at supper." Lars knew he had been less than an attentive host, but he was certain he would have noticed had the couple not been their usual affectionate selves. "Have you called it off?"

"No, sir, I still plan to marry your daughter. Our only argument was over when the wedding would be."

"Well, apparently it wasn't soon enough to suit her. You've got a fine horse, you could catch up to the train if you tried," Lars suggested helpfully.

"Yes, sir. I might be able to overtake the train, but that would be pointless since I haven't changed my mind, and it's plain Erica isn't about to change hers, either."

Lars regarded the earnest young man with a thoughtful glance before finally offering what he hoped was sound advice. "I've lost my Eva and there's no way I can get her back, but you're a damn fool if you let Erica go like this. As I told you, she was thoroughly miserable, but I misunderstood why."

"It can't be helped," Mark insisted sullenly. "Now may I please have that address?"

"Of course, but what can you say in a letter that you couldn't say better in person?"

Mark was sorely tempted to smack Lars right across the face with his handful of flowers but managed to restrain himself at the last moment. "Just give me the address, please, Dr. Hanson. I'll worry about what goes in the letter later."

Lars still wore a disapproving frown as he returned from his desk, but he handed over the address without further comment.

"I'll see you next week when we have to report, if not before," Mark called over his shoulder as he started out the door. He heard Lars mumble some sort of a farewell but walked straight to his buggy without turning back to wave.

Thinking the flowers too pretty to waste he drove to the church and laid them beside those Erica had placed on her mother's grave. Standing where he knew the pretty blonde must have stood earlier that morning, he prayed the war would soon be over and that the promises he had made her would swiftly come true.

# Chapter One

## July 1862

There were almost nine hundred people living in New Ulm, and by her third week in the city Erica was certain she had met every one. Located in southwestern Minnesota on the Minnesota River just north of the junction with the Cottonwood River, the city had been founded in the mid 1850s by German colonization societies from Chicago and Cincinnati. Her mother's younger sister, Britta, had married a German merchant who had done quite well for himself with a dry goods store there. While Erica had always enjoyed reading letters from her Aunt Britta and Uncle Karl, she had not met them or their sixteen-year-old son, Gunter, until the steamboat she boarded in St. Paul arrived at the docks of New Ulm.

Since it was no fault of theirs that she was so unhappy to be with them, Erica hid her heartbreak behind a façade of lighthearted charm. She did not describe how deeply her father still grieved for her mother, nor did she mention the fact that she had a fiancé, let alone the abrupt manner in which she had left him. That omission posed problems almost immediately, for the few bachelors who had not departed New Ulm to fight in the Civil War began to pursue her with an enthusiasm she found difficult to discourage politely. Unfortunately, they mistook her lack of interest for shyness and redoubled their efforts to impress her favorably.

In an effort to repay her relatives' hospitality, although they did not ask her to do so, Erica spent each morning working in their store. She had kept her father's accounts since her mother's death and found it a simple matter to apply her mathematical skills to the dry goods business.

15

She had quickly discarded her hooped petticoat in order to move more easily behind the counters, but her pretty gowns were still the envy of all their female customers as well as being greatly admired by the males. While she had never sewn more than a stitch or two herself, she was frequently called upon to provide advice on fine fabrics and the latest styles. Much to her aunt and uncle's delight, she swiftly produced a sizable increase in sales in all manner of fabrics and lace.

While she was far from content, Erica took pride in the fact that she was at least being useful. Like everyone else, she followed the news of the war, hoping daily to hear it had drawn to an end. When a letter arrived from Mark, she shoved it into her apron pocket, but the minute she could leave the store to read it in private she did so.

The thriving town of New Ulm was built upon two gently sloping terraces backed by a bluff rising some two hundred feet above the level of the river. Rather than turn in the direction of her aunt and uncle's home, Erica instead chose to walk down to the river. Having lived on the Delaware River all her life, she felt a far greater kinship with the water than she did with the people of New Ulm, and she often went for walks along the riverbank in the afternoon. The day was quite warm, but the woods at the water's edge offered an inviting coolness and she walked for a long way before finally choosing a comfortably shady spot to sit down and read Mark's letter.

Even after she had slit open the buff-colored envelope, Erica hesitated to remove the two neatly penned sheets of stationery. Tears filled her eyes, for all she truly wished to read was Mark's urgent plea that she return home to become his wife. Thinking herself impossibly foolish for harboring that hope, she finally forced herself to read what Mark had actually written.

While she did not suspect how many letters the level-headed young man had penned before mailing this one, Erica found its stilted tone deeply disappointing. Mark had not sent a reassuring declaration of love but instead a factual account of his first week in the army. If he were angry with the way she had left him, he did not mention it. He said he hoped she was happy and asked her to write to him soon.

Erica must have read the friendly letter a dozen times

before giving up all hope of finding something suggested between the lines that Mark had failed to state in words. Apparently he felt not a shred of remorse for refusing the love she had offered so eagerly. Her cheeks filled with a bright blush of shame at that memory and she quickly stuffed the letter back into its envelope. She would write an answer, that much was certain, but she knew she dared not say what was truly in her heart, as he had already heard that and disregarded it too many times to repeat.

Frustrated that their weeks apart had done so little to aid her cause, she tarried there at the river's edge, so lost in dark thoughts that she did not see the Indian who had entered the water to bathe only a few yards downstream until he began to splash about noisily. Then, fearing the man would find her presence objectionable, she sat very still and prayed he would soon finish his bathing and be on his way. Her dress was a soft blue and blended into the shadows provided by the overhanging canopy of leaves from the elm tree at her back, and she thought if she sat very still she had a good chance of going unnoticed.

Erica had had scant opportunity to observe Indians, and had not realized any lived so near the town. Despite her silent pleas that the man would be swiftly on his way, he was not simply bathing, but flinging water about with a flamboyant exuberance that astonished her. He was a muscular individual and appeared to be quite tall from what she could judge from his sleek proportions. His hair was so long it brushed his shoulder blades, and its deep ebony color reflected the same iridescent highlights as a raven's wing.

She knew she shouldn't be watcing the man, but since she had unintentionally violated the privacy he obviously thought he had, she was simply embarrassed rather than guilt-ridden. When he at last turned toward her, his glance was still focused upon the water but what she could see of his features beneath the flying spray of water and swirling cloud of black hair looked remarkably handsome. Her interest piqued, she gave no further thought to the fact that he would not appreciate her gaze be it openly admiring or not. The setting was idyllic, and she continued to watch him cavort about like a playful child, wondering if Eve might not have also observed Adam in such an unguarded moment. It was not until the man started to walk

17

out of the river that her innocent appreciation of him came to an abrupt end.

Water dripped from the Indian's thick mane of hair down over his broad shoulders and chest, following the contours of his powerful frame to form a central rivulet that slid past the taut muscles of his flat stomach and was lost in the dense curls which framed his manhood. Her attention now squarely focused where she was positive it shouldn't be, Erica realized the full extent of her folly. The daughter of a physician, she had satisfied her curiosity about male anatomy at an early age by simply consulting her father's medical texts. This man was a superb specimen in all respects, but she knew she should have had the sense to flee the spot while he was too far out in the river to give chase.

She had merely stepped off the path before sitting down, and Erica suddenly realized that, once dressed, the Indian might walk right by her. Since he couldn't fail to see her then, and know exactly how much she had seen, she dared not remain there a moment longer. Hoping he would pay as close attention to getting dressed as he had to bathing, she waited until he had put one leg in his buckskins before rising stealthily to her feet. When he did not look up, she breathed a sigh of relief, but as she took her first step toward the path she heard the loud snap of a dry twig and froze, praying the Indian hadn't heard the sound over the constant churning roar of the river. Then she heard an angry shout, and certain she would never be able to out-run the man and knowing she would simply have to bluff her way out of a most unfortunate situation, she turned around slowly to face him.

The Indian was not simply annoyed to find he had not been alone at the river's edge. He was livid. After fastening his belt buckle to secure his loose-fitting fringed pants, he drew his knife and covered the distance between them in a near flying sprint. Stopping within inches of her, he greeted Erica with a wicked snarl: "Have you seen enough, or should I come closer still?"

In Erica's opinion he was already standing much too close, but as she tried to move back she tripped over the hem of her gown, which without its hoop was several inches too long. She was forced then to reach out toward the Indian rather than fall, but had she not grasped his

18

wrist tightly to regain her balance, she would most surely have landed in the leaves at their feet, for he made not the slightest effort to catch her.

Mistakenly thinking the woman was making a desperate lunge for his knife, the well-built young man drew back his left hand intending to slap her aside. But Erica released her hold upon him before he could strike that intended blow. He was more puzzled than before, for he had never heard of an Indian brave's being attacked by an unharmed white woman, and he would not spread the tale that he had been the first.

That the Indian had come so close to striking her alarmed Erica all the more, and she raised her hands slightly to show she meant him no harm. Since the oaf at least spoke English, she tried to reason with him in a frantic whisper. "Please, put away that knife, and I'm sure we can settle this misunderstanding without either of us getting hurt."

The Indian's frown deepened, for he thought her daft to threaten him. "How could you possibly hurt me?" he asked with a currish sneer.

"I've no wish to hurt you! Certainly not," Erica assured him. Encouraged when he merely stared in response, she rushed on with what she prayed would be an adequate excuse to permit her to quickly escape him. Gesturing toward the elm tree where she had been sitting, she continued, "I'd been seated there for some time, perhaps an hour, before you entered the water. Rather than embarrass either of us I tried to slip away but—"

Apparently at least partially swayed by her explanation, the Indian slid his knife back into the beaded sheath at his belt, but he then folded his arms across his bare chest and continued to stare down at her with a threatening gaze. Each year the valley teemed with more of her despicable kind, but that he could not even wash without being spied upon disgusted him so deeply that he had no intention of allowing her to go until he had frightened her so thoroughly she would never again venture into the part of the forest he considered his own. "Why did you wait so long to leave?" he asked with a taunting grin. "Do savages fascinate you?"

Erica swallowed nervously, thinking the man's point well taken, for she had obviously waited much too long to

19

take her leave. She shrugged helplessly, hoping he would believe the truth. "Well, you must admit you were putting on quite a performance. You weren't bathing, nor swimming, but almost dancing in the water. Had anyone else been here they would have undoubtedly been as intrigued as I was." When he didn't laugh in her face for that remark, she seized what she hoped was becoming the advantage. "Had you taken the time to look around you would have seen me and gone elsewhere to do whatever it was you were doing. This is really your fault, not mine," she insisted proudly.

"My fault!" the Indian shouted in a hoarse gasp. He raked his fingers through his still dripping hair to push it out of his eyes and called her a name he could not equal for foulness in English.

"Yes, your fault, and whatever it is you just called me I'm certain you are far worse!" Erica turned away, thinking she would be able to just walk off, but the man reached out to catch her shoulder with such force that he easily spun her back around to face him.

She had spirit, and he admired that, but the Indian would allow no woman to turn her back on him in the midst of an argument. "You must apologize," he commanded firmly.

Appalled by that demand, Erica straightened her shoulders and lifted her chin defiantly. "For what? For being here first?"

"You know why," the man replied coldly.

Erica clenched her fists at her sides. She had done her best to fit in in New Ulm, which was the very last place she wanted to be. Her life was so far from the one she wished to be living that she dreaded each new dawn, and now she had absolutely no desire to spend the rest of the afternoon arguing with some ill-mannered Indian. "All right, I am sorry I interrupted your privacy, but you had intruded upon mine first!"

While many of the German immigrants who populated New Ulm were fair haired, he had not seen any woman so blond as this one. Her curls reflected the sunlight with the sparkle of new-fallen snow, and her eyes were more blue than the river for which the state was named. Her nose had a slight upward turn, imparting a saucy air to all her expressions. Her lips had a delectable rose hue and the inviting shape of a bow, but he did not like any of the words that poured from them. "You do not belong here. I do."

It had not occurred to Erica that she might be trespassing upon the Indian's land, and she hurriedly looked around for some sign of a house or cultivated gardens but saw none. "The Sioux reservation is much further up the river, isn't it?"

The Indian made an obviously derogatory response in his own language before replying in English. "I am not an animal who can be kept in a pen. I go where I please."

"Well, it just so happens that I also have that privilege, and if you'll excuse me I'll be going on home now." This time Erica hesitated a moment to be certain he would have no objection to her leaving in hopes of avoiding another bone-jarring blow to her shoulder.

"As soon as you apologize to me you may go," the Indian replied calmly.

"I already did apologize," Erica reminded him.

"No, that was no apology."

The man had relaxed sufficiently for his features to assume the more carefree expression she had glimpsed briefly in the water. No longer appearing so menacing, he wasn't merely good-looking but extraordinarily handsome. His skin was a warm bronze. His features were even and strong, and his teeth were a sparkling white she was certain would lend a heady masculine magic to his smile, if he were ever happy enough to smile. His brows and lashes were as black as his free-flowing hair, but his eyes were gray, not brown. When he had first come running up to her they had glowed with the same evil light as the polished steel of his blade, but now both his glance and stance had softened. The color of his eyes struck her as being odd, but she knew so little about Indians she had no idea what color his eyes should be.

The woman was regarding him with an open curiosity that the Indian found most offensive, and he urged her to speak her apology and be gone. "Your dress is very fine. Do you not have the manners to match it? Surely you can apologize to me without insulting me at the same time."

"You needn't have drawn a knife on me," Erica pointed out accusingly. "That scarcely showed any manners."

"You should be grateful I did not use it," the man responded sullenly.

Erica doubted respectable white women did much apologizing to Indian braves, but since the man was such an obstinent sort, she feared she might never get home if she didn't let him have his way. What possible difference did it make? she asked herself. They would probably never meet again. She picked up her skirt to be certain she would not trip a second time as she gave him the most sincere apology she could bear to speak. "I haven't been in New Ulm long, and I'll make a point of staying close to town in the future. I'm sorry we met under such unfortunate circumstances, but you can be certain I'll avoid this part of the river in the future."

The merest shadow of a frown passed over the Indian's finely chiseled features before he dismissed her with a curt nod and turned away. He went back to where he had left his belongings and when he glanced back over his shoulder, Erica was gone.

Holding her skirts well above her toes, Erica ran all the way back to the steamboat landing before adopting a more sedate pace. When she reached her aunt and uncle's home, she found her cousin seated upon the front steps attempting to whittle a small horse out of a block of wood. He was a strapping lad who towered above her in stature, but he always treated her with a respect bordering upon awe. She stopped in front of him.

"Hello, Gunter, what are you making?"

"It was to be a horse, but it looks more like a mule, I'm afraid," the boy admitted self-consciously. He had inherited his mother's fair coloring and finely shaped features, but the fact that he would one day be a remarkably handsome man had as yet escaped his notice.

"Call it a mule then, and no one will know what it was you intended." Encouraged by the warmth of his smile, Erica dashed on by him and ran up the stairs to her room. The homes in New Ulm were all remarkably similar: two-story frame houses with dormer windows in the attic bedrooms. She had been given the guestroom on the second floor. As she sat down at the desk, ready to begin a reply to Mark she suddenly realized she had lost his letter.

"Oh no!" Erica leaped to her feet and shook out her skirt before reaching into her pockets. She left her apron on its hook at the store and carried the letter in her hand when she left there, but what had she done with it when she had gotten up from beneath the tree in her futile attempt to escape the Indian? It had been in her hand then, too, she was certain of it. She feared she had dropped it when she had grabbed the man's arm to keep from falling. It had been insanity to reach out to him, she thought now, since she could so easily have cut herself on his knife.

Erica slipped back down into her chair, her expression forlorn. She would have no choice but to go back and look for the letter, but it was too late to go again that day. She had told the Indian the truth: she never wanted to stumble across his path ever again. Now she would have to go right back to his part of the forest the very next day. She folded her arms upon the desk and rested her cheek upon them. If she didn't find the letter she would have no way to send Mark a reply. He might think she no longer cared—especially after the way she had left him.

During supper, Erica's mind wandered so often to that afternoon's confrontation that she finally decided she ought to learn something about the Sioux reservations without giving away the fact that she had actually met an Indian brave. Since her uncle was so knowledgeable, she spoke to him about it at the first lull in the conversation.

"From what I understand, most of the land around here used to belong to the Sioux, didn't it?"

Karl was surprised by that question, but he had been in Minnesota long enough to know the state's history. "Yes, but the government has talked them out of so much all they have left now are two thin strips bordering the south side of the Minnesota River. The Upper Sioux Agency is the farthest away. It's near the mouth of the Yellow Medicine River, and the Lower Sioux Agency is below the Redwood River. That's about thirty-five miles northwest of here, up past Fort Ridgely."

Britta was a pretty blonde, if not nearly so elegant a creature as her sister and niece. She adored her husband, but that did not prevent her from arguing with him upon occasion. "The government paid the Sioux for the rest of their lands, Karl, don't forget that."

Karl had a stocky build and the rolling gait of a bear. His features, while neither handsome nor distinguished, were pleasant, and he was so good-natured that Erica liked him immensely. He simply laughed at his wife's comment. "Oh yes, they were paid at thirty cents an acre. Under the new Homestead Act the government is selling land at a dollar twenty-five an acre, so you tell me whether or not the Indians were cheated. Traders took a lot of the money to pay what they claimed the Indians owed them, don't forget that either. The Sioux were also promised annuities for fifty years, but Congress still hasn't voted them this year's money. After the poor harvest last fall, that's damn near criminal. The government's trying to make farmers out of them, but they are far better at hunting and fishing than anything else."

Erica nodded thoughtfully, thinking her uncle's points well taken. With the government treating the Indians so unfairly, it was no wonder the man she had met was so hostile. "Just how many Indians are there living on the two reservations?"

"About seven thousand, I think. Some of them have been persuaded to become farmers, but not many. The others don't like them, call them 'cut hairs' for adopting the white man's ways. I'm thankful I'm not a Sioux, I don't mind admitting that."

Taking care to project a nonchalance she didn't feel, Erica asked one last question. "Do you ever see any Indians around here?"

"I've seen some down by the river," Gunter offered, eagerly joining in the conversation.

"Well, don't you dare go near them, young man," his mother cautioned sternly. "You just let them be. No one is pleased with the fact that they wander so far from the reservation, so don't encourage them by being friendly."

"I don't," the shy boy insisted as he again focused his attention squarely upon his plate.

Erica allowed the conversation to drift to other subjects, but what she had heard disturbed her. If they were thirty-five miles south of the closest reservation, the man who had given her such a bad time had no business being so close to New Ulm, regardless of his claims that he went where he chose. He was clearly no farmer if he traveled about. But perhaps his nomadic ways would work to her advantage. Maybe he would be some distance away by the following afternoon and she could go back to search for Mark's letter without having to worry about meeting him. She kept hoping that would be the case, but she spent a restless night fearing that it wouldn't be.

24

# Chapter Two

## July, 1862

Mark Randall's well-tailored uniform fit him far better than the role of army officer did. Whenever he happened to catch a glimpse of his reflection as he passed by a mirror he was startled, for he had found the military clothing hadn't changed the way he felt inside. He backed President Lincoln wholeheartedly and thought it imperative that the Union survive, but when the war had begun he had thought that as an architect he would be of little value to the army unless they wished to put him to work building forts. Then one by one his friends had enlisted: attorneys, accountants, even college professors whom he knew could fire a rifle no more accurately than he. After the horrible losses suffered at Shiloh in April, 1862, his conscience had pained him so horribly for leaving the defense of the Union to other men that he had known he could no longer support the war effort with words alone. He had completed the work he had in progress as quickly as possible and had enlisted.

Since Erica held as strong views as he did about preserving the Union, he had not been prepared for the violence of their arguments after his enlistment. She had not wept, although he thought later it would have been far better if she had. After an initial stunned silence she had bravely accepted his decision and suggested they make plans to marry immediately. Since that was not something he would consider, from that day forward nothing had gone right between them.

That the carnage at Shiloh, in which more than seventeen hundred Union troops were killed and another eleven thousand injured, had also prompted her father to volunteer for the army had come as a further shock to Erica. Mark had not anticipated her father Lars's action, either, although he did not know how he could have changed his own plans once he had made them so that Erica would not have felt deserted by both her father and fiancé.

Now that he had been assigned to General John Pope's command he knew he would soon see action, and plenty of it, for the man had made a name for himself as an aggressive commander in the West. Mark knew he would have scant time to write to Erica and wasn't even certain she would reply. He had learned the hard way that it was difficult if not impossible to reconcile his ideals with the demands of her love, but he prayed Erica would continue to love him as dearly as he loved her when she no longer had the passion of his kisses to keep his image alive in her heart.

The whole morning Erica inwardly debated the wisdom of returning to the river. If she went back to where she had lost Mark's letter, she had no guarantee she would find it. Neither could she be assured she would not meet the arrogant Indian brave again. She wanted the letter but she didn't want to risk seeing him for a second time. Finally realizing she would never find the letter if she didn't conduct a search for it, she accepted the sorry fact that she had little choice in the matter. She would have to follow the same path along the riverbank, and if she chanced to meet the surly fellow who had given her such a bad time the previous afternoon she would simply step around him and go on her way.

She was wearing a dress of rose-colored chintz that day, one far more practical for walking through the woods than her blue gown, although it was still far too pretty for such informal wear. Erica had no less festive clothes, however. She hadn't wanted to have any gowns made in tailored styles from simple fabrics especially for wear in the store, since that would have been admitting she would be there for some months to come, which was an eventuality she still refused to accept.

As she reached the river and began the winding path alongside it, she realized she had paid such scant attention to how far she had walked the previous afternoon that she wasn't sure she could return to the same spot. She might not go far enough, or she might walk right past the elm tree where she had sat without recognizing it. She was furious with herself for having lost Mark's letter and traveled along scanning the trail so intently that she did not see the Indian she had hoped to avoid until she was within a few feet of him. She saw the brightly beaded tips of his moccasins first, and, startled, jumped back.

The Indian had been fishing, and recognizing the rustle of Erica's full skirt as she approached he had laid his line aside and risen to meet her. That she seemed flustered amused him, for he could think of no reason she would come back to the woods unless she had wanted to see him. He was accustomed to being popular with women, but certainly not with her kind. He did not greet her, but simply looked her up and down slowly, wondering again why she wore such fancy clothes. Her cheeks were filled with a blush as bright a pink as her gown, but he doubted she could be as shy as she appeared and pursue him so boldly. When she made no effort to greet him either, he finally spoke. "I know many of your men have gone to war, but if you are seeking me out because you are lonely, I—"

Erica interrupted before the arrogant Indian could complete the sentence with what she was certain would be another insult. "You are the very last person I wished to meet," she assured him emphatically. "I dropped an important letter I had with me yesterday and I'm looking only for that."

Her story sounded false to his ears, but the Indian did not call her a liar to her face. "A letter?" he asked skeptically instead.

Thinking the man did not understand what it was she had lost, Erica quickly described what she meant. "Yes, a letter. A message written on two sheets of paper. They're in a beige-colored envelope addressed to me. I must have dropped it while we were talking."

"Then why are you looking for it here?" the man asked with a sly smile, thinking he had trapped her into admitting she had been looking for him all along.

Puzzled, Erica wondered if she had misunderstood his question. "Well, where else would I be looking for it if I lost it here?"

"We were not here yesterday," the Indian replied, his smile widening into a taunting grin.

Erica looked around quickly, thinking the scenery looked no different than it had since she had left the outskirts of town. She wasn't lost, since all she had to do was follow the river back downstream to return to New Ulm. Exasperated, she looked to the Indian for help. "I'm sorry, but I've no real idea just where we were yesterday. Have I come too far, or not far enough?"

Her deep blue gaze seemed so truly innocent that the man thought she was either extremely clever or actually speaking the truth. He could not tell which. "We were closer to town. You have come too far," he advised her matter-of-factly.

Erica immediately lifted her skirts and turned away. "Thank you. I'm sorry I disturbed you again."

When she left him so suddenly, the Indian was too curious to let her go. He still doubted she had lost a letter and decided to make her admit she had come to see him instead. "Wait!" he shouted, meaning to call her bluff. "I will help you look."

Erica waited for him to overtake her, then refused his offer politely. "Thank you, but if you'll just point out the spot where we stood yesterday I'm certain I can search for it adequately by myself."

"I am tired of fishing," the Indian responded with a careless shrug. "The letter might have blown into a tree and be out of your reach."

"Oh, I doubt it would have blown away. The paper was an expensive bond so the envelope was fairly heavy." When the Indian seemed unconvinced by her words and did not turn back, Erica gave up her efforts to continue on alone, but she didn't speak to him again until he reached out his hand to stop her.

"You said you were sitting there, by that tree."

The elm looked like all the others she had seen that afternoon, but Erica took his word it was the one she was seeking. The grass along the riverbank was thick, and she spent several minutes looking through it before she looked up to find the Indian simply staring at her. "I thought you wanted to help me."

The man nodded and began a methodical search of the underbrush as well as the overhanging branches, but he kept his face turned away so she would not see his smile. He was beginning to get used to the way she looked and decided she was probably considered quite pretty by white men. From the slender lines of her throat and arms he guessed she might also have attractive legs, but like all white women she wore so many layers of clothing he had to rely upon his imagination for the details of her figure not exposed to his view. Fortunately, he had a very lively imagination. When he was satisfied they would never find the letter whose existence he still doubted, he straightened up and turned back toward her. "Why is this letter so important?" he asked.

Erica was also convinced the letter simply wasn't there and ceased looking for it to reply. "It's from—" she hesitated then as she noticed that the Indian looked far different that day. He was no less handsome, he just looked more like an Indian. He had braided feathers into his hair, and while his chest was still bare, he wore a leather thong around his neck from which were suspended a half-dozen of the longest, sharpest claws she had ever seen. Totally distracted, she had to ask him to repeat his question.

"I'm sorry, what did you ask?"

"Why is the letter important?" the Indian repeated in a louder tone, not understanding how she could have forgotten his question in the middle of answering it.

"Oh yes, of course." Eria felt very foolish then, but she still didn't want to reveal she had a fiancé, even to him. "It's from a friend who's in the army, and unless I find it I won't have his address to send a reply."

"His name is not enough?" the helpful man inquired.

"No, I need to know the number of his company, that sort of thing."

The Indian nodded as he stepped forward, still thinking it likely she had made up the tale about a letter as an excuse to see him. "Is the man your husband, or a lover?"

"Neither!" Ereica denied indignantly, tears stinging her eyes at the bitter irony of his question, but she quickly blinked them away

"Then why did you come so far from town to read it?"

the Indian asked as he moved another step closer.

Since that was none of his business, Erica began to back away, but bumped into the tree she had forgotten stood directly behind her. Embarrassed to appear so clumsy, she picked up her skirts to make ready to leave. "I enjoy privacy as greatly as you do, that's all. I've no more time to look for the letter now, though. I must be going. Thank you for your help."

Before she could turn away, the Indian reached out to stop her. He laid his hand lightly upon her arm as he tried to charm her with a ready grin every bit as dazzling as she had imagined his smile would be. "Will you come back tomorrow?"

His hand was warm, his touch light, and Erica saw something far different from hostility in his glance and grew frightened. What in God's name was she doing alone in the woods conversing with a half-clothed savage as though he were a gentleman?

"No. I probably could not even locate the right spot, and if we couldn't find the letter today, then surely it's lost and we never will."

Her reaction was not that of a woman who was inviting a man's attention, and surprised to see she had not enjoyed his touch, the Indian withdrew his hand and stepped back. He still thought her story a lie but went along with it. "If I find your letter, where shall I bring it?"

"You'd bring it to me?" Erica asked hesitantly, certain she should not provide him with the directions to her aunt and uncle's home.

"Well, if you do not want the letter then I will not bother to bring it to you," the man responded gruffly, clearly annoyed by her nonsensical question. Perhaps she had only thought she wanted an Indian lover and had changed her mind upon seeing him for the second time. It was an insulting thought and his expression became the stern one she had seen the previous afternoon.

Since she had not meant to insult him but obviously had, Erica quickly apologized. "I'm sorry if I said something to upset you. It was unintentional. If you do find my letter, would you please bring it to Ludwig's Dry Goods? Do you know where it is?"

The Indian nodded. "I know which store it is. Do you trust the people there to give it to you?"

"Yes, the Ludwigs are my aunt and uncle," Erica explained with a nervous smile. "If I'm not there, they will bring it home to me. Thank you!" she called over her shoulder as she hurried away. She doubted the Indian would find Mark's letter, or that he would bother to bring it to her, but the thought of his walking into the store and asking for her made her laugh all the way home.

The Indian returned to his fishing, but he was too deeply puzzled by the woman's behavior to regard their meeting in a humorous light. Pretty young women should not wander the woods alone. Indian maidens knew that, didn't white women? He did not recall seeing a letter the previous afternoon and still thought it had merely been an excuse to see him again. Yet even when she had seen him, the woman had not seemed pleased. What a strange person she was: pretty, but possessing no sense at all.

The next afternoon the Indian was restless. He kept expecting the woman to return, and when she did not he was more disappointed than he cared to admit. Thinking he had been out hunting and fishing alone too long, he told himself he had merely been hungry for a companion of any sort, even a reluctant yellow-haired woman. Deciding that that was a sign it was time to go home, he erased all traces of his camp but on an impulse returned to the spot where he had first met the woman. Simply to satisfy his own mind, he gave the area another thorough search, moving downstream to cover more ground than he had with her.

When he actually found the letter he was shocked to discover the woman had been telling the truth. The envelope was soiled, one corner chewed off by an ambitious squirrel who had apparently carried it some distance from where he had found it before discovering it wasn't something tasty to eat. The Indian turned the envelope over in his hands. It was damp near the river at night, and the ink had run so the name and address were too blurred to read. He knew it was not polite to read a letter meant for someone else, but since he could not make out the name, how could he be sure this was the woman's letter?

His only choice clear, the Indian removed the stationery, which, while somewhat wrinkled, was in better condition than the envelope. He had learned to read and write

31

English from a well-meaning missionary who had wished to convert him to Christianity. The religion of the white man did not interest him, but he had known even as a child that it would be wise to learn all he could about the white men who seemed determined to overrun his world. Squatting down by the river's edge, he read the letter with deliberate care, pronouncing each of the words in his mind. He had not heard the name Erica before, but spoke it aloud several times before deciding he liked it. Finding precisely what the woman had said it was, a letter from a man who appeared to be no more than a friend, he returned the stationery to the tattered envelope and straightened up.

He had said he would return the letter if he found it. He could toss it in the river, burn it, or take it home with him, and the pretty blond woman named Erica would never know he had it. He would know, however, and he had told her he would bring it to her. Why he had made such a ridiculous promise he didn't know. The question now was whether or not it would be wise to honor it.

The following day, Erica had just cut ten yards of lace for a customer when the usual hum of conversation that filled the busy store came to an abrupt end. As she handed the woman her neatly wrapped package and change, Erica saw what had caused the sudden silence. The Indian she had met in the forest had walked through the door and was making his way toward her. His expression was neither friendly nor menacing, but the rifle he carried in his right hand alarmed her. As her customer hurried away, she looked up at the man and tried her best to smile. "Good morning."

"I need some shells for my rifle," the Indian replied.

Erica was standing at the counter where yardage was sold, not bullets, but assuming the man was unfamiliar with the arrangement of the merchandise, she nodded toward the opposite side of the well-stocked store. "My uncle will have to help you, then, as I've no idea what you need." To the buckskin pants and moccasins she had seen him wearing the day before he had added a fringed buckskin shirt elaborately decorated with beadwork. It lent him a slightly more civilized air, but when he seemed confused she came out from behind the counter. "I'll come with you. I really should learn where everything is kept myself."

The Indian's eyes were focused upon the gentle sway of Erica's hips as he followed her across the store, but he did not complain that she could not see to his request herself. Knowing the store owner's first question would be whether or not he had the money to pay for what he wanted, he tossed the coins on the counter as he again asked for shells.

Erica noted the strain in her uncle's expression and thought it must be because they seldom had Indians come in the store. She made a point of noticing upon which shelves the shells were kept and tried to ignore the fact that the other customers were all staring at the Indian. Despite the fact that he was a good-looking man, obviously clean, and neatly dressed, the glances directed his way were hostile, and since he was behaving politely she thought that rudeness completely uncalled for.

After he had picked up the box of shells, the Indian turned toward the door, gesturing to Erica with a barely perceptible nod for her to follow him. When she did, he had difficulty hiding his grin, but he stopped before reaching the door. "I have your letter," he confided softly.

"You do!" Erica's deep blue eyes danced with excitement. "Well, where is it? Didn't you bring it with you?"

The Indian shook his head as he flashed her an enticing grin. "You'll have to come get it this afternoon. Don't be late, Erica, or I'll be gone."

With that surprising invitation the Indian strode out the door, leaving Erica both entranced by his smile and dismayed by his words. She was positive she had not told him her name, so he must have not only found the letter, but read it! When her uncle tapped her upon the shoulder, she jumped in surprise. "Oh yes, Uncle Karl, what is it?"

"What is it?" the man repeated, his gaze one of wide-eyed wonder. "Come in the back for a moment, I need to speak with you."

Erica feared she knew what was coming even before they reached the storeroom. If he had guessed she and the Indian were acquainted, she knew she dared not explain how they had met. Her mind searching frantically for some plausible excuse for knowing the brave, she was

33

enormously relieved when her uncle did not begin with a string of embarrassing questions.

"That Indian goes by the name of Viper, which suits him well. Being a city girl you might not ever have seen a snake, let alone a rattler like we have here. Rattlesnakes have no fears, and neither does that brave. That he'd march right in here and speak to you proves that fact. He's every bit as dangerous as those cougar claws he wears around his neck, and if he ever comes near you again, you come running straight to me."

Erica knew that the Indian had a fierce nature. He had swiftly proven that when they had first met. He also possessed a reasonable side, and she was far more intrigued by his request that she meet him again that afternoon than frightened, since his smile had held such a teasing warmth. That an Indian brave could be as charming as a white man was a surprise, and she wondered what else she might learn about him if given the chance. "What has he done that makes everyone seem so frightened of him?"

Karl leaned back against a wooden crate and folded his arms across his chest as he replied. "I told you New Ulm is more than thirty-five miles below the Lower Agency, so he ought to know better than to come hunting way down here. Oh, there are plenty like him who continue to roam around ignoring the fact this is no longer Sious territory, but few of them are mixed bloods like him."

"Mixed bloods?" Erica wasn't certain what that term meant.

"He's part white. Didn't you notice his eyes?"

Erica wasn't sure whether or not she should admit that she had, but she did. "His eyes were gray, but he certainly looks all Indian to me."

"I'm sure he considers himself all Indian too, but those light eyes give away his mixed heritage. What did he say to you as he was leaving?"

Now that Karl had finally asked the question she had been dreading, Erica blushed shyly and made up an answer she hoped he would believe. "He just thanked me for helping him get the shells and said I was pretty."

"You see what I mean?" Karl responded angrily. "No white man would dare talk to you that boldly."

Since her uncle had believed her lie, Erica relaxed

34

slightly. "Well, perhaps Indian girls expect compliments like that and he thought I'd be flattered. Now, since the store is full of customers, I think we better not neglect them any longer or they might take their business elsewhere."

That his attractive niece had proven to be such a practical young woman pleased Karl immensely, and with a hearty chuckle he followed her back out into the store where he found business as brisk as she had described it.

Erica thought she had met the Indian each afternoon sometime between the hours of one and two. She didn't foresee any trouble meeting him that day until her uncle invited the most persistent of her unwanted suitors, a young farmer by the name of Ernst Schramberger, to come home with them for the midday meal. Ernst was a tall, heavy-set man with blue-gray eyes and light brown hair that had begun to turn gray at the temples. Each time he smiled at her his desire was so undisguised that Erica felt as though she were actually being crushed in the bear hugs he was clearly quite anxious to give her. She would then have to lay her fork aside and take several deep breaths to reassure herself her imagination was playing tricks upon her, but she had seldom endured a more uncomfortable meal. It was not that the man was homely, nor was his personality unpleasant, but she simply did not find him appealing, and she couldn't wait for him to go so she could be on her way. When he finally left with her uncle, she helped her aunt clean up the kitchen, then slipped out the back door with her usual excuse that she wished to go out for a walk.

Since it had been past two-thirty when she had left home, Erica hoped the Indian had not been serious when he had warned her not to be late. She was already late, but she had taken only half a dozen running steps from the house when Gunter fell in by her side. First Ernst and now Gunter, she moaned inwardly. Was there going to be no way for her to enter the forest without being seen?

"I thought it a good afternoon for a walk. Where are you bound?" she asked brightly, praying her cousin was on the way to his parents' store.

Gunter shrugged. "I thought I would gather some wood

to make more carvings."

Her heart filling with dread, Erica was certain he was bent upon taking the same path she had hoped to travel without being followed. "Shouldn't you bring along a rope to bind it, or perhaps a basket to carry it?"

Embarrassed to admit he had not thought that far, Gunter had known only that his charming cousin sometimes went for walks and had wanted to go along with her. He tried to hide his oversight by agreeing with her. "Yes, of course, I meant to stop by the store to get a sack."

"Good, then maybe you'll be able to gather enough wood to make something for me." Erica was delighted to find he would have to make a stop at the store, but her compliments on his work were sincere for she thought it showed promise. "I thought the mule you did yesterday turned out very nicely."

Gunter could not help but laugh, since she knew he had hoped to carve a horse. "I think I'd be smart not to tell anyone what it is I am making until I am finished, but if you will tell me what it is you want, I'll try and make it."

They were nearing the corner where he would have to turn toward the store, while she intended to continue on down to the river. Erica thought for a moment and then knew exactly what she wanted. "Could you make me a cougar?"

"A cougar?" Gunter asked in dismay. "Well, I suppose I could try."

"Yes, you do that. I'm sure you can carve a magnificent cougar." Erica brushed his cheek with a quick kiss and hurried away before he recovered enough of his senses to follow her.

The Indian told time by watching the sun's progress across the sky. He knew the hour if not the exact minute, but he began to think himself a great fool for having looked forward to seeing Erica again. He thought of her by her name now, which made the embarrassment that her failure to appear caused him all the more acute. What a fool he had been to walk into town! He could always use more shells for his rifle, but still, had he not told Erica to meet him, she could not have stayed away to purposely disappoint him. He had planned to give her the letter and tell her good-bye, but the longer he waited the more furious he became with himself for ever growing interested in a white woman in the first place. Had she come to meet him, she would not have thrown herself into his arms. She would probably have taken the letter from his hand and with a coldly polite, "Thank you," gone back home.

Thoroughly disgusted with himself for being so curious about sampling a white woman's affection when Erica's indifference was obviously no coy act but sincere, he finally laid the letter beside the elm tree where he had first seen her and placed a rock on the corner to secure it. His belongings were few, and slinging them across his back, he started up the river, cursing his own conceit with every step.

Erica dashed down the path, looking for the landmarks she had taken the time to note the previous afternoon so she could slow down to a sedate walk before she came upon Viper's camp. When she found only the crumpled letter and no sign of the Indian, she was overwhelmed with disappointment. Why hadn't the man waited for her? Then she realized she had forgotten to bring money to reward him and felt even worse. Looking up the path, she wondered if she might catch sight of him if he hadn't had too great a headstart. Taking a firm hold on the letter this time, she lifted her skirts and continued to follow the river, hoping if she overtook an Indian that it would be he.

When the Indian heard peculiar sounds on the trail at his back he at first mistook the noise for a deer. Stepping behind a pine tree for cover he brought his rifle up to his shoulder. When Erica came into view, he set the rifle aside, and stepped out to greet her. "I told you not to be late," he scolded in so teasing a tone she knew he wasn't truly angry with her.

Out of breath, Erica swept her curls off her forehead and leaning back against the pine, used Mark's letter to fan her flushed cheeks. "I am so sorry. Not only am I dreadfully late, but I've forgotten to bring any money so I can give you a reward."

"I did not ask for money," the Indian exclaimed proudly. That she had plainly exhausted herself trying to catch up to him was so flattering a fact he decided she must like him more than her actions had shown. He still did not

37

forgive her for being so late, however. "Why did you wait so long to come find me?"

Still gasping for breath, Erica had a ready excuse. "We had a guest at the house for dinner and I couldn't leave when I usually do. I would not have kept you waiting intentionally."

Her bosom heaved most invitingly with each breath she took, and the Indian found it difficult to focus his attention upon her face rather than her enticing curves as he replied. "I did not wait," he lied, for indeed he had waited a good hour longer than he had wanted to.

"Well, I've found you to say thank you, and that's all that matters." Erica assured him with a nervous smile. He had discarded his shirt, and the sight of the cougar claw necklace lying upon his bare skin was still a most unsettling one. "My uncle said you're called Viper, is that right?"

The Indian stepped close enough to place his hand upon the tree at her back, and caressed her right cheek with his thumb as he replied in a husky whisper. "No, but it is as close as a white man can come to saying my name."

Erica found the directness of the man's gaze most unsettling. He didn't look at her as Ernst did: almost drooling, but the silver light in his gray eyes was nevertheless much too intense. With the tree at her back and him standing so near, she didn't see how she could avoid such close scrutiny, though. His touch was, as before, very light, but far too familiar. When she tried to brush his hand away he simply caught hers in a firm grasp and held it. "Please," she whispered, "I wanted only to tell you thank you for finding the letter, and if you are returning home to wish you a safe trip."

Her lashes were so long and thick they provided the perfect frame for her deep blue eyes. But he had not meant to fill them with fright. He kept her hand in his as he said, "You had your letter. You did not have to chase after me just to say thank you."

"Well, no, perhaps not, but—" As Erica looked up at him she suddenly recalled how the water had dripped off the sleek planes of his well-muscled body as he had left the river, and she found herself at a loss for words. She was still having difficulty catching her breath, but it wasn't

38

because she had been running so hard. She clutched Mark's letter tightly in her free hand, frantically trying to recall how handsome a man he, too, was, but his face wouldn't come clear in her mind. It wavered and danced on the fringe of her memory, refusing, just as he had, to become a part of her.

"Are you a virgin?" the Indian asked perceptively, thinking perhaps inexperience was causing her fright. She had come running after him, so clearly she liked him, but maybe she was too young to know what to do about it.

The impertinence of that question jolted Erica to anger so swiftly that she found it a simple matter to reply. "That is none of your damn business, Viper, or whatever it is you like to be called!"

The Indian thought again how much he liked her spirit and suggested another name. "You may call me Beloved, if you like."

"Beloved!" Erica nearly shrieked. The man was devilishly handsome, but obviously a rake through and through, and she yanked her hand from his. "I have never before met an Indian brave, but believe me, you have made me sincerely sorry I ever met you!" Again taking the precaution of lifting the front of her skirt, she shoved past him and dashed back down the trail with the same careless haste that had caused him to mistake her for a badly frightened deer. She was dressed in a yellow gown that shimmered in the sunshine, and suddenly he feared a hunter who lacked his cool head and sharp eyes might also mistake her for a deer moving between the trees and shoot her. Tossing his gear aside, he tore down the trail after her.

The Indian called her name in so frantic a shout that Erica turned back to face him. Her cheeks were still burning with shame, for she knew she had deserved that question about her virtue, since no respectable young woman would be tramping through the forest looking for a man who wore more feathers than clothes. That she was still a virgin through no fault of her own caused her an even more excruciating type of embarrassment.

"What is it now?" she demanded rudely.

The Indian was so thoroughly confused by the blond woman's hostility that he shouted right back at her. "You should not be walking alone so far from town."

"I'm not walking, I'm running!" Erica pointed out, but as she turned back toward the trail he reached out to stop her.

"Wait, I will go with you to see you reach home safely."

"I've seen no one lurking about the river but you, and if you go one way and I another then I will surely reach home without coming to any harm." Yet when she took another quick step, he came right along with her, exasperating her all the more.

The Indian had never apologized to a woman, but for a reason he could not even begin to understand, he did not want them to part enemies. "I have never talked with a white woman. If I said the wrong thing, I am sorry."

When Erica turned to look at him, she was shocked to find the Indian actually looked contrite. His woebegone expression made her feel so guilty, she slowed down to a sedate pace. "I'm sorry, too. Perhaps we are simply too different to be friends."

"I did not think it was a friend you wanted," the Indian admitted slyly.

Erica couldn't help but laugh, since what he had obviously thought was so plain, and in her mind completely wrong. "You were mistaken."

"Yes, I see that." Still, he could not ignore the nagging suspicion that if he were attracted to her, then she must feel some of that same sweet excitement when she looked at him. 'You need not worry, I will not walk you to your door. I will go only to the edge of the woods before saying good-bye."

The man did raise his voice rather often, but it had not been again the anger that had frightened Erica. Now that he was again speaking and behaving politely, she tried to erase from her mind the erotic images of him cavorting in the river, but unlike Mark's elusive memory, the Indian's stubbornly persisted to taunt her.

"You are a very handsome man," she announced suddenly. "You must have plenty of pretty Indian women waiting for you to come home."

"Indian women are very shy. None has ever told me I am handsome."

"Would they say such a thing to their husband?" Erica mused aloud, thinking it no wonder he thought her

40

forward if their customs were so different. She had been raised from the cradle to flatter men, and apparently Indian women weren't.

"I don't know. I will have to wait and see." The Indian thought his joke amusing, but when Erica did not laugh he offered a fact he thought perhaps she did not know. "There are some braves with white wives."

"Oh, really?" Erica mumbled nervously, certain she had again led their conversation in completely the wrong direction. She had not realized she had gone so far from town until they had started back. Perhaps it had been a good idea for the Indian to escort her most of the way. When they were within sight of the steamboat landing she stopped when he did. "Thank you again for finding the letter. It really is an important one I must answer."

"The man who wrote it did not say that he loved you."

Since she would never see the Indian again, Erica thought there would be no harm in telling him the truth now. "He does love me, though. We had an awful argument before I left to come here, and that's why he sounded so cool. You should not have read the letter, by the way, but I will forgive you since you returned it to me."

The Indian was tempted to ask if she loved the man who had sent the letter, but fearing what her answer might be, he posed another question instead. "May I have a reward, then?"

"But I told you I'd forgotten to bring any money."

"I don't want money."

The man was forever stepping too close to her, but this time Erica was too curious about what it was he did want to move back. "What did you have in mind?" she asked softly.

"You have kissed the man who wrote the letter?"

Erica looked away, thinking the afternoon one of the loveliest she had seen since coming to New Ulm. But it had also proven to be one of the most uncomfortable. "Yes, I've kissed him," she finally admitted, but didn't add that she had lost count of how many times.

"Then kiss me." The Indian did not wait for the slender blonde to argue, he merely slipped his arms around her tiny waist, and pulling her close, lowered his mouth to hers.

41

Taken by surprise, Erica couldn't decide what to do with her hands. First she placed them on the man's smooth bronze chest, then upon his shoulders, then, as his lips continued to caress hers with a heartbreaking tenderness she had never dreamed he would possess, she wound her arms around his neck and lost herself in the magic of his affection. When he drew away slightly, she deftly lured his mouth to return to her.

The Indian had kissed women, but never one who put such passion into it. But after his initial surprise, he enjoyed Erica's affection too much to complain that she lacked the modesty of an Indian maiden. He thought only that it was a great pity she did not want to make love, and tightened his embrace.

As the handsome Indian's kiss grew more fervent, Erica felt its searing heat burn all the way down to her toes and suddenly realized that, unlike Mark, he would have absolutely no reason to control his passions to protect her. She would never have to beg this man to make love to her. All she need do was continue to return his kisses with equal ardor and he would just do it. Shocked to think that should she lead him any further there would be no way to stop him except with the satisfaction of total surrender, she hastily disengaged herself from his arms and stepped back.

"You better go," she stated as firmly as her shaking knees would allow.

"I will come back soon," the Indian promised hoarsely, praying it would not take too many visits to convince her to share his blankets.

Erica didn't understand what had come over her, but knew she shouldn't encourage the Indian to think they would ever share more than that one nearly endless kiss. "No, I think you better stay closer to home." Mark's letter was now so thoroughly wrinkled she used both hands to try and smooth it out. "Please just go home and stay there."

The blue-eyed woman had said something far different with her kiss, and the Indian chose to believe her unspoken words rather than her softly voiced lies. Untying his necklace, he removed one of the wicked-looking claws. "Keep this, to remember me." When Erica seemed reluctant to accept it, he reached for her hand, placed it in her palm, and folded her fingers over it. "It will bring you good luck," he promised. He then draped the gruesome necklace back around his neck and retied the ends of the thong. Drawing his knife, he sliced off the end of one of the startled blonde's long curls before she could gasp a refusal. He laughed at her stricken expression as he replaced his knife in its sheath. "Did you think I would give you a claw for luck and then slit your throat?"

"Well no, but you might have warned me what it was you meant to do before you drew your knife." Erica watched him wrap the curl around his index finger and thought his hands as handsome as the rest of him. He definitely had the looks of a fine gentleman, even if not the manners. "Before you go, won't you please tell me what I should call you if Viper isn't correct?"

"Call me Beloved and I will answer." With a teasing wink, the brave bent down to kiss her slightly swollen lips lightly, then sprinted away so quickly he was immediately lost in the thick foliage that bordered the path.

Erica looked down at the claw and the letter, thinking the men the tokens represented were as different as two men could possibly be. But she couldn't deny that the warmth of their kisses filled her with the same indescribable longing for the fulfillment she had never known. Thinking that surely it couldn't be possible for the kiss of a savage to affect her as strongly as Mark's always had, she discounted the heady effect he had had upon her senses as the sorry result of loneliness rather than something far more unique. She would keep the claw, though, as it would lend credence to what she was sure would be the most amusing tale she would have to relate when she again saw her friends in Wilmington.

The piercing whistle of an approaching steamboat reminded her she had been away from home much too long, and she turned back toward the path into town. Before she had taken a single step, however, she saw her cousin, Gunter, standing not twenty feet away. He was looking at her with an expression of such agonized disbelief that she feared he had seen more than she could ever successfully explain away.

# Chapter Three

## July 1862

Gunter had dropped his sack of wood scraps and bolted before she could reach him and Erica could do no more than pray he had been so mortified by what he had seen he would not rush straight home to tell his mother. She had only just gotten to know her Aunt Britta, and out of regard for her own dear mother's memory she did not want the woman to think the worst of her niece.

As Erica hurried toward home, lugging the sack her cousin had left behind, she began to worry Gunter might have gone to his father instead. Her Uncle Karl had advised her only that morning to avoid the Indian, so undoubtedly he would be infuriated to learn she had been seen kissing the man in the afternoon. On the other hand, she was probably exceedingly lucky it had been Gunter who had seen her in the savage's arms rather than someone else.

She slipped her hand into her pocket to touch the cougar claw and thought that, despite the owner's promise, it most certainly had not brought her good luck. Knowing it might be wise to hurl it out into the river, she nevertheless kept it clutched tightly in her hand until she reached her aunt and uncle's home. She tossed Gunter's sack by the porch steps and entered through the back door.

Britta was seated at the kitchen table and looked up from the apples she was peeling to greet her niece. "It is such a lovely day. I wish I had chosen to work in my garden or to go for a walk with you rather than to bake a pie. Why don't you brew us some tea and sit with me a while?"

Erica was relieved to discover she had beaten Gunter home, but if he had gone to the store to fetch his father, then she was in serious trouble indeed. She knew there was an outside chance her aunt might be sympathetic to her plight, but her uncle surely wouldn't be. She washed her hands and put the kettle on to boil before taking the chair opposite Britta. She thought it might be wise to tell her what had happened before Karl rushed in to accuse her of carrying on with Indians, but her aunt spoke before Erica could summon the courage to make such an outlandish confession.

"I'm sorry you don't like Ernst as much as we do, dear. Is it only that you have no wish to become a farmer's wife, or has another man already stolen your heart?"

It seemed far too late to mention Mark was her fiancé, so Erica left his letter in her pocket and answered only the first part of her aunt's question. "It's not that I don't like Mr. Schramberger. The problem is I don't like him in the way he likes me. New Ulm is a nice town and I've found the people friendly here, but I won't deny how anxious I am to return to Wilmington."

"If only so many of our young men hadn't joined the army, I'm sure you would have found one who could have changed your mind about staying here. I know it is partly selfish of me to want you to live here with us, but you know you'll always be welcome in our home."

"Thank you." Startled by its piercing sound, Erica leaped to her feet with the tea kettle's first shrill whistle. She got out the china teapot, filled it with boiling water, then put in some tea leaves to steep while she took the cups and saucers from the cupboard. She knew honesty was a highly esteemed virtue, and deservedly so, but she couldn't bring herself to confide in her aunt. How could she explain any of her encounters with the Indian in rational terms when clearly the whole episode had been totally irrational? She would sound daft if she said she had been reading a letter from her fiancé, whom she had not bothered to mention, and had been so startled by the sight of a handsome Indian brave playing naked in the river that she had dropped it. That much was damaging enough, but to have had conversations with the Indian on three more occasions would very likely brand her as a harlot, if not simply mad.

Her mind made up, she served her aunt tea and decided in this case, honesty was the last thing she needed. She turned the conversation to the fabrics that had been ordered for sale in the fall while she waited anxiously for Gunter to appear. When he finally did come home, he was alone and he did not even glance her way before he dashed upstairs to his room.

Britta apologized for her bashful son's antisocial behavior, "I hope you'll forgive Gunter. I'm afraid he's more than a little smitten with you. It is a shame he is not the elder, for you two would make a very handsome pair."

While it was not uncommon for first cousins to marry, Erica could not imagine herself falling in love with Gunter regardless of his age. "I think he is very sweet, but you're right, there's a vast difference between a boy of sixteen and a girl of seventeen. I am a woman, and he is still a youth."

"I think Eva's death forced you to grow up a bit too fast, Erica. It's no wonder you're not anxious to marry when you had to take over so many of your dear mother's duties while you were still so young. I'm surprised we've not heard from your father. I thought he would write to you long before this."

"I know the army needed physicians very badly. I'm sure Dad's just been too busy to write." Since her Uncle Karl had not come home with Gunter, Erica assumed the boy hadn't told his father what he had seen and immediately seized upon the idea of relying upon his affection for her to insure his continued silence. "Speaking of letters," she said as she carried the now cold teapot back to the stove, "there are several I have neglected to write. If you don't need any help with the cooking, I think I'll go and write a few now."

"No, I'm fine. You go write your letters, dear."

Erica gave her aunt a kiss upon the cheek, then left the room at a sedate pace she had to force herself to set. She climbed the stairs as though she had not a care in the world, but rather than stopping at her room, she went on up to the attic to see Gunter. He was sprawled across his bed, his face turned to the wall, and she took the precaution of closing his door so their conversation would not be overheard.

"Gunter, I know what you saw shocked you rather badly, but I wish you hadn't left before I could explain."

"Go away," the distraught youth responded, his voice muffled by his feather pillow.

Since she couldn't allow him to sulk until his parents became suspicious as to the cause of his downcast mood, Erica moved closer to his bed and continued. "I know full well that respectable young women do not kiss Indian braves. I suppose they do not even know such men. I chanced to meet that fellow in the woods. He helped me to find something I'd lost and asked me to kiss him as a reward. I should have refused. I know that, but since I'll never see him again I plan to forget about that scene you witnessed this afternoon, and I hope you will, too."

Gunter was both embarrassed and ashamed. He was also appalled that he had run off like some witless child rather than ask his beautiful cousin just what the hell she was doing when he had seen her in an Indian's arms. Turning to face her, he sat up and hoped he would sound more like a man now. "If you had lost something, why didn't you ask me to help you find it?"

Since she had not even considered that possibility, Erica swiftly apologized. "That is precisely what I should have done, Gunter. I'm very sorry that I didn't do it, too. It's just that I'm used to walking down by the Brandywine Creek near my home where everyone goes for an afternoon stroll. I will try harder to remember this is the edge of the frontier and I shouldn't go wandering about alone."

Gunter's mother had underestimated her son's devotion to Erica. He was not merely smitten with her, he adored her. "I did not want to believe you preferred red men to white," he admitted shyly.

The Indian had been a handsome devil and his kiss a delight, but Erica was not about to reveal to Gunter that she had found scant difference between him and Mark. Instead, she smiled warmly at Gunter and assured him he need have no such worries. "This must remain our secret, Gunter, you understand that, don't you? Why the gossip about me would never cease if you told anyone what you saw. You haven't told anyone, have you?"

"Oh no!" the astonished youth exclaimed. "I will never tell that story. I swear it."

"Good. I brought your sack of wood home. Don't forget you promised to carve me a cougar," Erica reminded him as she moved toward the door.

"No, I promised merely to try," Gunter called out, his spirits soaring now that he had learned she and the Indian weren't lovers, no matter what his eyes had told him.

"All right, you promised to try." Erica gave him a charming smile as she left his room, but she did not draw a deep breath until she had locked her door behind her. She sat down at her desk and reread Mark's letter several times, still hoping to discover some hidden admission that he regretted not marrying her. Since there was no such message she soon found her mind wandering to thoughts of the Indian. She took his claw from her pocket, and after tying it upon a red ribbon to make it look less fearsome, she hid it in the bottom of her stationery box. She then attempted to compose a coherent reply to Mark, but she found the dashing Indian brave's stirring kiss surprisingly difficult to forget.

An amused smile played across the Indian's lips as he began the trek home. That he had taken a lock of Erica's pale blond hair would provide proof for his friends that he had kissed her. As he followed the river upstream, he rehearsed increasingly lurid versions of the tale, beginning with the instant he had discovered her spying upon him and ending with their kiss.

He had gotten so late a start, when darkness fell he was forced again to make camp for the night. His dreams were filled with the sad sweetness of Erica's parting smile, and he awoke with her image still fresh in his mind. By the time he arrived home the next morning, he found for some curious reason that while he had an intriguing romantic adventure to relate, he had no desire to share it. It wasn't like him to be so close-mouthed about his travels, but he described only the number of fish he had caught and how few animals he had seen, and his friends did not guess he had begun keeping secrets from them.

Two Elk scowled angrily as Viper spoke. "We no longer have good lands for hunting. The white men have taken them all. Now we must wait for them to give us money and food or we will starve. The trader Myrick will give us no more credit at his store. He says we can eat grass while he grows fat on the money we have paid him!"

"Were the annuity goods distributed or the gold we're owed paid while I was gone?" Viper asked with a skeptically raised brow. That question was met with bitterly voiced obscenities from his friends. He liked no better than they that the once proud Santee Sioux now had to depend for their livelihood upon the very white men who had stolen their land through unfair treaties. "I thought not. What news is there of the war?"

Two Elk lowered his voice and the small crowd that had surrounded Viper upon his return drew closer still. "When the Union Army is coming here to ask us to fight, it is plain the South is beating them badly."

"A promise of a full belly is not enough to make me want to fight for them," a young man called Growling Bear sneered.

"If the North loses the war, then we will never see our money!" Two Elk complained bitterly.

Squatting down in the dirt, the friends all wore similar expressions of disgust. Finally Hunted Stag spoke. "If the South wins, will they come here to make slaves of us?"

Viper laughed out loud at that question. "Not when they see what poor farmers we are!"

"You should not laugh!" Growling Bear scolded. "We have been shoved onto land where we cannot survive on our own. If the South wins, then even that may be taken from us!"

Taken aback by that warning, Viper's mood grew just as dark. "All right then, the choice is clear. We can join the Union Army and fight for a government which breaks all its promises and leaves us to starve, or we can wait and fight the South for the right to survive on whatever lands we choose!"

The air thick with tension, Two Elk offered still another opinion. "With so many white men gone from Minnesota to fight the war, we could drive out the rest if we struck now! Why have we no leader with the courage to do so?"

49

"This is the kind of talk we should do elsewhere," Viper warned as he rose to his feet. Like many men of his tribe, he was slightly over six feet in height and stood proudly. That a discussion of his travels had swiftly become a war council did not surprise him, for there was not a man among them who had any respect for the government of the United States. The chiefs had been wrong to give up their lands for promises of food and money, and he thought as his friends did that their situation had gotten so bad that not even war could make it worse.

As he turned away he saw Hunted Stag's sister, Song of the Wren, standing nearby. She was supposed to be minding her little sister, but clearly she had been watching him instead. Like all Sioux maidens she would not approach a brave who interested her, but the boldness of her glance held an unmistakable invitation. She was a pretty girl with large brown eyes, flowing black hair, and a shapely figure, but Viper had not courted her nor any of her friends. They were all pretty and sweet, but none had ever stirred his blood to the point where he wanted to make her his wife. He gave Wren no more than a slight nod as he walked away.

Wren was so disgusted that she had again failed to impress Viper favorably that she reached for her sister's hand with a rude yank. The little girl gave a yelp of pain, which Wren quickly hushed. Her brother would tell her where the handsome brave had been. Since she had not seen his friends teasing him, she knew Viper had not been visiting a woman in another camp. But that thought did nothing to raise her spirits. She was a very popular girl. Many braves came to her tepee in the evenings, but that Viper was not one of them filled her with a disappointment so deep it was swiftly becoming a black rage. It was time she took a husband, and no man but Viper would do! Dragging her whimpering sister along behind her, she returned to her family's tepee to ask her mother's advice in winning the heart of a reluctant brave.

Though seething with discontent, the Lower Agency to which Viper had returned would have appeared to the casual observer to be a peaceful encampment of tepees nestled between bluffs of the Minnesota River Valley. Overlooking the Indian camp stood a settlement of traders' stores, quarters for the Indian agent and other government personnel, along with shops, barns, and several other buildings, including a newly constructed stone warehouse. While the Sioux did not consider the feelings of the whites, the traders were as anxious as they were for the Indians' gold to arrive, since they had long passed the point at which they could operate on credit. Therefore, the summer of 1862 found no one at the Lower Agency happy.

Viper managed to remain home for one week before his spirit grew too restless to remain where every word spoken was a complaint. To the north lay the Upper Agency, which occupied far better lands for hunting. But he had no wish to trespass upon them. No, his interest lay toward the south, and without providing an explanation of his plans, he again slipped away before dawn so none of his friends could beg to join him or follow.

A loner by nature, he was comfortable in his own company, but when he reached the woods outside New Ulm he knew if he wished to see Erica again he would have to find a way to let her know he had kept his promise to return. Since he knew she worked in her uncle's store in the mornings, he decided to wait outside at noon and speak with her when she left. He had no plans for a lengthy conversation, but hoped all he need do was make her aware of his presence and she would know what to do next.

Viper's presence caused considerable stares, but since he was breaking no laws by standing outside Ludwig's Dry Goods, he returned the curious glances directed his way with a practiced nonchalance. His timing proved to be perfect. He had to wait only a few minutes before Erica came out the front door of the heavily trafficked store, but to his dismay she was not alone. Walking with her was a big man Viper thought to be several years older than he, but they went by him so quickly he scarcely caught Erica's eye. Disappointed not to have at least won a smile from the blonde, he returned to his camp by the river and sat down to fish while he waited impatiently for the arrival of the pretty young woman he could not be certain would appear.

When she saw the Indian lounging outside the store, Erica's heart leaped to her throat, lodging there so firmly

51

she could barely nod to show she was listening as Ernst described his hopes for a successful harvest. Her uncle had again invited him to eat dinner with them. While Erica had done nothing to encourage his admiration of her, Ernst's perseverance where she was concerned was leading her to think she should come right out and tell him she would never consider a proposal from him rather than politely to suffer his continued attentions. In fact, she began to hope he would mention marriage that very afternoon so she could refuse him and send him on his way.

The Indian's sudden appearance complicated her life considerably. Although she had gotten only a quick glimpse of him, it was enough to assure her he was every bit as handsome as she had recalled. Her whole body tingled with excitement at the thought of continuing their forbidden friendship. She had not really expected him to come back, or at least not so soon. She knew without being told where she could find him. The question was: did she truly wish to?

She struggled to make polite responses to Ernst as they ate dinner. Her mood was anxious, for she felt hopelessly trapped. The poor man tried so hard to impress her, but not only were his looks plain, but his personality and thoughts as well. He had none of her uncle's fun-loving charm, and while he was a solid, dependable citizen, Erica truly did not want ever to see him again. When finally he left the house and her uncle returned to the store, she felt far too tired to face a possible confrontation with an amorous Indian.

Britta studied Erica's pained expression throughout the noon meal and feared she was at fault for her niece's obvious discomfort. She hadn't repeated the beautiful young woman's comments about Ernst to her husband, and Karl apparently wasn't observant enough to notice Erica wasn't nearly so fond of the young man as he was. As soon as they were alone, she made what she thought was a considerate suggestion. "You look tired, dear. Why don't you go on out for a walk? You've been spending too much time either at the store or indoors here. Go on out, it will put some color back into your cheeks."

The thought of a walk was very attractive, but Erica feared her feet would carry her straight to the Indian and then leave her mind with nothing to say. "I like spending the afternoons helping you, Britta," she argued. "You remind me so much of my mother, being around you is almost like being with her again."

"What a sweet thing to say, Erica. But Eva was much prettier than I am. Now I insist you go out for a little while at least, since the afternoon is a fine one."

Finally pushed out the door by her well-meaning aunt, Erica dawdled along the path leading down to the river. Once she reached the steamboat landing she hesitated a long while before realizing that if she did not go see the Indian, he would probably wait for her outside the store again the next day and the next until she did venture out to the woods to meet him. By that time the whole town would be gossiping about the man and she would be fortunate if her name were not included in the same breath. Justifying her actions to herself in this way and convincing herself she was more eager to avoid drawing such unwarranted attention to their friendship than to continue it, Erica finally chose the path leading north and found the Indian fishing in the exact spot where she had first seen him.

Viper wound his line around a branch that jutted out over the river and rose to greet Erica when she waved to him. He had told himself repeatedly that she could not possibly be the beauty his memory had stubbornly insisted she was, but as she smiled shyly at him he realized he had been wrong. She was even more lovely than he had recalled. Her fair curls shone brightly, reflecting the sun's rays like a halo. The angels in the missionary's books had always been blond, pale, pretty creatures he had instantly disliked because they looked nothing like his dark-skinned friends and relatives. Yet here Erica was, looking like a living ray of sunshine, and he could find nothing to dislike about her.

The Indian's features had lit up with such unabashed delight when he had seen her that Erica felt the warmth of his pleasure wash over her. She was then pained with a sharp stab of guilt for having wasted so much time getting there. She scarcely knew the man, but all she did know about him suddenly made her long to know far more. While it was difficult to understand precisely why she had so little respect for the danger that knowing him presented, she did not hide the fact that she was happy to see him again, too. "If there's no hope I will get your name right in English, may I call you Viper as others do?"

While he had hoped Erica would run into his arms and cover his face with kisses, the Indian was so pleased to see her he did not complain that she had not shown enough enthusiasm in her greeting. "Viper is all right," he agreed. "Not as nice as Beloved, but it will do." He stood simply staring at her then, thinking the blue of her eyes far prettier than the summer sky. "Who was that man?" he finally had the presence of mind to ask, and instantly his smile vanished at the thought that he had a rival for her affections.

Relieved that he had not immediately tried to kiss her, Erica replied with a careless shrug. "His name is Ernst Schramberger. He's a farmer in need of a wife, and unfortunately he has set his sights on me. I have tried to discourage his attentions, honestly I have, but he just doesn't seem to notice I am not thrilled by them."

"You could tell him you are my woman," Viper offered graciously. "He would stop coming to see you then, wouldn't he?"

"Oh yes, he most definitely would!" Erica agreed with a sparkling laugh, for she could not even imagine herself saying such an outrageous thing. "But since it isn't true, I'll not use you as an excuse to avoid him."

Momentarily confused, Viper frowned slightly, then he reached out to take Erica's hand and drew her near. "What do you mean it is not true?" he whispered softly as he lowered his mouth to hers.

Erica had no time to reply before the Indian's kiss made a hopeless muddle of her thoughts. Again his gentle touch was remarkably soothing, while the feel of his warm, bare back beneath her fingertips provided a heady rush of excitement. His lips caressed hers sweetly, then his tongue slid into her mouth with the easy familiarity of a lover long held dear. The moment she had entered his embrace she had been overcome, as before, with the same reassuring sense of belonging Mark's presence had always created within her. Viper was not Mark, however, but a tender savage whose sensual magic enveloped her in a warm blanket of desire.

"This is wrong," Erica's conscience whispered faintly,

54

barely heard above her wildly beating heart. They were standing at the river's edge, in plain view of anyone going by in a boat, but the danger discovery presented failed to faze her. She was so lost in the Indian's delicious kiss that she ceased to care about anything save pleasing him. When he pulled her down into the soft grass at their feet the wantonness of her behavior still failed to shock her back to her senses.

She kissed the affectionate brave again and again, holding him so close she felt him shudder with the effort to keep his passions in check. Her hands moved down his back then over the soft buckskins that covered his narrow hips. In her mind's eye she recalled the perfection of his lean yet muscular build in such explicit detail it brought a bright blush to her cheeks. She felt his fingertips brush lightly over her breasts, burning her flesh with a possessive caress that seared right through the thin fabric of her pale green gown, making her long to feel her cool bare skin next to the fiery warmth of his. With irresistible affection he lured her to the very brink of rapture, before Erica recalled she could not even pronounce his name.

Viper held the blond beauty cradled in his arms as he lay stretched out by her side. His kisses grew increasingly insistent, but seemingly able to read the half-formed doubts that had suddenly filled Erica's mind, he sensed her reluctance to give their passions free rein and drew back.

"Tell me what is wrong," he encouraged with light kisses that teased her earlobes before sliding down the elegant curve of her throat. "Tell me."

Erica waited until his gaze again met hers before she tried to explain her misgivings tactfully. "I don't really understand why I came here today. I know nothing about you. You are very handsome, of course, and wonderfully affectionate, but—" she lost the thread of her complaint then as the gray of his eyes took on a hypnotic silver gleam. He seemed to see clear through her, past the glowing curls and soft silk gown, past the pretense fine manners required, past all subterfuge to the desolate depths of her heart. "I don't even know you," she whispered in a voice filled with wonder, for while she felt she knew nothing whatsoever about the Indian, somehow their souls had already touched, and each had found the joy of recognition in the other.

"Does it frighten you so that I am Indian?" When she did not respond he made a confession of his own. "It merely surprises me that you are white."

That was such an odd thing for the man to say, that Erica recalled something her uncle had mentioned and asked him about it. "My uncle says you must have white blood to have such light eyes. Is that true?"

"No," Viper replied with a teasing grin. "My blood is as red as yours."

Erica was certain he was only pretending not to understand her. "You know what I mean, Viper. Someone in your family must be white."

"Would that please you?" the Indian whispered as he continued to lazily nibble her earlobes.

Everything about the man pleased her, but she could not admit that, since it implied an invitation she could not give. Instead, she told him what no one else in New Ulm knew. "It would make no difference," Erica suddenly blurted out in a breathless rush. "I've already promised to marry another man."

"What!" It was Viper who was shocked then. He sat up quickly, and placing his hands upon Erica's shoulders he yanked her up into a sitting position facing him. "Is it that farmer? Is he the one you've promised to marry?"

"No, it's not he," Erica assured him with a shudder, for she would never agree to wed Ernst Schramberger.

Since he had no interest in playing guessing games, the Indian turned his argument in another direction. "You are lying! If you were in love with another man you would not be here with me!"

"Yes, I know that should be true," Erica agreed, as confused as he by the contradiction between her words and the wild abandon of her behavior.

"Well, if you know it, then why are you here with me?" the Indian snarled with a flash of the same evil temper he had displayed at their first fiery confrontation. He wanted to wring from her lips the confession that she preferred him to any other man, but, sadly, he failed.

Erica swallowed hard, for his fingers were digging into her flesh and sending pains shooting clear to her fingertips, and it was difficult for her to gather the breath to speak. "Oh, it is the damned war," she explained with

56

a half-choked sob. "The war has ruined all our lives!"

Huge tears welled up in the distraught blonde's eyes and then poured down her cheeks, but Viper did nothing but stare at her in mystified silence. Finally he released her with a disgusted shove and went to check his fishing line. The bait had slipped off the hook, so he added more and tossed the line back out into the river.

Erica could tell by the Indian's rigid posture that he was furious with her. She couldn't blame him, either, when she was furious with herself. She had been drawn to him by the most primitive of human needs, but she thanked God she had not satisfied them at his expense.

When the delicate blonde knelt down by his side, Viper asked angrily, "Why do you think I am fishing?"

"Because it is a relaxing pastime?" Erica guessed incorrectly.

"No! Because I am hungry. I thought you would end another kind of hunger, but now you say you belong to some other man!"

Erica reached out to touch his thick black hair lightly, the sight of his feathers and braids no longer strange to her. When he did not flinch at her touch she rested her cheek upon his bare shoulder as she tried to find a way to tell him good-bye. "Please do not think badly of me. It is only that I am so lonely and frightened that—"

"That savages seem amusing!" Viper taunted her rudely.

"No," Erica murmured softly. Fearing any explanation she offered would only make matters worse, she regretfully rose to her feet. "I think you are a fine man, with both a handsome appearance and a compassionate heart. I am truly sorry to have disappointed you so greatly." She waited a moment, hoping he would forgive her for beginning a romance she now had to end.

Viper's frown deepened to an angry scowl and he stared out at the river as though he were alone. Finally, certain he would never speak to her again, Erica turned away. The Indian heard a soft rustle as the hem of her dress brushed over the leaves, and he knew she had meant her good-bye to be a final farewell. He turned then to watch her until she had disappeared down the trail, but the fierce gleam in his silver eyes said something far different than good-bye.

# Chapter Four

## August, 1862

Erica was relieved when she didn't see Viper in town again. She knew she had handled their brief romance very badly and was grateful he had departed without taunting her with that fact. When Gunter presented her with a handsome carving of a cougar, she thanked him for the unique gift and immediately put it away in the box with the claw where she would not be constantly reminded of why she had asked for a keepsake of the animal. Even after several weeks had passed, her encounter with the amorous brave was still quite vivid in her mind, but she blamed embarrassment, rather than the heady joy of his kisses, as the cause.

Viper, however, made not the slightest effort to forget Erica. He kept the soft curl of her silken hair with him always, so whenever he was alone he could twist it slowly through his fingers. At those times he would recall the luscious taste of her kiss and the gentle swells of her figure until his whole body ached with longing. What did it matter that she had promised herself to another now that she had met him? Was he not fine enough a man for her? It was all too obvious that her answer to that question was different than his. Still, he remembered the startling blue of her eyes and the way the excitement of their arguments had brought a bright blush to her cheeks, and he knew fate would not have allowed him to meet such an enchanting woman if he were not meant to have her for his own. He knew that eventually a way to impress the white woman favorably would occur to him. He tried to be patient while he waited for such an inspiration, but unfortunately, he had very little patience.

Viper awakened the instant Two Elk's hand touched his shoulder. He had already drawn his knife before the young man spoke, but after recognizing his friend's voice he slid his weapon back into its sheath.

"What has happened that cannot wait until morning to be discussed?" he asked crossly in the dark as he swept his thick black hair out of his eyes.

Squatting down beside Viper, Two Elk inhaled deeply to have breath enough to explain all that had transpired during the night. "Four braves from Chief Red Middle Voice's Rice Creek Camp killed five settlers at Acton today. Two of them women!"

His full attention captured by that horrifying news, Viper sat up quickly. "Do we know the braves, or those who died? Tell me all you know," he urged hoarsely.

"It was those fools Brown Wing, Breaking Up, Killing Ghost, and Runs Against Something When Crawling. They chose shooting whites to prove their courage. The trader Robinson Jones, his wife, her son, a daughter, and another man all died."

Viper knew the braves, for while they had been Upper Sioux, they had married Lower Sioux women. Troublemakers all. He thought them crazy to have killed Jones and his family, for the man had always been friendly to the Sioux. "How did you learn of this?"

"Red Middle Voice has come here with Shakopee to talk with Little Crow about the killings and what must be done. They have sent for the other chiefs: Mankato, Wabasha, Traveling Hail, and Big Eagle. They are meeting in Little Crow's house right now. Come, we must listen, for the talk is of war."

"War?" Viper was now fully awake and needed no coaxing to follow his friend to the frame house the government had built for their chief, Little Crow. Two Elk was of medium height with a tough, wiry build. As they joined the warriors who had already crowded into the chief's dwelling, he jostled his companions this way and that, slipping between their ranks until he and Viper had moved to the front where they could not only hear, but also see the chiefs' expressions while they talked. It soon became apparent that the leaders of the Sioux were divided upon what course of action to follow. The two friends listened closely as Chief Red Middle Voice described what he had been told.

While the chief had only the word of the culprits as to what had happened, he reported it along with the fact that the four men involved knew they had created a great deal of trouble for themselves by choosing to prove their bravery by killing whites. They had stolen horses and hastily ridden back to Rice Creek, where their grisly tale had quickly stirred cries for an all-out war on whites. Since Shakopee's village was larger, Red Middle Voice had gone to consult with him about the incident. The two chiefs, unwilling to go to war without the backing of all the Lower Sioux, had then come to seek Little Crow's aid.

Viper shook his head, disgusted to think that dares exchanged among four men well known for making trouble had resulted in the senseless deaths of five whites. Regrettable deaths for which he knew they would all be made to suffer. "We will never get our annuity goods and money now," he whispered to Two Elk who nodded in agreement, for he was also certain the government would punish them all rather than only the four guilty men.

Recently defeated by Traveling Hail for the important post of speaker of the Lower Sioux, a bitter Little Crow at first refused to provide any advice on the dilemma the four fools from Rice Creek had created. He made only the dire prediction that white men so outnumbered the Sioux that any thought of war was simply the talk of foolish children. His ridicule did not stop the arguments in favor of an uprising to drive all white settlers from the Minnesota Valley, however. Wabasha and Traveling Hail also insisted it would be folly to make war on the whites, but while they were respected for their wisdom, even as chiefs their influence was limited.

Viper remained silent as the young men all around him spoke out in favor of war. While the killings at Acton had not been planned, hostility toward whites was so widespread that the incident appealed to many as the perfect excuse to go to war. Cries then went up to strike at the "cut-hairs," Indians who had adopted the white man's ways, as well. The gray-eyed brave watched as the younger men's hatred for whites grew increasingly virulent, until their cries for war overruled the far more cautious words of their chiefs.

"Little Crow will agree to lead us," Two Elk predicted accurately. "Then he will regain the prestige he lost when Traveling Hail was selected speaker."

Viper nodded, thinking a war resulting from deaths motivated by a stupid dare and led by a chief bent on regaining lost power was a foolish endeavor, indeed. Yet once overruled, the chiefs who had argued against war one by one agreed to go along with the younger braves' decision. The United States government had broken too many promises to the Sioux to deserve any loyalty, and in the majority view, war was long overdue. Whether or not it could be won no longer seemed important.

Once the uprising had been decided upon, Little Crow was eager to show off the military talent of which he was extremely proud. He quickly ordered an attack on the Lower Agency to take place the next day. As the conspirators spilled out of the chief's frame house they began to form war parties bent on killing the settlers, but Viper remained aloof from the others. He was a man who made his own decisions, but his friends soon surrounded him, expecting, as always, that he would be the one to lead them.

Growling Bear nudged Two Elk with a playful shove. "This is our chance to prove we are warriors worthy of the name! It is time we taught the white man to fear the Sioux."

"We can kill those at the agency, that is nothing," Viper warned pessimistically, "but what of the soldiers the army will send against us?"

"What soldiers?" Hunted Stag asked with a defiant sneer. "They have all gone to fight the war against the South. The army has no men left to send against us. Are you with us or not?"

Viper looked up at the eastern sky, which had already begun to lighten with the first rays of the coming dawn.

61

What choice did he really have? he asked himself. The government had stolen their lands with promises of food and money they did not send. His people had once been the proud masters of their own world. Now they were no better than pitiful beggars waiting for scraps to fall from the white man's table.

The Sioux mattered so little to those in Washington that clearly they did not care whether or not the Indians starved to death before their annuity goods were distributed. Viper cared though, and deeply. Even if they could not win a war against the United States, at least they would no longer be ignored. "I am with you," he finally replied, but his voice was filled with bitter resentment rather than pride.

Monday, August 18, 1862 was another warm summer day whose calm was swiftly shattered by the loud report of gunfire and the terrified shrieks of those desperately trying to flee the Indians' surprise attack. The first to die was James W. Lynd, a former state senator, who was clerking in the trading post of Nathan and Andrew Myrick. That he had recently deserted his Sioux wife and two children for another Indian woman may have made him a special target. The next casualty was also an employee of the Myricks', George W. Divoll. Andrew Myrick escaped from his store through a window on the second floor, but he died before he could reach cover. His corpse was found with grass stuffed in the mouth, the Indians' witty reply to his suggestion that they eat grass when he would no longer issue them credit.

The white traders were easy targets, for none was prepared for violence. François La Bathe died in his store. Two clerks died in the William H. Forbes establishment. A. H. Wagner, the superintendent of farms at the agency, was killed along with two of his employees at the urging of Little Crow when they foolishly tried to keep the Indians from stealing horses. The agency physician, Dr. Philander P. Humphrey, along with his wife and two children, fled to the other side of the river, only to be murdered there. Also losing his life was Philander Prescott, a fur trader whose wife was Chief Shakopee's mother-in-law. Thirteen died at the agency, and seven more as they fled for safety. Nearly a dozen people were taken captive, but when the Indians turned their attentions to looting the traders' stores, forty-seven others were able to escape with their lives, if little else.

Viper was an excellent shot, but he chose as his prey only the traders who had cheated his people and deserved to die. At one point he saw Growling Bear take aim at a fleeing woman, and he brought his hand down on his friend's wrist with so sharp a blow that the brave cried out in pain. "Let her go," he commanded firmly. "The women make valuable captives, but they are worthless dead."

While he did not argue the logic of that statement, Growling Bear was nonetheless insulted and stalked off to shoot whom he chose without having to listen to Viper tell him what to do. Two Elk watched their sulking friend depart, but he was so intrigued by the thought of taking a white woman hostage that he did not caution Viper to keep his thoughts to himself. "The women will run to the ferry. That's where we should be if you want to take captives."

While Viper had scant interest in taking prisoners, he had less in looting the trading posts, and so joined his friend in running down to the Redwood Ferry. Little more than a large raft, which was propelled across the water by a ferryman grasping a rope secured on either side of the river, the boat had already taken several groups of hysterical refugees across.

"It is thirteen miles to Fort Ridgely. Even if people from the agency run all the way there, the soldiers will not be here anytime soon." Two Elk seemed disappointed he would have no opportunity to kill any army troops for several hours.

Viper did not reply. Using a smooth hand-over-hand motion that belied his fright, the ferryman was returning his flat-bottomed boat to their side of the river in a brave attempt to carry more people to safety. With a deadly precision, Two Elk raised his rifle, took careful aim, and fired, making that crossing the last journey the ferryman would ever make. Viper turned away, sickened by the realization that the uprising would claim the lives of men

63

who had done them no harm as well as those who had treated the Sioux with contempt and deserved no mercy.

The first of the survivors of the attack to reach Fort Ridgely was J. C. Dickinson. He operated the boarding-house at the Lower Agency, and with his family had escaped in a wagon via the ill-fated ferry. Along with other terrified whites, he provided what details he could of the uprising to the fort's commanding officer, Captain John S. Marsh.

"In your worst visions of hell you could not imagine what horrors took place this morning, Captain." Dickinson was still so shaken it took him a great deal of effort to coherently describe their ordeal. "Yesterday was as peaceful a day as we have ever had. Then today there were armed Indian braves everywhere you looked. More than I have ever seen together. They must have come from a dozen different camps. They were painted up to look fierce and fired at everyone they saw. There were bodies lying all over the ground, houses in flames. It was pure hell, I tell you. That is the only way to describe the terror we escaped, pure hell."

While he had fought in the Civil War with a regiment from Wisconsin, the young army officer had no experience fighting Indians. "You've no idea what set them off?" he asked with a puzzled frown, certain so furious an attack must have had some provocation.

"None," Dickinson swore. "Oh, they were all mad about their money being late from Washington and the delay in distributing food, but that's no cause to go killing off every white at the agency."

"Certainly not," Marsh agreed, although he had had personal experience dealing with problems caused by the annuity goods' tardiness. Mistakenly believing Sioux warriors could be no worse adversaries than Confederate soldiers, he tried to reassure Dickinson he would soon have the situation well in hand. "I'll take some men out to the agency right now and put a stop to this before there's any more bloodshed." He did not alarm Dickinson by mentioning the fact that the fort was at the moment short-handed.

Only the previous day, Lieutenant Timothy J. Sheehan had left with fifty men of Company C, Fifth Minnesota, on the way to Fort Ripley on the Mississippi. Marsh hastily dispatched Corporal James C. McLean to recall them. He then left twenty-nine men at the fort with nineteen-year-old Lieutenant Thomas P. Gere, with orders to look after the survivors of the massacre at the Lower Agency as best he could. Taking forty-six enlisted men in wagons, while he and an interpreter, Peter Quinn, rode mules, the intrepid captain set out for the Lower Agency intent upon quelling the uprising in short order.

The Reverend Samuel D. Hinman was an Episcopal missionary. Only the day before Little Crow had attended his Sunday service. When the group of survivors with whom he was traveling met Captain Marsh and his men on the road, he quickly issued a warning.

"You'll be badly outnumbered, Captain. We had no warning of what was to come, but you should heed mine. Don't go any further without reinforcements."

Marsh was undaunted, however, and after thanking the priest for his concern, continued on. The soldiers passed homes in flames and saw bodies alongside the road, but it was not until they were within one mile of the ferry that Marsh had his men leave their wagons to march in single file. When they reached the landing, they found the ferry-boat tied up on their side. The captain was wary, however, for the tall grass and thick stands of hazel and willow on both sides of the river made it a perfect spot for an ambush. Fearing that if he and his men boarded the ferry to cross to the Lower Agency they would be picked off one by one, he waited to make certain the crossing could be made safely.

White Dog, an Indian referred to as a "cut-hair," since he had been hired by the government to teach farming to his fellow Sioux, then appeared on the opposite side of the river. He called out to the soldiers, and through Peter Quinn invited them to cross the river to hold a council.

Marsh, still wary of a trap, failed to give that order, however. His worst fears were then swiftly realized as scores of Indians sprang from their hiding places in the dense underbrush and began firing. Twelve of his troops and Quinn died almost instantly. His mule was shot dead, but the captain managed to leap from the saddle as the animal fell and rallied his men to fire upon their attackers. Urging them to take cover in the thickets at the riverbank, he led them back toward the fort. While they were sheltered from the Indians' fire as they worked their way downstream through the brush, when the vegetation came to an end they found the way to the fort blocked by still more well-armed braves.

Viper found fighting against soldiers far more to his liking than shooting civilians. The blue-coated men were armed and fought back bravely, making the contest far more sporting. The Sioux's argument was with the government, and the army belonged to the government, so their troops were the perfect opponent now that the greedy traders at the agency were dead. Thanks to the traders' well-stocked storerooms they now had plenty of ammunition, and Viper was careful not to waste a single shot.

While Viper chose his next target with care, John Marsh was growing increasingly desperate. Despite warnings from Dickinson and Hinman he had never expected to run into such vast numbers of Sioux warriors. To stand and fight was not an option when his pitifully small force was so greatly outnumbered that they would soon be overrun if they stopped moving. Thinking their only hope to escape total disaster would be to swim the river and approach the fort from the opposite riverbank, Marsh waded out into the water and began to lead his men across.

The captain was a strong swimmer and offered encouragement to the others, but before he could cross the river he suffered a severe cramp. As he doubled over with pain, water rushed into his lungs, choking him as he gasped frantically for air. While he would never have surrendered to the Sioux, the officer could not escape the deadly grip of the river, and it yanked him down deeper each time he fought his way to the surface. Despite the efforts of his men to rescue him, in the midst of his first Indian battle, Captain Marsh drowned in the Minnesota River.

Command of the beleaguered unit then fell to Sergeant John F. Bishop, a man all of nineteen years old. Despite his youth and inexperience, he succeeded where Marsh had failed and led fifteen survivors, five of them wounded, back to the fort. It was after nightfall before they finally reached safety. Later, eight more infantrymen who had become separated from the others managed to make their way back to the fort. Including Marsh and Quinn, twenty-four men had lost their lives in the ambush, and the Indians' strength would never again be so badly underestimated.

Earlier in August, war with the Sioux had seemed unavoidable at the Upper Agency. With his stone warehouse filled to capacity, the Indian agent, Thomas J. Galbraith, had refused to issue rations until the government had sent the gold due the Indians. New to the frontier, a political appointee lacking any experience for his job, he knew only that money and food had always been distributed together. He wanted to follow that tradition. It had taken Lieutenant Sheehan, who was on hand from Fort Ridgely with two companies of the Fifth Minnesota Regiment, to convince Galbraith to distribute pork and flour early. Captain Marsh had also arrived on the scene, and after assessing the tenseness of the situation, had persuaded the agent to distribute more rations after the army officer had secured the Indians' promise they would return to their villages to await the arrival of the money owed them.

Once calm was restored and the soldiers had departed, the ineffectual Galbraith decided to leave with a group of mixed bloods and agency personnel he had recruited to fight in the Civil War. Taking the name of their county, they called themselves the Renville Rangers, and on August 13 they set out for Fort Snelling, which was located near St. Paul.

When rumors of the uprising reached the Upper Agency the afternoon of August 18, there was no agent in residence and the whites at first found it impossible to believe reports of the massacre. At the same time, the Indians living in the vicinity of the Yellow Medicine River just below the agency were engaged in heated argument over whether or not to join the Lower Sioux in the uprising.

Urging peace was John Other Day, who was married to a white woman and had mixed-blood children. Also opposed to the war was Little Paul, the speaker of the Upper Sioux. When they could not sway the majority opinion to their view, they left to warn whites before the war council was over. John Other Day gathered the people at the agency into the warehouse, stood guard over them all night, then led them to safety across the Minnesota River the next morning. Little Paul made his way to the outlying missions of Dr. Thomas S. Williamson and the Reverend Stephen R. Riggs to spread word of the uprising and urge whites to seek refuge at Fort Ridgely. While his news was met with disbelief by the doctor and the missionary, his warnings were reluctantly heeded, and the white residents of the Upper Agency were spared the full wrath of the uprising their counterparts at the Lower Agency had suffered.

While the other braves celebrated their victory on the night of the eighteenth, Viper sat quietly by himself. He was leaning back against a tree, his rifle balanced across his knees. All around him men were getting drunk on the whiskey they had taken from the traders' stores. He had gotten drunk only once, but that experience had been enough to teach him he didn't want to drink whiskey ever again. He had been fourteen, out hunting with his uncle when the man had produced a bottle of whiskey. The vile stuff had burned his throat, but then warmed his insides sufficiently to inspire him to risk taking another drink, and then another. He could not recall the rest of the evening, but he had awakened in the morning so sick he had feared he was dying. His uncle had laughed at his pain and encouraged him to drink the last drops of whiskey left in his bottle, but Viper had refused. Now, more than ten years later, he still refused to take another drink.

He was not certain how many of the army men he had killed, since too many others had been firing at the same time. His friends had been right apparently: the army had few men to send against them. Those they had sent had died quickly. He had been impressed by the bravery of the officer who had led the troopers. That a man of such courage had drowned made it clear that the river had chosen to help them win the fight. That thought brought the first smile of the day to his lips, for Viper had a special fondness for the river.

While he would accept help from any quarter, Viper

knew the Army trained its men to be well disciplined, to follow orders, and to function as a group, whereas warfare was a far different matter for the Sioux. It was the heroic deeds of the individual, "counting coup," which mattered most to them. Despite their far more loosely organized structure, they had done very well that day. They had had the element of surprise on their side, though, in addition to a vast superiority of numbers. While his friends drank themselves into a helpless stupor, Viper sat by himself wondering just how long those advantages would last.

If the soldiers at Fort Ridgely died as quickly as those he had seen that day, Viper knew there would be nothing to stop them from retaking the entire river valley. The farmers at Milford would put up little resistance, and surely the residents of New Ulm would fare no better. Viper closed his eyes as memories of Erica suddenly flooded his mind. There wasn't a brave among them who was stupid enough to shoot a woman as pretty as she, but what if another man took her captive? That possibility filled his heart with dread, and the gray-eyed Indian swore to himself the slender blonde would fall into no man's hands but his own. He had not considered taking her against her will before that day, but he had not dreamed war was so close at hand, either. During a war, anything might happen. A white woman might even fall in love with an Indian brave if the man were clever enough to make it happen.

None of the advice Song of the Wren had gotten from her mother had proved of any help in winning Viper's heart, but the clever girl knew that when drunk a man might do many things he would not do when sober. If Viper were to get very drunk that night, she planned to seize that opportunity and make certain he awakened to find he was her husband. She felt a slight twinge of conscience at the thought of tricking the man into becoming her spouse, but she was tired of waiting for him to become enamored of her on his own. She was positive that if they could only spend some time together he would fall in love with her, since so many of his friends found her charming. Because of the war, she knew she had not a moment to lose. During the fighting he could easily meet a woman from another village but if he already had a wife, then he would come home to her at the war's end.

When she found Viper seated alone beneath a tree, Wren observed the stillness of his pose for a moment, then, certain he had joined the others in getting drunk before staggering off by himself, she rushed forward and knelt by his side. "Viper?" she whispered anxiously, hoping to lure him to a more secluded spot where either he would make love to her, or in the morning when he saw her tears, he would assume that he had, and offer marriage. It seemed the perfect plan, until Viper turned toward her and spoke.

"You should be with your mother tonight, Wren. I do not know half of these braves, and I am certain your parents would not want you to know them, either. I will find your brother to walk you back to your tepee." Viper was annoyed to have his thoughts interrupted by a young woman prowling about alone, but he had no intention of taking responsibility for her himself and rose to his feet.

Song of the Wren knew instantly she had made a terrible mistake, for it was now plain Viper had not been drinking at all. Fearing he would guess what she had planned to do, her face grew hot with shame. She leaped to her feet, but as she turned to flee, she slammed right into the broad chest of a brawny brave, who, looking for a place to relieve himself, had stepped away from his companions. He laughed when he saw she was pretty, and pulling her into his arms, he tried to kiss her.

Viper recognized the man as one from Shakopee's camp, but he did not hesitate before calling out to him, "Let the woman go!"

The brave, like Viper, was in his late twenties. A heavy-set individual, he scanned Viper's lean build and made the mistake of thinking he could fight him for the woman and win. "Is she your wife?" he asked first, for he would not cause any trouble over a married woman.

"It does not matter who she is," Viper responded. "Let her go."

"Clearly, she is looking for a man. If it is not you, then it will be me," the brave bragged with a deep chuckle.

Song of the Wren struggled to break free, but the pounding of her fists made no marks on the brute's chest and little impression upon his whiskey-clouded mind. She turned toward Viper, her tear-filled eyes imploring him to defend her.

The brave held Wren securely, and Viper dared not fire his rifle or draw his knife for fear of striking her. Why the silly creature had left her tepee at that late hour he didn't know, but he would not allow his friend's sister to come to harm. "This is not your camp, but mine. Release her, or you will not live to see the dawn."

Even in his drunken state, the seriousness of Viper's expression as he spoke that threat prompted the man to reconsider. He had been drinking a great deal and had wanted only to have fun, not make trouble. While he still thought he could beat the brave who faced him in a fight, he doubted the brief pleasure the woman would provide would be worth the trouble that would surely follow. With a disgusted sneer, he released Wren and went stumbling off to complete his original errand before rejoining his friends.

Mortified, Song of the Wren threw herself into Viper's arms and began to weep huge tears. She had wanted Viper to notice her, but not like this! Now her only hope was that he did care something for her and would speak of his own accord. She murmured soft words of praise for his kindness against his bare chest, but he did not respond as she had hoped he would.

Viper wasted no time in prying Wren's arms from around his neck, but rather than searching out Hunted Stag he escorted her back to her tepee himself. Without scolding, or wishing her a goodnight, he left her there and went to find a place to rest where his solitude would not again be interrupted.

Wren dried her tears before slipping inside the tepee. Her father was celebrating with his friends and her mother and sisters were sleeping soundly, so she knew the sorry fact that her plan to become Viper's wife had met with disaster would never be discovered. That thought did not console her, however. She still wanted the handsome brave for her husband, and vowed she would not give up until she found a way to melt the icy coldness of his heart with the warmth of her love.

# Chapter Five

## August, 1862

On Monday morning, August 18, curiosity about a commotion out in the street drew Erica from behind the counters of the dry goods store. The cause of the excitement proved to be a recruiting party getting ready to depart. The men were riding in several wagons and had brought along a brass band to better their chances of finding volunteers for the Union Army among the inhabitants of the outlying prairie farms. They were an enthusiastic group, and while there had been a time when Erica would have joined the other residents of New Ulm in waving and shouting encouragement to them, she no longer had any interest in seeing men go off to fight in the war and quickly returned to her duties.

Karl Ludwig saw his niece slip back into the store, but he made no move to follow her until the recruiting party had started on its way. The music had lured more than the usual number of people to the center of town, and any time a crowd gathered it had always proven to be good for business. Anticipating a profitable morning, he returned to work in an ebullient mood. He walked up to the yardage counter where Erica was busy sorting thread hoping to discover why she hadn't shown more interest in the unexpected entertainment. She spent so much time by herself, he was surprised she had not wanted to mingle with the crowd, as he had.

"What's the matter, child, don't you like music?" he

asked with a warm smile, which kept his question from sounding critical.

"I love music," Erica replied, "but I thought all the men who wanted to be soldiers from around here had already enlisted. Is there anyone left for that noisy bunch to recruit?"

"You've a point there, my dear," Karl admitted. "Of course, there are always boys like Gunter, who may have recently had a birthday and may now be old enough to join the Army."

That her shy cousin might have such a dream had never even occurred to Erica. "Gunter doesn't want to enlist, does he?" she asked with a worried frown.

"No, not yet, but he just might decide that's what he wants if all his friends do."

"Would you allow it?" Erica doubted that her aunt and uncle would, since they doted on their only child.

Karl shrugged as he supplied a philosopical reply. "When Gunter is old enough to join the army, I hope he will be man enough to make his own decisions."

"Well, yes, of course," Erica agreed. "But you'd try and influence him to say here, wouldn't you?"

"Of course I would, but like I said, he'll be a man soon, and a man has to listen to his own conscience rather than his father's."

The expected influx of customers interrupted their conversation then, but Erica simply couldn't imagine her bashful cousin ever having the courage to fire a gun at anyone. Not wishing to dwell on so gruesome a prospect, the lively blonde forced such dark thoughts aside and waited on their customers with her usual cheerful smile. She had gotten very good at hiding her thoughts, she realized with some amazement, but her heart had not softened one bit where Mark was concerned, and any talk of the war always reminded her instantly of him. She had answered his letter with an equally stilted reply and was yet still wondering what he would send in return.

Because of the increase in business, Erica did not leave the store promptly at noon. She was still in town when the recruiting party returned without having completed its proposed route. The men had traveled within five miles of Milford, a small town upriver, when they had been

73

ambushed by Sioux from the Lower Agency. The high-spirited group had just begun to cross a bridge spanning a ravine when suddenly they were caught in a murderous crossfire. With four of their number dead, the survivors had wheeled the wagons around and raced back to New Ulm. Following close on their heels were families who had hastily abandoned their farms to dash for the safety the German settlement would provide. They readily confirmed the recruiters' shocking report of an Indian uprising.

For the second time that day the residents of New Ulm gathered in the street, but there was no laughter on anyone's lips now. All were horrified to learn a rampage had begun at the Lower Agency and was rapidly spreading beyond its boundaries. The recruiters' wagons were splattered with the blood of the four victims. As the survivors excitedly recounted the tale of the ambush, Erica was stricken first with panic and then seized with nearly suffocating feelings of guilt. That she had befriended an Indian brave, kissed him quite willingly, suddenly seemed like such a horrible mistake that she felt like a traitor to her own kind. She and Viper had not been enemies then, so she knew she shouldn't think of herself as having betrayed her own people. Still, she feared she had unwittingly committed some terrible crime. She couldn't help but wonder if Viper had taken part in the ambush. Had he been one of the Indians hidden in the underbrush, lurking in the shadows, waiting for some unsuspecting traveler to appear? Would he stoop to treachery as low as that?

The handsome brave had made no attempt to hide his anger at the United States government. Apparently he was not the only one who could no longer hold his hatred in check. That the Indians would strike out at innocent farmers and hapless musicians nonetheless appalled her. Despite her fears that she knew one of the Indians responsible for the day's carnage, Erica remained in the street listening spellbound as the people pouring into New Ulm told stories of such barbaric butchery that she knew they had to be speaking the truth. Without warning the Sioux had gone on a wild killing spree, and with growing horror the distraught blonde realized that the Indians were moving south and that New Ulm lay directly in their path.

74

Karl put his arm around Erica's shoulders to turn her away from the crowd as he spoke. "I'm going to help Sheriff Ross and Jacob Nix organize the men with rifles. I want you to run home and tell Britta and Gunter to leave whatever it is they are doing undone and come to the store at once. Just tell them there's trouble with the Sioux, but don't waste any time giving them the details before they get here."

Erica nodded. "I understand." A nervous smile quivered briefly across her lips as she hurried away. "Dear God," she whispered softly to herself as she sped down the street. It had been a little more than ten years since the Sioux had signed over much of their lands to the government. Had such murderous anger as they had displayed today been seething in their hearts all that time? If so, the fury they had unleashed was long overdue but why had no one at the agency had the foresight to warn the settlers of the impending peril before it was too late? That question only added to her feelings of guilt, for if she had not shut Viper out of her life so quickly he might have warned her of what was to come. "Oh, I am being very foolish!" she scolded. The man was an Indian, and he would not have provided her with information that could be used against his people to save hers! Her head aching from a jumble of painfully conflicting thoughts, Erica dashed up the back steps of her uncle's home praying both her aunt and cousin would be there.

Britta was a perceptive woman and needed no more than one glance at Erica's terror-filled expression to fear that the worst had happened. "My God, Erica, what's wrong?" she cried as she rushed to her side. "Has something happened to Karl?"

Erica shook her head, out of breath from running and unable to find her voice for a moment. "Uncle Karl's fine. He wants you and Gunter to come down to the store at once. Indians attacked the Lower Agency this morning, then struck at farms and people on the road. Now come, you must hurry!"

Britta's fair complexion turned ashen as she listened to her niece's report. "But that's absurd! We've been here all these years and—"

Erica stepped behind her aunt to untie her apron. "Yes, and I'm certain you'll be here many more, but right now

75

you're needed at the store. Where's Gunter?"

"Down by the river I think. Oh no! Oh Erica, we'll have to find him!"

"I'll find him, don't worry. Now you go on down to the store and Gunter and I will be there in just a few minutes." While she had to take her aunt's hands and pull her out the door, Erica finally succeeded in setting the woman on her way. She then raced all the way down to the docks where talk of the uprising was as desperate as it was in town. Since goods for the store arrived by boat, it wasn't unusual for Gunter to be down at the waterfront, but Erica saw no sign of him. She walked up and down, waited a few minutes, then decided Gunter was smart enough to know he should look for his father the minute he had heard about the uprising. With that thought in mind she hurried the several blocks back into town where she found her cousin at work building barricades on Minnesota Street.

He waved when he saw her, and Erica gestured for him to come close enough for them to talk without having to yell. "Does your father know where you are?" she asked immediately.

"Yes," Gunter replied with an exasperated sigh. "Look, they need all the men they can find to set up barricades. You just go on back to the store and stay put. I'm needed here."

While she was surprised that her cousin suddenly considered himself among New Ulm's adult male population, Erica didn't ridicule him for it. He was obviously strong enough to be of real help, and in an emergency that was all that mattered. "I'm on my way there now," she replied in a far more polite tone than he had used with her. "I just wanted to make certain your parents wouldn't be worried about you."

"Well, just make certain they don't have reason to worry about you, either," Gunter warned pointedly as he turned away.

Erica nearly screamed in frustration, she was so insulted by that unwanted piece of advice. There was no reason for her aunt and uncle to be worried about her, none whatsoever in her opinion, but she knew why her cousin had said what he had, and her cheeks burned with shame at the memory of what he had seen.

Once she reached the store, Erica learned their situation

76

was even more desperate than it had at first appeared. There were no more than forty men with firearms, and while they had been hastily organized into militia units, that didn't change the alarming fact that their number was pitifully small. To lighten their nearly impossible burden of defending the city, it had been decided to gather everyone into the center of town, since the brick structures there would be far easier to defend than individual frame houses.

After checking with her uncle, who was busy taking an inventory of the ammunition he had on hand, Erica joined her aunt in the Dacotah House, a two-story frame hotel that had been designated as the meeting place for women and children. The hotel quickly became so crowded that the women began to discard their hoop skirts to make more room for later arrivals. That fashion was one of the first casualties of the war didn't surprise Erica, since she had already found the hooped garments ill suited to the way of life she had adopted in New Ulm.

Standing at the window of a second-floor bedroom gazing out at the homes that dotted the gently sloping landscape, Erica found it impossible to reconcile the peaceful scene before her with the threat of attack. From where she stood she could also watch the progress on the barricades. The workers were using barrels and planks and whatever could be found to enclose the central part of the city.

Erica felt deeply troubled that the ugliness of war might soon touch so tranquil a setting. When a little red-haired girl handed her an apple she whispered a strained, "Thank you," and slipped it into her pocket for later. Feeding everyone would be an immense problem, she knew, but she doubted any of them would have much appetite.

"How could it have come to this?" Britta asked her companions, but they all shared her shock and looked as helpless as she to explain the sudden outbreak of violence.

"The Indians were pushed too far," Erica finally responded when no one else spoke up. "They've been treated unfairly all along, but they should not have been expected to wait forever for their yearly payment of food and money."

The little redhead's mother, a buxom woman in a faded

77

green dress, took immediate exception to that remark. "You aren't taking their side, are you?"

When Erica turned to reply, she found every eye in the room was focused squarely upon her. None of the glances were friendly, either. Clearly this was not a group who wanted to discuss causes of the uprising in dispassionate terms. They were all too close. It was their farms that were being threatened, their neighbors who were being murdered. Feeling curiously detached from the other women's plight, she continued. "Certainly not," she assured the woman calmly. "Whatever has caused the uprising, I'm not condoning it. A war is rightly fought between opposing armies on a battlefield, not by unwarranted attacks upon helpless civilians." When that reassurance satisfied the group that she was not defending the Indians' actions after all, the conversation turned to more practical considerations such as feeding the children. Relieved to no longer be the center of attention, Erica decided she would be wise to keep her opinions to herself in the future.

She wasn't certain what had prompted her to mention the Sioux's grievances, although it had been her uncle, not Viper, who had explained them to her. Her comments had surprised her nearly as much as they had her companions, and she had swiftly learned she would have to be more careful to keep her thoughts to herself in the future. She had never been the secretive type until she had come to New Ulm, and the effort to keep so many things hidden was hurting her conscience badly.

As she remained at the window watching for the danger she prayed would not appear, she recalled the bitterness of Viper's expression when she had bid him good-bye. Did he ever think of her with any emotion except hatred? Whatever part he might be playing in the uprising, if he came to New Ulm would he look for her? That she had no idea whether he would want her dead or very much alive was so frightening that she shivered with dread and turned away from the window.

"I should have brought the quilt I've been working on," Britta remarked absently. The afternoon was warm, and simply waiting for the Indians to attack the town while her apprehension rose to paralyzing heights struck Erica as the very worst of pastimes.

When her aunt's comment provided an excuse to leave

the crowded hotel, Erica immediately took it. She knelt down beside Britta and whispered softly, "There's not an Indian in sight. I'm sure I could run home and get the quilt. Anything else you'd like to have?"

"Oh no. I can't ask you to go out on such a foolish errand." Britta was embarrassed even to have mentioned the quilt now.

"I won't be gone more than ten minutes. Now just tell me what to bring and I'll go and get it," the lively blonde insisted. "It will help us all to have something to do."

Britta chewed her lower lip nervously, not wanting to put her niece at risk merely to ease her own boredom. "Are you sure there's no sign of Indians as yet?"

"Positive," Erica swore convincingly.

"Well then, I would like to work on the quilt. You know where I keep my sewing. You ought to bring back what food you can carry, too; that new cheese would be good."

Erica patted her aunt's hands, thinking as she had so many times that Britta and her mother were very much alike. Her mother had been lovely, but she had never been given to deep introspection on any subject. Erica had learned at an early age that if she wanted sensible answers to her questions she would have to ask her father, for she had quickly surpassed her mother's store of knowledge. Now here they were, in the very real danger of being murdered by Indians, and Britta wanted to do a bit of quilting. Her reasons for volunteering to go home were far different, however. Erica had suddenly decided she wanted the claw Viper had given her, for surely this was the perfect time to rely upon the value of a good luck charm provided by an Indian. If it would work any magic at all, then she wanted to have it handy.

Certain her brief absence would not be missed, Erica sped out the back door of the Dacotah House. But before she had taken five paces Gunter grabbed her arm, stopping her in midstride. "Just where do you think you're going?" he asked, as though he had some right to know.

Erica was too embarrassed to admit the truth, so she made up a convenient lie. "We need something for the little ones to eat. I'm on my way to our house to pick up some food."

Gunter frowned slightly, then, after finding no threat in any direction, he decided to go with her. "I'm getting hungry myself. I'll go with you just in case there's trouble."

Rather than argue that he was unarmed and would be of little value should trouble in the form of hostile Indians overtake them, Erica accepted his company as unavoidable. "Let's hurry." She had to take two steps to each one of his, but once they reached their house she left him in the kitchen while she dashed upstairs. The claw lay right where she had left it in the bottom of her stationery box. That day its wicked tip looked even more fearsome than she had recalled, but she hurriedly shoved it into her pocket. Then on an impulse she scooped up the little carving of a cougar Gunter had made for her and dropped it into her pocket, too, thinking she could use some of the animal's fierce spirit as much as an Indian brave.

After making himself a generous sandwich, Gunter had put bread, cheese, and a ham in a basket while Erica had been upstairs. When he saw her carrying the fabric satchel containing his mother's sewing, it didn't occur to him that she had said she was coming to get food. "Let's go. We don't want to be caught alone here in the house." Yet as she slid past him to go out the door, the subtle fragrance that clung to Erica's clothes teased his senses so seductively that he suddenly wished there were some way for them to remain alone there together.

As they raced back into town, Erica had no idea her cousin's thoughts were focused upon her. She kept looking at the bluff behind them, thinking it provided perfect cover for an attack. "This is an awful mess, isn't it, Gunter? I never realized what the people in the South are going through with battles raging all around them."

Gunter dared not admit how little that prospect frightened him, that he had been so caught up in the excitement of preparing for an attack that he had had no time to be afraid. "Henry Behnke has already gone to get help from St. Peter and the other towns nearby. I think we'll be able to gather enough men to come out of this all right."

"Oh, so do I!" Erica agreed optimistically. "Just see you don't take any chances."

That she seemed truly worried about him pleased Gunter enormously. "I won't," he promised. When they reached the hotel, he carried the basket of food inside, then went back to work on the barricades.

As long as they had light, the women sharing the corner room with Britta and Erica joined in working on the quilt. When the hour grew late, none found it easy to sleep.


While the citizens of New Ulm frantically gathered their meager resources to defend their city, the situation that Monday was no less desperate at Fort Ridgely. Lieutenant Gere, the nineteen-year-old left in command by Captain Marsh, was ill with the mumps. Although it was a military outpost built to house army troops near the Sioux reservation, the fort had no stockade. It was a collection of detached buildings: a two-story stone barracks, a commissary, frame quarters for officers, the commandant, and post surgeon, a log hospital and log houses for civilians, and numerous other buildings with varying purposes. The main structures were grouped around a parade ground on open terrain, making them nearly impossible to defend. Deep ravines cut into the prairie on the east, north, and southwest, providing easy access for the Indians.

Around noon, when settlers seeking protection from the Indians were just beginning to reach the fort, a stagecoach carrying $71,000 in gold, the money the government owed the Sioux, arrived. Gere had the kegs of gold hidden, since, tragically, they had arrived one day too late to forestall the uprising.

The population of the fort had grown by more than two hundred with the influx of refugees by the time the first of Marsh's troops returned with the news of his tragic death. Lieutenant Gere then sent another dispatch to Lieutenant Sheehan entreating him to hurry his return. He also sent a rider to notify the commanding officer at Fort Snelling and Governor Alexander Ramsey, alerting them to their dire situation and requesting immediate reinforcements. While carrying that message, Private William J. Sturgis passed through the town of St. Peter, and finding the Indian Agent, Thomas J. Galbraith, there with his newly recruited Renville Rangers, sent them back to help out at the fort.

Had the Indians gone from the Lower Agency directly to Fort Ridgely, they would surely have taken it on

81

August 18. Fortunately for the few army personnel in residence, and for those others who had taken refuge there, the Indians paused first to celebrate their victories. When Little Crow and his braves drew near the fort on Tuesday morning, August 19, the chief, along with Mankato and Big Eagle, urged an immediate attack upon the fort. Many of the younger men had another goal, however, and wished to attack New Ulm, where there would be stores to loot and pretty young women to capture. While the Indians argued, Lieutenant Sheehan and his men arrived at the fort followed by Galbraith and his fifty Rangers. The beleaguered fort then had a hundred eighty men to defend it.

Viper coul not believe there were men among his friends who were more concerned with gathering spoils than with dealing the United States Army another stunning defeat. "Fort Ridgely is the most natural target," he argued persuasively. "It is the army who enforces the government's policies, and it is the army who deserves to suffer, not the fat shopkeepers of New Ulm!"

Growling Bear was not convinced. "If I am going to fight, it is my right to say where!"

Viper shook his head, for he could see the futility of arguing with so stubborn a man. Unlike army troops, Indian braves were not compelled to follow their leaders. They kept their independence at all times, even in the heat of battle. They might follow a respected chief on one day and not on another if they so chose. No man criticized another's actions, for all believed each man was accountable only to himself. How could one man hope to change the tradition of centuries? Viper wondered. "Look," he finally pointed out, "if we are going to sweep the white man from Minnesota, then we must destroy each army outpost on our soil. If we attack in full force we can take Fort Ridgely as easily as we did the agency, but we cannot fight half a dozen battles up and down the river until each man has stolen whatever booty he wants and goes home!"

"What is the point of fighting if I do not get what I want?' Growling Bear continued.

"What you want is not important," Viper insisted once again. "All that matters is that we defeat the army again today. Now, before reinforcements can arrive!" The Indian knew he was right. He knew what he was saying was the truth, and he was also wise enough to see his friends would never grasp the importance of a quick strike with deadly force. "We are not counting coup here, Growling Bear. No one will award you eagle feathers for touching a trooper. Instead, you must kill him. All that matters is that we take the fort so that the arms stored there can't be used against us."

Growling Bear would readily admit that Viper was far more eloquent than he. Tradition, however, did not demand that he persuade others to his cause with brave speeches, and he made no attempt to do so. "I will do what I think best, and you are free to follow your own conscience, Viper. That is as it should be."

"Not in a war, if we are to have any hope of winning!" Viper cried out in frustration.

That response amazed Growling Bear, and he shook his head sadly. "We have never had any chance of winning. Our only hope is to take what we can. That is what I mean to do."

Viper watched Hunted Stag follow Growling Bear as he walked away before turning to Two Elk. "Well, what about you? Are you going to stay here to attack the fort with Little Crow, or do you want to join the others headed for New Ulm?"

Two Elk was torn by indecision. He wanted the things he knew they could take from the prosperous town, but he also wanted to keep his best friend's respect. In the end, it was that desire that proved to be the stronger. "I will fight by your side," he announced calmly, and his heart filled with pride when Viper rewarded him with a grateful smile.

While neither his expression or his words showed it, Viper was also facing a painful dilemma. He truly believed, as Little Crow did, that striking the fort was imperative. He also had a better reason to go to New Ulm than any of the other braves, since he knew a woman there well worth taking captive. If he went with the group heading down the river, no one would criticize him for it, but he was not a man who put his desires before his ideals. As he walked slowly around the camp, he overheard at least a dozen repetitions of the same argument he had had with his friends. When finally the younger braves broke off from the others, he was positive their cause was doomed to fail. There were too few going to New Ulm to put the city in any real danger, and with no chief to lead them, they would be unlikely to plot a clever enough strategy to succeed.

When the small force of Sioux attacked New Ulm on the afternoon of August 19, they took cover on the bluff overlooking the city and began firing from well-protected positions. The newly organized militia, their number augmented by men from St. Peter, bravely held their own, although some had to leave the security of the barricades to drive back the attacking force. When a thunderstorm struck late in the day and the Indians withdrew, the citizen soldiers felt a substantial victory was theirs. That some of the houses at the northern end of town had been burned did not seem a great loss, except to the owners.

That night another one hundred twenty-five men, Frontier Guards from St. Peter and Le Sueur, reached New Ulm. With them were three physicians. When Dr. William W. Mayo of Le Sueur and William R. McMahan of Mankato chose one of the front rooms of the Dacotah House as a hospital, Erica quickly introduced herself and volunteered to help them.

"My father is a physician," she explained proudly. "I often helped him in emergencies, and since there are wounded to tend, I'd like to help you see to them." She knew she could be of real service, and the activity would keep her mind from dwelling on what she feared would be an inevitable confrontation with Viper.

Dr. Mayo glanced over at his newly acquired partner. The young woman's smile was so utterly charming he saw no reason not to grant her request, and he could tell from Dr. McMahan's appreciative glance that he agreed. "We're delighted to have your help, Miss Hanson. Why don't you see if there are any other women without small children to tend who would also be willing to act as nurses? There were five wounded this afternoon, and that's far too many for one young woman to tend."

"I'll go and ask right now," Erica agreed, but while she found two ladies who reluctantly volunteered to help watch over the wounded men, they were so squeamish a pair that she knew should the doctors have to perform any surgery, she would have to be the one to assist them.

There had been six fatalities that day, one of them a thirteen-year-old girl who had foolishly dashed out into the street in the midst of the battle. Erica felt Emilie's death had been senseless. She could not help but wonder if the girl had merely been hit by a stray bullet or if some brave had deliberately aimed for her. From the tales she had heard from the settlers who had fled their farms, the Indians had no qualms about killing women and children. That was so despicable a practice it sickened her thoroughly.

Unfortunately, Erica found that having useful work to do did not stop her from worrying. While enough armed men had been gathered to defend the town from the first attack, how would they fare if the Sioux returned again and again? Would the town eventually be overrun despite their best efforts to prevent such a crushing defeat? They were relying upon the men to protect them now, but what if so many men were wounded or killed that the women had to protect themselves? Would she be able to pick up a rifle and shoot an Indian if her life depended upon it? Perhaps the Sioux's hatred of whites had real justification, but she had no reason to despise Indians, although the violence of their actions terrified her. Would fear be a strong enough motivation to inspire her to pull the trigger? With a shudder of dread she realized those were not questions she wanted answered.

Her head aching from the turbulence of her fears, Erica remained awake all night, seated at the bedside of the most seriously injured man. Late that afternoon sixteen men had left the city to scout the farms along the Cottonwood River hoping to gather intelligence as well as to rescue survivors. Upon their return they had met with disaster when eleven of their number were slain in an ambush just outside of town. Erica knew they couldn't afford to lose any men, let alone nearly a dozen. She didn't even know how to fire a gun, but she couldn't shake the horrible premonition that she was going to have to learn, and fast. That her target would undoubtedly be Viper only added to her fright.

# Chapter Six

## August, 1862

Viper found it difficult to hide his smile as the braves who had been defeated at New Ulm returned empty-handed to Little Crow's camp. None wished to discuss their failed expedition, but they were now ready to join in the attack planned for the next day at Fort Ridgely, without argument.

The afternoon of August 20, while Little Crow took a smaller group to create a diversion in the west, Viper was with the main body of four hundred Sioux approaching the fort along the ravine on the east. With loudly shrieked war whoops they stormed the northeast corner of the fort, taking several of the outbuildings. The soldiers grouped on the parade ground were trapped by the braves' fire, until Lieutenant Sheehan ordered them to take cover and fire at will.

Squinting into the smoke that swirled about them, Viper chose his targets with his usual care, while all around him men fired their weapons indiscriminately. Being more observant than many of the others, he was the first to see the artillery pieces being rolled out, and while he was uncertain how much damage the two twelve-pound mountain howitzers could do, he swiftly found out as their shells exploded nearby with a thunderous roar. Knowing it would take more than rifle fire to seize more ground now, he joined the others in dropping back to the ravine.

Little Crow found himself facing cannon fire on the west and also had to retreat to a safe distance. Rifle fire continued until nightfall, however, when the Indians abandoned their positions and returned to the Lower Agency. The artillery pieces had frightened them all, for they had not anticipated that the army would have such powerful weapons. When rain kept them from attacking again on the twenty-first, the chief used the time wisely to gather more braves, swelling his forces to eight hundred. If he could not beat the army in firepower, he could nevertheless outnumber them and pray that advantage would be enough to insure a victory.

Friday, August 22 found Viper again ready to attack Fort Ridgely. With several others he crawled on his belly through the prairie grass to get close enough to shoot flaming arrows into the roofs of the buildings. Still soaked by the previous day's rain, the roofs stubbornly refused to ignite, and the few fires the Indians did start were quickly put out by the fort's defenders.

Now that Little Crow had doubled his strength, his strategy was a simple one: he planned to lay down a blanket of continuous fire, rush the fort, and defeat the whites in hand-to-hand combat. To begin the assault, a group of braves reached the stable, which provided fine cover, but when artillery shells set the buildings aflame, they were forced to retreat. Next to be set ablaze was the sutler's home when the Sioux attempted to use it for cover. Realizing that any other building they took would undoubtedly meet the same fate, they swiftly abandoned that strategy.

When Little Crow was wounded, Mankato took over leadership of the Sioux warriors and attempted an all-out attack through the ravine that lay at the southwest of the beleaguered fort. Again the braves were driven back by fire from the artillery pieces, which had been double-charged in a desperate attempt to stave off the attack. The Sioux were brave, but not suicidal, and the fort's defenses would not be challenged again. The Indians withdrew and made no plans to return.

Viper could not recall ever having been so tired, but as he gazed at the disheveled poses of the friends who had collapsed from exhaustion all around him he realized with scant pride that he had more stamina than most. At least he was still awake. He had agreed with Little Crow that taking the fort was the first step to ridding the valley of whites. Once the fort had fallen, there would have been nothing to stop them from reaching the Mississippi. It was now painfully clear Fort Ridgely was not going to fall, and no more time would be wasted trying to defeat men armed with artillery. He had known exactly what he wished to do when the enemy had been the army. Now he would have to redirect his anger toward any whites they encountered, and he was not convinced that was what he truly wished to do.

Using a twig, the weary Indian drew a faint line in the dirt at his side, lazily tracing the path of the river from the fort to New Ulm. The town would have no cannons. From what he had seen of the residents, there were few men to defend it, either. If the Sioux could move with the same determination they had shown that day, the city would soon be theirs. Just as they had at the agency, he knew most of the braves would turn to looting, but there was only one thing of value in New Ulm as far as he was concerned, and he whispered her name softly to himself. Erica must know about the war. Did she also know he would be coming for her?

On Saturday morning, August 23, lookouts at New Ulm saw huge clouds of black smoke coming from the direction of Fort Ridgely. Fearing the fort had fallen to the Sioux, they fully expected to be attacked from the north side of the river.

Now commanding the forces gathered to defend New Ulm was Judge Charles E. Flandrau. A member of the Minnesota Supreme Court, he had attended the state's constitutional convention and was a former Indian agent. A resident of Traverse des Sioux, he was the most prominent citizen of the valley, and his leadership had been readily sought and acknowledged. He had ordered the street barricades fortified with wagons and whatever else could be found to more effectively seal off the core of the city. There were now more than one thousand women, children, and men without firearms crowded into the barricaded structures. Many of them had been in their cramped basement quarters since the first attack on Tuesday and were not only frightened, but tired and hungry, as well.

Not realizing the Sioux had set the fires to give the residents of New Ulm the mistaken impression the fort had fallen, Flandrau sent a force of seventy-five across the river to defend the city on the north. Those men were quickly cut off by waiting Sioux and had to retreat to St. Peter. Flandrau then had only two hundred twenty-five armed men to defend the town.

While Little Crow recuperated from his wounds, the chiefs Mankato, Wabasha, and Big Eagle led a force of six hundred fifty braves to within striking distance of the town. The Sioux warriors approached to within a mile and a half, then began to fan out. As their charge increased in speed, the braves began to yell war cries so terrifying that the white men who had advanced past the barricades turned tail and ran for the center of the town, while the Indians used the vacant houses they had passed for cover. The firing then grew intense, with sharpshooters hidden in a large wooden windmill west of the business district keeping the braves from overrunning the barricades there.

Viper was surprised to find that the citizens of New Ulm had burned many houses to the ground to prevent them from being used as cover. He was on horseback that day, and, carrying a torch, rode swiftly to set other houses aflame so they could advance under the dense cloud of smoke fanned by the wind blowing from the direction of the river. They had the numbers to encircle the town, and as he moved forward setting fires, his friends kept up steady fire at the men who manned the barricades.

After having faced cannon fire, Viper found the assault upon New Ulm child's play. The men defending the town were relying upon the protection of wooden barricades that he felt certain would be far easier to ignite than the roofs at Ford Ridgely. He could swiftly turn that wooden wall of defense into a ring of fire, and while that idea struck him as nothing less than brilliant, he did not want to see all the residents of New Ulm burn to death in the inferno he could so easily create. He pulled his horse to an abrupt halt, then gouged his heels into the stallion's flanks when a bullet came so near his thigh it ruffled the fringe on his buckskins. There was a fine line between bravery and stupidity, and he wheeled his mount away and back through the veil of smoke as he tried to decide just how much more of the city he truly wished to put to the torch.

It had been so long since Erica had slept she felt only numb rather than fatigued. Enduring three seemingly endless days of waiting for the Sioux to return had been far worse torture than facing their first attack, but she could tell from the sound of the gunfire that this battle was much more intense than the previous one had been. Casualties were being carried to the back door of the hotel and brought inside as quickly as space could be found to accommodate them.

Like everyone else, she had been forced to wear the same clothes all week. That her pale blue dress was splattered with bloodstains was scarcely reassuring to her patients, but her manner was still calm and competent. Dr. Mayo had complimented her many times, for he had found she had a better knowledge of emergency procedures than most medical students. That also worked to her disadvantage, however, when he had to rely upon her to care for the more seriously injured before he could reach them.

Two hours went by, perhaps three. Erica had no reason to glance at the clock as she drew upon reserves of strength she had not known she possessed. Being tired seemed a small complaint when men who were seriously wounded lay on makeshift beds all around her. Stumbling out the back door in the vain hope that no more casualties would be found waiting, she saw two men approaching dragging a third between them. She rushed out to meet them and quickly provided instructions when she saw the profusely bleeding wound in the badly injured man's left thigh.

"Just take him right on inside. Carry him to the front room, but don't leave him until Dr. Mayo says you may go." The two able-bodied men turned fright-filled eyes toward her, fearing their friend might lose his leg, but she shook her head warning them not to ask that question out loud.

Erica held the door open as the trio entered, but she couldn't bear to follow them just yet and leaned back against the frame structure to catch her breath. Before she had enjoyed more than a few seconds' respite from her labors, she heard hoofbeats approaching rapidly. Assuming someone must be bringing in another desperately wounded man, she remained where she stood to greet them.

The horse was big and black and his flying mane obscured the rider's identity until it was too late for Erica to flee. Bright streaks of red war paint crossed the Indian's face on a diagonal slant resembling a fierce swipe from a cougar's claws, while his long hair flew out behind him like a wild crown of ebony fire. His bronze skin glistened with a light sheen of sweat, and the gleam that filled his eyes was again that of highly polished steel.

Paralyzed with fright, Erica could not even reach for the door, let alone gather the strength of purpose necessary to dart back inside the hotel. She stood transfixed by the Indian's piercing silver gaze, certain she was looking directly into the face of her own doom. Her worst fears had suddenly come to pass, and as the stallion's hot breath brushed her cheek she fully expected a bullet to rip through her heart. She shut her eyes tightly to spare herself the gruesome sight of her own blood splattering across the horse's flank.

Viper leaned down, and with the ease of a well-trained warrior he plucked Erica from the ground, then laid her across the horse's withers in front of him. Without breaking his mount's furious pace, he swept down the line of buildings beside the hotel, then leaped the barricade at the end and carried his struggling captive away before the men defending the city had the presence of mind to realize who he was and what he had done. Swiftly obscured by the blanket of smoke he had created, the Indian disappeared with the grace of a phantom at dawn.

"Jesus Christ!" screamed the man whose hat had been knocked from his head by the hind hooves of the fleeing horse as the animal had cleared the top of the barricade with no more than an inch to spare. "Who in the hell was that?" He jammed his battered hat back on his head before he turned to peer over the makeshift wall, but he could

91

make out nothing through the cloud of smoke that surrounded them.

Gunter had been helping Ernst Schramberger keep his two rifles loaded, having none of his own. He wasn't certain just exactly what he had seen, since the Indian who had sped by them had been little more than a blur of black and bronze. And light blue, he realized, with a sudden horrified suspicion that the bit of blue silk that had passed so quickly from his view might have been his cousin's dress. "It was a Sioux!" he screamed as he turned to Ernst. "But what was he carrying? Was it a woman in blue? Did any of you see what he had?"

His companions had all been facing outward and had seen little more than the black horse's flying tail before he and his rider had disappeared. All except Ernst were too busy to worry as Gunter did that an Indian brave might have just ridden off with one of their women.

Ernst reached for the rifle Gunter had just loaded as he spoke. "You think a brave just carried Erica off, is that your fear?" he asked with a barely concealed smile, for such a happenstance sounded preposterous to him. "Go on in the hotel and take a look around. I'm sure you'll find her with the doctors."

Gunter knew the man was making fun of him. He also knew he would get no answers there, and since being ridiculed was easier to bear than the nagging fear that his pretty cousin had just been taken captive by a savage, he crawled away from the barricade. He kept his head down until he reached the back of the buildings and could make a dash for the hotel. He bolted through the back door, and moving toward the front room, called out Erica's name as he searched the faces of the wounded and those tending them for some sign of her.

Dr. Mayo looked up from the wound he was suturing. "I don't know why you're looking for Erica, but I'd like to find her, too. She was at the back door a few minutes ago, and I need her in here."

The smell of warm blood turned the youth's stomach, but he couldn't tear his eyes away from the physician's gruesome task. The man had laid his patient upon an elegant mahogany table that had formerly been used for dining, but that struck Gunter as no stranger than the fact

92

that the town was surrounded by Indians screaming what he was certain were curses none of them could understand. "I'm afraid, I'm afraid she's been taken captive," he finally managed to stutter.

"Taken captive? You can't be serious!" William Mayo looked up again and saw immediately from the lad's stricken expression that he most certainly was. "God help us all," he prayed aloud. "Well then, you come here and help me. We won't be able to go after Erica until the shooting stops, and from the sound of it that won't be for some time."

There was only one thing Gunter wanted to do less than help the physician, and that was to find his parents to tell them Erica had been captured by some bloodthirsty Sioux riding a black horse. Swallowing hard to force back the nausea that filled his throat, he stepped forward. "What is it you want me to do, sir?" he asked bravely, as though he actually had the courage to follow through with any instructions he might be given.

That she hadn't been shot dead surprised Erica so greatly that she didn't at first realize how excruciatingly painful bouncing facedown across Viper's lap actually was. She found it nearly impossible to draw a breath, and each time she managed that feat she gagged on the dust kicked up by the black stallion's flying hooves. Oblivious of her discomfort, her captor rode mile after bone-jarring mile. Then to her horror he forced his mount into the river, but he did not pull her upright until her hair had already been soaked to the roots by the water. She had been certain he meant to hold her head down and drown her, but the fact that he had spared her from such a horrid fate at what appeared to be the last possible minute did not lessen her fears that he meant to do her great harm. She was still terrified of the man, but she clung to him tightly to keep from being swallowed up by the river.

The stallion was a strong brute, and Viper had been certain the animal could carry both of them across before he had entered the river. When they reached the northern bank he wasted no time trying to remove Erica's arms from around his neck, but instead allowed her to remain in the more comfortable pose and kept on riding. They reached the border of the thick stand of timber known as the Big Woods, then crossed the Minnesota River again above St. Peter and Traverse des Sioux. Only then did he allow the horse to strike a slower pace.

The woods cut a wide swath down the center of the state, extending all the way up to the Canadian border in the north, and Viper meant to stay lost in them for a good long while. He urged the stallion to continue until there was too little daylight left for the horse to make its way safely. Confident they would not be tracked this far from New Ulm, the Indian finally drew his mount to a halt in a small clearing surrounded by sugar maple trees and white elm. "We'll make camp here," he announced confidently.

She didn't dare look up at him for fear of what his expression would be, but after a slight hesitation Erica removed her arms from around Viper's neck. When she realized he had released his hold upon her waist, she looked down with an apprehensive glance. The horse was so large that the ground appeared at least ten feet below her, and she couldn't find sufficient courage after all she had been through to leap from his back.

There was still enough light for Viper to see the trails of Erica's tears upon her cheeks, and he raised his right hand to touch her damp curls with a reassuring caress as he spoke. "I will set you down on your feet if you promise not to try and run away."

Just as Viper had planned, Erica had seen no signs of civilization since they had left New Ulm, so she had no idea which way to run. Besides, she doubted her legs would hold her after such a harrowing ride. She would not admit either of those fears to Viper, however. "I won't run away," she promised in a shaky whisper. She had feared the man wished to kill her, but now another prospect loomed as the more probable, and the possibility of being violated was every bit as frightening as facing death.

Still not convinced the volatile blonde wouldn't bolt at her first chance, the wary brave slid down off the stallion's back first, then reached up to take a firm hold upon Erica's waist, and swung her down to the ground. "New Ulm will have fallen into our hands by now. When I saw you standing at the back of the hotel, I wanted to spare you that

94

ordeal. A woman of your spirit would suffer too greatly as a captive."

Since neither Viper's words nor gestures were threatening, Erica risked looking up at him now, but she found it impossible to believe his words, in spite of the fact that his tone was soft and reassuring. "What are you saying? That I have just been rescued rather than abducted?"

Viper smiled slightly as he nodded, apparently amused by the way she had worded her question. "Yes, you will be far safer with me than with any of the others. Remember that, and do not try and run off."

Erica surveyed their surroundings with a nervous glance, again seeing no possible way to flee. She was certain he could find his way through the dense woods, while she was completely lost. Even if she did have some idea which way to go, she knew it would be ridiculous to attempt to outrun a man who could so easily overtake her. From any point of view, her situation was hopeless: she was trapped, even if he did not have her bound. "What are you going to do?" she finally blurted out, thinking she could more easily bear her fate if she knew what to expect.

Viper had not meant to terrify Erica, as he so obviously had, but he was not all that surprised by her reaction to him. Pretending not to understand the true import of her question, he replied nonchalantly, "As soon as you gather wood, I am going to build a fire. Hurry before it gets dark," he ordered gruffly before turning back to see to the stallion.

Erica didn't know whether to laugh or cry she was so shocked by his command. Completely bewildered, she asked, "You kidnapped me because you needed a servant?"

Viper looked over his shoulder, his glance as cold as his tone. "No, I rescued you to keep you safe from harm, and I expect you to be grateful to me. Now stop wasting time and fetch the wood."

"Why do we need wood? Do you plan to cook?" Erica's voice had taken on a sarcastic edge as her anger swelled to overpower her fear.

Viper turned back to face her, his expression difficult to read beneath the bright streaks of war paint. "I have nothing to cook, but I did not want you to be cold. If we argue much longer, it will be dark. Go now and look while you can still find some wood."

Earlier that afternoon, Erica had expected him to kill her. There was still the very real possibility he might rape her, and, suddenly, wasting her breath arguing about gathering wood seemed absurd. Erica strangled a shriek of outrage as she turned away. She'd been taken captive, regardless of Viper's calmly worded denial to the contrary. She was his prisoner, not his guest. Had New Ulm actually fallen to the Sioux, as he had boasted? If it had, had the Indians continued their wanton slaughter of men and taken the women and children captive? Were her uncle and Gunter lying dead in the street? What fate had befallen her dear Aunt Britta? She was a pretty woman still. Had some brave claimed her for his own?

Tears splashed down her cheeks as she recalled how warmly she had been welcomed into her aunt and uncle's home. Now she did not even know if that home was still standing. Exhausted after a harrowing week and aching all over from the jarring ride, Erica leaned down to pick up a fallen branch and simply slid into unconsciousness, and like a rag doll that had fallen from a child's hand, she crumpled to the ground.

Although he had been pretending to care more about his mount than her, Viper had kept his eye on Erica as she crossed the clearing. She wasn't moving with the sprightly step he was used to seeing, but far more slowly. He saw her bend down, then with a slight sway she collapsed in a heap in the grass. He hesitated for an instant, thinking she was merely playacting to avoid doing her share of their chores, but when she failed to stir he grew alarmed and sprinted across the distance that separated them.

Kneeling by her side, Viper smoothed Erica's tangled curls away from her face, then felt for the pulse in her throat and was reassured to find it strong. He turned her over slowly so she could rest comfortably upon her back, still not understanding what had caused the pretty blonde to faint so suddenly. It was not until then that he really looked at her closely, and he was stunned by the dramatic change in her appearance since they had last been together. Her face was far thinner, and bluish circles marred the usually creamy ivory skin beneath her eyes. She was so pale that her long sweep of dark lashes provided her only touch of color.

She had always been well dressed and beautifully groomed, but she certainly wasn't now. While he recognized the blue gown, the skirt bore numerous dark stains he feared might be dried blood. Had she been wounded as they fled New Ulm? Moving down to her feet, he removed her soft kid slippers, then shoved her ruffled slips aside and slid his hands up her white silk stockings searching for some sign of injury. Her legs were as long and slender as he'd expected them to be. Her feet were tiny, her ankles small, her calves but a gentle swell in her shapely leg. He pushed his hands higher still to caress her thighs, and Erica moaned slightly. He drew back then, certain if she awakened suddenly she would not believe he had been looking for a wound rather than merely enjoying the beauty of her splendid limbs.

Not having any idea how to revive the young woman, but satisfied she was not injured, Viper rose and swiftly gathered enough firewood to build a fire. Once he had it burning brightly, he carried Erica over beside it and sat down with her cradled across his lap. She fit in his embrace as perfectly as he had recalled, and he hugged her close to his chest as he called her name in an insistent whisper. "Erica, Erica, you must wake up."

Erica heard her name in the same instant that she became aware of Viper's confining embrace. Awakening to find herself held so firmly in his arms, she struggled frantically to break free, but succeeded only in throwing him off balance. Rather than release her to avoid falling over backwards, Viper twisted to the side and rolled over on his stomach, easily pinning her beneath him.

Her deep blue eyes reflected the amber glow of the fire as she stared up at the Indian brave. Their faces were no more than a few inches apart, and for an instant she saw only the streaks of war paint rather than the man himself. The weight of his well-muscled body forced her flat against the earth, and while she was no less frightened than she had been upon awakening, he now held her so firmly she could no longer fight him.

Erica knew exactly what was going to happen to her now that she had no way to stop him. He would rape her as often as he pleased, then pass what was left of her on to his friends. She had not the slightest doubt of the horror she faced. She would never see those she loved, not ever again. Mark had feared he would die in the war, but she was going to be the one to die, if not that very night, then soon. Her worst fear was that it wouldn't be nearly soon enough, and tears again overflowed her lashes as she turned her head and shut her eyes tightly so she would not have to look at Viper's triumphant grin as he forced himself upon her.

Viper had little experience with women, but Erica had again confirmed his suspicions that she was a most peculiar female, indeed. He kept his hands upon her wrists as he spoke in the same soft soothing tone he had used with the stallion. "You must not run from me. I cannot protect you if I must spend all my time chasing you through the forest. Now stop crying and look at me."

When she did neither, he released her hands and cupped her cheeks between his palms, turning her face toward him. Resting his weight on his elbows, he gave a sharp command this time. "Erica, look at me!"

Erica shuddered with revulsion before slowly opening her eyes. She felt nauseous she was so tired, and while the thought that it might be possible to rip open Viper's jugular vein with her teeth flashed briefly through her mind, she knew she lacked both the strength and the resolve to do it. He was the savage, not she. The firelight danced in his strange silver eyes with the same bright flames she knew must fill the halls of hell, and she shuddered again, sorry he had made her look at him.

"There is blood on your dress. Is it yours?" Viper asked in a softer tone now that he had succeeded in getting her attention.

That question struck Erica as totally irrelevant. Why should he care? Didn't he plan to hurt her herself, and badly? Seeing no reason to reply, she kept still.

"Erica, answer me!"

"No," the bone-weary blonde finally replied in a shaky whisper as she again shut her eyes to forcibly remove his image from the nightmare to which she had awakened.

Thinking she had fainted again, Viper swore softly, then moved aside, sat up, and gathered her into his arms. She was completely limp, and he pressed her cheek against his chest and rubbed her back lightly. "I will see you come to no harm," he whispered into her curls.

When he did no more than hold her upon his lap, Erica suspected his gentle touch was a trick of some sort. Was he trying to lull her into complacency? Into accepting the unwanted advances she would have no choice but to endure? He was a strong man, and she was a young woman so exhausted by turmoil and fear that she was physically ill. "I'm going to be sick," she managed to warn him, and this time when she tried to break free of his grasp he let her go. She stumbled as she broke away, then dropped to her knees and gave in to the nausea that had plagued her all afternoon.

Viper looked up at the stars that now brightened the sky, fearing that Erica was proving to be far more delicate than an Indian maiden. He had uttered no threats, but clearly she was so terrified of him that she was ill. He waited until she had ceased to retch, then scooped her up into his arms. "There is a stream nearby. I will take you to it." When he placed her beside the swiftly flowing water, he apologized, "I have only jerky made from venison to offer you tonight, and I do not think you will be able to keep it down."

Erica splashed the cool water upon her face for several minutes, hoping the sight of her being sick had also upset Viper's stomach so much he'd leave her alone. "I don't want anything to eat. Just let me sleep."

Viper bent down to lift her into his arms again, but Erica pushed his hands away. "I can still walk," she insisted proudly, but as she rose and turned back toward the clearing she was so filled with dread she had to reach out to touch the trees to keep her balance, and her steps were painfully slow.

"I will put the blanket by the fire." Viper had only the one he had removed from the stallion's back, but the moment he placed it upon the ground Erica stretched out upon it and closed her eyes. He had expected her to complain that he had no fine buffalo robes to use for her bed, but her even breathing revealed that she was already sound asleep.

Perplexed, the Indian wondered if he had made a serious mistake in seizing the opportunity to take her from New Ulm. He had made his decision the instant he had spotted her at the back of the hotel. He had wanted her, and now she was his, but while he had anticipated her anger he had not expected her to be so frail and sick. What had happened to her to take the pink glow from her cheeks and the fire from all her actions?

Unable fully to understand his lovely captive's plight, Viper returned to the stallion, which was grazing contentedly, unconcerned by his new master's predicament. Viper had used a leather thong to hobble the horse and checked it now to be certain it would hold, since he did not want to lose the fine animal during the night. Satisfied the valuable mount would not stray, he returned to the fire, sat down, and began slowly to chew on a piece of jerky. He had a fine horse, a knife, a rifle, ammunition, a bow, a quiver full of arrows, a fishing line, and a few pieces of jerky. He was confident his few possessions were more than adequate to fulfill his own needs, but what of Erica's?

Even sound asleep the beautiful young woman fascinated him still. Her lips were parted slightly, reminding him of the delicious taste of her kiss, and he hoped she would be in a far better mood in the morning. When he finished eating his meager meal he went to the stream for a drink, then washed off what was left of the red paint he had used to create a fearsome mask for battle.

Returning to the fire, he paced restlessly until he had to gather more wood to feed the flames. He was still worried Erica would try and run away and considered tying her ankle to his while he slept. If she awoke first she might be able to untie herself, though, and whether she could elude him or not, he knew she would be furious he had tried to hobble her as he had the horse.

Since he was a light sleeper, Viper decided to lie so close to Erica that she could not stir without waking him. He thought that an excellent plan, until he stretched out beside her. Then she seemed so small and vulnerable he wanted to be closer still. Finally he turned upon his side and pulled her close so she could rest comfortably against the curve of his body. She made not the slightest protest, but he found the more tightly he held her, the closer they became, the more disappointment he felt at the depth of her slumber. He remembered the kisses they had shared and longed for more, but if Erica were not strong soon, he knew he would have no choice but to take her to where the captives were being held. The women there would be able to care for her if he could not. He wanted the vibrant beauty he had found it impossible to forget to share his nights, not a frail creature who shook with fear whenever he forced her to look at him. If her health did not improve soon, he would not keep her.

He thought of Song of the Wren then. He had seen her only once since the night he had nearly had to fight another brave to protect her, and she had quickly turned away as though she were ashamed rather than grateful for his help. Wren was pretty, but when she had thrown herself into his arms and wept he had found no pleasure in her nearness, no thrill in the feel of her lips against his bare chest. Sound asleep, Erica was more exciting than Wren would ever be, and he hoped the Indian maiden would soon set her sights on someone else, since he had no interest in her. It was true she was of his own kind, but while he was loath to admit it, Erica was, too.

Viper awakened often that night, and each time he found Erica snuggled against him sleeping peacefully. Her fair hair shone in the moonlight, her beauty taunting him with desire. He had wanted to talk with her, to recapture the rapport they had shared all too briefly, and his impatience for the coming dawn awakened him frequently. But the night passed with maddening slowness. When finally the sky began to lighten, he hoped Erica would awaken, too, but she continued to sleep so soundly he began to worry she might never return from the world of dreams. That the woman he wanted for his wife might be stolen from him as everything else he had ever treasured had been was too bitter a possibility to bear, and he greeted the new day in a mood far darker than the midnight sky.

# Chapter Seven

## August, 1862

The sun was high overhead when Erica began to stir. Opening her eyes, she saw a heap of blackberries on the edge of the blanket, and fearing she had been abandoned with no more than a pile of fruit, she sat up and quickly scanned the clearing. Her fears subsided, then returned full-blown when she saw Viper, comfortably seated with a maple tree at his back, no more than ten feet away. He was lazily plucking the brightly colored feathers from a pheasant's carcass. In the clear light of day, without his war paint, his ready grin was reassuring, until she recalled how she had come to be with him.

"I am glad you are awake. I did not want to eat this fine bird all alone. The berries are for your breakfast," he then remembered to add, delighted she had not awakened screaming.

Erica could recall little of the previous night's conversation, but she was certain they had not said goodnight on pleasant terms. She rose shakily, stepped into her slippers, which Viper had thoughtfully placed at the edge of the blanket, then attempted to smooth the wrinkles from her dress. That effort proved futile, however, and she stared in the direction she thought the stream lay. "I am going to wash," she announced firmly, as though she were still in control of her life rather than he.

"You will need my help," Viper offered generously. He laid the half-plucked pheasant aside, but before he could rise Erica refused his offer.

"All I need from you is some privacy," she responded coldly.

"Erica," Viper called out with a low chuckle.

Thinking he was making fun of the way she looked, which she knew had to be ghastly, the distraught blonde did not stop walking but merely called over her shoulder, "I am a grown woman. I don't need help to wash."

"The stream is the other way," Viper pointed out matter-of-factly, but he was relieved that she seemed to be feeling like her usual feisty self.

Erica wheeled around, horribly embarrassed she had not known that herself, even though her memory of the stream's soothing coolness was dim. "Thank you," she mumbled with a haughty toss of her tangled curls. She marched past him again, displaying the proud posture that proclaimed her a lady through and through. While she did not see it, Viper's grin grew twice as wide.

Once she reached the stream, Erica turned to look back over her shoulder to make certain she had not been followed. Birds called to one another overhead, while chattering squirrels scampered through the branches, but the only animal that concerned her was the Indian. Hoping he would give her a few minutes alone before he came searching for her, she slipped her dress off her shoulders so she could rinse the grime from her face, throat, and arms. She had been too tired to demand a softer bed than the ground had made, but she felt so stiff and sore that morning she vowed to find a better substitute before nightfall.

Her hair was so badly tangled she despaired of ever combing it free of knots. She bent over to drench her curls in the stream, thinking her hair would at least be clean, if not snarl free. When she finally returned to the clearing she was feeling so much better she nearly asked Viper for a comb, then caught herself and did not make so foolish a request. She doubted he would have one, and even if he did she did not want to share anything of his. Sitting down on the blanket, she turned her back toward him, and feeling surprisingly hungry, she began to pop the succulent blackberries into her mouth in rapid succession, pausing only long enough between bites to wipe the dark purple juice from her chin.

Viper was disappointed in Erica's pose, but rather than order her to face him, he simply got to his feet, walked over to her side, and joined her on the blanket. "Do you know how to clean a bird?" he asked as he made himself comfortable.

"Of course," Erica replied flippantly, although, in truth, she had watched others handle that task but she had never done it herself.

Viper removed the last few feathers, then tossed the limp pheasant her way. "Good. When you finish eating your breakfast, prepare the bird while I gather the wood to roast it."

The sunshine bathed the clearing in a charming golden glow, but Erica saw only the neat hole Viper's arrow had drilled through the pheasant's breast, and feeling chilled clear through, rubbed her arms briskly.

"Are you cold?" Viper thought it unlikely, since the day was a warm one, but he knew she was far more delicate than he and undoubtedly more sensitive to both heat and cold. He had no shirt, but since he seldom wore one in summer, he did not miss it.

Erica shook her head, then brushed her still dripping curls off her shoulders as she thought of a fact she was certain he had not considered. "My father is a wealthy man. You would be wise to ask for a ransom for me and find yourself an Indian girl to do your chores."

Clearly the defiant blonde still thought herself too good for him, and Viper rebelled instantly at that insult. His expression grew stern, and his gaze turned cold as he replied, "It is not money I want, nor another woman. You are the only prize I am after."

"Prize?" Erica asked incredulously, not about to be considered part of the spoils of the uprising. "The Sioux may have won a battle or two, Viper, but the army will soon send soldiers from Fort Snelling to defeat you rogues soundly, and then you'll suffer for kidnapping me."

"Your words are very brave this morning," Viper replied with an arrogant sneer. "But do you really think the army has enough soldiers to send some to look for you?"

"Yes!" Erica responded without a moment's hesitation, her deep blue eyes blazing with indignation. "They will chop down all the trees in this forest if they must, but they will find every single captive the Sioux have taken."

Having no wish to argue what he considered a ridiculous point, Viper drew his knife and handed it to her handle first. "Take the bird to the stream and clean it there. I will build a fire."

Astonished that he would trust her with a weapon, Erica stared at him wide-eyed. The young man had superb coordination. All his actions were characterized by a fluid grace. Could she move fast enough to plunge the blade between his ribs before he could block the blow?

Viper saw that murderous thought cross Erica's mind as a frown furrowed her brow. "I would break your wrist before that blade touched my skin. Do not take that risk. Not ever," he warned sternly. He rose to his feet, and turning his back on her, walked out of the clearing to begin fetching wood.

"You arrogant bastard!" the irate blonde muttered under her breath. Her appetite suddenly gone, she scattered the remaining berries with a broad sweep of her hand. She then picked up the pheasant and rose gracefully to her feet as though she were holding a bouquet of flowers rather than a dead bird. She was certain Viper was only trying to fool her by bragging that he prized her more highly than a handsome ransom, and she vowed to bring up the subject as often as necessary to convince him to think otherwise and set her free.

Viper was pleased to see Erica's health greatly improved after a night's rest, but he was still angry that she did not appreciate the reasons he had taken her away from New Ulm before it had become overrun by Sioux warriors. He had spared her the sight of much death and suffering. He had also saved her the humiliation of being taken captive. Why had that consideration not impressed her?

She had said her father had money. From what he had seen of her clothes he believed she was speaking the truth. Perhaps in her home servants saw to her every need. She had not refused to clean the bird, though, and that was to her credit. Still, her surly mood was making things far more difficult than he had expected. For the hundredth time Viper cursed his own ignorance where women were concerned, but he doubted experience with any other women, Indian or white, could ever have prepared him to deal with Erica.

The Indian's scowl did not lift as he built a fire. As he had told her, Sioux maidens were raised to be modest, and when they became wives they served their husband's every need graciously. What sort of wife had he expected Erica to make? Had the memory of the luscious taste of her kisses and the charms of her graceful body clouded his mind so greatly that he had not considered the differences between them to be any greater than those between any man and woman?

When Erica returned with the pheasant, Viper had buried the ends of two sturdy branches on opposite sides of the fire to hold a third branch he meant to suspend between them as a spit. He offered no criticism nor praise for the way she had dressed the pheasant, but simply threaded it upon the spit and placed it over the fire to roast. "My knife," he stated then, his softly spoken words a demand for the weapon's return.

Wary of him, Erica gripped the knife tightly, reluctant to surrender it. She knew damn little about the Indian, except for the fact that he was clearly strong enough to force himself upon her whenever he chose. Did he plan to wait until he had a full stomach to do so?

Viper turned to face Erica, his light eyes filled with a smoky haze that mirrored her confusion. "I will loan you the knife whenever you have need of it, but it is mine." He held out his hand, confident that if she tried to plunge the blade through his palm, his reflexes were sufficiently quick to spare him that injury.

Erica saw not only Viper's disappointment that she had not returned the knife without his having to ask for it, she also felt the heady current of tension that had, on all but a few brief instances, always flowed between them. She felt as though they were at opposite ends of an invisible cord stretched nearly to the breaking point. He was the most fascinating individual she had ever met. He was a handsome man, yet undoubtedly capable of the most hideous sort of violence. His name fit him well, she finally realized. He was as hypnotically compelling as a viper and twice as deadly, and she was his prisoner. With a thoroughly disgusted glance, she placed the knife across his outstretched palm and turned away.

Viper slid the razor-sharp weapon into the beaded

sheath at his belt, not understanding why he felt as though he had just lost an argument when clearly he had won. He was too hungry to dwell on the willful blonde's belligerent attitude, however. The pheasant cooked quickly, and he hoped she would enjoy it as greatly as he was certain he would. Since he knew food would improve his mood, he hoped it would also better hers.

When Viper carried the pheasant over to where she sat to carve it, Erica found it impossible to ignore the flavorful essence borne upon the steam that escaped the crisply browned bird. Her mind insisted stubbornly that she shouldn't eat a scrap of food he provided, but her body swiftly betrayed her and her mouth watered hungrily. Since they had no dishes of any kind, she laid the bird upon the grass and quartered it neatly. Erica managed to hold her tongue until she had taken several bites of the succulent breast he had handed her, but then she could no longer keep still.

"This is delicious, but we cannot live here in the forest like—" she was about to say gypsies when she realized he would probably not know what they were, but before she could think of a suitable substitute, he supplied an appropriate word.

"Indians?" he inquired with a sly chuckle, which grew swiftly into outright laughter, he was so deeply amused by her comment.

"What do you find so funny?" Erica took another bite, still too hungry to throw the half-eaten breast into his face, which was what she felt he deserved. "You can't expect me to live like this," she scoffed, her anger at his mocking laughter making her bold. "My dress is filthy. I had to sleep on the ground. I would rather have stayed in New Ulm and taken my chances with the others. You have done me no favors by bringing me here!"

Viper did not reply until he had finished the first piece of pheasant and laid the bones aside. "Wash your dress in the stream, and I will cut some branches to make you a bed. I am not used to having a wife. If there is something you need, all you need do is tell me."

"I am not your wife!" The absurdity of their situation proved too much for Erica, and she reached for a plump leg, wrenched it from the pheasant's carcass, and went to sit on the opposite side of the clearing to eat it by herself.

Not about to allow her to turn her back on him again, Viper picked up what was left of the bird and rejoined her. "The forest will provide for all our needs. When winter comes I will build you a house."

That the man would make such an outlandish promise infuriated Erica all the more. "I want to go back to New Ulm. I will see you receive a generous reward for taking me back. I promise I will."

The young woman was impossibly stubborn, in Viper's view. "I brought you here so you would be safe. I have no more need for reward now than I did when I found your letter."

He had received a reward, though, Erica recalled with chagrin. He had claimed a kiss, a long, slow, and delicious kiss. Feeling very uncomfortable with him seated so near that his bare shoulder brushed hers each time he took a bite, she finished the last bit of meat on the leg she'd taken and laid the bones aside. As she wiped her fingers on the grass to clean her hands she thought that it had been the most delicious pheasant she had ever tasted, but the meal, while most welcome, had not changed her feelings about going her own way. "I must go back to New Ulm, Viper. I simply must."

Viper's gray eyes narrowed slightly as he shot her a menacing glance. "What if your white lover does not want you now that you have been with me?"

"But I have not been with you!" Erica protested angrily, but she looked away quickly as she realized how swiftly he could make his statement true. "Mark would love me still," she insisted in a hoarse whisper, more to reassure herself than to convince him. Dear God in heaven, she thought. What would Mark say when he found out she had been kidnapped by an Indian brave? He would be horrified, of course. But would his opinion change if he discovered she had known the man, met him in the woods on more than one occasion, and even kissed him? Would he blame her then for having thoughtlessly encouraged the attentions of the savage who had abducted her? She could scarcely draw a breath she was so frightened at the realization that she would have no way to counter such a damaging accusation. What decent man would want a wife who chased an Indian through the woods until he caught her?

Mark prided himself upon being a gentleman. He would stand by her no matter what ghastly thing happened to her. Erica knew he would consider such loyalty his duty. She also knew her flirtation with Viper and its disastrous results would cause him a great deal of anguish. He would blame not only Viper, but her, as well. Perhaps the savage was right and her fate was already sealed. She had spent the night with an Indian, and who would ever believe she had not been raped, even if she denied it vehemently? She would never be believed, even if she had a doctor's word she was a virgin still. She hugged her knees tightly as her eyes filled with tears that swiftly spilled down her cheeks. Viper was right. Her reputation was already ruined beyond repair. She had begun the damage herself when she had made the mistake of watching him bathe in the river rather than fleeing before he had seen her. She had caused her own downfall, and now she somehow would have to find the courage to survive the humiliation that would surely follow.

Viper stared at the slender blonde, astonished by her sudden flood of tears. He had meant to curb her defiance with his question, but not so totally as this. It disgusted him to think she considered being with him so degrading that she was reduced to tears. "Go and wash your dress while there is still enough sun to dry it," he ordered gruffly. Not wanting to attract scavengers to their camp, he gathered up the scraps and bones left from their meal and rose to his feet. "Well, go on, hurry."

Erica was immensely relieved that he had not been waiting for a full stomach to ravish her, but that was scant consolation in her mood. Viper's long ebony hair caught the sunlight as he walked away, and she wondered how he planned to occupy himself while she did her laundry. He was not the type to hide in the bushes and spy upon her, but she was certain he would cut enough branches to create a bed before she could wash and dry her garments. Since he was right about the need for haste, she brushed away the last of her tears and hurried to the stream, again glancing back over her shoulder frequently to make certain she had not been followed.

The water was not deep enough for true bathing, but once she had removed her shoes, dress, stockings, and slip, Erica decided the only way she could also launder her chemise and pantaloons was to wade out into the stream while still wearing them. She splashed about, scooping up the sparkling, clear water and rinsing her lingerie as best she could before attempting to wash her other things. After searching her pockets, she put the carving of the cougar Gunter had made for her, along with Viper's claw, into her shoes. She prayed her cousin was still safe in the same breath that she cursed her own folly in keeping the claw, which had brought her nothing but the worst of luck, despite what its owner had promised. With that bitter thought in mind, she scrubbed her things with a vengeance, then laid the wet garments on top of the nearby bushes to dry. Feeling tired, although she had done little that day, she chose the boulder beside the stream most comfortably cushioned with moss and sat down to dangle her feet in the water.

Viper had given her a great deal to consider, but despite the fact that she could not predict how she would be received, and feared it would be with contempt, she still wanted to go home. How the Indian could have imagined she would agree to become his wife when she had told him good-bye so emphatically, she could not imagine. Now it seemed impossible to refuse his offer in terms he would not regard as insulting, and she knew insulting a man as proud as Viper was a mistake to be avoided at all costs. Her offer of a ransom had been a sincere one, but even if he continued to refuse money, wasn't it possible there was something else that might tempt him more?

Viper buried the bones some distance from the clearing, then cut enough small branches to form a comfortable mattress for their blanket. He stretched out upon it and propped his hands behind his head. Finding the makeshift bed to his liking, he hoped his companion would approve, since he intended to have her share it. The afternoon was warm, and he dozed off, then awoke abruptly, uncertain how long he had napped. When he saw Erica had not returned to the clearing, he rushed down to the stream to look for her.

Erica was still seated upon the moss-covered boulder, dressed only in her lace-trimmed lingerie. She sat with her arms wrapped around her right leg, her chin resting upon her knee. The sun's rays were filtered through the leaves overhead, imparting a romantic glow to her long, fair curls and peach-toned skin. Viper found her beauty a delight to behold and hesitated to disturb her. He waited a moment, expecting her to look up and see him, but her attention was focused upon the dancing waters rushing across her left foot and she did not notice him for several minutes.

It was the call of a bird that finally caught Erica's attention, but as she glanced overhead her eyes met Viper's and held. The setting was nearly identical to the one in which they had first met, but it was not anger that she saw reflected in his expression this time, but the unmistakable hunger of desire. Knowing if she rose to her feet she would only present him with a better view of her scantily clad figure, she did not stir. She lifted her chin as though she had every right to sit in the sun in her lingerie while the rest of her clothing dried.

Viper went to the bushes where her dress and slips lay and turned them over to place the damp side toward the sun. Her stockings were already dry, and he ran his fingertips over the silk, recalling fondly how the filmy fabric had felt on her legs. When that sensation brought a longing he was not ready to express, he moved to Erica's side, leaned back against the boulder upon which she sat, and folded his arms across his chest. "I will get you a buckskin dress. Then you will not have to do so much laundry," he offered considerately.

"I prefer to wear my own clothes, thank you," Erica insisted. He was again standing so close that their shoulders were touching, but she could not move over without toppling into the stream. His deeply bronzed skin was far warmer than hers, and she could not help but recall how smooth it had felt beneath her fingertips. That her captor was attractive was irrelevant, she told herself; all that mattered was that she convince him to set her free. "If it is not money that you want, then my father will provide whatever it is that you would like for my ransom."

"Unless you have a twin sister, he has nothing I want," Viper countered slyly.

That reply was stated in so taunting yet so emphatic a tone that Erica fell silent. Even when he rested quietly, the man's strength was a physical force she could not ignore. He had every advantage, while she had none, she thought dejectedly. As her eyes followed the winding stream, she suddenly realized it must flow into the Minnesota River. She could follow the stream's path to the river, then follow the river upstream until she came to New Ulm! She wasn't lost after all! Now she was sorry she had not put the afternoon to better use and tried to escape him. That was a foolish mistake she would not repeat. The next time he left her alone she would leave him. He appeared so comfortable lounging by her side that she knew such an opportunity would not present itself again that day. As the sun began to dip behind the trees she shivered, fearful of what the night would bring.

Viper could also feel the tension that existed between them, but whether it reflected hatred on her part, rather than desire, he didn't know. He wanted her to again want him as her wanton kisses had once told him she had. That everything had changed between them both confused and depressed him. "You were not afraid of me before. You have no reason to fear me now, Erica," he said.

"No reason?" Erica could not believe he had said that. She opened her mouth to point out how wrong he was in that statement, but then remembered her decision not to deliberately anger him and took a more moderate tone. "My uncle told me how unfairly the Sioux have been treated by the government. But just because the money and food you were owed were late was no reason to start slaughtering settlers when we have done nothing to harm you."

Since Viper agreed with that view, he did not attempt to argue but tried instead to win her sympathy. "In exchange for lands which will not support us, we were promised food and money. It was a bad bargain for us, but since the government has not kept their side, why should we keep ours? Did they think we would starve to death without complaint?"

"Wanton murder can scarcely be called a complaint, Viper." Erica glanced over at her clothes, wondering how she would be able to get dressed without him watching her. The prospect of debating the causes of the uprising in her lingerie struck her as a most indecent one. Like everything else she had done since she had met him, she scolded herself silently.

"I fought at the agency, and Fort Ridgely, but I came to

112

New Ulm only to find you. The settlers have already been frightened so badly they are leaving their farms. We don't need to kill them to take our lands back. I have not slain any women and babies; I refuse to do that."

Erica frowned slightly, surprised that Viper had such a highly developed sense of honor when clearly many of his kind did not. "While I am grateful for that, I wish that you had not killed any men, either," she admitted frankly.

"What of your lover? If he is in the army he must have killed Southern soldiers. Does that make him a murderer?"

They were treading upon treacherous ground, and again Erica chose her words with care, ignoring his reference to Mark as her lover. "No, Viper. During a war a soldier is expected to fight, to do all that he can to see that his side wins. For a soldier to kill an enemy in battle is not considered murder."

Viper nodded, glad that she at least saw some things as he did. "This *is* a war, Erica. I am a Sioux warrior, but my enemy is the army, not everyone who is white."

From the looks of him and the confidence of his manner, Erica couldn't help but wonder how much influence he had. "Are you a chief?" she asked apprehensively, wondering if he actually had the power to decide just who his enemy was.

"No," Viper responded with a good-natured chuckle. "But I do not have to blindly follow Little Crow the way army troops must follow their officers. It is my choice when and where I fight."

"What?" asked Erica, greatly intrigued. "You mean you can just come and go as you please? Fight in this 'war,' as you call it, one day, and not the next?" She wondered if the army knew that, for surely it would prove valuable for them to know, that the number of Sioux warriors varied from day to day.

Viper looked down at her, his smile taunting. "Yes, and since I am a very good shot it would be to your people's advantage to keep me here. Do you think you can do it?"

Badly embarrassed by that challenge, Erica's cheeks began to burn with the heat of a bright blush. Did he honestly expect her to throw herself at him in an attempt to distract him from returning to the uprising? That struck her as both a ridiculous and pointless sacrifice, since she was certain Viper would do exactly as he pleased no matter how she tried to influence him. Lifting her chin proudly, she countered with the demand she had made several times before, "All I ask is that you return me to New Ulm, and I'll see you are given any reward you choose."

Again Viper laughed at her offer. "You are all the reward I want, Erica, and I already have you."

Erica swallowed nervously, but she returned his level stare without flinching. You will never have me! she screamed in her mind, but she knew better than to voice that challenge out loud. "I want to get dressed," she blurted out instead, but as she tried to scramble past him he grabbed her arms and held her fast, pressing the soft fullness of her breasts against the hard planes of his broad chest.

"I mean what I say, Erica. I will not harm you, but there are others who would use you badly and leave you for dead. I have already risked my life to save yours. What will you give me in return?"

The terror that question caused filled the fragile blonde's throat and made any response impossible. She could do no more than stare up at the handsome brave with the same wide-eyed fright with which a cornered bird regards a snake. She was astonished then, when rather than throwing her to ground and dropping upon her, he enfolded her in a warm embrace. He inclined his head and kissed her, not hungrily, but as tenderly and sweetly as he had in the past. He surprised her anew with the depth of his emotion, and as before, she could not withhold the loving response he craved, nor did she even wish to deny him that victory.

Viper felt Erica's fright turn gradually to surrender as she relaxed in his arms, and he eased his hold upon her. She was clad in sheer silk garments that provided no barrier to his touch, and he moved his hands slowly down her back, then over her hips, to press her lithe body closer still. He considered her fair beauty as delicate as a wildflower's and did not want to crush it with clumsy enthusiasm. He wanted instead to cherish the vibrant young woman in his arms, to find the answers in her heart to all the questions that filled his own. He had no idea how long he had held her in his arms before her breathing became as erratic as his own, but when he drew back to look down at her, longing to see her smile, fear again filled her expression so swiftly that he knew he dared not seek more than fevered kisses from her that afternoon. With a sigh of regret he took her hand and led her over to her clothes.

"Get dressed," he ordered bluntly, instantly shattering the last moment of the blissful interlude they had just enjoyed.

When he made no move to leave, Erica grabbed up her slips with trembling fingers and stepped into them. She didn't understand how Viper managed to work the magic he did upon her senses. All he need do is kiss me, she thought as she fastened the ties at her waist. The instant his lips touched hers she was drawn into an enchanted world where nothing existed but him. It was a wildly pleasurable sensation, but also a very dangerous one. She looked for her corset, then remembered she had discarded it at the hotel, and reached for her dress instead. It was at least clean, if no less wrinkled.

As Viper bent down to hand her her slippers, he saw the little wooden cougar and the claw he had given her. Scooping them up into his hand, he broke into a wide grin. "I wondered if you had kept this. You see, it did bring you good luck."

The man's remarks were continually unsettling, but that he regarded her recent run of luck as good simply appalled Erica. She was grateful her blue gown buttoned up the bodice rather than down the back so she didn't need his help to dress. She didn't want to provide him with any excuse to touch her when the consequences were so very predictable. "On the contrary," she argued, "my luck has been nothing but bad since the day we met. Take the claw back, I don't want it anymore."

Had she struck him, Erica could not have angered Viper more. He stepped forward and dropped the red ribbon over her head so the claw he had given her lay comfortably nestled between her breasts. "You are alive and well, which is more than I can promise for the others from New Ulm." He slid his right arm around her waist then, and drew her close for a kiss of such savage intensity that when

115

he released her she stumbled and would have fallen had he not caught her. "You are a bright girl. Now can you tell the difference between good luck and bad?"

Not wanting any further demonstration on the subject of luck, Erica nodded. She raised her hand to her lips, knowing he had deliberately bruised her mouth and hoping he had also hurt himself just as badly. "My cousin made the little cougar for me. Please give it back."

Viper turned the carving over and examined it thoroughly before handing it to her. "It looks more like a house cat than a cougar."

Erica shoved the little animal into her pocket quickly. "It looks like a cougar to me," she stated proudly.

Viper shook his head as he laughed. "How many cougars have you seen?"

Erica licked her bruised lips before replying. "I have never seen a live one, but I have seen drawings of them, so I know how they are supposed to look."

"From drawings?" Viper asked skeptically. "A drawing is no more a cougar than that piece of wood is. We will need more wood for tonight's fire. If you can't find enough, we might have to burn your little pet."

With that offhand threat he turned away and started for the clearing, leaving Erica staring at his back and seething with anger over the way he had treated her. It was obvious he wanted her to cater to his every whim, but she wasn't about to bargain for her life with her body. He had sounded very convincing when he had sworn his only enemy was the army. But what proof did she have that he would not soon tire of her, no matter how agreeable she attempted to be? She took hold of the claw suspended from the ribbon necklace and was sorely tempted to rip it off and toss it into the stream. Wouldn't that show Viper how little she thought of his concept of luck? Her grasp tightened upon the claw, then relaxed when she realized what his response could very well be if she defied him so boldly as that.

The shadows were lengthening, and she was supposed to be gathering wood, not standing around idly while she thought of ways to avoid angering Viper. She might have survived the daylight hours with him, but she had nothing but dread for what the night might bring.

# Chaper Eight

## August, 1862

When she returned to the clearing with a heap of wood, Viper showed Erica where the blackberry vines grew and told her to pick some for their supper. She made no effort to converse while they ate the fruit she had gathered, and neither did he. He sat staring into the fire, occasionally tossing a berry into his mouth, his expression impassive, if not hostile, but she sensed the seriousness of his mood and worried even more about what might become of her.

While Erica sat contemplating the uncertainty of her fate, Viper was wondering what the chiefs' next move would be. Reinforcements would soon arrive to aid the army troops they had not been able to rout from Fort Ridgely. Then he would again be willing to fight. Until that time, he would not join the others in raids upon towns, nor would he roam about the countryside killing settlers. There was no honor in shooting helpless farmers and murdering their families that he could see, absolutely none. He wanted the white man gone from their lands as greatly as any of the others did, but he would be satisfied to let them live as long as they had the sense to go away and did not come back. Erica had scoffed at his insistence that each Sioux warrior could fight the war on his own terms, but he intended to do just that.

When he glanced over at his enchanting captive, he saw she was watching the flames with an expression of such hopeless despair that he could not bear to see it continue.

Song of the Wren would have made a far more agreeable companion, he was certain; it was unfortunate she was not the woman he had chosen for his wife. Since Erica was, he wanted her to be happy. "Stand up," he ordered as he rose to his feet. When she hesitated a moment before rising, he did not scold her for being slow, but merely went to fetch the blanket from their bed on the opposite side of the fire. When he returned with it he flashed his most charming grin.

"When a brave decides to court a girl, he goes to her tepee at dusk. If she likes him, she will come outside. He will wrap his blanket around her so they can be alone to talk. Like this." He draped the red and black blanket around her shoulders and pulled her close so they were wrapped snugly inside its folds.

When he had taken the first step toward her, Erica had raised her hands hoping to force him to keep his distance. He had ignored that gesture, however, and now her hands lay lightly upon his bare chest. She felt the beat of his heart, steady and slow, while the rhythm of hers was a wild, pounding frenzy. Hoping to distract him with thoughts of other women, she asked the first question that came to her mind. "There must be many pretty Indian girls. How many have you spoken with like this?"

Viper shook his head as his smile became the taunting grin she had so recently learned to despise. "None, Erica. You are the first."

Erica found it difficult to imagine standing on her front porch wrapped in a blanket with Mark. As usual, with the handsome Indian so close, she found it impossible to recall the details of Mark's face with any clarity. Viper's well-chiseled features filled not only her field of vision, but overwhelmed the memory of her first love with shocking ease, and she felt all the more ashamed. How could she possibly go back to Mark now? she fretted silently. Going back to him suddenly seemed as impossible as remaining with Viper, and the streak of defiance the Indian would never tame flared again. "You want Minnesota to belong only to the Sioux, but if all the white people are forced to leave, how can you keep me here? That doesn't make any sense at all. Why would you even want me here if you hate white people so?"

"I do not hate all your people," Viper responded softly. "I hate only those who laugh at our chiefs, break the treaties, and refuse to treat us as men."

Erica glanced away for an instant, certain she could think far more clearly if he were not standing so near. It was getting very warm inside the blanket, and she wished he would describe some other, less intimate, custom if he were in the mood to talk. "I must admit I have not followed the dealings between the Sioux and the government as I should have, but still I am certain killing civilians can't possibly improve the way you have been treated."

Viper raised a brow and regarded her with a quizzical glance. "Is this what you do with your lover? Do you talk about the war between the North and the South rather than of love?"

Erica did shove him this time. She pushed against him with all her strength, then realized that with the blanket encircling their shoulders he could not step back without pulling her with him. "Damn you!" she shouted angrily. "Let me go!"

Viper waited a moment and then let the blanket fall to the ground. "Indian girls have far better manners than you. They know how to say goodnight politely."

"How would you know?" Erica screamed right back at him.

Viper winked at her, for some perverse reason enjoying her fit of temper. "I know," he assured her. Before she could reply with another insult he replaced the blanket on the bed he had made and then returned for her. Taking her hand, he pulled her around the fire behind him. "It is time for bed. I will let you sleep on the side near the fire so that you will not grow cold."

Erica hung back, not wanting to lie down beside him, but he swung her around and nearly flung her down upon the softly cushioned blanket before she could break free of his hold. He then dropped down beside her and draped his arm over her stomach so she could not spring to her feet. "Go to sleep," he ordered firmly. "I am tired of fighting with you."

The startled blonde held her breath, again fearing a trick of some kind, but Viper lay still, his breathing even, as though he had already fallen asleep. Erica stared up at the stars, her whole body rigid with the tension the Indian created within her so often. With his lean body pressed close to hers, she could now recall something of the previous night and knew she had spent it in his arms. His behavior puzzled her thoroughly. Did he really plan to court her as though she were an Indian maiden? Was he trying to win her consent for a marriage she would not even consider? That thought touched her so deeply she bit down on her lip to keep from bursting into tears, but her mouth was so badly bruised she cried out in pain.

"What is wrong?" Viper opened one eye to ask.

"Everything!" Erica replied. Trying to put more distance between them, she turned on her side to place her back toward him. When he moved over, too, she realized the folly of her action, for lying on their sides their bodies fit together as perfectly as spoons in a drawer.

Viper again slid his arm around Erica's waist. His thumb caressed the swell of her breast, and when she pushed his hand away he laughed. "It is too late to be so modest, Erica. The last time I touched you there you purred like a kitten. You will again."

"Never!" Erica vowed through clenched teeth, but she could remember that afternoon by the river as clearly as he did, and her breath caught in her throat, preventing her from saying more. Even now she could recall each and every exquisite moment of that brief encounter.

She had swiftly discovered there was far more to Viper than the handsome appearance that had first fascinated her. He was obviously as committed to defending his beliefs as Mark was to fighting for his. Unlike Mark, however, he had not told her love would have to wait for the war to end. In fact, if she were to believe his words, he had turned his back on the uprising to be with her. She had not thought of his actions in those terms before, and now that she had, she was even more confused.

"Viper," she called out suddenly.

The Indian was enjoying her closeness far too much to complain that she was too talkative. "I am right beside you, you need only whisper and I will hear you."

Erica knew she had spoken much too loudly and apologized quickly. "I'm sorry, but Viper, did you mean what you said? Did you really go to New Ulm only to find me?"

Sensing his answer was important to her, Viper rose up on his right elbow so he could look down at her. He had wanted to go after her the first time the Sioux had attacked her town, but he did not wish to reveal what a dilemma she had posed for him then. "From nearly the first hour we met, I have wanted you for my wife. I saw no way to make that happen until the uprising began. I thought if your choice were death or me, you would choose me."

Erica turned to look up at him, more frightened than ever by his words. "Is that truly the choice? If I do not take you for my husband, you will kill me?"

She had whispered this time, but her breathless voice carried the depth of her fears to his ears. He raised his left hand to caress her fair curls. "No, I will never harm you, but in a war many innocent people die, and I did not want you to be one of them."

Erica had the eerie feeling a mystical force had been put into motion at the moment she and Viper had met, or perhaps long before, to insure that their fateful meeting took place. The attraction between them had always been strong, far too intense to deny, but she feared if she were to give in to it again, it would become an obsession that could destroy them both. "Oh Viper, I am so frightened. I am frightened for us both."

Viper leaned down to silence her fears with a soft, lingering kiss, caressing her bruised lips tenderly, until she raised her arms to encircle his neck. She clung to him then with a fierce desperation born of terror rather than passion. It was not fear he craved, however, but loving acceptance, and he did not take advantage of her sorrow and make love to her. Instead, he continued to kiss her lightly and hold her wrapped in his arms until at last she grew calm and fell asleep still cuddled in his embrace. He did not count the evening as wasted, though, for he felt at last he had earned her trust, and knew surely that was the beginning of love.

When Erica awoke she was alone on the blanket. She sat up slowly, expecting to see Viper seated nearby as he had been the previous morning, but except for the stallion who stood grazing in the tall grass at the far side of the clearing, the area was deserted. There was no sign of the Indian, nor of any of his possessions. Erica wasted no time wondering where he might be. She leaped up, and in a soothing voice called to the stallion as she grabbed his bridle from the low limb where Viper had tossed it.

As she approached, the big horse eyed the blond woman with an annoyed swipe of his long tail, for he had no wish to be ridden on that day or any other. He laid his ears flat against his head and backed away, but, undaunted by his obvious bad temper, Erica came straight toward him.

"I have no time to argue with you. We are leaving here right now," she commanded sharply. She grabbed a handful of his thick mane and deftly shoved the bit in his mouth, forced the leather straps over his ears, and quickly secured the buckles on the bridle. It was stamped with army insignia, and she realized Viper must have stolen the horse. She would not be stealing the animal, then, but rather returning him to his rightful owners. Not that her conscience would have bothered her for taking the horse. It wouldn't have, because she knew she had to get away from Viper while she still had an ounce of sense left. Whenever the man kissed her she could think of nothing but how wonderful it felt to be in his arms, but under the cool light of dawn she was determined to leave him while she could still see what an impossible choice remaining with him would be.

She untied the thong that had hobbled the stallion, then led him over to a stump, stepped on it, and climbed upon his back. She had ridden astride a horse upon occasion, and even if it had not been recently, she had not forgotten how to handle a mount, even a difficult one. The stallion recognized the confidence in her manner and touch, and ceasing to balk, resigned himself to being ridden. When Erica nudged him in the flanks with her heels, he turned in the direction she wished to go and carried her toward the stream.

Erica had not dreamed getting away from Viper would be so easy. She directed the stallion into the water to be certain the Indian could not track them. She prayed the first people she met would be white, but she had traveled no more than five minutes when she rounded a wide curve and came upon Viper. He was seated at the edge of the stream fishing for their breakfast. When he saw her he leaped to his feet, his grin a delighted one until he realized by her horrified expression that she had been running away rather than coming to find him.

Desperate to flee, Erica jabbed her heels into the stallion's hide, urging him to plunge past the Indian before he could wade out into the stream and stop them, but Viper was too swift to be eluded so easily as that. He lunged across the water, grabbed the huge black horse's bridle, and with a savage jerk brought the animal to a halt. Seething with rage, he then reached up for Erica's arm and yanked her off the animal's back. She slipped as her feet reached the moss-covered rocks of the streambed and fell forward into the water. As she struggled to get to her feet Viper laughed at her foolish attempt to escape him.

"You will not have to wash your dress today, nor take a bath, but I am afraid you have frightened away all the fish!" he snarled crossly. Leaving her standing in the stream, water dripping from her drenched hair and clothes, he led the horse a good distance from the water and tied his reins to a low limb. He then returned to his fishing line, and to his surprise found that during the commotion with Erica he had caught a good-size trout.

"We will have breakfast, after all, no thanks to you. Now stop playing in the water and come clean this fish. I am hungry."

Erica flipped her sopping tresses out of her eyes and came forward. This time when Viper held out his knife she took it and then made a lunge for him, but he easily sidestepped the blow and brought his hand down upon her wrist with a punishing force that sent the knife sailing into the air. It landed in the mud at the edge of the water, and he picked it up before she could make a dive for it.

He had not broken her wrist, but he had come so close her arm ached from fingertip to shoulder. "I hate you!" she screamed, but the words were a lie, and he knew it as well as she did. He returned her angry glare with an arrogant lift of his chin and again held out the knife.

"Clean the fish," he ordered a second time, "Or I will not share it with you."

The trout was flipping about in the mud, trying to reach the water, and with a quick kick Erica booted it back out into the stream. "I'd rather starve!" she screamed defiantly.

Viper drew back his hand, ready to slap some sense into her, but when Erica did not even flinch, he realized trying to break her spirit was pointless. It was the fire in her soul that kindled the flames of his own. Taming her would be like taming himself, and he found that thought as abhorrent as she obviously did. He was not above tricking her, however. He shoved his knife back into its sheath and spoke in a convincing tone. "Since you have talked of nothing but your desire to return to New Ulm, I will take you back as soon as we have cleaned up our campsite."

"What?" Erica's expression first mirrored her disbelief, then, seeing he was serious, she had to restrain herself from throwing her arms around his neck and hugging him to show her gratitude. "You mean it? You will take me home? You really will?"

Her innocent enthusiasm tore Viper's heart in two, but he nodded. "Yes. I will take you to New Ulm and tell you good-bye, if I must. As you say, there are many pretty Indian girls, and I will take one of them for my wife." He saw something new in her glance then, a light that might have been only a tiny spark of jealousy, but it was jealousy all the same, and that pleased him enormously. "Come, we must hurry." He turned away, knowing she would follow, but he had to hide his smile when she scampered after him like a frisky puppy. The happier she was now, the more she would need him later, if what he expected to find at New Ulm proved to be true.

Without arguing, Erica helped Viper sweep the clearing of all sign of their presence, even though she did not understand why they had to leave no trace of the time they had spent there. She was too excited about returning home to care if some work had to be done first. When Viper folded the blanket and laid it upon the stallion's back, she went to his side. "Do you want me to ride in front of you or behind?" She cared little what his preference was, she was so anxious to leave.

Viper had his few belongings slung over his back. He mounted the horse and then looked down at her. "I should make you walk," he stated matter-of-factly, but the

124

teasing gleam in his eyes let her know he would not make such a demand.

"If I ride with you, you will be rid of me all the sooner," Erica encouraged playfully.

Viper extended his hand and pulled her up in front of him. "Why should I wish to be rid of you when we get along so well?"

Erica again made herself comfortable astride the horse and took hold of its flowing mane so she would feel secure. When Viper wrapped his left arm around her waist, she realized she should have insisted upon being seated behind him where he could not touch her. She would know better next time, she thought, but she hoped this would be the last time they ever rode together. They did get along well, but only when she was in his arms. "Just take me home, Viper, as quickly as you can."

Her dress and hair were still damp, and he was reminded of the way she had looked when they had arrived at the clearing. They had spent only two days together, and for him, that was not nearly enough. "It will take all day," he replied. "There is no need to run the horse as I did on the way here."

Erica turned slightly to glance over her shoulder at Viper, but he did not smile as she had hoped he would, so she faced forward again. "You have been very kind to me. I would still like to provide a reward."

The handsome brave intended to have one, but again not the one she would have chosen. "You are not home yet," he pointed out as they left the clearing. "Be quiet, unless you have something more interesting to say."

Too happy to complain about that remark, Erica lost herself in her own thoughts as she prayed that somehow the men defending New Ulm had been successful. She wanted to find the peaceful community as she had first seen it, but she had no intention of remaining there. She planned to start back for Delaware on the first available boat. She would then put the horror of the uprising far behind her. She reached up to grasp the claw that lay upon her breast and knew she would not show it to her friends as she had once planned. Viper's memory would be a secret she would keep for all time.

Viper had not really expected Erica to keep still, and he

regretted telling her to be quiet when she remained silent. The day was another warm one. It was Monday, August 25, one week to the day from the attack at the Lower Agency. The Sioux had thrown the whole valley into chaos, and Viper made certain the route he chose back to New Ulm took them near no settlements where men might be stationed on lookout and shoot him in the back. They crossed the river, then continued west, skirting Swan Lake on the south before again crossing the river just below New Ulm where the Cottonwood River joined the Minnesota.

"We cannot enter the town on the main road," he warned softly. "I will circle around the bluff so we can see what has happened."

"I understand," Erica replied, breathless with anticipation. They had stopped several times to allow the horse to drink water and rest, but she had not complained when Viper had made no effort to provide any food for them. She was sorry they had not had the trout for breakfast, but reminded herself that had she not been so hostile, the Indian might not have agreed to take her home. Her stomach had been growling in protest for hours, but hunger seemed a slight discomfort to her when New Ulm lay so close.

Viper dismounted at the base of the bluff and then carefully set Erica down on her feet. Keeping her hand in his, he led her to the top where, hidden by trees, they could look down on the town, or rather, what was left of it. All the houses located outside the barricaded central portion had been burned to the ground. All that remained of the nearly two hundred homes that had once dotted the landscape were the chimneys and rectangular piles of smoldering ashes that showed where the structures had once been. The desolate scene gripped the lively blonde with a tormenting fascination. Even from their position on the bluff, she could tell the city was deserted. Everyone was gone. Had they all been taken captive, or worse yet, were they all dead? She scanned the streets with a fierce intensity then, but there were no bodies to be seen anywhere, not even one.

Viper wanted to shout with glee, for surely Erica would realize now that there was no turning back. She would belong to him without argument now. He was sure of it but when he saw the confusion in her expression, he was careful not to gloat. "Everyone is gone. I cannot leave you here alone."

Nor did Erica wish to be left on her own in the deserted remains of the once prosperous city. "Where have they all gone, Viper? Where are the Sioux taking their captives?"

Her deep blue eyes peered into his with so helpless a stare that Viper was not even tempted to tell her what she wished to know. He merely shook his head. "I will not take you there," he insisted firmly.

With the speed of lightning ripping through rain-clouded skies, Erica suddenly realized he had never meant to leave her in New Ulm, either. She did not accuse him of that treachery, however, since it was to her advantage not to reveal that she had discovered how clever his lies had been. He mistook the mist of tears that filled her eyes for evidence of her sorrow, but they were, in fact, tears of frustration and rage. "I need so many things," she announced suddenly, forcing her attention away from him to more practical matters. "If the town has not been looted, perhaps I can find another dress, a comb for my hair, a—"

Viper's deep chuckle interrupted her list. "You are going to loot the town if the Sioux did not?"

Erica frowned impatiently. "I will keep track of what I take and pay for it later. If there is anything left to take, which I doubt." With one last, anxious glance at the devastated town, she turned away, and after squaring her shoulders proudly, she started back down the bluff. When she saw five Sioux braves examining Viper's stallion, she halted abruptly, fearing her consistently bad luck had just taken a disastrous turn for the worse.

Viper was no more than two paces behind the blonde, and he had already seen the braves by the time she did. Unfortunately, they had also seen her. "Get behind me," he ordered quickly, "and do not argue with anything I say!" He strode on by her then, his rifle in his hand and a look of immense pride and determination on his face.

Erica fell in behind him. She was shaking so badly she wanted to cling to his arm for support, but since he had not offered his hand she did not reach out to take it. As they approached the braves eyed them with openly curious, if not hostile, stares. With each hesitant step Erica took she counted them again, but consistently found there were always five of them and only one of Viper. If these men demanded that Viper share her with them, would he do it? Was she being a fool to follow him down the bluff, when perhaps her only hope to avoid being raped or murdered might be to scramble back over the bluff and run away?

These braves had far coarser features than Viper. They were not in the least bit attractive, only frightening in appearance, and while Erica tried to think of some way out of confronting them, her mind was a hopeless muddle, and she decided to do exactly what Viper had ordered and keep still. When he reached the stallion, she remained behind him and prayed that his charm worked as well on men as she knew it did on women.

Viper recognized the tallest brave as the drunken fool who had kissed Song of the Wren. Hoping the brute would not also remember him, he greeted the group in his own language and followed with a statement and a question. "My wife had relatives living here and is worried about them. How many people were taken captive?"

Claw of the Badger stepped forward to reply. Despite having had too much to drink when he had last seen Viper, their meeting had impressed him so deeply that he remembered him well. "How many wives do you have?" he asked with a taunting sneer.

Realizing the man knew him, Viper laughed as though he were amused by that question. He reached out to catch Erica's hand, pulled her around beside him, then patted her stomach with a knowing wink. "This is my only wife. She carries my child, and I do not want her to worry about her family. If they have been taken captive, I want them treated well."

Erica had no idea what Viper was saying, since he had taught her not one word of the Sioux tongue. He appeared to be claiming her as his own, and she tried to smile at the five strangers, then quickly looked down when she recognized the hunger in their glances for the dangerous emotion it was. She feared they were in such desperate trouble that Viper would have to talk until sundown to get them out of it.

Badger looked at his companions, and when none objected he explained. "They fought well, and we took no prisoners here. At sunrise the people loaded their wagons and went east, toward Mankato. We let them go."

Viper nodded thoughtfully, amazed to learn that New Ulm had been abandoned rather than overrun. The Sioux had not won the decisive victory there that they should have, but since the result was the same, he would not criticize what had happened while he had been gone. "We will look for them there, then," he stated simply as he reached for the stallion's reins.

"Wait," Claw of the Badger demanded. "You have a white man's eyes and a white man's wife. If you have not already cut your hair, I think you soon will."

Viper scoffed at that insult. "I am no 'cut-hair.'" Preparing for the worst, he grabbed Erica by the waist and swung her up on the black stallion's back. He handed her not only the reins but also his rifle before he took the precaution of drawing his knife. When he turned back to face the five braves they had moved apart, and he was grateful he already had his blade in hand. "You are a disgrace to the Sioux if you think you can insult another brave's wife and go unpunished!" he challenged defiantly.

Erica held the horse steady, shocked to realize that Viper had just given her the means to flee when clearly he was determined to stand his ground and fight. That show of courage inspired her own, but since she had never fired a rifle, she considered this a poor time to try and learn how to hit her mark from horseback. She slung the weapon over her shoulder as he usually did, thinking that if she could do no more than force the stallion to trample the threatening braves, she would damn well do it. She took a firmer grip upon the reins and stared down at the braves with a determined look that bore a striking resemblance to Viper's own fiery glance.

Claw of the Badger was cold sober now. To his everlasting shame, Viper might have gotten the better of him with the Indian maid, but he was determined to come out ahead this time. Telling his friends to step aside, he drew his knife and uttered a challenge of his own. "That yellow-haired slut is no fit wife for any brave. We will all have our fill of her when I have finished with you!"

Viper moved toward the left, and without taking his eyes off Badger he called out in English to Erica: "Follow the river downstream. Go!"

Erica did no more than back the big horse out of his way. She did not distract Viper by arguing, but she had no intention of leaving him to face five hostile braves all alone. How could he even ask her to do that? she wondered. She would wait and watch. If he could wound the leader, then she was certain they could both get away in the confusion that would surely follow.

When the headstrong blonde did not gallop away, Viper cursed loudly, but he did not take his eyes off the heavy-set brave who stood opposite him with knife in hand. He did not mind fighting a larger man. In fact, he considered his leaner build an advantage, for his sleek body provided a smaller target than Claw of the Badger's did. "It is plain from your build that you have been eating at the white man's table. When will you cut your hair?" he called out.

Incensed by that taunt, Badger lunged for Viper, but the agile brave ducked the blow easily and continued to hurl insults, each one stinging Badger as badly as a jab from the point of his knife would have. Viper called him clumsy and stupid, delighting in the man's temperamental response, and he soon had the thick-waisted brave sweating profusely. He then started in on the man's lack of success with women, his jibes both cunning and obscene. Badger had the brute strength of a bull, but his wildly swinging lunges never came close to inflicting any harm upon Viper, who was carving him up each time he drew within range.

Erica watched in fascinated horror as the two men circled and lunged, blood and sweat dripping off them like spring rain. It had been clear to her from the beginning that Viper had both the skill and endurance to beat the larger man, and when it became obvious to his friends, she saw them confer briefly and knew they meant to join in the fight.

Viper had kept his eye on the four bystanders, not trusting them to let Badger and him settle the dispute between themselves. He saw one man draw his knife and then another, and he darted inside Badger's reach to stab the man brutally in the right shoulder, forcing him down

130

in the dirt where he lay howling in pain. Viper then went after the closest man with a fierce swipe, catching the brave off guard and leaving a deep slash running across his chest.

With that bloodshed Erica had seen enough, and gouging her heels into the black stallion's flanks, she forced the powerful animal into the midst of the fray. Badger was still down, screaming for help as he tried to stem the flow of blood gushing from his shoulder, and his four friends scattered to avoid the horse's flying hooves.

"Viper!" Erica called in a frantic command, and when she brought the horse to his side he leaped up behind her, wrapped his arms around her waist, and with a loudly shrieked war whoop urged the beast to a gallop and sent them on their way. The wind whipped her hair against her cheeks, but Erica had no time to brush it out of her eyes. She did not know who held the reins, but as they reached the Cottonwood River the stallion veered to the right to follow its path. They raced on and on as they had the day Viper had first taken her from New Ulm, but this time her mood was one of elation rather than paralyzing fear. He had given her the chance to leave him, and she had not even been tempted to go when that selfishness could so easily have cost him his life. She placed her hand over his, knowing that fate was making all the choices for her, and that she would cease to struggle against the powerful force she could not see but could feel to the depth of her soul. Viper had claimed her as his wife, and she knew in her own heart that she was ready to be his.

# Chapter Nine

## August, 1862

It was not until after they had ridden past the last of the farmhouses nestled along the Cottonwood River that Viper pulled the stallion to a halt. Without inviting Erica to join him, he slid off the horse's rump, quickly removed his quiver and bow from his back, and tossed them to the ground. On his way to the river he shed his buckskins and moccasins, then, with a careless tug, pulled the feathers from his hair. When he reached the water he dove in with a reckless splash, then swam out of sight, leaving Erica staring after him with her mouth agape. Then she began to laugh.

Her first impulse was to hide his clothes, but she doubted that inconvenience would faze him. She felt as hot and dirty as he must have and looked forward to also enjoying a refreshing swim. She still had a healthy respect for the horse's size, however, and dismounted with far more care. She tethered him where the grass was plentiful and left Viper's rifle lying nearby. She then removed her clothes with nearly the same haste Viper had shown. Unlike the Indian, she left her garments in a neat pile before wading out into the water. It was cool, but so soothing after a day spent on horseback that she didn't feel chilled.

She swam out a way from shore, but kept her eyes on the horse and their clothes while she scrubbed herself clean and washed her hair. She was sorry now that she had not asked Viper questions all day, since there was so much she wanted to know about him. She felt gloriously free, completely happy for the first time in months, and since her lighthearted mood was entirely because of him, she hoped he would hurry back so she could tell him about it.

When Viper returned to find Erica also bathing in the river he expected her to again be wearing her chemise. He swam by behind her and wrapped his arms around her waist before realizing she was as naked as he. While startled, he did not release her. He pulled her back against his chest as he planted wet kisses along her shoulder. She shivered slightly as his lips caressed her skin, but she did not try to escape him, which amazed him all the more.

Erica made no effort to elude Viper's embrace, because she had no wish to. She leaned against the handsome brave with a lazy insouciance, welcoming the affection she had always found so enjoyable but had also been reluctant to accept. "Aren't Indian maidens far too modest to swim with braves?" she asked, smiling.

Viper had no idea what had come over the lively blonde to make her mood so playful. He had expected her to slip from his grasp like a terrified fish. That she preferred to stay with him instead was a delightful surprise. "Yes, but you need not worry about what they would do. You need be only yourself."

Since that piece of advice suited her needs perfectly, Erica turned slowly to face him and raised her arms to encircle his neck. The water lapped against the fullness of her breasts, only partially veiling her graceful body from his view, but she seemed not to notice. "That is precisely what I intend to be from now on, only myself. I have been very foolish worrying about what will become of me, or what people will say. It is pointless to fret over what will happen tomorrow, when we may never live to see the dawn."

"It would be a great pity for a woman so pretty as you to die a virgin," Viper responded with a mocking grin. He still did not understand her mood, but her pose was too enticing to ignore. He slid his hands down her sides to caress the smooth line of her hips and found her body as perfectly formed as he had always known it would be.

Erica shook her head regretfully, certain from his teasing tone that he did not understand what she wanted

133

so desperately to say. "That would be a small tragedy," she finally replied flippantly. Now that she was looking into his cool silver gaze the words she needed to express the depth of her feelings refused to form upon her lips. How could she speak of love when he never had? "You've told me you want me to be your wife," she began hesitantly. "But you've never spoken of love. Don't Indian braves love their wives?"

Astonished, Viper responded with a question of his own. "Are you the same woman who tried to kill me this morning when I stopped you from running away?"

Erica nodded, ashamed to state out loud that she was. Her behavior had been as erratic as a madwoman's and she wouldn't deny it. That she had fallen asleep in his arms and then tried to leave him the minute she had awakened was evidence enough of lunacy, there was no other way to describe it. "I have no manners at all," was all that she was willing to admit, however. "It is no wonder that you do not love me." How could he? she thought. He had just jumped into the river without a backward glance. Obviously he hadn't cared if she had been there when he came back or not.

Viper did not know whether to laugh or cry, he considered her comment so ridiculous. She suddenly looked so utterly dejected that he feared she might burst into tears unless he provided the reassurance she seemed to need. He raised his hands to her temples to tilt her face up to his and kissed her, thinking that gesture a far more appropriate response than mere words. How could she fail to know how deeply he loved her? How could she possibly not know? he wondered as his tongue curled seductively over hers.

This time Erica did not resist the heady effect of Viper's affection. She let the blissful longing to know even more of him swell within her heart without restraint. She slid her fingers through his long black hair, loving the feel of the silky strands that fell in damp profusion over his broad shoulders. As always, his bronze skin held an enchanting warmth, and she leaned against him to press their bodies closer still. The river swirled around them, rippling with bubbles as light as laughter. It seemed to enjoy their passion for each other as greatly as they did. Since he had been in the water when she had first seen him, the lovestruck blonde did not think their surroundings in the least bit odd or strange. They were merely coming home where they belonged.

Now that Viper again had the delectable woman of his dreams in his arms, he planned to lead her with loving stealth to the realm of sensual pleasure and then to the glorious heights of passion that lay beyond. He wanted to create within her the same fiery sense of urgency that was fast heating his blood to molten flame. The coolness of the river provided his only link to reality, for he was so lost in desire that he was aware only of the fluid motion of the water and the beautiful woman in his arms. They were together, and again of one mind and heart, and he relished that remarkable fact to the fullest.

Viper did far more than merely kiss Erica. He wrapped her in affection warmer than his blanket while his hands covered her slender body with caresses as light as the day's last rays of sunshine. He molded her body to his own, drinking in the beauty of her creamy flesh through every pore. Her figure was as perfect as any woman's ever born, but it was the harmony of her spirit that fascinated him more. Her heart was a great prize, and he knew now that it was his for the asking. What he had done to change her indifferent defiance to love he did not know, nor care. His only concern was in pleasing her so deeply that she would never regret her splendid gift of love.

Without ending the stream of lavish kisses that had left her clinging to him, Viper lifted Erica into his arms. He carried her no farther than the thick grass at the river's edge before placing her upon that soft living cushion and stretching out beside her. He deepened his kiss then as he leaned across her. He wound the fingers of his right hand in her wet curls, meaning to have a ready hold upon her should her fears return. He would not allow her to escape him now, nor to fall asleep in his arms. By the time the sun set, he meant for her to be completely his. His for all time.

While his mouth never left hers, his left hand wandered over the soft swells of her breasts. His fingertips teased one pale pink nipple to a flushed bud and then the other. His hand then brushed over her ribs, moved across the flat planes of her stomach, and paused to trace smooth circles as he wondered how long it would take to make his boast that she carried his child come true. Still pondering that intriguing question, he parted the patch of blond curls below her navel, then slipped his fingers between her thighs. Her fair skin had been cool, but now that his touch had grown more intimate, he felt the pulsating warmth that radiated from deep within her lovely body and longed to lose himself in that enticing heat. His caress was still light, playful, yet knowing, as he satisfied his curiosity about her virginity and found his suspicions were true. He would be her first lover, and he also intended to be her last.

The overwhelming joy of Viper's loving touch made coherent thought impossible, and a multitude of images splashed through Erica's mind like a kaleidoscope of vivid dreams. She had not the slightest qualms about giving herself to him. At the same time her conscience reminded her that no proper young lady from Wilmington, Delaware, or anywhere else, for that matter, would behave so wantonly with an Indian brave. That Viper was an Indian was the least of her concerns, however. He was love itself in her mind: bright, handsome, strong, and so very brave. She was certain no woman had ever had a finer husband than he would be to her.

When his mouth left hers to bestow tender nibbles upon the swollen tips of her breasts, Erica's smile grew wide. She had already surrendered herself completely into his keeping, and as he drew her toward a perfect union, she was too breathless to do more than sigh contentedly as she longed for still more of his uniquely beautiful affection. Again her hands went to his flowing ebony hair holding his face close to her heart as his luscious kisses and knowing touch made her whole body tremble with desire. She moved her hips against his hand in a silent plea: more, she begged, give me still more.

Viper had never slept with a virgin, but he meant to show Erica the depth of love's beauty before he caused her the unavoidable pain their joining would bring. He wanted her drowning in pleasure so rich that she would not even flinch when he sought his own. With that goal shining through the clouds of desire that swirled within his mind, his lips followed the path of his hands. He released his hold upon her golden curls to encircle her tiny waist so she could not bolt when his tongue found her body's most exquisitely sensitive spot. Her taste was amazingly sweet, and the tremors of ecstasy his exotic kisses brought shuddered through her and then echoed through him, until he knew she could bear no more. He moved over her then, his lips again covering hers so she could not cry out, but he prayed she would not wish to.

Again enfolded in Viper's wondrous embrace, Erica's senses were still reeling, for she had not even known it was possible for a man to create the rapture he just had with his shockingly intimate kiss. She had known only the tender beginnings of lovemaking, while clearly he was a master in the full range of the art. With his gentle guidance she was as lost as he in the joy of their loving, until his first deep thrust tore through her loins with a searing pain. Like a sudden shower of ice cold rain, the agony that pierced her body rudely shattered the spell of rapture Viper had taken such care to weave. Tears of angry disappointment flooded her pretty blue eyes, for she had not wanted anything to spoil the beauty of their first time together the way the fiery burst of pain just had.

Viper stopped moving instantly, as disappointed as she that his effort to spare her that anguish had failed. "I am so sorry I hurt you," he whispered hoarsely, "but there is no other way."

Erica did not reply with words. Instead, she reached up to wind her fingers in his flowing hair and pulled his mouth back to hers. She then kissed him with a sad, sweet hunger that swept away the last of his restraint. He withdrew slightly, then began with a gentle rhythm to recapture the paradise he longed for them to share. He wanted her not only to be his wife, but to glory in the fact that they were now truly one.

A numbing warmth began to spread through her body and tingle through her limbs, but Erica held back, unwilling to again naively lose herself to Viper's magical affection when she was now afraid there might be still more unexpectedly painful surprises. Rather than her own feelings, she concentrated solely upon his. She felt a tidal wave of emotion surge through the Indian, then crest with a shuddering climax, but when he buried his face in her curls and lay relaxed in her arms she felt curiously

137

alone, just at the time she had wanted them most to be close.

Until that very minute Viper had never considered a woman's pleasure more important than his own, but he did not want to be selfish with Erica when she was so dear to him. Rolling over on his side, he pulled her into his arms and hugged her tightly. "It will be better for you the next time, and better still the time after that," he promised.

While she appreciated his thoughtfulness, Erica sincerely hoped his prediction would prove true, for she refused to believe nature could be so cruel as to allow women to fall in love with men only to receive pain. She was angry not with Viper but with the basic unfairness of life itself. Love should bring only happiness, in her view, never sorrow and pain, but as she had done with so many of her thoughts since coming to Minnesota, she kept that opinion to herself as she cuddled closer to Viper.

It felt rather strange to lie nude in his arms, not at all unpleasant, but it was a strange sensation all the same. His sleek body was so warm she didn't feel chilled, even though the sun had dipped below the trees and it would soon be dark. When her stomach began to rumble noisily, she was embarrassed until she realized they had not eaten all day. "Aren't you hungry?" she asked shyly.

Viper laughed as he tousled her damp curls. "I am hungry only for you," he replied as he rose up on his left elbow, his ready grin reflecting the love that overflowed his heart. "Now do you understand how much I love you?"

When he began to trace lazy patterns on her bare stomach she laced her fingers in his to make him stop. "If you say that you love me, then I will believe you."

"You did not believe it before now?" Viper inquired incredulously.

"Most men like pretty wmen, Viper. I did not think you would be any different," Erica replied with a melancholy shrug.

Something was wrong, Viper was certain of it, but rather than curse the fact that she was such a wretchedly contrary female, he leaned down to kiss her lips sweetly. "Is it still impossible for you to admit that you love me?"

Rather than answer his question, Erica suddenly asked

one of her own. "You never intended to leave me in New Ulm this afternoon, did you?"

All trace of humor left Viper's expression as he told her the truth. "No, but I knew unless you saw the town with your own eyes, you would not believe me when I said you could not go back. You are my wife now, Erica. Your life will never be the same."

"I know that," the blonde replied wistfully. "My only hope is that it will be better."

Since she still had not spoken the words he longed to hear, Viper prompted her anxiously. "Erica, do you love me or not?"

Sensing she at last had something he valued with which to bargain, Erica began to smile. "First you must tell me who you are, and then I will decide," she insisted with an impish giggle.

"You know who I am!" Viper protested loudly. He then looked around to make certain their privacy had not been invaded by others. "You know me," he then argued in a softer tone.

"I do not," Erica insisted stubbornly. "I know almost nothing about you. Tell me why you have such light eyes, if your blood is pure Sioux without a trace of white." The hostile change in his expression frightened her then, but she knew that was too important a question to remain unasked or unanswered.

Viper stared down at Erica for a long moment. He was tempted to refuse her request, then remembered he had just taken her for his wife. Since he thought a man should trust his wife, he knew he would have to trust her. "That is too long a story to begin here," he explained curtly. He stood up, then took her hands and drew her to her feet. Again sweeping her up into his arms, he carried her back out into the river to wash away all evidence of their romantic interlude.

Now that she had mentioned food, he realized he was hungry, too, and when he was satisfied they were both clean he hurried her out of the water. As he pulled up his buckskins, he thought out loud. "It is too late to hunt or fish. Let's go back to the last farmhouse we passed and see if we can find something to eat there."

The idea of searching abandoned farmhouses for scraps

wasn't in the least bit appealing to Erica. "That's another thing, Viper. Where are we going to live until the uprising is settled? Or for that matter, where will we live when the war is over?" She had yanked on her chemise and pantaloons, but took the time to shake out her slips before she stepped into them.

"I had forgotten you are a rich girl." Viper shook his head wearily. "All the farmers along this river have left their farms. If you must have a house, then we can live in any house you choose."

"And if the farmer returns?" Erica asked apprehensively. "What will we do then?"

Viper laughed at that question. "I do not think any smart farmers will ever return, and I can deal with a stupid one."

Erica sat down to pull on her stockings, certain that was no way to make plans for the future. "I don't want to live in another man's house. I want a home of our own. You told me there were braves with white wives. Do they live in tepees or houses?"

Viper was already dressed and stood staring down at his bride, who, in his estimation, was proving to be far too demanding. "The men with white wives are all farmers. They are 'cut-hairs' and half-breeds who have taken up white men's ways. I will never do that. That is why I am fighting. I would rather be dead than have to live as white men do." He could not forget Claw of the Badger's taunts, however. He had chosen a white wife without thinking how much criticism that action would bring. Or what responsibilities Erica would create, either. As she glanced up at him she looked so pretty and sweet he was sorry he had spoken so harshly and softened his tone. "After we have found something to eat and a place to rest, I will tell you my story. I hope then you will understand."

When he offered his hand Erica took it, and she stood quietly as he buttoned up her dress When he stepped back, she leaned forward to kiss his cheek. "I do love you, Viper. I didn't mean to tease you about something so important as that, but I do want to learn everything I can about you."

The brave nodded thoughtfully, understanding that she was bright and therefore curious. "Yes, we each have much to learn about each other," he offered agreeably, but

140

he was already wondering how to make his story sound better than it truly was. Before he could even begin with those thoughts, however, the stillness of the gathering dusk was broken by a low, threatening growl. The animal was not yet close, but close enough to inspire him to hurry. "That is a cougar. I wanted you to see a live one but I do not think this is a good time."

"A cougar!" Erica cried out in alarm. She scanned the riverbank with an anxious glance, hoping against hope that she would not see the animal running toward them. "Where is he?"

"The animals come to the river at night to drink. If you are ever alone, do not make your camp close to the water or you will have company you did not invite," he advised slyly.

Viper was grinning happily, as though being stalked by a cougar were a trifling matter. "You know so many clever things which I do not, but I will make it a point never to camp anywhere without you, be it by a river or anywhere else." She scrambled up on the horse's back without his help, but she didn't feel secure until he was seated behind her and they had returned to the road. It was nearly dark and growing cold. "We should have found a house before we," she blushed deeply then, "well, before we went swimming. What if we can't find one in the dark?"

Viper looked up at the sky. The first of the night's stars was twinkling brightly and he was certain there would be light enough to see something so large as a house. "I have hunted nearby often. I know where the closest house is. You must trust me, Erica. I will take good care of you."

The man apparently owned little more than the scant clothes on his back and a rifle, yet Erica did not doubt that he could indeed take care of her. "Life is very strange, isn't it? If someone had told me at Christmastime that I would move to Minnesota and fall in love with an Indian I would have thought them crazy for making such an absurd prediction. Yet here I am with you, and it does not seem strange at all."

Viper hugged her more tightly. "We may seem a strange pair to others, Erica, but we need listen only to our own hearts, not to theirs."

"Yes, you are right. I know you are." Erica peered

ahead, certain the last house had to be close. She opened her mouth to restate her objection to sleeping in another man's bed, but then thought better of it. In the midst of a war conventional manners seemed totally out of place. They needed somewhere to sleep, Viper had promised to find one, and she would not complain. "Just up ahead, isn't that a house? Do you see it?"

"That is not the best house, but it is the farthest from New Ulm." Thinking they would be safe there for the night, Viper turned the horse into the yard and pulled him to a halt. There were no lights showing, and from the eerie stillness that filled the air, he was certain the house was deserted. He slipped off the stallion's back, then helped Erica down. "I hope these people left too hurriedly to gather up all their food."

"So do I," Erica agreed, as she continued silently to battle her conscience about trespassing. She moved up on the porch, then turned the handle and pushed the door open wide. A small furry creature dashed past her ankle, and, startled, she jumped back into Viper's arms.

"It was only a cat," he assured her with a deep chuckle. "The people must have fled in a great hurry to leave their pet behind."

"Are you sure it was a cat, not a skunk or raccoon?" Erica asked as she turned back toward the door.

"No one mistakes a skunk for a cat, Erica." Thinking of the animal's disagreeable odor, Viper made a face as he moved past her. "Let me go inside first."

Not wanting to be left outside all alone, Erica took his left hand and followed him over the threshold. When he found a lamp hanging on a peg near the doorway and lit it she relaxed only slightly. The single room was in a shambles, the floor littered with all manner of debris from torn linens to moldly bits of cornbread.

"Do you see what a bother a house is?" Viper asked in his familiar mocking tone. "If this were a tepee we could simply move it to another place and start over with everything clean."

Erica shot the handsome brave a skeptical glance. "Well, this isn't a tepee, as you can well see. If you will build a fire in the fireplace I will look for a broom and begin cleaning."

142

Viper turned away to hide his smile. He was not used to taking orders from a woman, but Erica had not really ordered him to build a fire, so he would do it without argument. The stone fireplace had already been laid with wood and he had the fire blazing long before Erica had located a broom. "Let me help you," he offered, not wanting her to be too tired to enjoy the night that lay ahead.

"Indians must have made this mess. Will they come back?" Erica didn't want to watch him fight any more braves after the ghastly confrontation she had witnessed that afternoon.

Viper plucked a feather pillow from the floor and tossed it toward the bed. "I do not think so, but if some do I will send them away."

"Like you did this afternoon?" Erica looked over the top of the quilt she was folding so she could study his expression as he answered.

"Yes. I should be very angry at you for not doing as I said," the brave mused softly, for he still did not understand why she had not run away when he had told her to go.

"But for some reason you aren't?" Erica coaxed coquettishly.

"No, staying with me was a very brave thing to do," Viper complimented her sincerely, and then he began to laugh. "I will not scold you when I may need your help again on another day."

Erica continued to move about the one-room house, picking up as best she could while they talked. She was delighted when she found a hairbrush, but laid it aside to use later. "Those braves were Sioux, weren't they? Why did they want to fight with you? Was it over me?"

"Are you so spoiled you think all men wish to fight over you?" Viper teased playfully.

"Yes, I am. Now tell me the truth. Why did those men want to fight with you?"

Viper thought it wise not to mention Song of the Wren as he explained, "Badger is a bully who will make up an excuse to fight if there is no reason. It was the horse he was after today, not you," he lied convincingly.

"Oh, I see," Erica commented softly, embarrassed to

143

think she had misunderstood the cause of the fight. "Just where did you get that horse, Viper? His bridle belongs to the army. Did you steal him from the fort?"

Insulted to be called a horse thief, Viper went toward the door. "The stallion was a gift from Little Crow. The bridle I took off a dead mule. I must go see the animal has a place to spend the night, too," he called over his shoulder as he stepped out the door. He needed to be alone enough to rehearse the tale she wanted to hear, and caring for the horse was reason enough to go outside. He found the barn empty, and left the horse in the first stall where someone had thoughtfully left hay for another animal. He then went outside and sat down by the door.

All his life he had fought to be considered wholly Indian, and now, at his first opportunity, he had taken a white wife. That made no sense at all. Yet what man of any color would not want a woman like Erica for his wife? Unable to find the answers he sought, Viper continued to badger himself with questions until the rumblings in his stomach drove him back into the house. To his amazement Erica had something cooking in an iron kettle over the fire. "What is that?" he asked incredulously.

Erica was disappointed he hadn't noticed how nice the house looked. True, it was small, with little room for anything other than the bed and a table and chairs, but she had spent considerable effort straightening it up. "I found some potatoes and I am trying to make soup. It smells very good, but I don't know how it will taste. I think it needs milk. Did you find a cow in the barn?"

"No, the barn is empty except for our horse." Viper walked over to the fire and looked down into the bubbling pot. The aroma was delicious, and he picked up the ladle to give the soup a stir. "Are you a good cook?"

Erica was embarrassed to admit she had very little experience in the kitchen. "We had a housekeeper who cooked all our meals. My mother used to order the groceries and plan the meals, but Mrs. Ferguson did all the cooking. After my mother died, I was the one who did the planning, but I've never really tried to cook anything myself."

Viper nodded thoughtfully. "It is time you learned."

"Well, I always thought," Erica began, but then she thought better of arguing with him and fell silent.

144

Intrigued, Viper wanted to know what she had been about to say. "You always thought what? Tell me," he ordered as he crossed the room to face her.

Erica was tempted to say anything but the truth, until she realized there were probably dozens of things he would expect her to be able to do that she hadn't learned. "I always thought I'd marry Mark and have servants to do all the chores," she finally admitted. "Do Indians ever have servants?"

Viper could not help but laugh at that question. "We used to make slaves of captives, but I do not think anyone caught during the uprising would make a good servant for you."

"Well, of course not," Erica agreed. "I'd set them free!"

"Yes, I knew you would. Now let's see what we can do to make your soup worth eating." Viper returned to the fire, hoping boiled potatoes would not taste too bad by themselves, but to his surprise, they were quite good.

Erica watched Viper as he finished the last drop of soup in his bowl. While he did not have the most polished of table manners, it was plain that it was not the first time he had eaten at a table. "Let's sit by the fire," she suggested, but before she could move her chair he grabbed the quilt off the bed and placed it on the floor in front of the hearth. Since he obviously saw no reason for chairs, she took his hand and sat down crosslegged to face him. "Tell me about yourself. You promised you would."

Viper sighed softly, reluctant to begin, but when Erica reached out to give his knee a sympathetic pat he knew he could not disappoint her. "It is my grandfather who would interest you most. He was born in France, but his parents were not married." He paused then, hoping she would not be too shocked by that fact, but the pretty blonde only nodded, as though everyone's grandfather were a bastard.

"His father was rich and sent him and his mother to live in Montreal. The man sent them money, but they never saw him again. When his mother died, my grandfather started trapping. He came down through the Great Lakes and into the Minnesota Territory. He learned the Sioux tongue and when he fell in love with a Sioux woman he never went back to Montreal. He and my grandmother had two sons: my father and his younger brother. My parents both died young, so it was my uncle and grandfather who raised me. My grandfather liked to pretend he was Sioux, but my uncle liked to go up to Canada and pretend he was a Frenchman. I went with him once and watched him do it. The women would have nothing to do with an Indian, but if a Frenchman had money, they would do anything he asked. I hated them for that," he revealed, without realizing how bitter he sounded.

Erica knew exactly to what type of women Viper was referring, and she couldn't help but blush. "It isn't so strange that people are frightened of Indians, but not of their own countrymen. Is that why you won't admit to being part white? Do you think people will see only an Indian and hate you?"

Viper looked toward the fire. "I do not care what people think of me, Erica. My grandfather taught me many things about the world, my uncle still more. The missionaries taught me to speak English and how to read and write. I learned their lessons so that I would know more than any white man did, not because I wanted to be white myself. I have made the same choice that my grandfather did: I want to live my life as a Sioux. There is nothing about the white man that I admire."

The hatred that glowed in his eyes frightened Erica badly. Then his belligerent attitude made her angry. "Nothing except his women," she pointed out with brutal honesty. "If you really believed what you are saying, then I would be the last woman you'd ever wed. You're lying, Viper, and you know it."

Viper's hand flew to his knife, then, disgusted at himself that he would even be tempted to use it on her, he sprang to his feet. "Do not call me a liar ever again. Perhaps a white man would take that insult from his wife, but I will not!"

Erica watched him stride out the door, uncertain if he would ever return, and at that moment, she didn't care whether he did or not. She hugged her knees and stared into the flames, wondering if their brief marriage were already over. When she grew sleepy, she looked longingly at the feather bed, and knowing she did not want to sleep in it alone, she reluctantly admitted that despite all their problems, she hoped Viper would come back, and soon.

# Chapter Ten

## August, 1862

Viper did not go far. He wandered aimlessly around the yard for a while, then sat down again in front of the barn and leaned back against the door. He hoped he had told Erica enough to satisfy her curiosity for the time being. If she found out more about him later, then he would deal with her questions then. Tilting his head back, he closed his eyes and tried to imagine what a blissful paradise her life must have been compared with his. He had not simply married a white woman, he groaned inwardly. He had married one who had been raised like a princess. It would be funny were he not so hurt about her curiosity about his background. Clearly it pleased her to think he was at least partly white, while that fact disgusted him completely. It was a flaw, which set him apart, and he did not wish to live as an outcast in anyone's world. The Sioux regarded him as a man. Whites called him a filthy Indian. Was it any wonder he scorned that part of his heritage?

He felt a tentative tug at his thigh, and looked down to find the cat had returned. Without waiting for an invitation it climbed into his lap, turned around twice to get comfortable, then curled up in a tight ball and went to sleep. Viper was surprised the animal had approached him since he was a stranger, but the tomcat seemed so content with him that he began to pet it lightly. The cuddly animal had a striped coat like a tiger, and Viper traced the pattern of his fur with a lazy caress. The cat

147

purred then, a deep rumbling hum that made Viper smile, and his anger with his headstrong bride gradually melted away.

Without knowing exactly what he would say to Erica to excuse his long absence, Viper lifted his new friend into his arms and rose to his feet. The cat opened one yellow eye, then, seeing they were approaching the house, closed it and went back to sleep. He was a plump fellow, a good mouser who lived off field mice when there was no one at home to feed him scraps.

Erica was adding wood to the fire as Viper entered, and his annoyance showed clearly as he spoke. "You should have waited for me to do that," he criticized with an exasperated sigh. Did the woman think he would shirk his share of their work?

The feisty blonde was tired, and covered a wide yawn as she directed her attentions to the cat he held rather than her maddeningly critical husband. "I was afraid it would be an all-night wait, and I would have gotten very cold."

"It is not that cold tonight," Viper contradicted her. He dropped the cat on the foot of the bed before crossing the room to stand at her side. Now that he was with her again, he knew he had to do something to earn her sympathy as well as her respect. They could not argue forever when there were so many more amusing things for a man and woman to do with their time. "Have you heard of the Indian, Inkpaduta, Scarlett Point?" he asked casually as though he had left the house for a stroll rather than in nearly a blind rage.

"No. Is he a friend of yours?" Erica inquired curiously.

"No, he is no friend of mine," Viper scoffed with a frown. "He was an outlawed chief who led a band of Lower Sioux renegades in the spring of 1857. They murdered more than thirty settlers in Iowa, then returned to Minnesota and killed a few more before they escaped into the Dakota territory. The army tried to catch them, but could not. The Indian Office then made the Sioux responsible for capturing Inkpaduta. They said we would not get our annuities until we brought him in. I went with Little Crow to search for the renegades, but we could not find them, either. We finally got what was owed us, but Inkpaduta went unpunished for the settlers' murders.

148

None of us forgot how we were blamed for his deeds, though. We knew then that those in Washington lacked any real power, but would use any excuse to avoid paying us the money and food we were promised." Viper took Erica's hand and pulled her down beside him on the quilt before he continued.

"Five settlers were murdered in Acton last week. Since we knew we would all be blamed again, not just the four killers, many believed it was a good excuse to go to war, but I did not agree. I do not hate all white men, but I am tired of being treated like a child. I am a man. Why can't I live where I wish to live, as white men do? Why should I let the government tell me I must stay on a tiny patch of land where I will soon starve? Why must I do that?"

Erica could not help but believe that the fiery anger which glowed in Viper's eyes was completely justified. "I am ashamed to tell you how little I knew of your plight before coming here. In Delaware, our only concern was the war between the North and South, not what was happening here in Minnesota."

Viper nodded in agreement. "We knew that, too. So many men have left their farms to join the army that there were few here to fight us. The army had little real strength, either." Viper glanced into the flames on the hearth for a moment, desperately wanting to make her understand his reasoning. "This is not a fight between Indian and white, Erica. We are in the right, and we want only the respect that is owed us. You will never be my enemy. It is only the government, which tells us nothing but lies, that I despise."

"I don't blame you," Erica agreed. "But still—"

"No," Viper interrupted emphatically, "I have not turned my back on my people by taking you as my wife. Do not say that ever again. Do not even think it. I can love you and my people, as well. I do not have to make a choice, and neither do you."

While his words were wonderfully reassuring, Erica still had another concern. "Are you certain all those braves wanted this afternoon was the horse?" she asked with clear feelings of apprehension. "I could have sworn—"

"It was the horse," Viper insisted stubbornly. "They were from another camp and do not like me. You do not

149

need to worry. My friends will not bother us."

Erica was still not convinced that was true, but she dropped the matter, since she had still another concern. She rubbed her thumb lightly over Viper's knuckles, then laced her fingers in his. "Will the Sioux consider us married now? Do we need to do no more than live together to be husband and wife?"

His eyes were on their hands. His were deeply tanned, while hers were fair. The colors of their skin blended together well in Viper's view, and he gave her hand a loving squeeze. "A white man may take a wife in the same way," he pointed out.

"Yes, that is one type of marriage," Erica admitted reluctantly. "I would rather be married in a church ceremony, though. Would you do that for me, Viper? Would you marry me in a church?"

Viper drew in a deep breath then, let it out slowly. While that delay did not influence him to change his mind, it provided sufficient time for him to gather the composure to answer politely. "No. No words that any priest or missionary could ever say would make any difference. You are already mine."

That was not the answer Erica wanted to hear. To be Viper's common-law wife simply didn't satisfy her sense of propriety. If she was going to have an Indian brave as a husband, she wanted their ties to be legal ones that would be recognized by everyone. She was proud to be his wife and didn't want to have to make any apologies to anyone about the circumstances of their marriage. She began to argue, then realized that even if she managed to talk Viper into agreeing to marry her in a church, they would be unlikely to find a clergyman who had not fled the uprising to perform the ceremony. Surely the war couldn't last too long, and then she could ask him again to marry her in a church. She smiled as she looked up at him, but it was a smile of subtle surrender, not defeat. "I love you," she said sweetly, and she was enormously pleased by his answering smile.

With an agile grasp, Viper pulled Erica across his lap. "You brushed your hair," he finally noticed. Her curls were now attractively styled to softly frame her face and cover her shoulders rather than merely falling free down her back. "Your hair is so pretty," he murmured softly as he buried his face in the glorious blond cascade. "You look like an angel."

Erica was certain she had seen the same illustrations he had and could not help but laugh. "I am very seldom good! No one ever mistakes me for an angel."

Viper gave her a lingering kiss before arguing that point. 'I think you are good, very, very good."

Erica knew exactly what he meant and responded with a throaty giggle. "You are better than good, Viper. Your kisses taste marvelous." She hugged him enthusiastically then, content to rest in his arms, but she soon realized rest was the last thing on his mind.

With a deft touch Viper undid the buttons on Erica's bodice and slipped his hand inside her camisole to caress the pale, creamy smoothness of her breasts. His fingertips brushed the tips gently, teasing them to flushed peaks. "Let me undress you this time," he murmured against the soft curve of her cheek.

Before she could agree or object, he lowered his mouth to hers, silencing any response she might have cared to make. He loved everything about her: the delectable sweetness of her kiss, the enticing softness of her skin, the incredible oneness they had found in each other's arms.

He trailed light kisses down her throat, then nibbled at her ears until she began to giggle. "Do you like that?" he whispered.

"No!" Erica insisted as she gasped for breath. "Well, yes. It is nice, but it tickles." She reached up to bite his earlobe then, but he didn't laugh. Instead, he lowered her down upon the quilt, nuzzled her neck playfully, then pushed her already open dress aside to shower the lush fullness of her breasts with tender kisses.

Erica had never expected to spend her wedding night in so small and humble a dwelling. Nor had she ever dreamed she would spend it with a passionate Indian. Her well-ordered life had been turned upside down since she had left home. Yet the fact that Viper was now all she knew of her future home did not frighten her.

The amorous brave sat up to remove her slippers and then her silk stockings. He was tempted to toss the sheer stockings into the fire, but since he had not provided the buckskin clothing he had promised, he dared not diminish the small wardrobe she had. Laying the stockings aside, he stretched out beside the lithe blonde and again pulled her into his arms. He was in no hurry this time. He wanted to savor each minute they shared, to make the night last forever in both his memory and in fact.

"Why don't you undress me first?" he offered generously.

"Undress you?" Greatly intrigued, Erica snuggled against him as she reached for his belt buckle. "This won't take long, since you wear so little."

"Indian girls do not complain I am poorly dressed," Viper teased.

"I did not say you were poorly dressed, my beloved," Erica responded with a musical purr, her comment as teasing as his. "I said you did not wear many clothes. There is a difference."

Viper caught her hand and brought it to his lips. "I understand. My clothes are very fine, but few. Is that it?"

"Precisely," Erica agreed. His eyes held a smoky warmth, and she reached up to pull his mouth back to hers, her efforts to help him disrobe forgotten for the moment. "I will never tire of kissing you," she vowed softly. "Not if I live to be one hundred."

"I think you will be as beautiful an old woman as you are a young one." Viper's words were not spoken as empty flattery, but were sincere. "It will be very nice to grow old with you."

Erica's eyes sparkled with mischief as she thought of the years ahead. Surely they would be paradise with him by her side. "It will be a very long time before we are old, Viper, years and years and years." She lost herself in his kisses then, preferring to glory in the beauty of the moment than dream of what lay ahead.

Between both playful and loving kisses they managed to remove each other's clothing, but the warmth of the fire was so inviting they did not leave the quilt to move to the bed. The golden light thrown by the flames illuminated the planes of Viper's deeply bronzed body in high relief. Like a classical statue, he was perfectly proportioned, and his muscular body radiated strength even when his pose was relaxed.

"I will never tire of looking at you, either," Erica mused aloud. "You are so very handsome." Running her fingers through his hair, she let it fall about his shoulders like an ebony cape. "I have seen only a few Indians up close. Are there many Sioux braves who are as handsome as you?"

Viper laughed as he replied, "No, I am the only one. You need look no further for a husband."

"I didn't plan to," Erica whispered seductively as she leaned across him. The tips of her breasts brushed his chest and he wrapped his arms around her waist to hold her tight. The lissome blonde kissed his eyelids, then his cheeks, before her mouth returned to his for a long, slow kiss that filled his heart to overflowing with desire.

Capturing her in a fond embrace, Viper rolled over to pin her beneath him, but despite the intensity of his need he was still determined to be considerate of her. His lavish kisses gave silent proof of his abundant love, while his tantalizing caresses led Erica's senses on a wildly pleasurable journey that skirted the very brink of madness. He allowed her to hover there on that narrow precipice, her body trembling in anticipation of the rapture she had but glimpsed when they had first made love. When he was certain her body would welcome his, he entered her only partially, then withdrew and slowly entered her again. It was a pattern he repeated, taking her with an exquisite stealth, until the ecstasy he had awakened within her cried out to be released. He abandoned himself in the beauty of their union then, quickening his pace to keep time with the furious pounding of his heart. Lost on the cresting wave of passion, he rode it to the shimmering shores of paradise and then, his ardor spent, he lay still in her arms, more in love than ever with the astonishingly responsive woman he had wed.

"I promised you it would be better this time. I was right, wasn't I?" he whispered when at last he had the breath to speak.

Curled against his sleek body, for a long moment Erica was too content to reply. Then she agreed. "Yes, if making love felt any more glorious than this, I don't think I would survive."

"Yes, you would survive, and want even more," Viper assured her.

153

Snuggled in his arms, surrounded by the lulling warmth of his love, Erica had no wish to argue that point and drifted off to sleep, but when he left her side to add wood to the fire she awakened, her hunger for him unquenched. "You are right," she murmured as he returned to the quilt. "I do want more. I will never have enough of you."

With a sly grin, Viper pulled her into his arms, then slowly, tenderly, and with a remarkably sensuous grace, he made love to her again. "You are my wife, Erica. For all time you will be mine," he vowed as his lips brushed her ear. He buried his face in her golden-blond curls and wondered how he had found the strength to exist before he had met her. She filled his life with meaning the way the sun filled the day with light, and he knew he would never stop loving her.

When Erica awoke, she did not at first recall why they had slept upon the smooth plank floor when the small house had a perfectly good feather bed. She stretched languidly and then decided it mattered not at all where she and Viper slept as long as they were together. As she wrapped the quilt around them she finally took the time to notice the beauty of the pattern. Called Ocean Waves, triangular pieces of contrasting dark and light shades of blue and gold cloth had been pieced together to create the lively rhythm of the sea. It called to mind the lovely quilt her aunt had been making, and grabbing the intricately stitched fabric blanket to cover her breasts she sat up and shook Viper's shoulder roughly. "Wake up!" she cried in so anxious a tone he was instantly awake and alert, expecting to find himself facing some terrible danger.

"What is wrong?" he asked with a menacing scowl when he saw nothing amiss. He was understandably displeased at having his dreams interrupted so rudely.

Erica did not bother to apologize before she explained her reason for waking him. "Yesterday you refused to take me to where the captives from New Ulm have been taken. But you simply must. How can I be content with you when I don't know if my relatives are alive or dead?"

At that question, Viper's dark expression lightened to a teasing grin. "You are content with me, do not lie. If these relatives were truly precious to you, you would have

154

remembered them before now."

Embarrassed that she could not argue with that logic, Erica grew contrite. "Yes, I know. It was very selfish of me to think only of us when they may be suffering terribly. Won't you please take me to them so I can see for myself they are alive and assure them that I am also?"

Viper lay back and propped his head upon his hands. He considered her request a long moment, then decided she deserved to hear the truth. "The braves we met yesterday said there were no captives taken at New Ulm. The people were allowed to leave."

"What do you mean, 'allowed to leave'? Where did they go?"

"Down river toward Mankato," Viper replied calmly. "I cannot take you there, and you know why. If your relatives are alive, they are alive. If they are dead, they will stay dead. It is not worth risking my life to satisfy your curiosity."

Erica chewed her lower lip with nervous nibbles, knowing he was right. At the same time, she was also certain she had to let her aunt and uncle know she was alive. "They must be beside themselves with worry, Viper. There's my father, too. He must have heard of the uprising and be terrified that something might happen to me."

"Mark will not worry?" Viper taunted sarcastically.

"Oh, he will worry even more than the others, because he knows how little I wanted to come here." Remembering their repeated arguments, Erica pushed her curls away frm her face with a saucy flip of her head. "He will never forgive himself for this," she predicted softly. "Never."

Viper's scowl returned as he sat up to face his troubled bride. "Never forgive himself for what? That you have taken up with an Indian?"

Exasperated that he had misunderstood her, Erica leaned forward to give Viper a reassuring kiss. "I'm sorry. I didn't mean to insult you, but that wasn't what I meant at all. I wanted to marry Mark and stay in Wilmington. He wanted to postpone the wedding until after the war. That's what will upset him. That we did not marry when I wanted to, and now he has lost me."

Viper's keen gaze searched Erica's expression for some sign of regret, but he found none. "You are not sorry to be my wife instead of his?"

155

Erica shook her head as she began to smile. She wrapped her arms around his neck and gave him an enthusiastic hug. "I will never be sorry I fell in love with you."

Before Viper could respond, the tomcat bounded across their legs. Hoping for breakfast, the rascal began to meow loudly and dance in circles to get their attention.

"Do you suppose he's hungry?" Erica reached out to pat the cat, and he rubbed his head against her hand, begging to have his ears scratched.

"Yes, he is hungry, and so am I. It's early. The fish should be easy to catch."

Erica watched with an admiring glance as Viper stood up and pulled on his buckskins. He then donned his moccasins, retied the cougar claw necklace around his neck, and seemed satisfied he was dressed for the day. "Do you think I should come with you?"

Viper leaned down to tousle her curls. "No, I will not be long."

The cat followed the brave out the door, but Erica remained seated on the floor. Viper hadn't built up the fire, so she'd do it to heat some water to bathe. Despite the fact that it would be wonderful to have soap and hot water for a bath for a change, that was not a sufficiently inspiring thought to encourage her to get up and begin the day. Instead, she sat tracing the triangular patterns of the quilt with her fingertips as she wondered who had made it. Surely she must have met the woman at the store, but she had no idea which family had lived in the house she and Viper were now occupying. There was a trundle bed that pulled out from under the large bed, so there must have been a child or two, but no toys had been left behind when the family had fled, and she hoped the people had gotten away without mishap.

Thoughts of the uprising made her shiver with dread. Quite unknowingly, she had entered an entirely different world when she'd come to Minnesota, a world poised on the brink of disaster. That Viper had appeared out of that tumult to become the central force of her life still amazed her, yet she felt so comfortable with him she knew she would never feel any need to explain to others why she had wed an Indian brave. She knew it would shock her family and friends, but since it did not shock her, she saw no reason to dwell on the matter. For the time being, Viper and she would have to live each day as it came and pray tomorrow would take care of itself.

Reluctantly, Erica put aside the pleasant thoughts of her husband and rose to her feet. She stretched her arms above her head, and feeling slightly stiff, vowed to make it a point to sleep in the bed that night. It took her a long while to get the fire started from the dying coals that remained from the night's blaze. Then she realized she would have to fetch water to bathe. It seemed silly to get dressed to bring water, then undress to bathe, so she merely wrapped herself in the quilt, picked up the wooden bucket sitting on the ledge by the fireplace, and went outside to find the well. When it was not in view, she hiked up the end of her makeshift garment and started around toward the back of the house. The bushes and shrubs had been cut back to allow for a path, but she circled the structure without finding the well. Since she knew there had to be a source from which to draw water somewhere, she decided to try the far side of the barn.

The morning air was chilly, and she hugged the quilt more tightly to her throat as she approached the barn. The path was a well-worn hollow, and she was certain if she just followed it she would soon find the well, but as she turned the corner of the barn she came to an abrupt halt, for not ten feet away sat what she was certain was a cougar. The big cat was eyeing the stallion through a crack in the barn wall. His tail was swishing back and forth with a menacing beat as his tongue swept over his whiskers in a hungry slurp that carried clear to Erica's ears. She began to back up slowly, hoping to escape the predator's notice, but the animal saw her out of the corner of his eye and turned his full attention toward her.

Armed only with a bucket, Erica hurled it as she shouted a threatening curse, but rather than frightening off the cougar, she succeeded only in angering it. He was a handsome beast, his fur a dark yellow on his back and sides, his muzzle and belly white. He snarled at her, then, with a wobbling gait, started for her at a run, swiftly gathering the speed necessary to lunge for her throat.

Not about to provide the cougar with a tasty breakfast, Erica threw off the quilt, and while the beast was momentarily blinded in its thick folds, she turned toward the house. Crossing the yard in a furious sprint, her blond hair flying, she was an amazing sight. Viper had just entered the yard with three large trout, and seeing his lovely bride dash nude into the house, he did not stop to ask what had frightened her so. He tossed the fish on the porch and drew his knife. By the time the cougar shook off the quilt and rounded the corner of the barn, Viper was ready for him. With a scream more terrifying than any banshee's, he challenged the beast to a fight to the death.

Sighting the Indian, the cunning cat slid to a halt, then spun on its hind legs and loped off into the underbrush, but not before Viper had seen the wound in his left hind leg. Thinking that the injury must have accounted for the animal's daring in venturing out in broad daylight, the brave returned his knife to its sheath and picked up the fish on his way into the house. Erica had pulled on her dress, but her pretty blue eyes were still filled with fright as she greeted him.

"Did you see the cougar?" she asked breathlessly.

"Yes, I saw him, and I saw you, too," he added with a devilish chuckle. "It is no wonder the cat was chasing you if you were parading about without your clothes."

Erica blushed deeply at that remark, but she was still too frightened to be offended by his teasing. "I was looking for the well. I was dressed too, in the quilt."

Viper pulled her into his arms and pressed her face close to his chest as he listened to her tearfully relate the rest of her tale. "You are safe, and that is all that matters," he assured her. "Cougars hunt at night. That one was wounded or he would not have been out now, nor would he have come so close to the house. I will have to go after him before he comes back. Wounded animals are dangerous, and I cannot let him roam free when next time you might not be able to outrun him."

Erica was still shaking. "I've never had to lug water from a well. Not once in my whole life. Where is the damn well, anyway?"

Viper released her and looked around for the bucket. "I'll go and get the water. Did you leave the bucket outside?"

The distraught blonde wiped her eyes on the back of her

hand as she tried to recall what had happened to it. "It must be by the barn. I'll come with you."

"Are you sure you want to?" When she nodded Viper took her hand. They recovered the bucket and quilt, then located the well hidden behind a shady elm tree across from the house. "I will chop the wood and bring the water, Erica. I do not want you to have to work harder as my wife than you did as your father's daughter. I want you to be happy with me."

"I am happy," Erica insisted proudly. "It is only that I know very little about being a farmer's wife."

"I am no farmer," Viper replied curtly, insulted that she might consider him one. "I like to hunt and fish for my food, not wait for it to grow out of the ground."

"Will we be able to eat the cougar?" Erica wondered out loud, the prospect most unappetizing.

"No, we will keep his pelt, but not eat his flesh." Viper picked up the bucket in his left hand and again took her hand in his right. "Now let's have breakfast and worry about trapping the cougar later."

With Viper's instructions Erica managed to fry the trout in the cast iron skillet the owners of the house had left behind. He then showed her how to peel the tender white meat away from the bones and carried their two plates to the table. While he thought the meal delicious, he could tell by her preoccupied stare that Erica thought otherwise. "You do not like fish?" he asked.

"Oh, yes, I do, and this is very good," Erica insisted as she toyed with the remains of her trout. "I was just trying to think of some clever way to convince you to take me hunting with you. I don't want to sit here all day with nothing to do. The fact is, I'm afraid to stay here by myself. So, won't you please take me along with you?"

Viper frowned slightly as he considered her request. "You will only be in my way."

"No, I wouldn't," Erica argued. "I promise to stay behind you and be very quiet. You could even let me carry your bow and arrows if you like, or the rifle, whichever you won't need."

"I planned to take both," Viper confided. "The cougar is hated by farmers because he will get into a herd of sheep or goats and kill more animals than he can eat. Unlike

159

other animals, he has a need to kill, rather than only a need to satisfy his hunger. In that way, he is like man." He looked up then, and found the innocence of Erica's deep blue gaze unsettling. "I do not wish to give him a second chance to kill you."

"Well, neither do I," Erica agreed. "But I won't be safe here alone if someone comes. There may be more braves out looking for horses," she reminded him, although she still didn't think the man he had fought had wanted their stallion.

Viper nodded thoughtfully, afraid what she said might well be true. "All right. Finish your breakfast and I will take you with me. We must track that cat before his trail grows cold."

Erica leaped to her feet. "I'm ready. Let's go now." She sat down on the ledge of the fireplace to pull on her stockings and shoes, then looked up with a triumphant smile.

"How am I to hunt when you are so pretty?" Viper inquired, his question far more serious than he knew she would believe.

"Maybe you can find other game, too," the excited blonde suggested, taking his question for a compliment that required no reply. "We really should have more in the way of food."

Viper rose to his feet, then scraped the fish left on their plates off into a bowl he placed outside on the porch for the cat. Turning back to her, he ordered gruffly. "Take off your slips, that way you won't make so much noise when you walk."

The perceptive blonde knew she wasn't welcome on the hunting trip, and since she had had to talk him into taking her, she didn't think she could demand he be more charming. "I suppose your buckskins are quiet?" she asked instead.

"Like the whisper of the wind," Viper assured her. He watched as she discarded the lacy undergarments, then slung his quiver and bow over his shoulder. He picked up his rifle and opened the door. "Stay right behind me. If I raise my hand, stop. Do not speak to me unless I first speak to you."

He was so serious about their mission that Erica did not

argue. "I will be like your shadow, quiet but always nearby."

That promise brought a smile to the brave's lips. "If I had a pretty wife who was as quiet as a shadow, everyone would envy me."

"Everyone will envy you whether I am quiet or not, now let's go." Erica slipped past him to go through the door, then waited for him to lead the way. The tomcat looked up only briefly, then went back to devouring the last bits of trout in the bowl.

Viper had certainly filled her life with adventure, Erica thought as she followed him into the forest, which lay on the north side of the barn. The farmer's cornfields were on the south, and she wondered who would harvest his crop. She didn't know the first thing about picking corn in the fields, and from what Viper said, neither did he. Well, they'd soon learn, she swore to herself, because surely it would be a sin to let the corn rot in the fields when his people were going hungry.

Unaware of the practical slant of his wife's thoughts, the brave walked with a light but sure step, stopping frequently to study the breaks in the underbrush for clues to the cougar's direction. The animal had run only a short distance then had lain down to rest before moving on. It was traveling steadily north, but Viper hoped to overtake it before it reached the safety of its lair. They walked one hour, then two. Viper turned back often to make certain Erica was keeping up with him, but she was never more than an arm's reach behind. She, too, had worn her cougar claw necklace, and he winked at her, thinking them a very strange hunting party, indeed.

When Viper heard the big cat moan, a low, mournful sound off to the right, he raised his hand to warn Erica he was about to stop and change direction so she would not run into his back. The underbrush was thick, but up ahead he caught a glimpse of the cougar they had been tracking sunning himself on a rocky ledge. Blood was trickling from the wound in his back leg and he turned his head to lick it away.

Viper could not get a clear shot from where they stood, so he gestured to a tree with an overhanging limb. Erica nodded that she understood, then held his rifle as he

161

climbed up and found a secure place from which to shoot. Regaining possession of the weapon, he took careful aim, then suddenly changed his mind and handed her down the rifle. Taking his bow and an arrow from his quiver, he then again took aim at the wounded cougar.

Erica didn't want to watch the animal die, even though she understood why he could not be allowed to live. She told herself it was the humane thing to put him out of his misery, but she turned away as Viper drew back his bowstring. A slight movement in the bushes behind them caught her notice, and she realized to her horror that the cougar's mate had begun stalking them. Before she could shout a warning to Viper, the female broke through the foliage and came running toward her, mouth open wide, her wickedly sharp teeth gleaming with the bright threat of death as she sprang into the air. Without allowing her total inexperience with a rifle to affect her actions, Erica pulled the trigger and watched in terrified fascination as the female's snow-white belly turned a brilliant red. In the same instant an arrow pierced the cougar's throat. Slain twice, the animal fell to the ground only inches from the blonde's feet, twitched convulsively, and died.

Erica turned to look up at Viper and found his astonished glance filled wtih admiration. His first arrow had also found its mark, and he leaped down from the tree to join her. "You were right," he shouted enthusiastically, "everyone will envy me!" He picked her up off her feet and spun her around, then set her down and kissed her soundly. "It is not every brave's wife who has the courage to shoot a cougar at point-blank range."

"Your friends will be impressed?" Erica whispered weakly.

"Yes. You are not only pretty, but also brave. They will like you," Viper assured her with another fervent kiss.

"Oh good," Erica mumbled as he drew his knife to begin skinning the first of the dead cougars. She then collapsed in a heap at the base of the tree, the rifle balanced precariously across her knees. She felt faint and sick to her stomach, but as long as Viper was proud of her, she would not complain.

# Chapter Eleven

## September, 1862

One week melted into two, and Erica grew accustomed to the easy routine Viper had set. Each morning he would catch fish for their breakfast. Since she had proven her value, if he went hunting later, he would take her along. Sometimes they gathered berries together in the woods, always eating more than they ever managed to carry home. In the afternoons they would ride the stallion to the river to swim or merely to sit under the trees and enjoy each other's company. The evenings were spent in front of the fire, where Viper would recount the more colorful adventures from his youth to amuse his adoring bride. She had enticed him into sharing the feather bed at night, but it was clear to her, despite the fact that they were enjoying the comforts of the small farmhouse, that the man still considered himself an Indian through and through. It was a placid life, which gave them both pleasure, but it also had the elusive quality of a beautiful dream, and they each knew it could not last.

Often when they were together, Viper would be so preoccupied that Erica knew better than to disturb him with idle conversation. She respected his privacy and did not pry, since she was certain he was silently dwelling upon the course of the uprising. She knew they were honeymooning in a valley torn by warfare, but she did not force the issue by asking him to discuss it any more than he already had. She enjoyed the hours they shared too greatly to spoil them with talk of bloodshed, but she said prayers each night that the Sioux and the white men would soon be able to again live in peace.

After repeated washings and days spent in the sun, Erica's only dress had faded to as pale a shade of blue as that of a robin's egg. The soles of her slippers were nearly worn through, and she could scarcely imagine how they would survive the winter if they did not find heavier clothes and a source of food. The fall weather was lovely, but she had heard the winters were harsh in Minnesota, and she did not want to spend several months wrapped in their one quilt huddled in front of the fire.

As they rode to the river one afternoon, Erica could no longer keep her worries to herself. "Where did your people get things like flour and salt, Viper? Were there stores at the Lower Agency?"

Viper was not unaware of the source of her concern, for he too had spent considerable time wondering how they would pass the winter months. "The government gave us flour and salt as part of their bargain to pay for our lands. Traders at the agency sold food, but they cheated us and charged more than it was worth. Then the Indian agents ignored our complaints and paid the traders' claims out of our money. Everyone cheated us. It was like a joke to them, but not to us."

"I certainly don't find it amusing, either, but if a shortage of supplies was a problem before, won't the uprising have made the situation even worse?"

"Yes," Viper agreed, "but now that we can hunt again on land the settlers have left, we at least have a chance to provide for ourselves. We had none before."

Every word he spoke was so damning, Erica was amazed the uprising had not taken place several years earlier. The Sioux had shown remarkable restraint, in her view, when they had been treated so badly. She was riding behind him that day and rested her cheek upon his shoulder. "You are so bright, Viper, you would make a fine spokesman for your people."

Viper disagreed. "No, I would not, for I know my words would be wasted. We have sent the wisest of our chiefs to Washington. Their pleas were heard but quickly forgotten. Talking does no good at all."

"And the killing will?" Erica asked skeptically.

"We will have to wait and see," Viper responded thoughtfully. "I should find my friends and learn what has happened."

"Will they still be living at the Lower Agency?"

Viper hesitated a moment, then, certain she would never betray him, told her the truth. "There was talk of moving our camp up past the Yellow Medicine River so the warriors' families would be safe."

As they reached their favorite spot on the river, Erica looked around apprehensively. She never relaxed until she was certain there were no signs anyone had visited the site since they had left the previous afternoon. "Isn't the Yellow Medicine River a long way from here?"

"Yes," Viper agreed with a sly grin. "If we were to follow the Minnesota River, it would be a long trip. But if we followed the Cottonwood to its source and then went north it would be no more than a day's ride." He slid down off the stallion and then helped her down to her feet. "You were not afraid the first time you talked with me. Would you be afraid to visit my camp?"

While Erica thought she would be wise to be cautious where his people were concerned, she did not want to admit the thought of meeting them frightened her witless. Without answering his question, she started walking toward the river, unbuttoning her dress with a carefree nonchalance as she went. They always swam nude, and she liked the feel of the water against her bare skin. She liked the way Viper's body felt against hers, too. Swimming nude would have created a scandal at home, but here in the woods it seemed a very natural thing to do.

Viper tethered the stallion where the animal could graze, then followed his bride down to the water. They spent so much time out of doors that her fair skin had turned a light golden tan, and if possible, her hair seemed even more blond. He walked up behind her, wrapped his arms around her narrow waist, and gave her a loving hug. "I must go soon, Erica. Do you want to come with me, or stay here?"

"You know I cannot stay here alone," the troubled blonde complained. "If you leave, then you will have to take me with you." She placed her hands over his, wishing with all her heart he would choose to stay there with her instead.

"Your dress is nearly worn out, our food is scarce. We will have to find the others before winter comes." Knowing each day he remained with her would make it all the more difficult to leave, he forced himself to make a painful decision. "Tomorrow we will go to the Yellow Medicine River. We will learn all we can, and then decide whether to go or stay."

Erica sighed regretfully, "I like it here, Viper."

"So do I," the brave readily admitted. "I do not mind living in a house if I do not have to be a farmer, but I am a warrior, and I cannot leave my friends to fight alone."

"I understand," Erica murmured softly, glad he could not see the tears that filled her eyes. She broke away from him then, hurriedly stepped out of her clothing, waded out into the river, and began to swim.

He knew her moods so well it was plain to Viper that Erica did not understand at all. Quickly discarding his buckskins, he swam out to her. With a flip of his head he sent his hair out of his eyes, then leaned forward to give her a light kiss. "It is not a choice of loving you or being a warrior, Erica. I do love you, and I am a warrior. You have always known I am Indian."

"Just as you have always known I am white," Erica reminded him. Now that they had finally taken up the subject she had been so afraid to discuss, she did not back away from it. "When other whites are being held captive, how can I ride with you into Little Crow's camp? I can no more go there than you could go to Mankato with me to look for my aunt and uncle. Each of us would be seen as the enemy by the other's people. You know we would."

Viper frowned slightly, for while he knew in his care she would not be in danger, he did not want her own people calling her a traitor. "I will take you with me, but leave you hidden nearby and enter the camp alone. The captives cannot be wandering about freely. When I am certain you will not be seen, I will return for you. Now stop worrying about meeting my people. They will not spit on you, even though your kind has never treated us well."

It was the bitterness of his tone that convinced the worried blonde to be still. She had chosen to become his wife when she had realized she loved him too dearly to forsake him. Every action in life brought consequences, some good, some bad, and she knew she would simply have to face them. "I could not bear to lose you," she confessed in a shaky whisper.

"You never will," Viper promised. He swam a few yards away and then came back to steal another kiss. He teased her until she began to laugh and join in his game of tag. She knew how to swim, if not nearly so well as he did, but he would let her catch him rather than take pride in how easily he could get away. They played until his mood became more passionate than playful, and then she no longer tried to slip from his arms.

Viper gripped Erica's hands and towed her toward the shore where a soft blanket of moss made an inviting bed. As he dropped down by her side she did not pretend ignorance of his intentions, but entwined her legs in his with a seductive purr, her joy in his love having grown deeper with each new day. He might have known far more about making love the first time they had been together, but she was an imaginative young woman who had led him with an enticing eagerness to learn even more. She met his every kiss and caress as though it bestowed a flood of rapture. Her whole body seemed alive with the essence of her love, making her endlessly responsive to his every gesture.

Viper had known Erica was a great prize even before they had made love. Now that her happiness had become as important as his own, he treasured her all the more. There was not an inch of her sun-kissed flesh he had not explored with his adoring fingertips and lips, and yet he never tired of the glorious quest to know her lithe body as well as his own. He watched the water trickle from her damp curls, slide over her breasts, then form a pool in the hollow of her stomach. He swept the moisture away with his hand, then buried his face between her breasts to savor their softness. He licked one delightfully puckered nipple and then the other, thinking the perfection of her body would fascinate him till the end of his days. "I love you," he murmured softly, the sound of his deep voice muffled by her glistening flesh.

Erica gazed up at the leaves, which provided a shimmering canopy for their mossy bed. The day was warm, the sun bright, the sound of the river bubbling with nature's own harmonies, and she breathed deeply of the fresh scent of the forest air. Had she and the man she loved been floating upon a billowy carpet of clouds, she could not have been more content. "And I love you," she responded dreamily.

Viper's sweet kisses traced intricate patterns over the lush swells of her bosom before his lips sought hers for a far more intimate exchange. He felt her fingertips lazily gliding over his back, following the rhythmic motions of the muscles as he shifted positions. She was never passive, never still. She was like the spirit of love itself, enfolding him in her arms while the luscious flavor of her kiss lured him ever closer to surrendering not only his heart, but his mind and soul as well. In her embrace, he was so totally lost in the magic of her loving spell that he wished with all his heart that the rest of the world would simply cease to exist. What need had they for anyone else when each was complete in the other?

Erica's hands slid down Viper's sides, encircled his trim waist for a moment, then lay relaxed upon the curve of his hips. Her toes toyed with his before she opened her legs in a silent invitation she knew he would not ignore. He ended his kiss and rose up slightly to look down at her, his gray eyes filled with a smoky haze of desire. Rather than wanton, he regarded her as merely being as honest with her emotions as he was with his. They were in many ways an unusual pair, but he found their multitude of differences only made their love more exciting. Recapturing her mouth in a fervent kiss, he moved with a gentle ease to fuse their two separate bodies into one ageless being whose brilliant aura rivaled the sun for light.

As always, the rapture Viper created with the rhythmic motions of his powerful body was shared fully by Erica. Like an endless spiral the ecstasy swirled through him to Erica, curling like flames that seared them both with passion's delectable heat. Their hearts beat wildly, and yet in perfect unison, until the stunning splendor of their union burst forth within them, leaving them awash in the beauty of perfect contentment and peace.

When at last Viper lay with Erica cradled in his arms, he traced the elegant line of her throat, the shape of her lovely face, then the outline of her lips, until she kissed his fingertips sweetly and caught his hand in hers. "I have no need to find others," she whispered softly. "They would only be in our way."

"You will find my tepee as private as a house. No one will bother us when we wish to be alone."

Erica took a deep breath, then ended it with a lazy yawn. "I will always wish to be alone with you."

Viper knew of no way to allay her fears before she actually met his people, but he hoped that once she had had a chance to know them, she would not feel out of place. He loved her dearly, but he knew the life he would give her was very different from the one she had known. He could only hope, as she had once confided, that it would be better.

When Viper returned from the barn with the stallion the next morning and found Erica holding the hairbrush, the quilt off the bed, and the tomcat, he could not help but laugh. "Bring the quilt if you must, but we cannot take the cat. He would only get lost and be eaten by one of the creatures that dwells in the woods."

Knowing he was right, Erica regretfully gave the good-natured cat one last hug and set him down on the porch. "Do you think he will be all right here?" she asked nervously.

"He'll catch mice in the fields and live in the barn. He'll not suffer at all without us." Viper leaned down to give their striped pet's ears a final scratch, then smiled at his bride. "We have little to take with us, two cougar pelts and a quilt." He shook his head as though their possessions should rightly be more numerous.

Erica folded the blue and gold quilt over her arm and patted it fondly. "I don't want to leave this here where someone might come along and rip it to shreds."

Viper was certain what she really meant was that an Indian might tear it up or burn it, but he didn't ask her to describe who she had in mind. "I want you to ride in front of me so we can talk."

Erica was so reluctant to make the trip that she didn't care where she sat, so she didn't argue. With his help she mounted the horse. She slipped the brush in her pocket, then folded the quilt and the hides he handed her across her lap. When Viper climbed up behind her and turned the horse toward the river she looked back toward the little farmhouse, her deep blue eyes filled with a mist of regret.

169

"I hope our next home is as happy as this one," she said wistfully.

"If we are together, it will be." Now that they were under way, Viper found his mood soaring, but he was wise enough to stifle his enthusiasm out of respect for Erica's feelings. He pointed out landmarks as they rode along, whistled to birds, and laughed at the antics of the squirrels that bounded through the trees, but his bride's interest in their surroundings remained slight. At midmorning they stopped to fish and eat breakfast, but Erica was still unnaturally quiet, and he gave up his efforts to amuse her.

After that brief rest they continued on, taking the northeast branch of the river when they came to a fork. By late afternoon they had yet to find the river's source, and Viper drew the horse to a halt. "We will stop here and find a place to make camp. Do you remember what I told you?"

For a moment Erica's mind was a blank, but then she recalled his advice. "Yes, we shouldn't make camp too near the river, or the animals going for water at night will disturb us."

While he was certain disturb was not the word he had used, Viper gave Erica a hug and agreed. "Yes, we will be safer away from the water's edge."

As Erica slid off the horse's back, she could not help but recall the days they had spent in the Big Woods. While here there were many trees growing along the riverbank, they gradually gave way to rolling meadows, and the terrain was far more open than the Big Woods had been. "This is a pretty spot," she called out when they had gone some distance from the water.

Wanting a concealed campsite rather than a picturesque one, Viper agreed but led the stallion to a rise shielded on the north by a stand of birch and a thick tangle of old vines. He pulled the blanket off the horse, then hobbled him and removed his bridle. "Let's sleep on the quilt this time. Then we won't smell like the horse in the morning."

Erica looked down at the wrinkled folds of her faded dress. "That might be an improvement. How can you introduce me to your friends looking like this, Viper? They will think I am a captive you have mistreated rather than your wife."

The handsome brave laughed at her worried frown. "I promised you a buckskin dress. I will have my aunt fetch

170

you one and let you change your clothes before anyone sees you. Will that please you?"

Erica tried to smile. "Yes, a new dress of any kind would make me feel better."

"Find us some wood, and I will catch more fish for supper," Viper called over his shoulder as he started back toward the river.

After stretching to shake off the fatigue of their long ride, Erica began looking around for dry wood, not once stopping to complain that she had again been given that task.

After Viper had threaded the fish he had caught onto the spit he had fashioned and placed it over the fire, he realized Erica might find some of his people's ways very strange. "When I am hunting alone or with other men, I do not mind cooking, but when we are in camp the women prepare all the food."

Since he had always helped her, Erica frowned slightly. "I'm sure it will take me some time to learn how to cook the dishes you like to eat. Won't you still help me?"

Viper shook his head. "No, my aunt will teach you how to cook. I cannot do it."

"Cannot or will not?" Erica asked perceptively.

Viper shot her a warning glance. "Our men hunt, the women cook. It is not so different in the white man's world. Your men do not cook, either."

"They do if they have a wife like me who has never learned how!" Erica took a few steps away, and then after a fierce inner battle to gain control of her temper, she turned back to face him. "I understand; I will do my best not to disgrace you."

Viper was disgusted with himself for not explaining his point so she would not feel insulted. At least she had not reminded him she had been raised to rely on servants to do all the household chores. "Do any white men sew clothing?" he asked, hoping to make her see her customs were not unlike his.

"Yes, there are men who sew. They are called tailors, and they make men's clothing rather than women's, but I understand what you are saying. There are some things women do and other things men do. Perhaps I should be quiet unless we are alone, that way I won't embarrass you publicly with my questions."

171

Viper flashed a disarming grin at that offer. "Do not worry. Many do not understand English as well as I do, so they will not know what you are saying."

"Good," Erica replied, a bit too emphatically. It was growing dark, and while she kept pacing restlessly, she stayed within the ring of light thrown by the fire. The fish cooked quickly, and when Viper summoned her to eat she went to his side and sat as close as she usually did. "Is your aunt your mother's sister or your uncle's wife?"

"My mother's sister." Viper held his breath, knowing that with Erica's curiosity, more questions were sure to follow. "My uncle had no wife."

Erica waited a moment for him to continue, and when he did not she spoke. "What happened to your parents, Viper? You said they died young. How did it happen?"

Viper waited until he had finished eating, then looked around for the cat to give him the scraps before he recalled they had left him behind. "I was a baby when they died. I have heard tales, but they were only tales."

Intrigued, Erica licked the last bits of fish from her fingers, then encouraged him to continue. "You know I will not repeat the story. Tell me what you were told."

Viper leaned back on his elbows, his pose relaxed, even if his mood was not. "My uncle and my father courted the same woman. She was very popular, and many men wished to make her their wife. She is still remembered for her beauty. When she chose my father, my uncle was very unhappy. He kept to himself, but everyone knew what was wrong with him."

Erica nodded sympathetically, understanding how the man must have been heartbroken. "There were no other women he cared to court?"

"No, never." Viper took a moment to gather his thoughts before he attempted to relate the most difficult part of his story. "One day when I was two, my mother went down to the river to fetch water. Some white trappers saw her, and being fools, did not think she would fight them as she did."

Erica reached out to touch Viper's arm. "You mean she was raped?"

The brave nodded. "Then murdered. My father and uncle went after the trappers. They found them, but only my uncle lived to tell how they had killed them. From that day to this some people have thought he murdered his older brother for not guarding the life of the woman they both loved."

"And that is the man who raised you?" Erica gasped in disbelief.

Viper's glance was dark as he replied. "He was a good father to me. My grandfather did not believe one of his sons had murdered the other. Neither do I. I told you it was only a tale. Are there not white people who spin evil tales about others?"

"Yes, and plenty, but Viper, that must have been a terrible burden for you as a child." Erica stared at her husband, wondering how he could have become such a charming man if he had grown up surrounded by such horrid gossip. "Your poor uncle, what a tortured life he must have led."

Viper had to disagree, "He liked fun more than most. He did not walk around weeping."

"But still," Erica began.

"Do not ask me about him again," Viper cautioned.

"I won't. It's just that I think it must have been horrible for the man to live his whole life under such a dark cloud of suspicion."

Viper did not argue. He was grateful she had not guessed that it was his uncle's white blood which had often been blamed for his tragic fate. He remained silent until the flames had grown so low he had to get up and add wood to the fire. "The women bring the wood, too," he remarked absently.

"You must think me a total failure as a woman, Viper, since I was raised to be no more than an ornament in my husband's life."

"An ornament?" Viper asked, clearly not understanding the word.

"A decoration, something pretty, with no value at all other than as something to admire."

"No, you have a mind and can think for yourself. You are no ornament."

"Well, thank you," Erica responded as she rose to her feet. "You tanned the cougar hides yourself. Am I supposed to know how to do that?"

"Yes, that is women's work." Viper watched his bride pace to and fro, thinking her beauty undiminished by the

173

faintness of the light. Her spirit glowed with an inner radiance that lit all her actions with a taunting hint of her passion's fire. "The night is the best time of the day. Let's not waste it," he called out as he walked toward her.

Erica slipped her arms around his waist when he reached her. "Your people are going to think me the most useless bride you could have wed."

"So what?" Viper agreed with an amused chuckle. "You need only please me."

"And do I?" the lively blonde inquired through seductively lowered lashes.

"Very much." He ended their verbal play with a deep kiss, grateful she was so easily distracted. His right hand moved down the buttons on her bodice, swiftly freeing her from the garment so that with but a few brief tugs it fell to the ground. Her lingerie was whisper-soft from repeated washings, and he slipped the straps of her camisole off her shoulders. "You would please any man."

"I want only to please you, though," Erica murmured softly as she snuggled against him. He was as handsome as the night. The black of his hair like the ebony sky, the silver gleam in his eyes as bright as the stars. Think only of the joy of tonight, she cautioned herself. Tomorrow will bring cares enough of its own.

Viper combed her thick curls through his fingertips, vowing never to make her wear her glorious golden hair in braids. She was unique, precious, and, dressed in buckskins or fine silks and lace, she would still be his wife. Only through her had he begun to understand the depth of the love his uncle must have felt for his mother. There was no way to replace love so profound as that. When it was lost, it was gone forever. He stepped back slightly as he shared the secret he had kept hidden in his heart. "My uncle would never have killed my father. He and I were all that was left of my mother's love, and that would have been as precious to my uncle as she was. I have always thought my father killed the trappers, and then himself. My uncle carried the blame for his murder rather than the shame of his suicide, but there should be no shame when a man chooses to die for love."

That was so bittersweet a legacy that Erica was moved to tears. Unable to speak, she covered her husband's face with kisses. She clung to him, knowing from the sadness of her

174

father's life how deep a man's love for a woman could be and how eager he could be to join her in death. When Viper pulled her to the ground they made love with a passion born of remembered sorrow, but that made the ecstasy of their union no less deep, and the peace of their dreams no less sweet.

With her heart in her throat each step of the way, Erica tried to be better company for her husband on the second day of their journey. They left the Cottonwood River when it narrowed to a stream spilling forth from the ground, and turned north once again. When they came to another river, she could barely swallow her fears long enough to speak. "Is that the Yellow Medicine River?" she asked hoarsely.

"No, it is the Redwood, if we are not lost. The Yellow Medicine still lies ahead." Thinking they would reach it by that afternoon, Viper asked Erica if she would like to stop and rest, but she was too nervous to postpone the arrival at his camp for any reason, let alone fatigue. They crossed the Redwood River, then kept up a steady pace until the Yellow Medicine River came in sight.

"Where will your people be?" Erica turned to look up at her husband, her eyes filled wtih a bright glow of fear rather than curiosity.

"Near the Upper Agency I think. I can leave you here and come back, or you can come with me. You may have your choice."

Erica looked down at the horse's mane, nervously pulling the coarse black strands through her fingers. "I would rather hide on a rise so I can watch you enter the camp. I want your rifle, too."

Viper thought her first request reasonable, even if her second definitely was not. "I will leave you my knife instead. That way I will not have to worry about your shooting me when I return."

"I would never shoot you!" Erica protested, her feelings hurt by his remark.

"Not on purpose, I know." Viper's mind was already made up. She could defend herself, if need be, with a knife, but not injure him by accident with it. As it turned out, their discussion proved to be premature, for Little Crow had moved his camp farther north, to the banks of the Chippewa River, which lay several hours' ride away.

175

When they found no trace of his family and friends near the Upper Agency, Viper knew they would have to ride on. While he was disgusted by the unexpected delay in returning to his camp, he could readily see in Erica's every glance and gesture that each extra minute only served to heighten her dread.

They camped along the western bank of the Minnesota River late in the afternoon. Viper again caught fish for their supper. He tried to lift Erica's spirits, first with amusing stories and then with passion, but even as the rapture he had always been able to create swept through them, he could still feel the depth of Erica's fear and thoughtfully kept her cradled tenderly in his arms until dawn.

The next morning Erica was so tired she could barely stay awake. On this third day, their journey now seemed endless, and she could easily imagine them spending the rest of their lives roaming the world looking for a home. In midmorning they crossed paths with braves from Red Iron's village, who greeted them in friendly fashion and told Viper where he could find Little Crow. They then had to cross the Minnesota River to the eastern bank, which only made Erica thoroughly wet as well as miserable.

As they neared the confluence of the Chippewa and Minnesota Rivers, they came upon a sentry. Recognizing his good friend Two Elk, Viper called out to him.

Two Elk stared first at Viper, then at the blond woman riding with him. "Where have you been?" he asked curtly, clearly disappointed by the warrior's long absence.

Erica was trembling so badly Viper gave her a loving hug before whispering. "He is my friend." He answered Two Elk in his own tongue. "I have been amusing my wife as best I can. She is too shy to ride into camp with me. May I leave her here with you while I go see where we might live?"

Two Elk's mouth dropped open. "A wife? You have taken a wife?" He tried to get a better look at the blonde, but she appeared to be as shy as Viper described her and kept her head down so he could not get a clear view of her face.

"Yes. She is a young woman from New Ulm who had already caught my eye."

"And you caught hers?" Two Elk asked skeptically.

176

"Oh, yes." Viper had to laugh at that question, since it described how they had met so well. He slid down off the stallion's back, then pulled Erica down beside him. "This is my good friend, Two Elk. He speaks but a few words of English, but if you wish him a good afternoon he will understand you."

Erica kept a firm hold on Viper's hand with her left hand and gripped the quilt tightly with her right as she forced herself to look up at the brave. Like Viper, he had a quiver of arrows and a bow slung across his back and held a rifle in his hands. He was dressed in buckskin breeches and moccasins and his hair was braided and adorned with feathers. While not nearly so well built nor so handsome a young man as her husband, his good-natured grin seemed sincere. "Good afternoon," she managed to whisper nervously.

It was the vibrant blue of Erica's eyes that held Two Elk transfixed. Like the summer sky, they seemed infinite in their beauty, and he envied his friend his choice. "Good afternoon," he finally remembered to respond.

Not about to let anyone stare dumbfounded at his wife, Viper spoke to wake Two Elk from his trance. "Claw of the Badger said the people of New Ulm were allowed to leave in peace. Is that true?"

"Yes." The brave forced himself to look at his friend as they continued their conversation in their own language. "They fought bravely, and we had captives enough without them."

"And the army? Have you fought them again?"

Two Elk broke into a wide grin as he illustrated his remarks with expansive gestures. "I was with Little Crow's brother, White Spider, two weeks ago, when Gray Bird, Red Legs, Big Eagle, and Mankato surrounded soldiers camping at Birch Coulee. They fought for two days and killed many men and nearly one hundred horses. They would have slain all the troopers had more not come from Fort Ridgely with cannon."

"And what were you and White Spider doing while this happened?" Viper asked with a puzzled frown.

"We were on our way to attack Forest City, but as before, there were arguments about what we should do. Walker Among Sacred Stones took braves who wished to raid other towns, but we met again and together fought

177

soldiers sent to guard the towns along the Big Woods. We did well, too," he claimed modestly. "Forest City now has a stockade. The settlers have built stockades around all their towns, and we could do no more than burn the homes they left behind."

That was something Viper had not anticipated. "The settlers are not leaving then, as they left New Ulm?"

"No, they mean to stand and fight," Two Elk replied with a shrug, as surprised as Viper by the white man's courage.

Erica tugged on Viper's hand. "What is he saying?"

"The fighting hasn't stopped," Viper responded, choosing to keep the gist of Two Elk's remarks to himself for the time being. Again addressing his long-time friend, he continued, "May I leave Erica here with you until I have a place to take her? Truly she is frightened of what she might find in our camp, and I want to be certain she is welcomed."

Honored to be asked such a favor, Two Elk quickly agreed. "I will guard her life with my own," he vowed proudly.

"See that you do." Viper then reached out to touch the cougar claw necklace he had fashioned for his wife to wear. She still wore one of his claws, in addition to her own. This time he spoke in English so she would understand. "Erica is very brave. She killed the cougar whose claws she wears herself, so be careful not to insult her." He then handed Erica his knife so she would have the comfort of a weapon while he was gone. After giving her a brief kiss, he pulled himself upon the stallion's back, and with a sly wink, bid her good-bye, "I will be back soon. Use that knife only on white men. Two Elk is too good a warrior to lose."

Embarrassed, as well as exasperated that he would tease her about turning the knife on his friend, Erica was tempted to say she did not see any humor in his advice, but Viper turned the horse away before she could speak and was gone. She could do no more than smile nervously at her companion then. The brave seemed as embarrassed as she, and considering that a good sign, Erica moved out of his way, chose a sunlit spot, and sat down on the quilt to anxiously await her husband's return.

# Chapter Twelve

## September, 1862

Not wanting to keep his beautiful bride waiting for long, Viper hurriedly entered Little Crow's camp, found his aunt, and in as few words as possible told her of his marriage. She had been a child when her sister was slain, and while also slender and attractive, with luminous brown eyes and glossy black hair, she had never possessed the murdered woman's remarkable beauty and charm. All her life she had suffered from that comparison. Childless herself, she envied the fact that her lovely sister had produced so fine a son, and, as a result, she and Viper had never been close.

She surveyed her handsome nephew with a long, slow glance before offering her opinion. "If you have decided to follow the white man's way, then you should not have brought this woman here."

Out of respect for his aunt, Viper did not shriek obscenities before he replied to that piece of unwanted advice, but he was sorely tempted to do so. "I am the same man I have always been. The color of my wife's skin does not change mine. I wish to fight again with Little Crow. Will you be a friend to Erica and teach her all she must know to be one of us?"

"I do not speak her tongue," his aunt responded, her enthusiasm for the project obviously slight.

"She is a lady with fine manners. I thought you were also." As Viper turned away, his aunt reached out to touch his arm.

"Bring her to me," she offered after a sigh of reluctance. "I will do what I can to make her welcome."

While that was scarcely the joyous response he had hoped the news of his marriage would receive, Viper nodded. "Thank you. Please find her a dress and moccasins. Your size should fit her, too." He left her then to prepare for his return, but he took the time to find several of his friends in order to hear what their version of the news of the uprising would be. In each case, they told the same tale Two Elk had. With astonishing speed, settlers had built stockades to protect their cities. They were not fleeing Minnesota as the Sioux had hoped, but digging in for a long fight. The army could still be surrounded and beaten, but many of the chiefs were tired of fighting and were talking of making a truce.

"On what terms?" Viper asked with a deeply furrowed brow, for he recalled vividly how the older chiefs had opposed the uprising in the beginning. Given the chance, they would surely end it now.

"Sibley is commanding the volunteer army. He left a message for Little Crow at Birch Coulee. He is willing to talk peace, but only if the captives are freed first," Hunted Stag explained.

"Little Crow did not agree?" Viper knew who Henry Sibley was. A former fur trader, he had been the Territory's first delegate to Congress and then had been elected the first governor when Minnesota became a state in 1858. He was a man who spoke their language and understood their customs. He was no young army officer who, ignorant of Indian ways, would lead his troops right into their traps.

"No, why should he? It is to our advantage to keep them. We can bargain with their lives, or kill them. If we give them back, we have nothing."

While Viper understood the value of having hostages for bargaining purposes, he did not like the mention of their possible deaths. "Killing the captives would prove nothing," he argued.

Hunted Stag shrugged. "There are some, like Wabasha's son-in-law, Rdainyanka, who think they should die. He says the war has gone on too long to end in a truce. He thinks we must fight to the death, and kill all the whites we can. The prisoners will die with the last of us."

Viper swallowed hard, knowing the uprising had begun for a ridiculous reason, but not wanting so badly to see it end as apparently Rdainyanka did. "I have brought a white woman back with me. She is my wife, and I do not want her frightened by such talk."

Hunted Stag was as startled as Two Elk and his aunt had been by that news, but for an entirely different reason. "Wren would have made you a fine wife," he uttered with a disgusted sneer. "Keep the white woman as your captive until you tire of her. She need not be your wife."

Viper reached for his knife, then realized too late he had left it with Erica. "Erica is my wife," he replied in a menacing whisper. "If you dare to insult her again, I will have your life for it!"

No coward, Hunted Stag still took the precaution of moving back a step before he issued a challenge of his own, "If your white blood calls so loudly to you, you no longer belong with us. There are many mixed bloods among the captives. Perhaps you and your white wife belong there also!"

Viper went for him then, using his fists to make the point he had failed to score with words. A crowd quickly gathered around, not caring what had caused the fight, but eager to watch it. Hunted Stag and Viper were evenly matched in size, but Viper's righteous anger gave him the advantage. With but a few decisive blows, he won an apology from his former friend, then left him bleeding in the dirt. He stalked off then, still too angry to acknowledge the cheers or greetings of the bystanders.

Knowing he could not return to Erica before he had bathed, Viper went back to the tepee where he had found his aunt for a change of clothes and also picked up the clothing she had gathered for his wife. He hoped that if he brought Erica into camp dressed as an Indian, his intentions to remain with his people would be so clear even the fools among them could see he was still a Sioux.

Two Elk saw Viper coming down the trail and called to Erica that her husband had returned. He then saw his friend's deep scowl and grew worried, but Viper's expression changed to one of delight as he swung down from his horse and greeted his bride.

"Did you miss me?" he teased. His hair was still damp from his bath. Dressed in new buckskins and smiling broadly, he appeared to be completely free of care.

"Miss is not a strong enough word," Erica replied. She gave him one enthusiastic hug after another, unmindful of Two Elk's chuckles at the joyousness of their reunion after so brief a separation.

"I have brought you the dress I promised." Viper unrolled the soft buckskin garment and held it up for her to see. "I have moccasins, too. Will you wear the clothes for me?"

Not realizing how important her manner of dress was to her husband, Erica readily agreed. "Yes, if it will please you. I told you I would be happy to have anything new." She glanced down at her faded blue gown and noticed to her surprise that the bloodstains near the hem, while now faint, were still visible. "Yes, I definitely need something new." She looked around then, not wanting to bathe and change her clothes in front of Two Elk.

Understanding her desire for privacy, Viper offered his hand. "Come with me, there is a better spot for bathing up ahead."

As she moved past Two Elk, Erica glanced up at him shyly. "It was nice to meet you," she paused to say.

Not certain how to reply, the embarrassed brave merely nodded and smiled broadly. He watched as Viper helped her onto the horse and then led the animal away. He was still surprised that his friend had taken a wife and wondered what their other friends had said. Since he would surely find out that evening, he reminded himself to take his duties as a sentry more seriously, and tried to put Viper and his remarkable bride out of his mind.

When they arrived at a suitably secluded spot, Viper stopped the horse and helped Erica from his back. A sly smile graced his lips as he began to unbutton her bodice. "Save this dress. It will give us many memories."

Since not all of them would be pleasant, Erica would have preferred to burn the worn garment, but she did not argue with his request. He sat at the river's edge while she bathed. After she had finished and put on her own lingerie, he helped her to don the buckskin dress. The fit could be adjusted with the laces at the shoulders and neckline, and he worked until he was satisfied the garment was as flattering as her other dress had been. Still, even attired in the graceful buckskin dress, his lovely blond wife did not even remotely resemble an Indian woman.

"Sit down in front of me and I will brush out your hair," he offered politely but he took the precaution of making certain no one was nearby to observe him at the task. Wet, her hair hung in dark ringlets he knew would relax into soft curls when dry. It was finer in texture than his own hair, and he concentrated on brushing it over his hand as it dried, distracting himself from the darker thoughts that filled his mind with heart-rending confusion.

Impressed by the softness of her new dress, Erica toyed with the fringe on the sleeves and hem while her husband hummed softly to himself. "You found your aunt, then?"

"Yes. She is the one who makes my clothes. She will teach you how to make your next dress yourself." Then curious, he thought to ask, "You do know how to sew, don't you?"

Erica peeked over her shoulder at her husband, both her manner and expression apologetic. "Well, actually, no. My mother taught me the various stitches for embroidery, but all our clothes were made by seamstresses."

Viper nodded. "Of course. Rich women do not sew their own clothes. I should have known that without asking."

Objecting to his condescending tone, Erica was quick to defend herself. "I do know how to thread a needle, Viper. I am certain sewing hides is nothing like sewing fabric anyway, so even if I were an accomplished seamstress there would be lots for me to learn. I am not stupid. You needn't worry your aunt will laugh at me."

"That is the least of my worries," Viper confided sincerely. "Her name is Flowers of Spring, and since she is only eight years older than I, she has never tried to take my mother's place. She is a widow, and childless, so her life has not been a happy one."

"Just how old *are* you, Viper?" Erica was shocked to realize she had never even asked that question.

"I am twenty-seven," he responded with the teasing chuckle that often filled his deep voice. "How old are you?"

"Seventeen." Erica laughed too, then, thinking it odd they had never before had any curiosity about their ages. "Your aunt is only thirty-five, then. She could marry again and have a family, couldn't she?"

"Yes," Viper admitted rather reluctantly, "but it is unlikely."

"My father is only thirty-nine. I wish that he would marry again. It broke my heart to see him so sad and lonely." The moment she mentioned the man who was so dear to her, Erica was overcome with painful feelings of guilt, for she still had thought of no way to send him word that she was not only safe, but married.

"Would he like an Indian woman? Flowers of Spring can sew and cook well, and she is so quiet he would not tire of her company," Viper boasted proudly.

"Are you tired of mine?" Erica turned again to inquire. "Is that all Indian men want, a woman who can do chores well and keep quiet?"

Knowing he was treading upon dangerous ground, Viper shook his head. "It is nice if a woman is also pretty, even better if she likes to make love. A slave can do chores. A wife's duties are different."

"Do Indian women consider making love to their husbands only a duty?" While she knew there were white women who held such a pathetic view, she had always felt sorry for them. Since her parents had been so blissfully happy, it had been obvious her mother enjoyed making love as much as her father did.

"I hope not," Viper replied with a teasing grin, thinking they had discussed the subject long enough. He looked up at the sky then, wishing night would fall swiftly so he could escort her into camp without attracting too much notice.

Her hair was nearly dry now, and as Erica took the brush from Viper's hand she noticed he had scraped his knuckles. Alarmed, she knelt in front of him. "Were you fighting with someone? Is that how you hurt your hand?"

Viper thought of the many secrets he would have to keep and decided to tell the truth, or at least part of it. "I often disagree with my friends. A brave said something I did not like, so I hit him. I won the fight, so he will keep his thoughts to himself around me."

Erica pursed her lips thoughtfully, certain there had to be more to the story than that. "Just what did the man say?"

"I will not repeat his insults," Viper vowed stubbornly.

"Well then, were they about me?"

"Why would he insult you? He does not even know you," the wily brave replied, hoping to satisfy her curiosity with questions of his own.

Erica was too bright to fall for his trick and continued to pester him to explain. "He doesn't have to meet me to tell you what he thinks of your marrying a white woman, Viper. Is that what he did?"

"Where is my knife?" Viper asked, suddenly recalling he had wanted to plunge it into Hunted Stag's throat.

Erica reached into the pocket of her blue dress to remove it and returned it to him. "Here. Now finish your story."

"I already did," Viper insisted as he slipped his knife into the beaded sheath at his belt. After dropping the two cougar-claw necklaces over her head, he rose to his feet and drew Erica up beside him. "The war has given everyone a short temper. The fight is over and will soon be forgotten. Do not worry about it."

The stern set of his jaw convinced Erica it would be pointless to try and get more information out of him. She still had the little cougar Gunter had carved for her. She left it in the pocket of her blue dress along with the hairbrush, and after folding it up with her slips, she squared her shoulders proudly and announced she was ready to go. "Just as I promised, I will do my best not to disgrace you or your family, Viper, but if people choose to hate me just because I am white, there is little I can do about it."

That was something the brave already knew, and he drew his pretty bride into his arms and kissed her so passionately she would have followed him anywhere, even through the gates of hell.

In spite of the fact that she was expecting a white woman, Flowers of Spring was still shocked to find Erica so astonishingly fair. Recognizing that she possessed that rare beauty all braves would long to have for their own, she warned Viper in their own language. "This woman is too pretty to be anything but trouble. What can I teach her that

185

she would want to learn?"

Viper smiled widely, pretending for his bride's sake that his aunt's comments had been compliments as he replied in the language Erica could not understand. "She is a smart girl and not lazy. Do not insult her when you do not even know her."

While she was positive she did not want to know her, Flowers of Spring said no more. She pointed to the covered iron kettle sitting upon the stone hearth at the center of the tepee. "There is venison stew for you to eat. I will make my home elsewhere while you are here." She left then, without giving Erica so much as a polite nod of farewell.

While the tepee was much larger than she had anticipated, Erica was not so fascinated by the dwelling constructed of buffalo hides that she had failed to notice his aunt hadn't seemed pleased to meet her. She tried to smile as she reassured her husband that things were bound to improve. "I know it will take time for everyone to accept me. I will just have to be patient. After all, if I took you home to Wilmington, you would receive some peculiar looks too."

Erica continually amazed him, and he was greatly relieved that she had not been insulted by the chill of his aunt's attitude. "Tomorrow I want to ride with the others. Spend as much time as you can bear with my aunt, then come back here and rest. I am certain the other women will be curious about you, but most are shy, and they will not be rude."

"I won't be rude, either," Erica promised sincerely. "I'll do my share of the work, and if I have any complaints to make, you are the only one who will hear them."

"Let's hope they are very few. Are you hungry? My aunt's stew is usually good."

"Even if it isn't, I am too hungry to care," Erica responded with a sparkling laugh. She was no less apprehensive, but as always, Viper's good-natured humor was infectious.

Using wooden bowls and spoons made of buffalo horn, they quickly finished one serving of stew and began another. Seeing his bride's interest in the tepee, Viper began to tell her about the portable dwelling. "The tepee is more than a home to us. The floor reminds us of the

186

earth; the sides, which reach toward the heavens, are the sky. It is round like the sacred life circle, with no beginning and no end." He paused for a moment, hoping he did not sound daft, but Erica's expression was one of polite interest, not disdain. "Tepees can be taken down quickly and moved easily. It is the perfect home for people who move often to follow game, but when we were forbidden to move, the sight of them always made me sad."

"I understand," Erica responded sympathetically. "To live in a hunter's home and not be allowed to hunt would sadden anyone."

They finished eating in companionable silence, then Viper reached for Erica's hand. "Come outside with me. There is something I want you to see."

She had attracted so many curious stares when they had ridden into camp that Erica would have preferred to remain hidden, but knowing she would have to make the effort to venture out the following morning, she rose to her feet. Viper did no more than lead her a few steps outside before he moved behind her and wrapped his arms around her waist. Night had fallen, and all around them the tepees shone with a soft red glow from the fires within them. Like mystical lanterns of some ancient gods, they provided an enchanting sight, one the pretty blonde was glad she hadn't missed.

"How peaceful everything looks," she whispered softly.

"We once had the perfect life," Viper replied. "There was a harmony among all living things. We did not clear the land of trees. We did not wantonly slaughter animals. Then the white man came, and he did not respect any of our beliefs. He wanted the land for his farms, the trees cut into logs to build his houses. He shot animals for sport, or took their hides and left their carcasses to rot while we went hungry. Every year the damage the white man does spreads, while the ways of the Sioux are forgotten. Now all that is left of the beauty we once knew is the red glow of a tepee at night."

Tears spilling over her lashes, Erica turned in Viper's embrace. She threw her arms around his neck and sobbed as though her heart were broken, for she feared he had lost more than her love could ever give him.

Viper had not meant to overwhelm his bride with his own

187

desperate longing for bygone days. She was a woman of the present and the future, not the past, and he knew that. He drew her back into the secluded warmth of their tepee and pulled her down upon the thick buffalo-skin bedding he had already unrolled to serve as their bed. He kissed away her tears, then stilled her trembling lips with the pressure of his own.

"You should never have married me, Viper. How can I raise your children when I have none of your beautiful memories of your tribe?"

"Our children will be fortunate to have your memories, too. They will have twice as many reasons to be proud, not half. You were never meant to be Indian, only to be my wife."

As she looked up at her husband, Erica thought him the dearest man alive. She had never imagined a man regarded as a savage by so many could have such a tender and loving heart. "I do think I was meant to be your wife. It is just that I am afraid I will make you a very poor one."

"No, you are perfect." Viper raised his hand to the laces at her throat and slowly began to untie them. "You will never guess how much time I spent dreaming about making love to you here."

A slight frown crossed Erica's brow, for indeed she had given no thought to making love to him while they were apart. Deciding she need not admit that, she began to smile. "Well, now that I am here, I will do my best to make all your dreams come true."

"You already have," Viper whispered as his lips brushed her ear softly. He did not speak again as he removed her moccasins, then, with a touch lighter than a whisper, he peeled away the buckskin dress and her soft silk undergarments. In the dim light cast by the dying embers of the fire her fair skin took on a rich, golden glow, gently reflecting the warmth of his adoring gaze. She had assumed a graceful pose, and her supple figure beckoned seductively, her body calling to his with an ageless feminine allure he would never wish to ignore. Quickly casting off his own clothing, he stretched out beside her. He pulled her close, so there was not an inch of his deeply bronzed flesh that did not touch her creamy, smooth skin, but that was only the beginning, not the end of his need to

188

be close to her.

Perhaps it was the beauty of the night, or the sorrow of his memories that had aroused her passions, but Erica also wanted a new type of closeness. Rising up on her right elbow, she ran the fingers of her left hand down the length of his right arm. "You have the most beautiful body a man could possibly have." She leaned forward then and brushed his shoulder with her lips. "You are so very handsome. You know it, too, don't you?" she asked with a throaty giggle.

"I am not blind," was all Viper would admit. He knew his looks would appeal to a white woman. Since his grandfather's time, the males in his family had inherited the finely chiseled features of the French aristocrat, rather than the distinctively Indian facial characteristics of the Sioux.

"I like the color of your eyes, too. Sometimes when we're swimming they seem to reflect the color of the water and they appear almost blue. At night, they are a warm, smoky gray, though, like the sky just before dawn."

Viper sighed contentedly, very glad he had taken the time to master English, since he enjoyed hearing her compliments so greatly. He slipped his fingers through her curls to pull her mouth to his and thanked her for her praise with one of the long slow kisses he gave so often. As always, the delectable sweetness of her kiss made him want still more, and a long while passed before he released her. "I love everything about you," he revealed as he dropped his hand to her breast where his thumb began slowly to circle the tip until it became a firm, flushed bud that begged for his kiss. "The pale yellow of your hair, the deep blue of your eyes, the beauty of your smile just before you laugh, I love every bit of you," the Indian vowed in a voice slurred by desire.

They had made love on riverbanks, in front of a fire, in a feather bed, and under the stars, but the close confines of the tepee created a new type of intimacy that was not only altogether different but quite wondrous in itself. Since her mood was so open and loving, Viper knew she would not object to any request he made. "There are many ways we can give each other pleasure. I have taught you only a few."

That remark made Erica curious, but not as Viper had hoped. "Just how do you know so much? Who taught you?" she asked as she laced her fingers in his so he could no longer fondle her breasts as he replied. She wanted nothing to distract her from hearing his answer.

"I told you my grandfather was French. He took great pride in his skill as a lover. He told me many things none of the other boys ever heard. If you think I have put his lessons to good use, he would be very pleased."

Erica licked her lips thoughtfully as she nodded. "I understand. You wish to keep your memories private."

"No, you do not understand. I want my memories to be only of you." Keeping their hands together, he rubbed her fingertips lightly over his chest, then down the flat planes of his stomach. "I enjoy the feel of your touch and kiss just as much as you enjoy mine." He moved her hand lower then, and while he provided the motions, it was the light pressure of her fingertips he felt.

Erica was not in the least bit shy with her husband. She adored him and knew whatever brought him pleasure would please her as well. Her fingertips caressed the velvet-smooth tip of his manhood before encircling the hardened shaft. Her eyes never left his as the exotic magic she worked with his unspoken instruction made his breath quicken to deep gasps. Her intuition told her he would not have spoken of kisses unless he had wanted them also. Since she had promised to fulfill his erotic dreams, she slid down beside him. She then spread feather-light kisses over his stomach before using her tongue and lips to ignite flames from the splendid heat she had created so easily with the loving motions of her hand.

Viper wove his fingers in Erica's flowing curls, spilling the silken mass over the quivering flesh of his stomach. It took every ounce of self-control he possessed to contain the rapture that now swelled within him and threatened to swiftly overflow. The ecstasy continued to build, cresting in shuddering waves that fought for release, until he knew he had to give in to it or lose any hope of remaining sane. He reached for Erica then, pulling her astride him so the exquisite sensation she had drawn forth could be shared. With his hands gripping her waist tightly, he showed her how to move until he was no longer capable of conscious thought, and with a low moan of surrender, he finally allowed his powerful body's will to become his own.

Her own senses reeling, Erica stretched out upon Viper's chest, her cheek cradled upon his right shoulder as the joy she had given him spread through her lithe body like liquid fire. It was not simply warmth, but a compelling heat that fused not only their bodies but their spirits, as well, into one blissfully content being. It was a long while before she became aware of Viper's hands moving slowly over her back in a soothing massage. "That feels wonderful," she purred sweetly. "Are the French good at giving massages as well as making love?"

"The word massage *is* French, so what do you think?"

"I think with you as my teacher, I am going to learn many truly remarkable things." She raised her hand to cover a wide yawn, then closed her eyes, thinking his well-muscled body made the nicest bed she had ever found. The steady beat of his heart provided so soothing a lullaby that she was soon fast asleep.

Erica's weight was so slight it was like a living blanket rather than a discomfort for the Indian brave. He was on the verge of falling asleep, too, but he could not stop smiling and congratulating himself for having the wisdom to marry so fascinating a young woman. How could she even imagine he would remember other women, when the pleasure they shared was so complete? "I love you," he whispered softly, and with a contented sigh he joined her in the land of dreams where the beauty of love never ends and the hours are always happy.

When she awakened the next morning and found Viper gone, Erica's fears of visiting his village not only returned but increased tenfold, twisting her stomach into painfully anxious knots. The tepee, whose warmth had been so comforting at dusk, was now only a strange, cold, and totally foreign dwelling. Viper had thoughtfully covered her with a warm buffalo robe, but that consideration did not lessen the icy tentacles of fear that gripped her heart.

How would she ever pass the day without him? They had been together not quite three weeks, but she could not imagine how she would fill the long hours that lay ahead without his charming company. He had said she should spend her time with his aunt. Would the woman come to her, or should she go and look for her? Glancing about the tidy interior of the tepee, her eyes fell upon the dress and slips she had brought with her. Washing them would give her an excuse to walk down to the river, and if she saw no sign of Flowers of Spring, then she would just stay by the water all day. Anything would be better than being cooped up inside the tepee when she could readily imagine that everyone walking by was pointing and whispering about the woman Viper had brought into camp.

With the practical goal of doing her laundry in mind, Erica got up, put on the flowing buckskin dress and the moccasins, then brushed out her hair. She then picked up the bundle of soiled clothing, threw back the flap of hide that served as the tepee's door, and stepped out into the sunshine. The savory aromas wafting from nearby cooking fires made her very hungry, but she knew she could scarcely go from tepee to tepee looking for Flowers of Spring in hopes that the woman would share whatever she had for breakfast. Viper had shown her how to recognize their tepee by its distinctive markings, and she looked at it again to make certain she had memorized the brightly painted designs that adorned it. He had said the paintings told stories he would relate later, but it was enough for now that she could distinguish this dwelling from the others.

There were children nearby who stopped their play to stare at her, but Erica smiled sweetly in hopes they were too young to think her an enemy simply because of the color of her skin. The youngsters, however, stared at her with mouths agape, then scattered as though they feared she might chase them. Thinking it perhaps a blessing that she saw no one else about, she turned toward the river. Bracing herself for possibly one of the worst days of her life, she hoped only that she could wash her clothes and find some safe place to quietly spend her time until Viper came home.

There were other women at the river. They stole furtive glances at Erica and whispered amongst themselves, but none smiled at her in a friendly fashion or tried to begin a conversation. When she had washed her well-worn garments, she took them away upstream to lay them upon bushes to dry, then, grateful for a few moments of privacy, she sat down in the sun hoping Flowers of Spring would come along, or that some other chore would occur to her. But none did. When her dress and slips were dry, she folded them neatly, but still tarried by the water. She wished she had thought to bring Viper's fishing line with her, then realized that since she had not seen other women fishing, that was probably something the women did not do.

"Well, just what is it they do do?" she asked herself aloud. Despite the warmth of the sun, she felt very lost and alone. She had tried not to think of the captives' plight as they had entered the village, but now she could not help but worry about them. Were they bound and kept under heavy guard? Was there any way she could possibly free them? That had been Viper's fear, she knew: that she would disgrace him by seeking to set free the settlers who had been taken captive. She closed her eyes and said a fervent prayer that the captives' lot was not too difficult and that the uprising would soon end. When she heard the shuffle of footsteps approaching she leaped to her feet fearing the worst, but it was Flowers of Spring, not a stranger.

"Good morning," Erica greeted her happily, relieved it was not someone who had read her traitorous thoughts and had come to drag her off to be confined wherever the hostages were being kept. "It is a lovely day, isn't it? So bright and warm." The Indian woman looked only puzzled, and Erica gave up her efforts to communicate. Flowers of Spring was holding a basket, and she gestured for Erica to follow. Erica picked up her clean clothes and tagged along behind her. They went some distance before reaching vines laden with plump blackberries. Readily understanding that she was to help pick the fruit, Erica laid her bundle aside and began to work. She was so hungry she could not resist the temptation to sample quite a few, but when she caught her Indian companion looking at her with a disapproving frown, she forced herself to concentrate upon filling the woman's basket rather than her own painfully empty stomach.

They worked until the basket was nearly overflowing, and then Flowers of Spring handed it to Erica to carry as they made their way back to the camp. When they passed the place on the river where the other women had been, an attractive young woman in a buckskin dress heavily

193

decorated with beadwork called out to them. When Flowers of Spring stopped to speak with her, Erica had no choice but to stand holding the heavy basket and wait. She expected some sort of an introduction, but the two women carried on a private conversation for several minutes, making her feel most uncomfortable and left out. She would have gone ahead and carried the berries back to the tepee she and Viper had shared, but the two women blocked the path and there was no polite way she could slip past them.

Knowing their words would not be understood, Song of the Wren bombarded Flowers of Spring with questions. She could not believe that the outrageous tale her brother had told her could possibly be true. Even after Viper's aunt had confirmed the story of her nephew's marriage, she refused to accept it. Finally she brushed by the older woman so she could get a better look at the white woman who had gained the place in Viper's heart she had been determined to win for herself.

Erica smiled sweetly, hoping the pretty young woman was another relative or someone who might become a friend. They appeared to be about the same age, which she took as a good sign, thinking it would give them similar interests. "Good morning," she tried again. "I hope you speak English, as I know not one word of Sioux."

Wren's flashing black eyes narrowed, for she realized instantly that the blonde possessed many valuable assets which, unfortunately, she did not. How dare she be not only fair and lovely, but confident enough to greet me as a friend? she wondered angrily. She wanted only to hurt this smiling outsider as badly as Viper had hurt her by his neglect. "Why would I want to speak to a white whore?" she responded in the precise English she had also learned from missionaries who had been dedicated to the task of spreading the gospel among her people.

Shocked by so rude an insult, Erica looked to Flowers of Spring for an explanation as to why the young woman would say such a mean thing. Viper's aunt merely shrugged as though she had no idea what had been said, and Erica realized that, sadly, she was on her own. As a precaution, she shifted the basket of berries to her left hand along with the bundle of clean clothes. "I have no idea

194

who you think I am, but you are mistaken. I am Viper's wife, and he would be most displeased if I repeated your insult to him."

Wren tossed her braids over her shoulders as she stepped closer. "Viper may let you think you are his wife, but you are only his whore. You'll die with the other captives. I hope he saves you until last, so you can hear the others' screams and know what horrible pain awaits you!"

While horrified by so vile a threat, Erica would not permit it to go unchallenged. "You insufferable little bitch," she screamed, and at the same instant she slapped the smirk from Wren's face with a fierce backhanded blow. Trying to avoid being hit again, the Indian maiden dodged to the side, lost her footing in the slippery mud of the riverbank, and slid into the water where she proceeded to scream that she was being murdered.

"Shut up, you little fool. Nobody's trying to kill you!" Seeing Flowers of Spring rush to help the girl, Erica felt doubly betrayed and dropped the basket of berries scatttering them all over the trail. Clutching her clothes tightly to her breast, she sprinted back down the path the way they had come. She ran on and on, not caring how far she had gone from the village, for she had no wish to return to a place where she had been greeted with cool indifference and hostile threats of death.

When she could run not a step farther, she stripped off the soft buckskin dress and quickly pulled on her own clothes. "I am no captive!" she swore to herself, but her heart was still racing wildly, for what if what the obnoxious girl had said about the captives were true? What if the Indians had killed them all? Filled with dread, she sank to her knees and sobbed pathetically.

Viper had sworn to her that he had not killed women and children—but how many men had he slain? How many more would he kill that day? Where had her mind been? she asked herself over and over. Were the Sioux so filled with hatred that they would slaughter their poor captives and laugh at the sound of their dying screams? Worse yet, how could she call a man husband who would let such a tragedy occur? Not knowing what to do or where to go, she remained beside the river. She sat hugging her knees, trembling with fear, and crying for the handsome young brave she now feared she ought not to love.

# Chapter Thirteen

## September, 1862

Rather than his bride, Viper found his aunt waiting for him at their tepee. In an attempt to defend her own actions, she provided an imaginative interpretation of the day's events, relying on her own bias rather than the truth for inspiration. "The white woman wasted most of the morning dawdling by the river. I planned to teach her how to make pemmican, but when I took her to pick berries she ate more than went into my basket."

Viper raised his hands to stop her tale as he began to laugh. "She was probably hungry. She is used to picking berries with me, and must have thought the fruit was to be eaten then. Where is she?"

"I do not know," Flowers of Spring replied evasively. "After she shoved Wren into the river, she ran away."

"What?" Viper reached out to grab his aunt's shoulders and yanked her so close their noses were nearly touching. "Why are you prattling on about berries if Erica has run away? I left my wife in your care. Now tell me what happened!"

While Flowers of Spring was badly frightened by her nephew's fiery burst of anger, she stubbornly refused to accept any blame for Erica's disappearance. "It was as I said. We were coming home with the berries. When Wren spoke to your woman, she slapped the girl and shoved her into the river. Then she ran off. I had to pull Wren out of the water myself or the dear child would have drowned."

"Wren is of no consequence here!" Viper shouted, losing all patience with the coldness of his aunt's attitude. "Now tell me which way Erica went, and I will go find her while there is still enough light to search."

"She went north, up the Chippewa," Flowers of Spring replied, then, gathering courage, she rushed on boldly. "She knew she should not have hit Wren. That is why your woman ran away. You should be glad she is gone. I told you she would bring you nothing but trouble."

Further outraged by that vicious outburst, Viper responded in kind. "Wren caused the trouble. Don't deny it. What did she say to my wife?"

Flowers of Spring merely shrugged innocently. "I speak no English, so I do not know. You will have to ask Wren."

Viper shook his head. "I will ask Erica for the truth when I find her." He left the tepee at a run, then, thinking his bride had had the better part of the day to flee, he decided to ride his horse. He had had an exhausting day and had looked forward to spending another evening in his wonderfully loving bride's arms. Now he felt like a fool for leaving her with Flowers of Spring. He should have known his aunt would not be friendly. He had clearly made a serious error in judgment, but if he could not rely upon his own aunt to accept his wife and treat her with kindness, then who would? He was also chagrined that Erica had apparently behaved like the spoiled rich girl he had to keep reminding himself she was. "Damn!" he swore as the stallion reached the banks of the Chippewa River. "Why are women such impossible creatures?" he asked his mount, but the horse did no more than snort and toss his head in reply.

This time Erica recognized the black stallion when he came racing toward her. She stood and waved, hoping Viper would see her before the horse ran her down. When her husband drew the beast to a halt and leaped from his back, she scanned his expression with an anxious glance, hoping for a clue to his mood before she spoke. When he appeared to be as distressed as she was, she backed away as she began to explain. "None of it was my fault. I tried to be friendly, honestly I did."

While Viper was relieved to find Erica so near the village, he was disappointed she had not run to him as she had the previous afternoon. He stood still, holding the stallion's reins lightly in his hands and wondering how he could make everything right. Since she had not gone far, he knew she had not been trying to run away. Grateful for that, he tried to smile. "What did Wren say to upset you so?"

"Is that her name, Wren?" When Viper nodded, Erica looked away for a moment. She had practiced dozens of ways to ask her next question, but the dread of what his answer might be nearly choked her now. She coughed to clear her throat before she looked up at him. "I love you," she began, "so dearly that I refuse to believe I am no more than a captive you might one day tire of and kill."

"Is that what that little bitch said to you? I'll wring her neck for insulting you like that," Viper swore convincingly. "You should have not only tossed her in the river. You should have held her head under!"

Erica dismissed his remarks with a wave of her hand. "It was her own clumsiness that caused her to fall in the water. I can't take the credit for that. It doesn't matter what she said about me, since I know it isn't true. It was what she said about the captives that frightened me. If there is even the remotest chance they might die, then I can't stay here with you. I won't. Too many innocent settlers have died, and I won't be a part of any more bloodshed. If your people are going to murder the captives, then I must go, now, this very night."

Viper stared at his bride, his expression as grave as hers. "If you truly wanted to leave, you would not have been sitting here beside the river waiting for me."

Erica had shed too many tears that day to weep again, but the thought of leaving him still threatened to tear her heart in two. "You are my husband. I could not leave without telling you why I had to go."

Viper turned away for a moment to tie the horse's reins to the closest branch. He used the time to try and find a way to deal with her accusation without admitting it held at least a grain of truth. Discovering that was impossible, he gave up the effort. He then took Erica's hand and led her back to the thick patch of grass where she had been sitting before his arrival. He sat down and patted the place at his side. "We must talk," he stated firmly, his invitation an emphatic one he hoped she would not dare refuse.

Erica sat down beside him, taking care to arrange the skirt of her worn dress so it did not brush the dirt at the edge of the grass. "What is there to discuss? I have heard all your arguments and you know I sympathize with them. Your people have every right to be outraged at the way you've suffered at the hands of the government, but I cannot condone wanton murder. You cannot ask me to live here and close my eyes to what happens to the captives."

Viper reached for Erica's hand and laced his fingers with hers. His gesture was filled with affection, but it was merely a precaution to keep her from leaping to her feet and again running away. "You are the first woman I have trusted with the thoughts which fill my heart. Listen carefully to me now, and then we will decide what to do."

He had always been able to command her undivided attention, and Erica squeezed his fingers as she moved slightly closer. Her whole body ached with the bittersweet longing to again feel his love, and at the same time she feared this might be the last hour they would ever spend together. "Say whatever you wish. I will never repeat it to the others," she promised in a voice husky with the threat of tears.

As Viper had said, placing his trust in a woman was something entirely new for him, but he knew Erica had earned that honor many times over. It took him a moment to overcome the natural reserve that made him reluctant to share his thoughts and explain what he had learned that day. When he spoke, his voice was soft and low, barely above a whisper. "I have always found that if I listen quietly to others, I can learn what I wish to know without arousing curiosity. I rode with a scouting party today, and while we found no soldiers nearby, my time was not wasted. Men like to talk just as women do, but today the braves spoke only of the war. Little Crow has refused to turn over his captives before talks of peace begin. While there are some braves who think the captives ought to die, there are two powerful chiefs, Wabasha and Taopi, who want to bring the war to an end. They will see the captives come to no harm."

"What?" Erica found Viper's comments difficult to

comprehend. "You mean the chiefs are openly disagreeing with Little Crow?"

"Yes, they have all along. I told you a Sioux is free to follow his own conscience even in time of war. Little Crow has still another problem, though. He commands those here who wish to fight, but the chiefs Red Iron and Standing Buffalo are Upper Sioux who want no part of the uprising. They will not allow Little Crow to move farther north and cross their lands."

"And the army is moving up from the south?" Erica asked, a bright flicker of hope now lighting her eyes.

"Yes," Viper was pleased she had grasped the situation so easily and he relaxed enough to smile.

"What of the settlements east of here, those near the Big Woods?"

Realizing she had not understood Two Elk's words, Viper explained quickly so she would also know about the stockades. "There is no point in raiding east now that the towns are so heavily fortified. With the way north blocked by Red Iron and Standing Buffalo, the way south blocked by the soldiers at Fort Ridgely, and by the chiefs here who are anxious for peace, how long do you think Little Crow will continue to fight?"

"I suppose that will depend on how proud a man he is," Erica replied perceptively.

"He is very proud," Viper admitted, "and he has beaten the army many times."

"He knows everything that you do?"

"No, he does not know that when he sent his message refusing to free the captives to Sibley, the man who commands the volunteer Army, Wabasha and Taopi sent along a message of their own. That is a secret they think only their mixed-blood messenger knows," Viper revealed with a sly grin, "but he has friends."

Erica stared at her husband for a long moment, wondering if she should have been so quick to promise his words would go no further. But surely Sibley would realize from the conflicting messages he had received that there was a great deal of dissension among the chiefs. "By seeking peace on their own, aren't those chiefs guilty of treason?"

Viper shook his head. "They are free to do what they

think is right. They want the war over."

In the gathering dusk, Viper's eyes appeared dark, without the smoky haze she had grown to love, and Erica could barely find the courage to speak. "Then the real question is, what do *you* want to do?"

Viper looked out over the river, envying the bubbling waters their endless rush toward freedom. He had joined in the uprising with grave misgivings, and he had them still. Since Erica already knew how hopeless their cause had been, he readily admitted it. "I thought it important to fight, even though we might never win back all we have lost. I have done all I can to make those in Washington hear our pleas," he explained slowly, the depth of his commitment to his people clear. "If they do not understand our desperation now, they never will. I do not need to kill another soldier, or the dozen I might kill in a week or two, if the uprising lasts that long. I would like to go back to the valley of the Cottonwood River and wait there for the peace talks to begin. Do you want to go with me?"

"Back to the little house, you mean?" Erica asked excitedly, her answer to his question already plain in her delighted expression.

"Yes, or another one, if you find one you like better," Viper offered generously. "If everything is settled by spring, we can build our own house then."

Tears of happiness made Erica's eyes sparkle brightly as she threw her arms around Viper's neck. Forgetting the terror of her fears in the warmth of his embrace, she vowed fervently, "Oh, how I love you! I knew you would make everything right. I just knew you would."

While Viper was very flattered to find she had such confidence in him, he had done little other than gather intelligence and draw conclusions from what he had learned. The end of the war was near, and the aftermath was bound to bring the worst sort of confusion. He wanted to spare her that. It would be far better for them to begin their life together now than to wait for the government to right all its wrongs, since he feared that might take more years than they had to live.

Viper lay back in the grass and pulled Erica down with him. He pressed her cheek to his bare chest and began to comb her flowing curls through his fingers. "My aunt is jealous of every woman who is happily married. I expected too much of her. I don't blame her, but myself, that you had such a difficult time today. It will not happen again."

While Erica could understand the silent hostility Flowers of Spring had shown her, she wondered what had made Wren so mean. "And Wren? Is she merely jealous, too?"

"Oh yes, she sounds very jealous," Viper agreed without hesitation.

Laying her arms across his chest, Erica rose up slightly so she could look at him as he answered her next question. "Does she have any right to feel that way?"

Viper frowned slightly, not understanding her concern. "What do you mean? Nothing would give her that right. She is no more than the sister of a friend." Or the sister of a former friend, he reminded himself, since he and Hunted Stag hadn't spoken since their fight.

"Well, there has to be more to it than that. Does she care for you? Was she hoping to become your wife?"

"How would I know what is in the silly girl's head?" Viper protested a bit too strongly.

Seeing she was upsetting her husband needlessly, Erica ceased to pester him and rested her head upon his shoulder. "No one has ever spoken to me like that, Viper, not in my whole life. I had never seen her before today, and yet she despised me. The hatred was dripping from her mouth like venom, and I silenced her the only way I could. I slapped her, and hard, but it was her own fault she fell into the river. If there is any trouble because of it, then it was of her own making, not mine."

Viper felt he had revealed enough confidences for one day and did not tell Erica that Hunted Stag's anger may well have fed his sister's hatred. More than one brave had warned him that Claw of the Badger was looking for him, but he doubted the man could harm him in a second fight, since he had not touched him in their first. He could scarcely criticize his wife's behavior, he realized, when he settled his own arguments with either his fists or the sharp edge of a blade. "I was not there, or I would have done worse to her myself," he stated calmly. "But I will see she apologizes to you before we leave."

"Do you think that's wise? Can't we just let the matter drop?"

"No. She has insulted you, which means she has insulted my entire family. An apology is the least she owes us."

Erica was now so curious she had to sit up so they could converse face to face. "How many people are there in your family? I have met only your aunt. Are there many more?"

Viper propped his hands behind his head as he ran through a lengthy mental list. "My grandfather's relatives are all in France, so I know none of them, and they do not even know I exist. My grandmother had four brothers and two sisters. Each of them had children. I was my parents' only child. My father's brother was childless, as is my mother's sister, but there was also an older brother in her family, and he had several children."

"So you have quite a few cousins, then?" Erica had tried to follow along, and thought it sounded like cousins were all he could claim. "I didn't mean to start a feud, Viper, but Wren deserved what she got. Truly she did."

"I believe you," the amused brave assured her. "You needn't worry. We are all too busy with the uprising to begin a feud."

While she adored her husband's enchanting grin, Erica did not think he should tease her about Wren when the woman's threats had been so vile. "When are we leaving?" she asked abruptly.

"In a few days. We do not want anyone to think you are afraid to stay here."

"I don't give a damn what anyone thinks of me," Erica vowed as she lifted her chin proudly.

"Not even me?" Viper asked with a quizzically raised brow.

"Oh, of course I care what you think. Don't be silly." Erica reached out to lay her hand upon her husband's chest and he drew it to his lips. He covered her palm with affectionate nibbles, then pulled her back into his arms.

"I know it will be difficult, but try not to give anyone else the opportunity to insult you. We cannot be together all day, so you must watch for trouble and avoid it. There will always be people who will be eager to hate us, for an Indian is not expected to have a white wife."

"But you told me there were braves who do," Erica reminded him.

"Yes, and almost all were taken captive with their families. I will not allow anyone to make me a prisoner, nor you."

Erica tried to sit up again but Viper held her fast. "Then why must we stay here even another hour? Why can't we leave for the Cottonwood River tonight?"

"Because I do not want to be called a coward," Viper replied curtly. "Neither of us can afford to look like cowards, since that insult would haunt us forever."

"Must we stay here even though you do not want to, just so no one will talk about us after we are gone?" Such a precaution made no sense at all to her.

"Yes," Viper replied with the calm self-assurance he always displayed. "We will leave at the time we choose, and it will be soon."

Erica nibbled her lower lip thoughtfully, knowing she ought not to argue when Viper had already promised to take her away. She was so seldom quiet, however, that he began to worry.

"Erica?"

"Hmm?"

"You can bear to stay here a few more days, can't you?"

"I will have to," the lively blonde replied in a dreamy whisper. "I love you, so I really have no choice at all."

"Yes, you had a choice, and you chose me," Viper reminded her. With the agility for which he was well known, he rolled to his side, and in the next instant pinned her beneath him. He lowered his mouth to hers, wanting her to think only of the joy they had found together rather than the seemingly insoluble problems that confronted them at every turn. "I love you," he whispered between hungry kisses. "I will love you forever."

As Viper began to unbutton her dress, the thought briefly crossed Erica's mind that it was remarkable he had not scolded her for wearing it again, since it loudly proclaimed she was a white woman rather than one of his tribe. As his fingertips brushed the tips of her breasts she ceased to worry about the design of her apparel and instead let her spirit soar aloft with his. Once again she found it impossible to dwell upon her cares under his delicious

204

onslaught of affection. The grass was soft at her back, the lilting music of the river soothing, her husband's taste and touch so enchanting that she thought the moment perfect for making love.

Erica wound her fingers in Viper's flowing hair, pressing his face close as his lips and tongue continued to tease her nipples, until they became so sensitive the joy he imparted was of the most exquisite sort. As he continued to peel away her clothes, his kisses traced the path of his fingertips with a soft, sweet tongue of flame. Fed by the fires of his own desire, he caressed her smooth, creamy skin until he could feel the flames of her passion become an unquenchable heat that burned only for him.

His mouth slid over the flatness of her stomach, then returned to her navel where his kiss tickled and drew a throaty giggle from her lips. Enjoying her playful mood, he shoved the last of her garments aside before turning his attention to the elegant shape of her legs. His hands moved from her ankles to her waist in a gently adoring sweep before he rubbed his cheek against her thighs, parting them eagerly so he could nuzzle the pale, blond curls, which were but a soft promise of the tantalizing secrets her glorious body kept hidden still.

As he moved to lie between her legs, the sweetness of her body's own natural perfume beckoned seductively, overwhelming his senses with her fair beauty and daring him to draw closer still. Lured on by her unique fragrance, he parted her tender folds with his tongue and delved deeply into the now unveiled cleft. He felt the first faint tremors of her response tingle within her loins, then swell until the rapture he was taking such care to create sent ripples of warmth up her spine, threatening to sweep through her limbs with a blinding heat. When she began to writhe beneath him, he pulled away for a moment to let the waves of pleasure subside before the crest so her need for him would be all the more intense. When she called out his name in a throaty whisper, her slurred words a hoarse plea for release from that torment of desire, he did not tease her. The tip of his tongue returned to caress her most sensitive nub of flesh, tenderly bestowing dazzling gifts of ecstasy, until the delectable essence of her femininity spilled forth in a welcoming rush. Knowing how deeply he had satis-

205

fied her thirst for love, he then sought to quench his own in the wondrous pleasure she would create for him.

As Viper's mouth covered hers, Erica could taste her own sweetness mingled with the flavor of his. She clasped his shoulders tightly, holding him close as she moved her hips in time with the deep thrusts that threatened to pierce her very soul. It was not until he had buried himself so deeply within her that she thought they would spend eternity entwined that she felt him surrender himself to ecstasy's most compelling spell. They were now lovers so finely matched, that that beauty not only shuddered through him but roared through her with a raging splendor as well. She had never dreamed making love could provide so fulfilling a glimpse of paradise, but then she had never dreamed of loving him, either.

The moon was high overhead before Viper again felt a compelling need to talk. Erica had fallen asleep in his arms, and while he hated to disturb the peace of her dreams, he did not want to sleep by the river when they did not have to. "Erica, wake up," he called softly as he brushed her curls away from her face. He kissed her cheeks lightly, then her eyelids, hoping to wake her with thoughts of love. "Wake up."

Erica stretched languidly. They were lying on their sides and she drew her knee up over his. She wanted to make love again and again. That was the only valid reason she could see for waking, and she yawned before opening her eyes. "Let's make love all night long, Viper, until dawn," she suggested with an alluring smile.

Not wanting to refuse so delightful a request, Viper gave her an enthusiastic hug before he sat up and spoke. "At dawn, we might be embarrassed by men coming to fish, or hunt, to say nothing of women and children who might be up early to gather wood and berries, or to bathe. If you want to make love all night I will be happy to do it, but we must return to the tepee first." Before she could argue, he rose and went to the river to wash.

Hating to bring their romantic mood to a close even temporarily, Erica sighed sadly, but knowing he was undoubtedly right, she followed him to the water's edge. Still in a playful mood, she was tempted to push him in, but decided merely to splash him instead. As she scooped up a handful, she thought the water's slight chill invigorating, but Viper did not. With an indignant howl, he grabbed her around the waist and carried her out into the river with him.

"If you want to play, then you must get wet too!" he insisted as he pushed her under. The moonlight danced on the water, and as Erica broke the surface her flying curls reflected the bright glow of the stars in a shimmering cascade. Her lush breasts shone with a seductive sparkle as the water trickled down her pale skin, and Viper realized that had he wanted to postpone making love, he had chosen the wrong way to go about it. He wanted her again, right then and there. Reaching out for her hands, he pulled her so close she could not fail to understand the depth of his need. When she raised her arms to encircle his neck her kiss was as hungry as his. Breaking away for an instant, he put his hands on her waist and easily lifted her off her feet. "Wrap your legs around me," he ordered hoarsely.

Viper continually surprised her, and Erica did not object, but as she followed his directions she could only marvel at the ease with which he entered her. He was quite strong, and she was a slender woman, so her weight was no barrier to the enjoyment of making love in this new pose. Supporting her tenderly in his arms, Viper used the slow undulating rhythm of the river to create a warmth deep within her, which burned ever more brightly, until her breath escaped her lips in shallow gasps. Despite the coolness of the water, her very bones seemed to melt from the fiery intensity of this sudden, feverish union, leaving her clinging limply to her dashing husband's powerfully built frame. It seemed to matter not at all how they made love or where, the pleasure born of their love grew ever richer, deeper, until Erica could not imagine that any sensation more pleasurable could possibly exist. When at last Viper released her to place her upon her feet, she continued to lean against him, too enthralled with the heady magic he worked upon her senses ever to want to let him go.

Song of the Wren brushed the hot tears of anger from her eyes as she watched the passionate scene being played out in the water. She had wanted only to hear what the blond woman would say about her to Viper and had followed him there never dreaming there would be far more to see than to hear. She knew only one way for a man and woman to make love, and her shock at what she had seen that evening would be a deep and lasting one. "It is the woman!" she swore under her breath. "She has bewitched him, turned him into a demon who will do anything to satisfy her desires!" Horrified by the abandoned passion she had observed, and yet afraid she might miss something even more scandalous if she left, the dark-eyed maiden remained hidden in the bushes until Viper and Erica had gotten dressed and mounted his horse. When they had turned back toward the camp, she darted away. They had spoken in voices too low to overhear, but she would never, ever, forget what she had seen transpire between the fine brave she loved and his wanton white whore.

Before he left the next morning, Viper made certain his aunt understood that she was to treat Erica like a dear daughter rather than an enemy. He then had her tell him what she wanted Erica to do that day, so he could explain the task in words his wife would understand. With both women present he described the making of pemmican, while he silently prayed that Erica would not refuse to help make it. She had put on the buckskin dress without his having to ask her to, and he took that as a good sign. "My aunt will need more berries. Then you will help her mix them together and mash them up, with bits of fat and meat. That is how we make pemmican. It makes a good food for braves to take on the trail."

Erica frowned slightly, but his words and gestures had given her a fairly clear idea of what was to be done. "I think I understand. Pemmican must be something like mincemeat. That's made with chopped apples, spices, suet, raisins, and meat, for a pie filling. It's baked, of course."

"Well, pemmican isn't cooked," Viper informed her, grateful the nourishing dish didn't sound too horribly strange to her.

Erica had another more important question, however.

"Just which braves will this pemmican be used to feed, Viper?"

Viper knew what her objection would be without having to hear it. "We will eat it ourselves on our travels. It won't feed braves who are fighting the army. Does that please you?"

Greatly relieved, Erica rewarded him with a lovely smile. "Yes, it does. Please be careful today. I don't want you to be hurt now, or ever."

Viper leaned down to kiss her cheek lightly. "Do not worry. I am clever, and my horse is swift. I will come to no harm."

As she watched him walk away, his long, easy strides were filled with the masculine grace that marked all his actions, and Erica's heart swelled with pride. She adored her husband, but as she turned to smile at his aunt, she saw only the same aloof curiosity she had seen the previous day. Knowing she would be leaving soon, Erica refused to allow Flowers of Spring or anyone else's unfriendliness to affect her. Picking up the basket they had used to gather berries, she smiled at the woman and gestured toward the river. "Shall we go?" she said brightly, and when the woman started down the path, she followed right behind her.

Flowers of Spring had not expected Erica to show her face that day. The young woman had courage. She had to admire that quality even in a white woman, and while she could not imagine having so blond a daughter, she had given her word to Viper and she would try.

When he returned to camp that evening, Viper found Erica waiting in their tepee. She had been stirring the stew simmering over the coals, but she jumped up to welcome him home with an enthusiastic hug and a flurry of sweet kisses. Relived that she appeared to have passed the day without incident, he was quick to return her show of affection. "You had no problems today?"

"No, none at all. I didn't see Wren. I hope she is too embarrassed to come near me, because I certainly don't want to see her again."

"You know I meant to have her apologize to you, but when I went to her family's tepee today I was told she has gone to visit relatives in one of the other camps. I do not

209

want to take the time to look for her."

Relieved by that news, Erica was swift to agree. "I think that's a wise decision. We have trouble enough without having to search for it. Are you hungry? This is another of your aunt's dishes, and it certainly smells good. I think she was trying to be more pleasant today. It's somewhat difficult to tell, because she seldom smiles at me, but I think she was trying as hard as I was to get along well."

After she had ladled the stew into bowls and sat down to eat with him, Viper began to chuckle to himself. He thought Erica was both beautiful and charming, but he knew others might think different. "It is a good thing my friends cannot see us now, for an Indian woman prepares her husband's food and then eats her own when he is finished."

"Really? What a curious custom," Erica replied, too hungry to consider adopting such a practice herself. "Isn't that rather lonely for them to eat separately?"

When Erica looked up at him, her eyes were such a lovely shade of blue that Viper knew his world would be a desolate place without the joy her presence gave him. "I think it began as a show of respect, but yes, it would be lonely. Had I taken an Indian wife, though, I might not have noticed."

Understanding his joke, Erica laughed with him. "I know, Indian women are quiet, while I am talkative, but to whom can I talk if not to you? Perhaps it is a good thing your friends are not here, because I would not want to embarrass you."

Viper hesitated a moment, hoping he had not hurt her feelings. "I like talking with you, since you have important things to say. We have always shared our meals together, too. I follow few of the old ways, Erica, so I hope you will not find it difficult to live with me."

Surprised his mood had so suddenly turned serious, Erica reached out to caress his thigh. While his buckskins were soft, she could feel the toughness of the muscles beneath, and giving him a loving pat, she withdrew her hand before thoughts of his sleek body made her forget what it was she had wanted to say. "These are difficult times, Viper, but I am very happy with you. You are a wonderful husband. Truly you are."

210

That the enchanting creature at his side thought so highly of him made Viper very proud. "Since Wren has left, we need stay here no longer. Can you be ready to leave in the morning?"

Erica was positive he was teasing her then. "I know your aunt will be disappointed, since I am such a wonderful helper, but yes, I think I can be ready to leave when you are."

"Good, because I do not want to leave you behind."

His hearty laughter gave that threat away for the joke it was, and Erica laughed again, too. "You see, you need me to eat with you. Who else would laugh at your jokes as often as I do?"

Viper put his arm around her shoulders to give her a loving hug as he replied, "If you think I need you only to laugh at my jokes, you are very wrong."

As he flashed a wicked grin, the love that shone so brightly in his eyes provided all the reassurance she would ever require that his need for her more than equaled her own for him. Tomorrow they would embark on a journey that was bound to be fraught with peril, for there would be the ever present danger they might be stopped by the army. They had managed to elude patrols on the way north, but that might prove to be far more difficult when traveling south. Yet Erica's heart was so filled with love for her handsome husband that she had little room for fear. She was certain whatever trouble they encountered, he would be able to protect them both.

While Erica's trusting smile was a delight, Viper prayed that by following his conscience he had not chosen a path that would endanger her life as well as his own. Since he had no way of knowing what the dawn would bring, he promised to make the night another they would never forget. "Let's go down to the river," he suggested as he set their empty bowls aside, and knowing exactly what he had in mind, Erica was as eager to go as he.

# Chapter Fourteen

## September, 1862

In September, Mark Randall returned to Washington when General John Pope was recalled to account for the disastrous defeat the Union Army had suffered at the Second Battle of Bull Run. It was then that the conscientious lieutenant received his first news of the two-week-old uprising in Minnesota. His initial reaction was one of stunned disbelief, swiftly followed by stark horror as he realized his beloved Erica must surely be in the most terrible danger possible.

He had had his fill of the brutality of war and could not bear to think the woman he loved might have witnessed the very same senseless carnage he had been forced to view time and again since enlisting in the army. He had truly believed she would be safer living with relatives in Minnesota than remaining alone in Delaware while he and her father were away serving in the army. All his thoughts had been focused upon protecting her from the pain of needless suffering while the war raged, but he had never dreamed the choice he had forced her to accept might cost her her life.

"How could I have been such a stubborn fool?" he cried out in an anguished sob. Erica had wanted so desperately to marry him and create a home in Wilmington, a home in which she would have been completely safe, if only he had let her impassioned pleas and tears sway him. Had she known what lay ahead? Had she had a premonition of the danger that awaited her in Minnesota? Had any of her tears been caused by dread of the future rather than by the sorrow of their parting? Those questions pierced his heart with the pain of the sharpest of arrows, for he feared he might never be able to ask them, nor ever again hear the sweet sound of her voice as she replied.

To add to his heavy burden of guilt, Mark knew that in all of Minnesota Erica could not have gone to a worse place than New Ulm. He read the newspaper reports of the battle there until he had memorized each gruesome phrase, for they provided a fascinating, if grim, account of the citizens' heroic defense of their city. Thirty-four had been killed and sixty wounded, but there was no list of names attached to those frightening statistics. Not knowing whether the vibrant young woman he loved was alive, dead, or gravely injured was the worst torture Mark had ever been forced to endure. Praying her father would have more information, he hurried to the army hospital where Lars Hanson had been assigned, but it took him more than an hour of combing the overcrowded wards to find the physician.

The Union's losses at the Second Battle of Bull Run had been massive. In the final days of August nearly two thousand men had been killed and more than eight thousand wounded. The injured were still being sent from field hospitals to Washington for care, and Lars was so numb from overwork and lack of sleep that he did not recognize the tall lieutenant striding down the hall until Mark was within six feet of him. He then reached into his pocket for the telegram from the Ludwigs, which his housekeeper had forwarded to him. Knowing the moment he had been dreading had finally arrived, he took the precaution of directing Mark outside where the air did not reek of the vile stench of death before he handed the young man the brief message.

"Erica was taken captive on August 23. I've received no further word from her aunt and uncle." In an attempt to judge Mark's commitment to his daughter, Lars studied the young man's expression closely as he read the wire, but he could discern little other than the same sense of horrified shock he had felt upon learning of Erica's plight. He had had several days to consider his only child's fate, and his voice was bitter as he continued. "There are so many wounded in need of medical care, my request for leave was denied. If you wish to go to Minnesota to search for Erica yourself, I must warn you to be prepared for what you may find."

Mark could not help but notice the change in Lars's appearance and manner since they had left Wilmington together in June. While they were both a good deal thinner, the physician's attitude had always been friendly, never bordering upon open hostility as it seemed to be that day. While the subject of Erica's survival certainly demanded a serious response, Mark was nonetheless alarmed by Lars's mood. Confused, he scanned the physician's stern expression, hoping for clues to help him identify the emotion that had prompted the unexpected warning. The intensity of Lars's dark blue gaze only puzzled him further, however. Mark had always considered Lars charming, if somewhat aloof, but there was not the slightest trace of charm in the man standing opposite him that day. Did Lars no longer turn to brandy to dull the pain of his existence? Was that what he was seeing? Mark asked himself—a man who now faced the worst life had to offer without constantly trying to escape it in the numbing warmth of alcohol?

Thinking perhaps he had never really known Lars Hanson at all, Mark refolded the telegram and returned it to him. "I'll not find the fighting there worse than what I've already seen. I'll ask for a leave within the hour. If it isn't granted, then I'll simply go without it, but I'll not leave Erica in the hands of savages a minute longer than I have to," he declared emphatically, taking his clue from the blackness of Lars's mood and allowing it to darken his own.

Realizing the young man had completely misunderstood him, Lars gestured toward the path that led to the carefully tended rose garden at the rear of the hospital. "Come take a walk with me." As Mark fell in beside him, he tried to put the cause for his depression into words that would be more easily understood. "Do not think me unfeeling, for I love my daughter dearly, but there are some ordeals from which a young woman never fully recovers. If Erica has been abused, she may turn away from

214

all men, even those who love her. It is possible she will not be grateful if you are the one to rescue her. Your presence might only deepen her shame."

Infuriated by the physician's remarks, Mark clasped his hands behind his back to force back the nearly overwhelming compulsion to throttle Lars Hanson. "If by abuse you mean rape," he began between tightly clenched teeth, "I will show Erica such loving kindness she will soon realize she has no reason to fear me. I would not taunt her with cruel reminders of what she has suffered, but instead provide her with hope for a future filled with love. I wish to God we had been married in June. If we had, then she would not have come to the slightest harm. I will never forgive myself for postponing our wedding. Never. My reasons were simply ludicrous in light of what has happened to her."

"You blame yourself for this, then, and not me? After all, I was the one who insisted she go to New Ulm. You were merely going along with the decision I made," Lars reminded him.

Lars's sorrow was deeply etched in his expression and echoed hollowly in his melancholy tone. Mark was suddenly ashamed of himself for thinking his own pain outweighed his companion's. He reached out to touch Lars's sleeve and draw him to a halt. "Perhaps the idea was yours, but I agreed with it wholeheartedly, and I will deal with the consequences. Do the people in Wilmington know Erica is one of the captives?"

"No," Lars replied without hesitation. "The telegram was sent to my home, but Mrs. Ferguson sent it on to me here unopened. No one can possibly know more than what was printed in the newspapers, and her name wasn't given."

Mark nodded thoughtfully, grateful for that bit of luck. "I'll leave for Minnesota as quickly as I possibly can. Once there, I promise you I will find Erica. Regardless of what has happened to her, and I pray it has not been so horrible as you imagine, we can be married there, and I'll bring her home as my wife. We will never speak of what occurred in Minnesota, and I'll make certain not a breath of scandal is ever attached to her name."

Encouraged by Mark's confident vow, Lars agreed his

215

plan was a most sensible one. "Yes, I'm sure you're right. The war has caused so much confusion that an Indian uprising in Minnesota will swiftly be forgotten. I'm sorry if I misjudged you, but you must realize not every man would make such a generous offer. There are many who would simply pretend they had never met a young woman, rather than marry her after—"

Mark interrupted then, unable again to listen to the man recite his fears whe he hoped with all his heart they would prove unfounded. "I love your daughter, sir. She swore she would love me no matter what awful thing happened to me during the war. I can treat her no differently."

They had stopped to talk near a wooden bench placed at the edge of the garden. Too weary to remain standing, Lars went over to it, sat down, and leaned forward to cradle his head in his hands. "I hope you do not have to desert, and I also hope you understand why I can't turn my back on my responsibilities here to go with you."

While it would not be easy for Mark to leave the men with whom he had grown close during the many weeks of fighting they had shared, he understood the uniqueness of Lars's situation. Knowing he had at least a few minutes to spare, he chose to spend them with the man he hoped would soon be his father-in-law. Taking the place at his side, he offered Lars what reassurance he could. "I understand completely. The most difficult part of this war has been hearing the screams of the wounded and knowing I can do nothing to ease their pain. You are needed here far more than I am, for you can alleviate suffering, while I am merely a hastily trained officer who can easily be replaced."

Lars gave a rueful laugh at that compliment. He sat up and crossed his arms over his chest to get comfortable, but he knew he would have to get back to the hospital soon. "All too often I can do little more than allow a man to die in peace. How many limbs do you think I amputated while I was in practice in Wilmington?"

Uncertain, Mark shrugged, but gave the best guess he could. "I have no idea, perhaps two or three?"

Lars shook his head. "None. I never saw anyone so severely injured as to require amputation. But here, I have lost count of how many times I've had to use a saw on a young man's arm or leg. I hear their screams even in my sleep. On the rare occasions when I can fall asleep, that is."

Mark could readily see how tired Lars was, for his fatigue showed clearly in his slumped pose and dejected expression. He was not yet forty, but looked a good ten years older than his actual age that day. "This war has been hard on us all. I had only a vague idea of what serving in the army would be like when I enlisted. I knew the Union's cause was a just one, but I find it impossible to think of causes when men are dying by the thousands and an end to the war is not even in sight."

Lars heard his own bitterness voiced so loudly in Mark's words he couldn't listen to any more. "Put the war out of your mind, if you can. Just go to Minnesota, find Erica, and bring her home." Forcing himself to return to duty, he rose to his feet and straightened his shoulders proudly. "Tell her I've given up my reliance on brandy. That should please her. She was always too sweet to call me a drunk to my face, but that's all I've been since her mother died. Or rather, that's all I was until I came here and found I'd have to use a saw more often than a scalpel. The least I can do for my patients is to be sober, and unfortunately, all too often that's all I *can* do."

As Mark stood, he doubted brandy would be of any help if he lost his beloved Erica. The pain of not knowing she was safe was so excruciating, he knew if he found her dead his life would no longer be worth living. Feeling a kinship born of their mutual despair, he grabbed Lars in an enthusiastic bear hug. "I'll find her, sir. I promise I will."

While Lars could not recall the last time someone had tried to comfort him in so physical a fashion, he found Mark's hearty embrace not unpleasant and smiled as the young man pulled away. "I'm sure you will. Take care of yourself, and send word the minute you have news of any kind."

"I'll do that," Mark agreed, and cheered that he had Lars's support, he bid him farewell, confident he would have good news soon. With a determined gait he went to demand rather than request a leave so he could rescue the woman he loved more dearly than life itself. To his amazement, he found General Pope had just been

217

reassigned to Minnesota as commander of the newly created Military Department of the Northwest and given the task of battling the Sioux. While the general felt he was being banished and angrily protested his transfer, Mark was the first officer to volunteer to accompany him to his new headquarters in St. Paul. And soon after their arrival there, the earnest lieutenant left for Fort Ridgely, carrying a message from the general to Henry Sibley that encouraged the colonel to vigorously pursue the Indians and bring the uprising to a swift end.

Sibley had more need for lieutenants than for stirring messages. The loss of nearly one hundred horses at Birch Coulee and the departure of most of his volunteer cavalry had left him with too few mounted troops to challenge the Sioux. When two hundred seventy newly paroled infantrymen of the Third Minnesota Regiment who had been taken prisoner in July in Tennessee had arrived on September 13, their officers were still Confederate prisoners. "I can send someone else to carry messages back and forth to Pope. I need officers too badly here to let you go," he quickly advised Mark.

Since he had prepared several convincing arguments to make his stay at the fort sound imperative, Mark quite naturally agreed. "I'll be proud to serve under your command, sir. My fiancée is being held by the Sioux, and the sooner this cursed uprising is over, the sooner we can be married."

"Good Lord," Sibley moaned sympathetically. "I had no idea." At a loss for words, since he had made no progress toward the captives' release, he shook his head sadly. Then, knowing he had no way to guarantee the young woman's safety or anyone else's either, he said a silent prayer for her and explained to Mark how his presence would enhance her chances for survival.

On September 19, when Colonel Sibley left Fort Ridgely, Mark had been promoted to the rank of captain and given command of one of the companies of the Third Minnesota. With nine companies of the Sixth Regiment, five companies of the Seventh, a company of the Ninth, thirty-eight Renville Rangers, twenty-eight mounted citizen guards, and sixteen citizen artillerymen, there was a total of 1,619 men. The missionary, Reverend Stephen R.

Riggs, went along as the group's chaplain, while the Indian who had saved so many white lives at the Upper Agency, John Other Day, served as the scout.

Following the government road toward the Upper Agency, the determined group marched for four days to reach Lone Tree Lake, which they mistook for Wood Lake, which lay farther west. Three miles below the agency, they camped on the shores of the lake on the night of September 22. A stream flowing from the lake had cut a deep ravine to the northeast, and the Sixth Minnesota camped to the left of it. The Third Minnesota took the crest of the ravine opposite them, while the Seventh took a position at the rear forming a triangular encampment. Mistakenly believing the Sioux were farther north, Colonel Sibley chose to post the guards close to their positions. Little Crow, with a force of between seven hundred and twelve hundred braves, was only a few miles to the north, however. The chief considered attacking the troops at night, but decided it would be far wiser to wait until the next day when the soldiers would be strung out along the road as they continued their march.

At dawn, the Indians were hidden in the tall grass at the side of the road when several enterprising men of the Third Minnesota Regiment who had left the camp without permission came rolling by in wagons. Intent upon gathering potatoes from the fields at the Upper Agency to add variety to their meager rations of salt pork, hardtack, and black coffee, they had not considered their errand dangerous. When the wagons strayed off the curving road to make better time, the Indians had no choice but to rise up and fire their weapons to avoid being run over.

Hearing gunfire as the wagons inadvertently triggered the ambush, Mark was as confused as the other officers as to what had happened. Before any orders could be given, many soldiers had picked up their rifles and gone running to their friends' aid. The Indians withdrew momentarily as the Third Minnesota made their daring, if unauthorized, advance; then the braves gathered their forces to attack the army's flank. Sibley immediately recalled the Third and ordered fire from a six-pound cannon to blanket the ravine before companies of the Sixth and

Seventh regiments opened fire to keep the area clear.

After two hours of fighting, in which seven soldiers died and thirty-three were wounded, the Indians withdrew, carrying with them the body of Chief Mankato, who had failed to dodge a cannon ball. They left the bodies of fourteen others behind. Sibley claimed the battle of Wood Lake, misnamed because of the confusion as to their location, so decisive a victory that he accurately predicted the Sioux would not attack the army again. While he would have preferred to pursue the fleeing Indians, he lacked sufficient cavalry troops to do so, and he remained at Lone Tree Lake for two days to care for the wounded.

Fearing that Little Crow might kill the captives if he returned victorious from his latest battle, Christian Indians and others friendly to whites moved them into the camp of Chief Red Iron, who had vowed to keep Little Crow and his braves off his land. They were prepared to defend the captives, but when Little Crow returned after suffering another defeat, he gave no thought to the captives' fate. Along with the Chiefs Shakopee, Red Middle Voice, and Medicine Bottle, Little Crow and many of his followers gathered their families and left for the Dakotas, where they thought they could elude the army as easily as the renegade Inkpaduta had done.

Wabasha, Red Iron, and Taopi, along with Gabriel Renville, an influential man of mixed blood, sent a mixed-blood prisoner, Joseph Campbell, to inform Henry Sibley that the captives were safe and that the army should advance to receive them. The troops left Lone Tree Lake on September 25 and marched fifteen miles past the Hazelwood Mission, which had been the Reverend Riggs's home. There they found a hundred and fifty lodges filled with Indians from Wabasha's and Taopi's camps, plus numerous Lower Sioux, who, knowing the war was lost, were prepared to surrender.

While Mark Randall readily understood Colonel Sibley's desire to enter the Indian camp in dress uniforms to the accompaniment of their drummers' loud and stirring cadence, the wait until two on the afternoon of September 26 was sheer agony for him. He cared nothing for colorful flags, elaborate ceremony, or the stern speech Sibley delivered to impress the Sioux that those guilty of

220

participating in the uprising would be severely punished. He wanted only to see Erica, to hold her in his arms, and make her his wife before the day was out. He had been so encouraged by the news that Christian Indians had protected the white prisoners during their captivity that he had already asked the Reverend Riggs to perform their marriage ceremony. Yet when he saw the first of those being released, his heart fell. Even though the women and children were weeping for joy, their faces were gaunt, the thinness of their bodies clear evidence of how close they had come to starvation. After nearly six weeks of captivity, their clothing had been reduced to such tattered shreds that many of the soldiers were prompted to remove their coats and give them to the women rather than allow them to continue going about nearly naked.

At the close of the meeting, ninety-one whites and a hundred and fifty mixed bloods had been released, but there was no sign of Erica Hanson. Mark spoke with each of the women who had been freed, describing his fiancée and asking for word of her, but he received no more than sympathetic apologies, until he found a woman who recalled meeting the pretty blonde in her uncle's store.

Although tired and hungry, Harriet could not ignore the urgency of the handsome captain's pleas and offered the only help she could. "I can tell you only that I know who Erica is, but she has never been with us. If she is a captive, then she must have been held elsewhere." She gave Mark's arm a comforting pat and moved on, eager to see if one of the civilians might have word of her husband.

Sick with fear, in the following days Mark waited as sixteen more white captives appeared at the army encampment, which had been appropriately named Camp Release, but again, all he received in response to his queries were blank stares. No one had seen his fiancée since the day she had been abducted, more than a month ago. Then, finally, it occurred to him to begin interrogating the Indians who had surrendered, for surely if Erica were being held by a Sioux brave, others would have seen her.

Song of the Wren had been in Chief Red Iron's camp when the uprising came to an end. Her father and her brother, Hunted Stag, had fled with Little Crow, while she

221

had been left behind to care not only for her little sister and her pregnant mother, who was in poor health, but for an aging aunt and uncle as well. That was a sorry situation, which Wren bitterly resented. When she had seen an army officer moving about their camp asking questions, she had no interest in speaking with him. They had all been badly disappointed to find the army planned to put the braves who had taken part in the uprising on trial rather than treat them as prisoners of war, and she would volunteer no information that might harm one of those who had surrendered. Then a curious friend had discovered that the inquisitive captain was looking for a blond woman named Erica, and Wren knew she had to speak with him.

Mark had all but given up his quest for clues as to Erica's whereabouts when he saw a slender Indian maid incline her head as her eyes met his. She turned away, then looked back over her shoulder at him as she started toward the river. Intrigued, if not certain she had been encouraging him to follow her, Mark brought the conversation he had in progress to an abrupt end and started after her.

Wren paused frequently, delighted to see the handsome officer was in close pursuit. She waited until she came to three sugar maple trees that grew so close together they would screen their meeting from curious eyes, and stopped to wait for him there. When Mark reached her side, he did no more than raise a brow as if to ask what she had wanted, but she had no intention of giving him the information he needed until she learned how he planned to use it. "I have seen you asking questions," she began with a deceptively innocent smile. Her teeth were straight, a sparkling white against her dark skin. She knew she was attractive, and hoped Mark, like other men, would think so, too. She brushed her long hair off her shoulders, thinking he could not fail to notice how long and shiny it was.

Mark knew very little about Indian women, but since this one seemed so friendly, he leaned back against the nearest maple and repeated the description he had given so often he thought he could probably repeat it in his sleep. "My fiancée was taken captive in New Ulm. Since she was not among those freed here, I am hoping someone might have seen her and be willing to tell me where she is. She is very pretty, slender, and no taller than my chin. She has long, curly blond hair and eyes of an unusual dark blue. Her name is Erica Hanson. Have you see her, or heard anyone mention a white captive with her name?"

Wren scuffed the toe of her moccasin in the dust of the trail. "Perhaps she does not wish to be found," she suggested shyly.

Mark straightened up, suspecting the young woman wished only to flirt with him, and he had no patience for that. "If you should hear something, please let me know. I will provide a generous reward to the person who helps me find Erica."

Money was something her family would need desperately, since it did not look like their annuity would be paid that year. Keenly aware of that, Wren reached out to touch Mark's sleeve, hoping to keep him talking a while longer. "Let me see the money first. Then I will decide if I wish to help you."

Seeing he had her sincere interest now, Mark smiled as he replied. "I plan to pay the reward in gold, and I do not carry that around with me." Taking a ten dollar bill from his wallet, he folded it nonchalantly as he made what he hoped would be an enticing offer. "Tell me what you know, and I'll give you this. If it leads me to Erica, then I will see you get one hundred dollars in gold." Mark was a wealthy young man and would gladly have promised his entire fortune to set Erica free, but he thought ten dollars would be enough to tempt an Indian maiden to confide in him.

Wren eyed the money for a long moment, then, wanting to be rid of Erica for good, she said, "I know the brave who has her, but you must promise me he will come to no harm."

Perplexed by that demand, Mark wondered if the girl wanted the brave for herself. "He has obviously taken part in the uprising, or he couldn't have taken my fiancée prisoner. He will have to stand trial with the others."

Wren shook her head slowly. "I cannot help you, if it means he will be captured."

Mark frowned angrily, convinced by her reluctance that she did indeed have valuable information, but not knowing what he could promise that would sway her to reveal it. "If you tell me who and where he is, I will try and

223

convince him to hand over Erica willingly. I will testify to that at his trial. That he turned over a captive without a fight will be in his favor."

Wren now faced the most difficult choice of her life. The officer provided not only a means of ridding their lives of the blond witch, but also a way to earn the money she knew her family would need to buy food for the winter. Still, she did not want to see Viper put on trial. It was a dilemma that made her head ache, and she did not know what to do.

Mark could see the girl was as deeply troubled as he was, and he grew certain the brave holding Erica must be the man she loved. "If I am the one to find this brave, I will give you my word he will live to stand trial. Search parties are being organized to look for more captives. If someone else finds Erica, they might kill the brave who has her. Do you want to take that risk? You will never see the man again if he is shot dead for what he has done. I will give you my word he will be brought back for trial. We are bound to catch him sooner or later. His best chance to live is if I find him. Now where is he?"

Wren's eyes filled with tears as she looked up at Mark. "He has done nothing wrong. Your woman bewitched him. She used her beauty to make him her slave. She is not his. I want only for you to take her away. Viper is the one you will be setting free."

"Viper?" Mark whispered hoarsely. "The brave's name is Viper?" The day was warm, but he felt a sudden chill. Someone stepping upon my grave, he told himself. He had never liked that expression, and he abhorred it now. It was the brave's name that had alarmed him, for surely a man with such a menacing name would be an evil brute. An evil brute he had just promised to see live to stand trial.

Wren nodded. "He and your woman were here with us, but they have gone south. If there is anything left of New Ulm, they may be there now."

Mark handed her the ten dollar bill. For all he knew her tale was a complete fabrication. It was possible Viper did not exist, or if he did, he might not have Erica. It was the only clue he possessed, however, and he would use it. "Thank you. Tell me your name, so I can find you to pay you the reward."

224

"I am Song of the Wren, but you must tell no one that I am the one who has spoken to you about Viper. No one!"

She reached out to grip his arm tightly, and Mark did no more than look down at her hand until she released him of her own accord. "I understand. If I give you the money, you can tell everyone you earned it by being my whore." With that rude farewell, he left her among the trees and returned to Camp Release. Seeing John Other Day talking with a group of troopers, he called him over.

"Is there a Lower Sioux by the name of Viper?" he asked without making an attempt to disguise the anger of his mood.

Other Day knew, as all the others did, that Captain Randall was seeking news of his fiancée. "Yes, there is such a brave. He is cunning and quick. If you meet him, be very careful. He would make the worst of enemies."

"I thank you for your warning. I won't forget it." Viper's existence confirmed, Mark went straight to Sibley's headquarters.

Colonel Sibley listened with interest as Mark requested permission to take a search party out to scour the area near New Ulm for captives. "Of course, take as many men as you need. There are so many people still unaccounted for, you are bound to find someone in need of rescue. I hope one of them is your fiancée. I am looking forward to meeting her. We all are."

Mark rose quickly to his feet, anxious to be on his way. "Thank you, sir. She is a lovely young woman, and I am certain she will enjoy meeting you, too." He could not face the prospect that she might be changed in any way. As Mark left to make the arrangements to get his search party under way, he could not get Wren's comments about Erica out of his mind. Erica was an enchanting creature. Men always found her appealing, but could she actually have bewitched a cunning Indian brave by the name of Viper? He needed only a moment's reflection to decide she could have done such a thing for only one purpose: to save her life and come back to him. He swore to himself that no matter what wretched thing she had done, or been forced to do, he would still make her his wife, and proudly.

# Chapter Fifteen

## October, 1862

Erica sat crosslegged on the grass at the side of the house, the striped tomcat cradled in her lap as she watched Viper chop wood. He worked with an effortless ease, swinging the axe with a lazy rhythm, splitting the logs without appearing to feel the slightest bit of strain. As usual, his chest was bare, and she found the sight of his muscular body as deeply pleasurable as his charming company. "Since gathering wood for the fire is the woman's responsibility, I'm surprised you did not tell me to chop the firewood for the winter," she teased happily.

Laughing with her, Viper paused for a moment to rest. "Gathering wood is women's work," he agreed. "But since white women insist upon living in houses and cooking on cast iron stoves, they need logs to burn. What would you say if I told you to go out and gather logs?"

"I would say that I might be gone a very long time." They often talked about the differences between his life and hers, but it was always with humor, never with one insisting the other's way of doing things was wrong.

"It would not take you long to find a man to do your work," Viper responded with a sly grin. "Just be careful he does not ask to be paid before the work is done."

"And how would you expect me to pay him?" Erica scratched the cat's ears playfully, but her eyes never left her handsome husband's face.

"With money, of course. How else?" Yet Viper's

suggestive glance said there were far more intriguing possibilities than his teasing question implied.

"I think I am very lucky you are willing to chop the wood," Erica remarked with an enchanting smile.

"Yes, you should remember that." Viper picked up the next log and placed it on the stump, eager to finish his day's work so he and his wife could get on to far more exciting things. He looked up often and smiled, silently promising the delights he planned for them to share soon.

Nearby, Mark Randall raised his hand, preparing to signal his men to move up into position. They could hear the sound of someone chopping wood as they approached the house stealthily, and while the possibility that an Indian brave would be doing such a chore struck him as ridiculous, the newly promoted captain was nonetheless primed to discover just who was. This farmhouse was the last along the Cottonwood River, and if they did not find Erica here, Mark had no idea where else to look. At his command, from either end of the house armed troopers moved out swiftly to encircle Erica and her husband. Their rifles aimed for Viper's heart, they instantly blocked any escape the brave might try and make.

"Throw down the axe," Mark called out loudly, so excited by the unexpectedly delightful sight of the woman he adored that he could not possibly speak below a shout. That she was dressed in a buckskin dress and moccasins, with gruesome necklaces of strange claws around her neck, shocked him, but he was thankful she had obviously been treated far better than the pitiful captives he had met at Camp Release. "Get up, Erica, and come here to me." Having once glanced in her direction, Mark kept his Colt revolver trained on Viper. "I said, drop the axe," he called out again, infuriated that the brave had not immediately followed his order.

"Mark? Is that you?" His hat partially shaded his face, but she recognized his voice instantly. Erica could scarcely believe her eyes, she was so startled by the sudden appearance of her former fiancé and a dozen armed soldiers. "Tell your men to drop their rifles instead," she directed as she leaped to her feet and sent the tomcat scurrying. "This man is my husband, and you've no reason to threaten to shoot him."

Since he was the only husband Mark intended Erica to have, he dismissed her claim as some absurd delusion resulting from the ordeal of her captivity. "Whatever desperate game you've been forced to play, it's over, Erica. This man is under arrest. I've promised to bring him in alive to stand trial for his part in the uprising, but if he doesn't drop that axe this minute, I will forget that pledge and take his body back instead."

While Erica's manner of dress had shocked him, Mark was totally unprepared to accept this man as one called Viper. His imagination had painted a far different picture of the savage, whom he had expected to be repulsive in the extreme. This Indian, however, was powerfully built, if lean, with features so finely chiseled that not even his unruly mane of coal-black hair marred the elegance of his appearance. That his eyes were a light, pale gray was also astonishing, but their unusual color did not hide the arrogance of his glance. Not about to allow that unspoken challenge to go unanswered, Mark called again to Erica.

"Come here to me so his blood does not splatter all over you when I shoot him. Even if he does not speak English, he must understand what it is I told him to do."

While she thought Mark was merely bluffing, when Viper kept a firm grip on the axe handle Erica did not allow the men's idiotic standoff to continue. She rushed to Viper's side and wrenched the axe from his hand. Carrying it over to Mark, she dropped it at his feet. "There, you have the blasted axe. Now stop bullying my husband. He's committed no crime and there's no need to take him anywhere for trial. Tell your men to drop their rifles. Put your pistol away, too, and I'll be happy to introduce you."

Mark took his eyes off Viper only briefly to glance down at the woman he loved. Her hair was loose, the blond curls tumbling down over her shoulders, and he thought she looked ridiculous in buckskins adorned with primitive jewelry when a woman of her fair beauty belonged in fine silks and satins worn with precious jewels. "I thought you might need clothes, so I've brought some for you. I'll unpack them while you bathe." He then turned to the man standing at his right.

"Sergeant, take the Indian's knife, tie him up, and keep him under guard. We'll leave for Camp Release at dawn, and I don't want to have to waste any more time looking for him."

"Mark!" Erica couldn't abide the high-handed manner in which he was treating them. Gesturing toward Viper, she attempted again to explain their true situation. "Have you suddenly gone deaf? This man is my husband. I will not allow you to tie him up. You have no right to do that. He's not done anything wrong." Before Mark could catch her, she dashed back to Viper's side and wrapped her arms around his waist. "You'll have to tie us up together, because I won't let you treat him like a criminal when he's done nothing wrong."

Mark gestured with his Colt, bringing the ring of troopers in a step closer. "If he's innocent, then he'll have no reason to fear a trial. Step aside or I will tie you up, too, but not with him. Now move!"

In response, Viper slipped his arm around Erica's waist and pulled her closer to his side. The insolence of that gesture was more than Mark could bear, and with a nod to the man directly behind Viper, he issued a terse order. "Knock him out."

Erica screamed as the butt of the soldier's rifle slammed into the back of Viper's head. With her standing in his arms, the Indian had had no chance to dodge that vicious blow, and he fell forward into the dust, unconscious.

The horrified blonde knelt by her husband's side, her tears falling upon his cheek as she felt for the pulse in his throat. Reassured he had not been killed, she began to scream hysterically at Mark. "How dare you treat him so? How dare you? He has done nothing to deserve such a beating."

"I want him securely tied," Mark repeated to the sergeant. He then shoved his revolver into his holster, went to Erica's side, and yanked her to her feet. When she struggled to break free, he swung her up into his arms, and as his troops cheered, he carried her into the small house and tossed her down upon the feather bed. Before she could spring to her feet, he slung his hat aside and fell across her. Grabbing her wrists, he effectively subdued her efforts to flee before he spoke.

"You needn't tell me what's happened to you. It's more than plain, but it's over. Do you understand me? It's over. That savage will be put on trial, and you will go home with me to Wilmington. This is all my fault, not yours, so I'm not blaming you. Now if you will promise to stop fighting me, I'll let you go."

Seething with rage, Erica barely heard Mark's words. "Let me go, you bastard!" she screamed. He was much too heavy to dislodge from the bed, far too strong for her to escape, but she did her damnedest to do it. "Get off me!" she shrieked.

"Did you ever say that to your redskinned lover?" Already knowing the answer, Mark lowered his mouth to hers, stifling her stream of insults with the hungry kisses he had waited far too long to give. When Erica did not respond, but instead stiffened rebelliously, he gave up the effort to turn her anger to passion, but he did not release her, nor move away.

"This husband of yours, where did you marry him?" Mark asked accusingly.

Jolted to reality by the full import of that question, Erica turned her head away as she stubbornly refused to answer. In my heart, she whispered silently to herself, in my very soul, but not in any ceremony Mark would recognize or understand. Hot tears of despair poured down her cheeks as she thought how cruelly he had treated the man she loved. "I am sorry. I know this must be an awful shock for you, but Viper truly is my husband."

Seeing her apology was sincere, Mark sat up and pulled the weeping blonde into his arms. While he had searched for her, he had repeatedly promised himself that he would not blame her or lose his temper with her, no matter what she had been forced to endure, but he had failed miserably in that vow. He patted her back and hugged her tightly as he pressed his lips to her temple. Her fair skin was now lightly tanned and wet from her tears, but as delightfully soft as he had remembered it to be. "The brave kidnapped you from New Ulm, Erica. There were witnesses, your cousin, for one. I've spoken to him, and he told me Viper carried you off kicking and screaming. That was no elopement, but a brazen abduction."

Unable to deny the apparent truth of his words, Erica

snuggled down in Mark's arms, hoping with all her heart she could make him understand what had really happened. "Gunter is all right, then? What about my aunt and uncle?"

"Yes, they are fine. With the uprising over, they were with those who returned to New Ulm with plans to rebuild the city. There are not many with that courage, but they are among them."

Erica bit her lower lip nervously, uncertain how to phrase her next question. "Did Gunter tell you that I knew Viper? That he and I were friends before the uprising began?"

Astonished by that question, Mark placed his fingers under Erica's chin to tilt her gaze up to his. "What do you mean? How could you possibly have been friends with an Indian brave?"

"Gunter did not tell you?" Erica asked again, her lower lip trembling as huge tears continued to escape her thick lashes and flow down her flushed cheeks. "He said nothing about seeing us together?"

"My God, Erica, were you so angry with me for refusing to marry you that you would stoop to disgracing yourself with an Indian brave to get even?"

"No! It was nothing like that!" Yet Erica found Mark's piercing gaze impossible to return, and looked down at the shiny brass buttons on his coat instead. Tears continued to slide down her cheeks as she tried to explain how she had met Viper. She took care to make the tale as innocent as possible. The story sounded plausible to her, since it was so close to the truth, but when she said the brave had come to New Ulm to rescue rather than kidnap her, Mark laughed out loud.

"So you were flirting with an Indian brave. Is that it? You considered it a harmless pastime, no doubt, since you are so very good at it, but Viper took you up on it. Well, your little escapade is over, Erica. Don't call the man your husband ever again, because he was never that. Since he seems to have treated you well, I will thank him for his kindness, but I am taking him back to stand trial and then I am taking you home. I told your father I would marry you here, and he agrees that is the best course."

"You and my father have decided again what is best for

231

me?" Erica asked resentfully. "Well, the answer is no. I will not go back to Wilmington, and I will not marry you!"

Mark's eyes narrowed as he recoiled from the hostility of her words. He could think of only one reason she would think she had to remain in Minnesota, and he quickly moved to satisfy his curiosity. "There's been time. Are you carrying that savage's child? Is that why you think you must stay with him?"

Mortified that he would ask so personal a question, Erica shook her head violently. How she had escaped conceiving she did not know, but she had. "No, there will be no child." At least not yet, she told herself.

"Thank God for that," Mark responded emphatically. He remained seated upon the bed, holding her in his arms as he tried to think how best to reason with her when she was in a totally unreasonable mood. Since the situation was so far removed from the one he had expected to find, he decided to go slowly, to carefully lead her where he wished to go taking one small step at a time. "We need decide nothing today, Erica. There will be plenty of time to make our plans after we reach Camp Release where the Indians are being tried."

"I'm staying with Viper," the defiant blonde vowed stubbornly. "I don't care what you and my father have planned for me, I won't leave him."

"Do you realize how swiftly I could make you a widow if you keep insisting you are that savage's wife?" Mark inquired with a slight smile, as though he would not think twice about shooting Viper.

Terrified by that threat, Erica again tried to escape his grasp, and again failed. "How dare you make such vile threats to me? How dare you? He would never treat you in so despicable a fashion."

"I doubt an Indian's principles can be any higher than mine," Mark responded confidently, but he had not meant to upset her needlessly when he would never execute a man for the crime of loving her. "Now I want you to take a bath, a long, hot one to wash away every trace of your Indian lover's touch, and then you'll put on the gown I brought for you to wear. We'll have dinner together, and in the morning we'll leave for Camp Release. If after his trial you

232

still want to remain with Viper, and he still wants you for his wife, we will make whatever decisions must be made then."

Mark released her and rose to his feet. "I'm glad you've not been tortured or abused, but I won't pretend I'm not bitterly disappointed that you seem to care more for some savage you've known a few brief weeks than you do for me. I still love you with all my heart, and I always will."

Erica remained on the rumpled bed, her emotions a painful confusion of guilt and despair, for she knew she had betrayed Mark's trust in the most cruel of ways. Drying her eyes on the back of her hand, she made an attempt to use his affection for her to make him see her love for Viper was neither a hasty infatuation nor a sordid affair. "Viper and I have known we belong together almost from the hour we met. He knew I was engaged to you, but that did not prevent us from falling in love. We knew there were bound to be problems at the end of the uprising, but we were prepared to face them. If you love me so dearly, can't you help me now? Can't you put your jealousy aside and help me to find happiness with the man I love?"

That Erica would prefer some half-naked savage to him was more than Mark could bear. He reached for her hand, pulled her off the bed, and drew her close. "What happened to the love you swore you felt for me? You were heartbroken when I postponed our wedding, and now you expect me to casually kiss you good-bye and allow you to live with a Sioux? You ask too much, but I have a question for you. Can you tell me with all honesty that you feel nothing for me anymore? Nothing at all? Can you look me directly in the eye and say that?"

Erica swallowed hard, forcing back the wave of uncertainty that question brought. Not knowing how to respond, she tried to change the subject. "I know it must have hurt you when I left without telling you good-bye."

"Hurt doesn't begin to describe the pain. That's a dead issue, however. It's done, over. I want to hear you say you don't love me. Can you do that, or not?" he demanded sarcastically. "Or have the last few weeks been so difficult for you that you no longer know what you want, or whom?"

Erica could not deny that Mark was very handsome. His light brown hair had been bleached by the summer sun until it now glistened with streaks of pale gold. His skin was deeply tanned, complementing his well-shaped features. The soft brown of his eyes still held a world of emotion, while the love that shone so brightly from their depths was unchanged. She could not even recall the time she had not loved Mark, but once Viper had entered her life, he had simply ceased to exist. Yet here he was demanding to hear the truth of her feelings, and she had no idea what to say. "Don't ask me to say that I do not love you, for I always will. It is only that now I love Viper more, and I wish to live my life as his wife rather than yours."

The muscles along Mark's jaw tightened menacingly. He had absolutely no intention of surrendering the woman he loved without a fight, and at present the advantage was his. "The man will have to stand trial, Erica. Hundreds died in the uprising, and those who took part are being called to account for it."

"The war was not going well for the Union when last I heard news of it. If the Confederacy wins, do you expect to be put on trial for being on the losing side?"

"Of course not," Mark denied with a dark frown. "Don't be absurd."

"Then why are the Sioux to be tried? The uprising was every bit as much of a war as the war between the states is. That they lost is punishment enough."

Mark laughed derisively. "Save your arguments for the trial. I think Viper will need them. Now heat water for a bath while I fetch the gown I brought."

"I don't need a bath, nor a gown. I want to be with my husband. He's been hurt and I don't want him to be all alone when he's in pain."

"He'll feel nothing for hours. Now I suggest you see to your bath or I will scrub that delectable body of yours clean myself when I return."

He slammed the door as he left the house, and Erica had the uncomfortable feeling he meant exactly what he said. After a moment's hesitation she flung open the door and carried the bucket to the well to draw water. As she returned to the house, she saw someone had moved Viper into the shade at the side of the house, and, grateful for that show of kindness, she braced herself for her next confrontation with Mark.

Just as Mark had predicted, it was nearly dark before Viper regained consciousness. His head was aching painfully. He tried to raise his hand to his forehead, but found his arms bound tightly behind his back. Half a dozen men were playing poker nearby, while the others napped or cared for their mounts. He'd been propped up against the side of the house, but by moving slowly, he managed to shift his position slightly. Unfortunately, he soon discovered there seemed to be no way he could find a comfortable pose.

His mouth still tasted of dirt. He remembered being struck from behind while Erica had stood by screaming as though she were the one who had been hit, but nothing else. There was no sign of her or the hostile officer. Mark, Erica had called him. So that was Mark. Imagine that! Mark had come for her and obviously did not like what he had found. That would not change what was, however.

One of the troopers looked up then and noticed Viper was awake. "Hey, chief, how ya' feelin'?" he called over to him.

Knowing it would be useless to reply, Viper looked away, his gesture a contemptuous one. He had not expected to be treated so badly, but now that he knew what the army's attitude was, he would not cooperate in the smallest degree. He began working at the ropes that bound his wrists. With luck, by nightfall he could set himself free. With that thought firmly in mind, he watched the men playing poker, his glance as arrogant and disdainful as it had always been when he had to deal with whites.


While Mark helped himself to another serving of venison, Erica continued to argue. She had bathed and dressed in the fine lingerie and pale pink gown he had provided, but she felt no differently than she had before she had changed her clothes. "I want to be with my husband," she stated firmly. "You had no reason to separate us."

"Nonsense. I had every right. The man's under arrest, you are not. I'm pleased to see you've learned to cook passably well. Not that you will ever have to do the

235

cooking in our home, but it will help you to direct the woman who does more knowledgeably."

"If all of the army's officers are so pig-headed as you, it is no wonder the Union is losing the war!" Erica cried out with an exasperated sigh.

"We are not losing," Mark contradicted sharply, then seeing no point in debating that issue since he could not support it with facts, he changed the subject abruptly. "Your father wished me to tell you he has quit drinking. If you think I am livid over your choice of mate, try and imagine introducing that savage to your father. Do you think you will ever succeed in winning his blesssing for such a ridiculous union?"

Erica straightened her shoulders proudly. She had yet to touch her dinner, but she had no appetite whatsoever for food. "That an Indian and a white woman would choose to marry might be unheard of in Wilmington, but it is not here in Minnesota. We plan to stay here."

"Moving from one humble dwelling to another as the owners return to their farms?" Mark inquired snidely.

"I've made no claim that this is our house. We have brought in the farmer's crop, though, and he should be grateful for that," she pointed out quickly.

"Why you would wish to marry a man who will dress you in hides and make you work in cornfields is beyond me. That is not the decision of a sensible woman, Erica, and you were always a most sensible sort."

"Until I wished to be married before you left for the war?" she replied sarcastically. "Was that when I took leave of my senses?"

"I have apologized for that," Mark admitted readily. "Had we married, we would not be sitting here in this tiny house arguing over your choice of husband."

"I want to see him," Erica demanded once again. "Post guards around the house, if you must, but I want him to spend the night here in the house with me."

Mark started to laugh and found it difficult to stop. He raised his napkin to cover his mouth as he tried valiantly to recover his composure. "You'll not spend the night with that heathen ever again, Erica. If it's a man you want in your bed, it will be me."

"You wouldn't dare!" she hissed.

"Not without an invitation, no, but as I recall, I have already received one." Mark smiled slyly, thinking he had just caught her in her own trap.

"That was a long time ago, Mark Randall, before I met Viper and became his wife. You had your chance, and you missed it."

"So, you are simply trying to pay me back for that imagined insult!" Thinking he had just scored an important point in their verbal battle, Mark's eyes glowed with fiery sparks of triumph.

"That was not an 'imagined insult,' it was a very real one." Disgusted with herself for remembering so clearly the shame she had felt that night, Erica turned her chair to the side so she did not have to face him.

She had combed her hair into a marvelous upsweep of radiant curls, and the style set off the exquisite beauty of her profile so perfectly that it took Mark a full minute to recall what they were discussing. By that time, all he wished to win was her love, not some ridiculous argument. "I went to your house the next morning. I had hoped to make things right between us, but you were gone, and I had no chance to apologize for upsetting you so badly. Will you forgive me now?"

"Don't you think it's a bit late for such a display of remorse? Why didn't you beg my forgiveness when you wrote to me, if you were so eager to make amends?"

Mark wadded up his napkin and tossed it upon the table. "Because I have as much pride as you," he responded regretfully. Rising to his feet, he circled the small table, took Erica's hands, and drew her up to face him. "We are a perfect match, my pet, and you know that as well as I do." He leaned down to kiss her, but Erica turned her head to avoid his lips, and his affectionate gesture landed upon her cheek.

"Please don't," the lovely blonde beseeched softly. "Just accept things the way they are and don't try and change them."

"You are asking the impossible," Mark responded truthfully.

Erica refused to allow herself to react to the tenderness of his manner and continued to voice her own pleas. "If you'll not let Viper spend the night here with me, will you at least let me go see him? I can scarcely be expected to carry on a coherent conversation with you when I am so worried about him."

Mark frowned darkly, disgusted that nothing he said had the slightest effect upon the willful Erica, but then it never had. "You may see him, but not alone."

When Mark turned toward the door, Erica hurriedly followed. He carried the lantern, and holding it aloft, lit her way. Viper was still sitting where he had been all afternoon. Cold and hungry, he had been given nothing to eat or drink when the soldiers had had their evening meal. He lifted a weary glance to Erica's face, and then, startled by the sight of her elaborate coiffure and expensive gown, he frowned. "If you have come to see me, madam, the least you could have done was bring along a few crumbs from your table. It is what I am used to eating."

In spite of himself, Mark Randall could not help but laugh, the Indian's request was so humorous. "Sergeant," he called out promptly. "Give the prisoner food and something to drink. We have plenty."

"Yes, sir," came a cry from the shadows near the fire the men had built to cook their rations.

Intrigued, Mark knelt down beside Viper, and still holding the lantern aloft, he looked him over closely. That the brave was so handsome was still unsettling, but now he realized he was bright, too, and that alarmed him all the more. "If you speak English so well, why wouldn't you talk with me earlier? It would have saved you a bad headache, if for no other reason."

Viper did not reply. Instead, he looked up at Erica, his glance a curious one as it again swept over her stunning apparel. She had on new slippers, and as she was holding her skirt slightly above her feet, he could see she was wearing new silk stockings as well. She looked like a princess, while he had been treated without the slightest respect. He had only to remind himself that she was white and he was Indian. Nothing would ever change that, nor the difference in the way they would always be treated. "You have already made your choice?" he asked sullenly, wanting to hear the words from her own lips.

"What choice?" Erica asked, confused by his question, but when Viper cast a significant glance toward Mark, she suddenly understood. Kneeling beside him, she wrapped her arms around his neck and buried her face in his ebony hair. "To love you is the only choice I will ever make. How can you doubt my love? Do you think if we are parted for a few hours I will forget you or how dearly I love you?"

That impassioned declaration of love was more than Mark could bear. He rose, and taking a firm hold upon Erica's arm, he yanked her to her feet. "That's more than enough of that disgusting display. Tell the savage goodnight." But before Erica could speak those words, he had pulled her away.

When Viper's hands were untied so he could eat, the soldier guarding him failed to notice how loose the rope had become. As he ate the unappetizing food, the brave reconsidered his plan to escape. It was clear to him that Erica was under as heavy a guard as he was, and while he still thought it likely he could make good an escape, he would not abandon her. The mention of a trial both puzzled and perplexed him, for he had never expected to be put on trial. If he was charged only with kidnapping Erica, he was certain she would say she had not been held against her will. If she were allowed to speak in his defense. On the other hand, he would not deny he had fought in the uprising when he had fought, and fought well.

The trooper guarding him took Viper's empty plate, then allowed him to relieve himself before he was again securely bound. This time Viper made no effort to break free. He would face whatever was to come as he always had: bravely. Erica would not desert him; he was certain of her love, but why hadn't she realized how her dressing in such elegant clothes would hurt him?

When Mark followed her back into the house, Erica moved as far away from him as she could. "Stay away from me," she warned. "I'll not share my bed with you, and if you force yourself upon me I'll see you're tried for rape."

"I mean only to see that you have all you require to spend a comfortable night." As though to prove that point, he added another log to the fire, then began to stack the dishes upon the table. "You didn't touch your dinner. I will leave it here in case you are hungry later."

"Please go." His presence in the house she had shared with Viper made her horribly uncomfortable, and Erica wanted to be alone with her thoughts. When Mark turned and walked toward her, she tried to back away, but she found the north wall of the small dwelling at her back.

A slow smile curved across Mark's lips as he made one last request. "I will leave you alone until morning, but only if you will kiss me goodnight."

Erica clenched her fists angrily at her sides. "I am Viper's wife, not your fiancée. Can't you accept that?"

"No," Mark replied in full honesty. "As far as I am concerned, you've had an Indian lover, not a husband. While I consider that regrettable, I told you I'd accept the blame for it. I also intend to make certain that our marriage will be a legal one, and that you'll never have need of any man but me ever again."

Erica did not try and escape him as his arms encircled her waist. His lips were soft and warm as they brushed hers, calling forth bittersweet memories of the love she no longer felt. She stood unyielding, showing not the slightest shred of emotion, until, finally discouraged, Mark dropped his hands to his sides and stepped back.

"I'm sorry," he apologized. "You've been through a terrible ordeal, and perhaps the worst is yet to come. I'll try and have more patience. Goodnight."

Erica watched him go without responding, for while the first days of the uprising had indeed been a horrible ordeal, the weeks she had spent with Viper had been paradise. She could not bear to think the man she loved would be placed on trial. "He is innocent, though," she whispered softly to herself. Then she realized that while his part in the uprising might have been brief, he must have fought as fiercely as any of the other braves. To make matters worse, surely the judges would be white, and after the despicable way the Indians had always been treated, what chance would Viper have in such a biased court?

Suddenly terrified by that thought, Erica ran to the door and called for Mark. In a moment he appeared, his expression a most puzzled one. "Yes, what is it?"

"Just what sort of trials are planned for the Indians who took part in the uprising?" Erica inquired breathlessly, her fears plain in her voice and anxious manner.

Disappointed she had not wished to say something personal to him, Mark became defensive. "I paid little attention," he began, "since my only concern was in finding you. The braves are being tried by a military commission. The trials had just begun when I left, so I know very little about them."

"A military commission?" Erica did not like the sound of that at all. "What punishment would such a prejudiced group think appropriate for the Sioux?"

She was already so upset, Mark did not want to add to her worries. "I told you, I paid scant attention to the trials. When we reach Camp Release you can get all the details you want."

When he turned away, their brief conversation over in his view, Erica ran after him. "No, wait. Tell me what little you do know," she implored him.

Mark turned slowly back to face her, his expression grim. "I heard they sentenced some braves to prison terms, while others will be hanged."

"Oh, dear God!" Erica cried, her heart leaping to her throat. "You'll have to let Viper go! Set him free. Say he got away from you. I'm the one you want, not him! Oh please, let him go!"

Mark was fast growing accustomed to taking the distraught blonde's arm and leading her into the house, and he did so again. As he closed the door, he cautioned her to be more discreet, while his own mood bordered upon rage. "I don't think any of the troopers overheard you. At least, I hope not. Viper is my prisoner, and I intend to see he is returned to Camp Release to stand trial. The commission will decide his guilt or innocence. Don't ask me to do it, because I would just as soon beat him to death with my bare fists as set him free. Now goodnight."

Before he could open the door, Erica threw herself against it to block his way. "You've seen how proud he is. Viper will never plead for his life, but I certainly will." The man she loved would hate her forever for what she was about to do, but he would be alive, and that was all that mattered to her. "Let him go and I'll do whatever you ask. I'll marry you tomorrow if you like. I'll go back to Wilmington and be the wife I once wanted to be to you. I promise I will. Just let Viper go, do it now, tonight!"

241

Mark was sorely tempted to take her up on that bargain, but he wanted her to come to him out of love, not out of misguided devotion to some devilishly handsome Sioux. "What has the man done that makes you so frightened for his life?"

"He's done nothing more than fight to insure the Sioux's right to exist. The government has broken all its promises to his people, and now to try them for protesting that mistreatment in the only manner left to them is obscene!"

Mark knew very little about the causes of the uprising. What he did know, however, was that hundreds of white settlers had been slaughtered. He was amazed that she would take the Indians' side against her own kind. "What is obscene, my darling, is to murder innocent women and children to make a point in a political argument. Think about that while you are packing whatever you wish to bring with you tomorrow. We are leaving at dawn, and I'll expect you to be ready to go."

Her spirits crushed after Mark had not even responded to her offer to marry him in exchange for Viper's life, Erica asked in a barely audible whisper, "Do I mean so little to you that you won't even consider setting Viper free?"

Rather than respond with words, Mark pulled her into his arms and kissed her with such brutal passion that he left her lips bruised when he pulled away. "No, my angel, I love you far too much to make you my wife for any reason save love." Having dashed her hopes completely, he left the house, but he took the precaution of posting a sentry at her door so she could not set Viper free herself now that he had refused to do so.

# Chapter Sixteen

## October, 1862

Neither Mark nor Viper slept well, but that Erica had not slept at all was readily apparent when the captain went to her door the next morning. Lavender circles marred the delicate skin beneath her eyes, and her thick lashes did not hide the fact that her lids were puffy as a result of too many tearful hours. While she held herself proudly, she seemed on the verge of tears still.

Not wanting to begin another round of arguments, Erica had chosen to wear her faded blue dress, since the new pink gown was far too fine for riding and she knew without asking that Mark would make her change her clothes if she tried to wear her buckskin dress for travel. She had taken care to pack the soft Sioux garment, the new gown, and the fine new lingerie in a pillow slip, and she had put Viper's extra clothes in the brightly painted rawhide carryall known as a parfleche, which he had brought with him.

She already knew the tomcat would be unwelcome on the trip and would have to be left behind, so she had left him the scraps of venison from the previous night's supper. Thinking the owners of the farm might return soon, she had left the quilt she had admired folded at the foot of their bed. She had kept the little house spotlessly clean, so she hoped when the farmer and his wife returned they would not be angry to find someone had lived there while they were gone. *If* they returned, she reminded herself, for it was possible they might be dead, or too

243

frightened of the Sioux to ever return.

"I'm ready to go," she announced wistfully, plainly reluctant to leave the small house in which she had been so happy. "I want to bring Viper's bow and quiver, and his rifle, too, but I don't know where they are."

"They were on the porch yesterday. I've already packed them with my gear." That the beautiful young woman he had found the previous afternoon had suffered so horribly during the night disturbed Mark greatly, for he wanted her always to be happy, as long as that happiness included him. She had obviously already executed Viper in her mind, but how long could she possibly grieve? he wondered. She was a sensitive young woman. Would she mourn for her Indian lover for several months, or as long as a year? That was a depressing thought, but Mark was confident he could eventually rekindle the fiery passion that had once burned so brightly within her heart when he had held her in his arms. That she had not been able to say she did not love him cheered him sufficiently to allow him to simply ignore the dramatic change in her appearance.

"Since they lost their home, your aunt and uncle are living in the back of their store while the town is rebuilt. I promised we would stop by to see them when I found you."

"No, that's impossible," the slender blonde pointed out sharply, greatly alarmed by that suggestion. "We can't take Viper there. It would be far too dangerous for him."

Mark placed his boot on the edge of the porch, striking a casual pose as he tried to appear calm while he forced back the angry outburst he wanted so badly to yell. Finally, he got control of his temper and responded matter-of-factly. "I'd say the people of New Ulm have every right to despise the Sioux, since so many of them lost not only everything they owned, but precious members of their family, as well. I don't want to create any kind of an incident, however. You and I will go into the town alone and leave the men in a secluded spot to guard your Indian."

"Yes, he is my Indian," Erica agreed with the first true smile Mark had seen from her. "I wish you would try and remember that." ·

"A poor choice of words," Mark apologized. "I brought along a horse for you. She is a gentle mare, and you should enjoy riding her."

244

Erica closed the door behind her, and without looking back, stepped off the porch. "Were you that confident you'd find me?"

Mark stood up straight, removed his hat to brush the hair off his forehead with his fingers, then replaced it and pulled the brim down low to shade his eyes against the morning sun. "Yes, I was. I swore that if you could be found, I'd not return to Camp Release without you."

Erica did not reply, for she knew Mark to be a determined individual who did not stray from a course of action once he had chosen it. He was dependable to a fault, which was commendable, but she wished just once that she could sway him to her point of view, since she knew her arguments were every bit as valid as his.

Having no clue as to her thoughts, this time Mark took Erica's arm in a tender clasp and escorted her over to where the men had tied their horses. "I would prefer to make Viper walk, but because I know you would give me no peace for it, I will allow him to ride. Don't encourage him to try and escape us, because none of us would think twice before shooting him in the back."

Even with the heavy burden of her own sorrow, Erica had noticed Mark had changed a great deal since they had parted. He was no less handsome, but there was a hardened toughness about him now, which was new. She did not like it, either. "What's happened to you, Mark? Is it now so easy for you to kill a man that it requires no second thoughts?"

Mark looked down into her beautiful blue eyes and feared for a searing instant that he might actually drown in their azure depths. Then he realized she was waiting to hear the answer to her question. "I'll admit it was difficult to shoot a man the first time I had to do it. The most difficult thing I've ever had to do, really, but after that, it was no different than shooting ducks. The Confederate soldiers are nothing more than human targets," he explained, without the slightest show of emotion to lighten the deadly import of his words.

Not wanting to hear any more talk about death, Erica turned her attention to the horses. "Is this the mare you brought for me?"

"Yes, we call her Sweetheart. I hope you like her."

"I'm sure I will," Erica agreed, but she quickly turned to

search the faces of the assembled men to find her husband. When she finally saw him at the end of the line of horses, he grinned and winked at her. In return, she mouthed only one word of warning: run. When he frowned then and shook his head slightly, she wanted to scream the word so he would understand it was the only chance he had.

That Erica and her Indian were communicating without words was obvious to Mark, and he moved to stop it immediately. He quickly gave Sergeant Maguire the order to mount up and keep a firm hold on the rope on Viper's stallion. Mark and Erica would ride two abreast behind the Indian with the troopers following them. The determined captain secured Erica's makeshift luggage and Viper's parfleche behind her saddle and helped her up upon the mare's back. The gentle chestnut horse responded readily to a light touch upon the reins, and confident Erica would have no trouble handling her, Mark mounted the dapple-gray gelding he had taken from Camp Release and got this rescue party under way.

The morning sun gave Viper's flowing black hair a radiant halo, and Erica did not take her eyes off him as they rode along. He was riding the stallion bareback as he always did, his posture proud and yet relaxed. How he could relax when they were in such terrible trouble Erica didn't understand. She could think of nothing but the trial that lay ahead, and she vowed she would testify until the judges grew so tired of listening to her extol Viper's virtues they would set him free. That plan did not raise her spirits, though, for she feared the judges would be swayed neither by the truth nor by reason where a brave was concerned.

Mark glanced over at Erica frequently, hoping to catch her looking at him, but she appeared to be completely absorbed in the Indian who preceded them. "He has a very fine horse," Mark stated, abruptly interrupting her solitude, knowing Erica would know exactly who he meant. "Do you know where he stole him?"

Erica turned toward Mark then, but her gaze was filled with fury rather than shining with the love he could not forget. "Viper is no horse thief," she responded emphatically. "The stallion was a gift from Little Crow."

"Ah yes, Little Crow." Mark nodded thoughtfully at the mention of the chief's name. "That bandit has fled to the Dakotas, leaving most of his braves to face the consequences of the uprising alone, while he mistakenly believes he'll go free. He's wrong. He'll be caught soon and sentenced to hang with the rest of them."

While the mention of hanging made Erica shiver with dread, she was anxious to learn more about Little Crow. "How did the uprising end, if Little Crow did not surrender?"

Mark described the Battle of Wood Lake, in which he felt he had played no significant part. He did give the Third Minnesota Regiment credit for triggering the ambush, however, and foiling Little Crow's plan of attack. "It was no more than blind luck that a few men took it upon themselves to go to the Upper Agency to gather potatoes. If they hadn't, we would have been gunned down while we marched along the road that morning. Little Crow could have claimed a stunning victory and the uprising would still be going on today. As it happened, though, when the chief was beaten he turned tail and ran, leaving the Sioux behind without the heart to continue a fight they must have known was futile at the outset."

"To fight meant far more to them than the eventual outcome," Erica mused aloud. Since Mark seemed interested in discussing the uprising, she briefly listed the Sioux's complaints, thinking if he understood their grievances more fully he would be more sympathetic to Viper's plight.

As he listened to the lithe blonde describe the treatment he had to admit was negligent, if not downright abusive on the government's part, he still could not agree that taking up arms had been the correct way to bring about an end to a long string of injustices. "The Indians' gold reached Fort Ridgely on August eighteenth, Erica, the very day the uprising began. If they had had the patience to wait one more day for the money owed them, none of this would have happened. Hundreds of lives could have been saved, but no, they did not wait."

Knowing it had been the senseless murders in Acton that had sparked the uprising, Erica felt doubly sad, for it now appeared the Sioux had made one bad decision after another. "They never had a chance," she whispered dejectedly. "Not from the day the government decided it wanted their land."

Mark opened his mouth to argue, then knew without

247

speaking that she would regard anything he might wish to say about opening up new lands for white settlement as indefensible. Perhaps it was, he had to admit, but only to himself, not to her. When they reached the point where the Cottonwood River flowed into the Minnesota, he kept his promise and left Viper there with the cavalry troops. He provided a stern warning that they were not to allow the wily brave to escape them, nor were they to harm him in any way. Satisfied the Indian would be safe for an hour or two, he then escorted Erica into what was left of New Ulm.

With little more than the commercial buildings on Minnesota Street left standing, the once thriving town looked lost and forlorn in the morning sun. As Erica dismounted in front of the dry goods store, her aunt came running out to meet her, tears streaming down her face as she greeted her dear niece.

"Oh Erica," she cried as she hugged her tightly. "We thought we'd never see you again! We're so happy to have you home." Britta turned then to Mark. "Did you kill the bastard who kidnapped her? Did you kill him?"

"No, ma'am, but he's my prisoner, and I'm taking him up to Camp Release for trial," Mark replied without daring to look at Erica, since he was certain he could accurately predict her reaction to that statement.

Karl Ludwig and Gunter came outside before Erica could speak, but she knew she could not allow her relatives to think she had been kidnapped when she had become Viper's wife instead. As shopkeepers from the adjacent stores came out to welcome her home, she was distracted for a few minutes as she responded to their greetings. The first minute she could, though, she suggested to the Ludwigs that they all go into the store to talk privately.

Mark slipped his arm around Erica's waist as he moved to her side. "As you can imagine, your aunt and uncle were amazed when I introduced myself as your fiancé." He flashed a taunting grin then, still hurt she had not told her relatives of his existence.

"Yes, we certainly were," Britta agreed, "but Ernst Schramberger was badly hurt by the news. He then assumed your engagement must have been the reason you'd always been so cool to him. Why did you keep such a secret, dear?" The charming woman led the way to the rear of the store where they had been forced to create a home

248

for themselves in the storeroom.

Chairs were brought for everyone, and as Erica sat down, she found herself the uncomfortable focus of three pairs of inquisitive eyes. She smiled shyly. "You all look well." They did, too, for all they had been through. It was Gunter's appearance that surprised her the most, for he had lost the last traces of his boyish innocence during the uprising. Clearly no longer the youth she had remembered, he was now a man, if still a young one. The handsomeness she had suspected he would one day have was even more pronounced than she had anticipated. She looked over at Mark then, uncertain how much to relate in answer to her aunt's question.

"Mark and I had a rather serious argument before I left Wilmington, and I was still so upset over it when I arrived here that I didn't feel engaged." That was at least the truth, even if it sounded like a feeble excuse for her behavior. She hoped someone else would have something to say, but her relatives simply sat regarding her with rapt gazes, while Mark sat silently at her side.

"There's something I must explain," she finally blurted out, no longer able to keep her love for Viper a secret.

"I wouldn't, if I were you," Mark warned darkly.

"But I must," Erica insisted. Gathering all her courage, she revealed how she had met Viper in the woods by the river and how when he had taken her from New Ulm she had stayed with him quite willingly, out of love. When she looked over at Gunter, she encouraged him to substantiate her story. "I still have the little cougar you made for me. In fact, I killed a cougar on my own, and Viper made me a necklace like his from its claws." Rather than respond, Gunter got up so quickly he knocked his chair over backwards as he rushed toward the back door, but the bitterness of his expression dashed what little hope she had that he would ever wish to see her again. Outwardly he might have become a man, but his first impulse was still the childish one to flee when confronted with a situation he couldn't accept.

Ignoring her son's hasty departure, Britta dried her eyes on her apron. "I don't know what to say. We were so frightened for you, and now to learn you actually enjoyed that monster's company, well, it is a blessing my sister did not live to hear about this disgrace."

"Aunt Britta, this is no disgrace," Erica contradicted her proudly. "I love Viper, and I plan to do all I can to see any trial he receives is a fair one, and that he is acquitted of all charges. He is my husband. I want to stay here in Minnesota, where I hope we'll be able to see you all often."

Karl rose from his chair as he angrily refused that request. "I can't listen to this rubbish a moment longer. I warned you that brave was no good the day he came into the store and had the gall to speak with you. Just look around. The shelves are all empty. We've precious little left to our names. We have to start all over again, because the years we've lived here don't add up to nothing now. If you think I'll invite one of the heathen dogs responsible for what we've suffered to share my table, you're dead wrong. Now go, get out of here before I call you the whore you obviously are!"

Mark leaped to his feet to defend his love from that hate-filled attack and his first punch caught Karl squarely on the chin. It did not knock the solidly built man down, but it staggered him. Britta began to scream as she moved between the two men and did her best to keep them apart. Knowing the store would rapidly fill with spectators for a fight, Mark grabbed Erica's hand and pulled her along behind him as he headed for the front door.

"Does that satisfy you? Every time you tell that ridiculous tale people will call you a whore, or worse! You can't go around claiming to be Viper's wife and get any respect at all!" He nearly threw her into Sweetheart's saddle, and knowing she would follow since they were returning to where Viper was being held, he rode out of town at a furious gallop.

While Sweetheart lacked the speed of the gray gelding, Erica kept Mark in sight as she followed. She was horribly upset at her aunt and uncle's reaction to her story, but she did not feel the slightest trace of shame. She was proud to be Viper's wife, and she would tell everyone who would listen what a fine man he was. Unfortunately, she feared few people would be willing to listen to praise for an Indian brave when the uprising had left no one in the Minnesota Valley unscathed.

Viper sent Erica a questioning look as she returned, but she did no more than shake her head sadly, and he knew whatever she had found in New Ulm, it had not been good.

After another meal of what he considered inedible rations, he was again given a boost to enable him to mount his horse with his hands tied, and their journey continued. When they crossed the river, he knew they were bound for Fort Ridgely, and he recalled how digusted he had been with their failure to take that important military outpost. They could certainly have used the cannons there so that they would not have been so badly outgunned time and again. As they rode along, he reviewed each of the battles in which he had fought. He had done his best to see they won, but after their initial victories, which he thought a result of the army's foolish mistakes rather than their own skill as warriors, the tide of the war had run steadily against them.

When they reached the fort, Viper was swiftly separated from the group and placed under a heavy guard. When Erica overheard a soldier remark he had seen the brave among those who had attacked the fort, she fought back her tears. She wondered how many other soldiers would remember her husband and be quick to testify against him—five, ten, perhaps dozens? She stood holding Sweetheart's reins until Mark came to her side. Her pain was nearly impossible to bear, but she was so weary from lack of sleep and the day's travel that she no longer had the energy to cry. "I've never heard of Camp Release. How far away is it?"

"It's another two days' ride if we make good time. I'd appreciate it if you would put on the gown I gave you and join me for dinner. There are other women staying here. Many lost husbands and children, so I'd advise you to keep the fact you do not despise Viper to yourself. I'm not simply trying to save you any further embarrassment, I think you might easily come to harm."

Disappointed that what he said was undoubtedly true, she nodded. "Yes, I understand. Viper will be under guard, so they will not be able to get to him but they could kill me quite easily."

While she was being far more melodramatic than he would have liked her to be, Mark agreed, "I'm glad you've decided to be sensible for a change. Perhaps that wretched scene in New Ulm had some value, after all."

"Don't you start on me, too, Mark. I've done nothing wrong, and neither has Viper." Following one of the soldiers stationed at the fort, Erica carried her small bundle of clothing to the enlisted men's barracks, which had been converted for use by women who needed temporary lodging. She said only that she was from New Ulm and turned all further questions aside, for she knew Mark's advice was worth heeding.

She bathed and dressed, attempting unsuccessfully to ignore the other women's envious glances when she donned her new clothes and piled her lustrous curls atop her head. When Mark came to escort her to supper, however, she found the few officers left at the post after Sibley's departure weren't so easily discouraged in their curiosity as the women had been. While too polite to ask her directly to recount in detail how she had spent the weeks of the uprising, they made many oblique references to the plight of captives, obviously expecting her to contribute her experiences to the store of tales they had heard from others. That she was so lovely a young woman, with such fine manners, only served to whet their appetites for her story, since they were certain it would be a very exciting and dramatic one.

Erica had no illusions about the officers' opinion of the Sioux, and she dared provide not even the smallest clue as to her feelings as she attempted to divert the conversation in another direction. "Frankly, I hope the uprising will soon be forgotten, so we can all carry on with our lives and look forward to happy futures," she offered with the most bewitching smile she could display.

Stymied in their attempts to enjoy her confidence, the officers exchanged disappointed glances and went on to discuss the Union's latest efforts to defeat General Lee. Relieved that she had finally succeeded in ending talk of the uprising, Mark reached beneath the table to give Erica's hand a comforting clasp. Her fingers were frightfully cold, and he kept them clasped tightly in his for a long moment before finishing his supper. At his first opportunity, he excused himself to walk her back to the barracks, giving the early hour of their departure as the reason for their brief stay in the officers' mess.

"I'm sorry," Mark apologized sincerely. "I expected them to show you more courtesy than that. Most of the captives are so overjoyed to be rescued that they have told their wretched tales again and again without any

252

prompting. It's clear those fools are not used to the company of a lady and put their curiosity above their manners."

"The only reason they considered me a lady is because I didn't reveal the truth," Erica reminded him. "I hated being so evasive, Mark, I just hated it. I can't keep the truth to myself at Camp Release when I want so badly to tell it to help Viper. If everyone wants to call me his whore, it won't matter. My reputation is a small price to pay for his life."

As they reached the door of the barracks, Mark drew Erica into his arms and whispered softly so his response would not be overheard by those inside. "It won't come to that, since I'll allow no one to insult you so rudely while I'm alive to prevent it, my darling. We can use the fact that you are so obviously a fine lady to request that you give your testimony to the commission in private. They are gentlemen who will keep your remarks in the strictest of confidence."

Even with that assurance, Erica's gaze was still filled with sorrow. "I can't let anything happen to Viper, Mark. Had it not been for me, I think he might be with Little Crow now. He'd be safe instead of facing a ridiculous trial before a commission that can't help but be biased."

Mark held her still more tightly, forcing her to rest her head upon his chest. Because of his hopes that they would soon marry, he found himself unable to say anything against the Indian when he knew it would displease her so greatly. "I will do all in my power to see he is given a fair hearing, Erica."

"Will you really?" the fearful young woman asked breathlessly. "I would be so grateful if you would help us. I have no one else to whom to turn."

That the radiant light of hope that suddenly lit her eyes came from her love for another man was still a painful sight, but Mark managed to nod. "I want you to be happy, my love. Can't you remember that?"

Erica reached up to kiss Mark's cheek. "Thank you. Maybe there is some hope for us, after all."

Greatly encouraged, she broke away from his embrace and hurried inside the barracks, leaving Mark aching with a loneliness he couldn't abide. He walked over to the stables where Viper had been left to bear the indignity of being housed with the horses. He excused the troopers

253

standing guard over the Indian for a few minutes, and as soon as they were alone, he hauled the well-built brave to his feet. Viper's hands were bound behind his back, but Mark considered that no reason to show him any mercy.

"I just promised Erica I would see you got a fair trial, but that's all I'll promise her." Mark then gave in to the furious impulse he had fought ever since he had first laid eyes on the arrogant brave. He drew back his fist and hit him with the most brutal punch he could throw.

Viper turned his head so Mark's fist caught him on his chin, or the blow would surely have broken his nose. Though dazed, Viper glared at Mark as he issued a challenge of his own. "Coward. If you want to fight, cut my hands loose."

"You aren't worth the trouble," Mark replied with a hostile sneer, but he had gained a strange sense of satisfaction from knowing he must have hurt Viper even if he hadn't knocked him down. "Erica Hanson is a fine lady. You're not fit to kiss her feet."

"I have done far more than that," Viper taunted him coldly. He saw Mark's next punch coming and tried to dodge it again, but it caught him above the left eye. His knees buckled, and he slid down into the straw. It infuriated him to know the only choice he had was to pretend to be unconscious if he didn't want to be beaten to death while his hands remained tied behind his back. He held his breath, forcing back the wave of nauseating dizziness that threatened to engulf him, until he heard Mark leave the small stall and the troopers return. One bent down to give his shoulder a rough shake, and he spit at him rather than warn him with words to keep his distance.

Since the captain had had the fun of abusing their prisoner, the trooper saw no reason not to follow his example. He straightened up, and taking careful aim, gave Viper a brutal kick in the ribs. "Sweet dreams," he taunted sarcastically as he turned away, and Viper could not draw the breath to insult him in reply.


As they prepared to leave the fort the next morning, Erica took one look at Viper's black eye and broke away from Mark to rush to him. A deep purple bruise marred the smooth flesh of the brave's left side, and she was appalled by the shocking evidence that he had suffered another beating.

"Who did this to you?" she demanded to know, clearly ready to give the culprits the same brutal punishment they had dealt out to him.

Viper did not reply, but his eyes narrowed as he looked toward Mark who was rapidly striding their way. Erica kissed him quickly, then whispered in his ear. "When I cause a disturbance, you must get away!"

Mark was at her side before Viper could acknowledge that plea, and she turned the full fury of her anger on him. "Is this how you promised to help us? Well, is it? Do you just plan to beat him so badly he'll not live to see Camp Release? Is that how you mean to see he avoids standing trial?"

While he was certain he wasn't responsible for the damage to Viper's side, Mark couldn't deny he had given him the black eye. "He and I had an argument last night. It doesn't concern you, though. Now let's get on our way."

When he reached for her arm, Erica pulled away to elude his grasp. "You bastard, you lied to me!"

"No, I did not," Mark insisted, disgusted to have her make such a scene in front of his men. She was high-spirited and used to speaking her mind, but no officer could keep the respect of his troops if he allowed a woman to give him a tongue-lashing in public. Knowing that, he spoke sharply to her. "We are leaving here immediately. If you aren't ready to go, then you will be left behind." He turned his back on her then, gave the order to mount up, and swung himself up into the gray gelding's saddle. "Well, are you coming with us, or not?" he called out to her, his tone still abrasive.

Erica looked up at Viper, her glance imploring him anew. She paused to give him another hasty kiss and again whispered, "You must get away." She then hurried to mount Sweetheart, but she refused to ride beside Mark. Instead, she maneuvered the mare in front of his horse, again following Viper as the troopers moved into place to begin the day's journey. Clearly distraught, she made no attempt to hide the blackness of her mood as she frantically searched her mind for a scheme that would create enough excitement to allow her badly battered husband to get away while he still had the strength to flee.

255

# Chapter Seventeen

## October, 1862

As they rode along, Erica's eyes strayed frequently to the river. Sweetheart seemed surefooted, but the determined young woman hoped that if she forced her too near the water's edge, the docile mare might slip in the mud. She would then have a split second to appear to lose her balance, slide from her mount's back, and topple headlong into the river. She was positive Mark would dive in after her, and Viper would have the chance he so desperately needed to break away.

As on the previous day's journey, Erica spent most of her time on the ride studying the play of muscles across her beloved's back. The brave's hands were tied in front of him and he rode as easily as he had the previous day, his fingers entwined in the black stallion's long mane. She was certain that were he to jab the horse in the flanks with his heels, urging him to break into a run, the powerful animal would be impossible for Sergeant Maguire to hold in check. Surely the stallion was far more swift than any of the mounts the army had provided, and he could swiftly elude the soldiers before they could either fire or give pursuit. The plan seemed plausible to Erica, and since the need for action was desperate, she began looking for a likely spot to carry it out.

Since Erica had taken pains to ride ahead of him, Mark kept his distance. He was not pleased, however. Viper's face and sleek body were deeply tanned, so he had not expected the punches he had given him to leave him so badly bruised. That was unfortunate, since he had promised Song of the Wren that he would say the brave had surrendered without a fight. Viper's appearance made that claim difficult to believe, but actually, the Indian had not tried to fight them when they had surrounded him at the farmhouse. It would have been far better if he had, for then Mark knew he would have been justified in shooting him. "I'll get you yet, you gray-eyed devil," he vowed softly under his breath. His right hand strayed to the smooth burl walnut handle of his Colt as he hoped the Indian would be foolish enough to give him a reason to use it.

When they reached the Redwood Ferry, Mark spent several minutes trying out various strategies in his mind before he gave the orders on how their crossing would proceed. He first sent Erica to the opposite side of the river with half the troopers. When the ferry was pulled back to the northeastern shore, he drew his Colt and kept it trained on Viper as the remaining troopers tugged on the rope to carry them across. He smiled at the Indian, silently daring him to try an escape, but Viper kept his eyes trained on the opposite shore where Erica stood waiting for them.

Once the group had reassembled on the southwestern bank of the Minnesota, they mounted their horses and continued the trip following the same order of march they had begun that morning. Erica drew the ends of Sweetheart's reins through her fingers as she took the place behind Viper. She was biding her time, but growing increasingly anxious. They had ridden only a few minutes past the ferry when she saw a cluster of trees ahead and was certain she would never find a better spot to pull off her ruse.

She pulled back on the mare's reins, gradually slowing the horse's pace to increase the distance between herself and Viper. She waited until Sergeant Maguire and the Indian had passed under the low-hanging limbs and were partially hidden from view before she gave her mare's reins a fierce yank, sending the good-natured horse careening backwards into Mark's gelding.

Sweetheart tried to avoid slamming into the gray horse by dancing sideways, and just as Erica had hoped, the mare lost her footing in the slippery mud at the water's edge. It was a simple matter then for Erica to throw up her hands as though she were terrified. She screamed and kicked away the stirrups, then simply rolled sideways off the mare's back and plummeted into the river. Kicking as best she could in the confining folds of the blue dress, she let the rapid current carry her out into midstream.

Having heard how Captain Marsh had tragically drowned not far from the ferry, Mark took the precaution of swiftly removing his hat, jacket, boots, Colt, and holster before he followed Erica into the water. His only thoughts were of her. A powerful swimmer, he began to close the distance between them swiftly, but he was astounded to discover she seemed to be swimming with the current in an effort to elude his grasp. He realized then in an instant what she had done, and cursed his own stupidity that he had not been smart enough to have one of the troopers ride between her and the river since she had refused his company.

While Mark pursued her, Erica floated easily downstream, not struggling, but gliding through the rushing water as though she were a freshwater mermaid fully at home in the river's depths. Her hair streamed out behind her creating a shimmering golden cape. When Mark at last overtook her she found the most difficult part of her plan was in attempting to appear grateful.

It was impossible to slap the gentle smile from her face in the water, but the instant Mark had succeeded in towing Erica to the shore he dragged her up on dry land and shook her so violently he nearly snapped her neck. "You crazy little fool! Grown men have drowned in that river," he screamed. "Is that damn Indian worth the sacrifice of your life?"

Erica stood reeling in Mark's savage embrace, fighting back her tears as his fingers dug into the tender flesh of her upper arms. "What do you mean?" she asked innocently when she was able to catch her breath and speak.

"What do you mean?" Infuriated by her feigned innocence, Mark shook her again, flinging droplets of water in all directions from her sopping curls. "You know damn well what I mean! You didn't fall into the river, you jumped, and you could have drowned. That brave isn't worth one minute of your time, let alone your life," he complained bitterly as he gave his jealousy free rein.

The bedraggled girl did no more than shrug. "I'm sorry you were so badly frightened, but to think I intentionally jumped into the river is ridiculous. Why would I do that?"

Before Mark could reply, they heard the sound of gunfire in the distance, and the terrified look that filled Erica's eyes told him all he wished to know. "I hope to God that was Maguire sending that blasted Indian to his reward." Taking her hand he started off in the direction they had come, but a trooper rode up with their horses before they had taken more than half a dozen steps. It was then Mark noticed the worn fabric of Erica's blue dress was nearly transparent, but since he had thrown off his jacket he had no way to restore her appearance to the modest one it had been. What his men must think of her he was disgusted to imagine, but knowing he would soon leave them behind when he returned to Delaware, he did not worry over their opinions of his beautiful, but maddeningly willful, fiancée.

When they reached the spot where Mark had left his clothes, there was no sign of the other troopers or Viper. Ignoring his wet socks, the irate captain jammed his feet into his boots, slammed his hat on his head, and strapped on his holster. He then tossed his jacket to Erica, who thought he meant for her to carry it and merely placed it across her lap.

"Put that on!" Mark insisted in a hoarse rasp. "Unless you want the men gawking at your breasts until your dress is dry."

Erica looked down, and finding the damp folds of the sheer garment outlined her curvaceous figure far too well, she pulled on the dark blue jacket without argument. Anxious to find out who had fired the shots and at whom, she started on up the path, but Mark overtook her and yanked Sweetheart's reins from her hands.

"Oh no, you don't," he cautioned belligerently, "I don't trust you not to try that stupid stunt again." He placed his gelding next to the river and led Sweetheart by his left side. "I will consider you a prisoner, too, since that is the way you behave."

Erica made no effort to deny his accusation, since she didn't care what he thought of her. When they rounded a curve and found Viper sitting in the dirt surrounded by the troopers, she didn't wait for Mark to give her permission to dismount, she leaped off the mare's back immediately and went to her husband's side.

Viper was attempting unsuccessfully to stem the flow of blood from the jagged cut his teeth had gouged in his lower lip when he had fallen from his horse. At that moment, he didn't know which galled him more, that he had been thrown, or that Erica seemed to think it was her responsibility to arrange his escape. He was a Sioux warrior, and a fine one. He didn't need a woman, and a white woman at that, to plan strategy for him. He had allowed her to do it simply because he had had no opportunity to argue wtih her about it. Still, he was disgusted with himself for failing to make good on his escape, since she was so determined to set him free. When Erica placed her hands on his shoulders, he pushed them aside and glared as angrily at her as he had at Maguire.

Misinterpreting the reason for the rejection of her attentions, Erica turned a furious glance toward the sergeant. "What did you do to him?" she asked accusingly.

"Why, I didn't do nothing, ma'am," Maguire replied with a satisfied smirk. "Your screams spooked his horse and he fell off. He must have hit his mouth when he landed in the dirt. I figure he'll be all right in a minute or two."

While Mark recognized that story as most definitely an exaggeration if not an outright lie, since it offered no explanation for the gunfire they had heard, he was wise enough not to ask Maguire for the truth while Erica was within hearing. "You look all right to me now, Viper. If you can't manage the stallion, then you can walk, but I've no more time to waste here. Get moving."

Erica didn't think twice before arguing with that order. "Can't you see the man's been injured? We might as well stop here to rest and have something to eat before we go on. We'll all feel more like making good time then."

"I am in command here," Mark reminded her sarcastically, but he had to admit they could all do with a rest. It would give his clothes a chance to dry, if nothing else, and since it was damned uncomfortable to ride in damp pants, he agreed. "We'll wait half an hour and no more, Erica. If Viper isn't up to sitting his horse by then, I'll tie him across the stallion's back like a sack of flour." Nodding to

260

the sergeant, he led the man away from the group and demanded he reveal the truth of the situation.

"Soon as your woman started to scream, the brave let out a yell that would have curdled the blood of an ox. He lurched by me and ripped the rope on the stallion clean out of my hands, but I managed to get off a couple of shots before he was out of range. Missed the Indian, but I nicked his horse's rump, and the critter started to buck something fierce and shook that red devil off into the dirt. He must have hit his mouth on a rock or a root, but I sure as hell can't take credit for his getting hurt."

"Your shot hit his horse?" Mark moaned in despair. "If you get another chance to fire at him, aim higher!" He stalked off then to inspect the stallion's wound. The horse would make a fine mount for a soldier, and the army was too short of horses to wound one accidentally. Fortunately, he found the animal had only been grazed by the bullet, but his glistening hide would be marred as badly as though he had been carelessly branded.

The stallion shied away from Mark's touch, his glance as suspicious as his owner's had always been. "Don't worry," the captain offered in a soothing tone, "the salve we use on the men will surely work on you, too." He went to his saddle bags for the jar of medicinal cream, but he tossed it to Maguire and told him to see to the horse rather than taking care of Viper's stallion himself.

Erica paid no attention to the activity of the troopers as they prepared to eat the midday meal a few feet away. She continued to kneel in front of her husband, hoping they would have a few minutes to discuss their next move without being overheard. That Viper had fallen from his horse's back made not the least bit of sense to her, since she knew him to be an excellent rider. Of course, with his hands bound, he would not have had his usual balance, and she thought perhaps that had caused him to be unnaturally clumsy. Whatever his problem had been, she feared she would not have another chance to distract Mark from what he seemed to consider his sacred duty to deliver Viper to Camp Release for trial.

Viper watched Mark walk off with Maguire, then spoke to Erica in a hoarse whisper. "Do not try to help me again. Did you really think I would leave you with Mark? Had I gotten away, I would only have had to come back for you."

261

While Erica was stunned by the bitterness of his tone, she wasn't ready to give up her efforts to set him free. "You don't understand. If you are tried for taking part in the uprising, you could hang! I would jump in the river a hundred times if I could keep you from reaching Camp Release, because I don't trust the army to give you a fair trial."

"No trial for an Indian has ever been fair," Viper agreed with a sullen frown. "But I must be the one to say where and when I will break free, if I decide I must."

"You already know that you must!" Erica scolded, for she had no patience with his domineering attitude when his situation was so dire. "I'll try and think of something else, some other way to help you get away," she whispered anxiously.

"No, it is too dangerous for you," Viper insisted, his mood deadly serious, too. Then seeing by her determined expression and knowing she would do as she pleased, he realized he would have to refuse her help more emphatically. "No Sioux warrior wants his woman fighting his battles. Do not disgrace me by doing so ever again," he commanded with an arrogant sneer. With a display of his usual agility, he rose to his feet before finishing what he had to say. "I will tell you what to do, but you are never to tell me!"

Overhearing that remark, Mark couldn't help but laugh. "You are wasting your breath arguing with Erica. Haven't you learned that much by now?"

Viper spit at the ground, clearing his mouth of the last of the blood from the deep cut in the tender flesh of his lower lip. Considering that rude gesture his reply to Mark, he turned his back on Erica and walked over to the trooper who usually brought him his food and waited for him to untie the rope that bound his hands and give him something to eat.

Embarrassed that Viper had walked off and left her, Erica gratefully accepted the hand Mark offered to help her rise to her feet. He had taken off his shirt and laid it over a bush to dry, and the sight of his bare chest with its thick mat of tawny curls startled her. She was used to seeing Viper without a shirt, and while his deeply bronzed chest was smooth and hairless, he had never looked nearly so undressed as Mark did now.

Seeing the surprise in her glance, Mark accurately guessed its cause. "I did not think it would bother you to have me go without a shirt, since that savage never bothers to wear one."

Since Mark's build was an attractive one, the sight of him half clothed was not unpleasant, but Erica had no wish to pay him compliments, since they would only encourage the attentions she did not wish to receive. "You just surprised me, that's all." She looked down at the front of her dress rather than meeting his gaze. The fabric was still damp and stained where she had knelt in the dirt.

"Do you want to put on your other dress?" Mark asked considerately, knowing how fastidious Erica had always been about her appearance.

Surprised that he would suggest such a thing, Erica failed to realize he meant the pink gown rather than the buckskin. "You wouldn't object to my wearing it?" she asked rather shyly, still finding it difficult to lift her gaze above the broad expanse of his bare chest.

"Why should I object? There's still enough time for you to change your clothes and have something to eat."

"All right, thank you." Erica hurried to Sweetheart and untied the pillowslip that contained her other clothes. She moved behind the clump of bushes where Mark had draped his shirt and quickly tore off the damp blue gown and replaced it with the soft buckskin dress. She had lost her old slippers in the river and she put on her moccasins to replace them. That her undergarments were damp couldn't be helped, but she felt so much better to be wearing a clean dress that she was smiling as she returned to the men. When Mark looked at her with a menacing glare, she realized instantly that they had not understood each other.

"The pink gown is far too special to wear for riding. I'm sorry if you thought that was what I meant to put on."

Hearing a snicker, Mark turned to find Viper smiling widely despite the cut in his lip, which had now begun to swell. The bastard was actually gloating over the fact that Erica had chosen to wear the dress he had given her rather than the pink gown, which had been a present from Mark. That was more than the usually supremely confident captain could bear in silence. "Just what are you staring at, Indian?"

"My wife," Viper responded, finally replying to one of Mark's questions with words rather than a darkly challenging stare.

Mark would have gone for him then and there, but Erica grabbed hold of his arm so tightly he could not shake her free. "Come sit with me while we eat," she invited graciously, but she would not have turned him loose had he refused.

Cursing under his breath, Mark grabbed enough jerky and biscuits to share and followed Erica to a shady spot some twenty feet away from the others. "That is the most obnoxious man it has ever been my misfortune to meet. How can you stand to be around him?"

Erica laughed at that observation, since it held more than a grain of truth. "He can be obnoxious, I'll grant you that, but he is also very bright and fun loving, as well."

"And I am not?" Mark asked pointedly.

Erica had no wish to fight with her former fiancé and again placed her fingertips upon his arm, her touch light and sweet this time. "You have many wonderful qualities, too, Mark, but really there is no comparison between you and Viper. It would be easier to compare smoke to wind than you to him."

"Of course, I am the smoke," Mark remarked with an exasperated sigh. "Do I do nothing more than blacken your clothes and bring tears to your eyes?"

Since jerky had never been one of her favorite foods, Erica handed the strip he had given her back to him and nibbled upon one of the hard biscuits instead. "Those were merely two things that are difficult to describe, Mark. I do not think of you as smoke and Viper as wind."

"Should I be pleased by that?" Mark inquired snidely before ripping off another bite of the tough dried meat.

"Suit yourself," Erica responded disappointedly, for she had no patience with his self-indulgent mood. The flavorless biscuit broke apart in her hand and she tossed the crumbs away for birds to gather, since she found it so unappetizing herself. "Let's not play games with each other. I meant what I said, I'll make whatever bargain I must to convince you to set Viper free. You don't care what part he played in the uprising. You hate him only because he fell in love with me. That's no crime, Mark. Set him free tonight while the others are asleep. They won't guess the truth if you don't tell them."

Mark laid the jerky aside as he appeared to give her words more serious consideration than he had the first time she had made that astonishing offer. Finally he turned to face her, his gaze mirroring the depth of his disappointment that she seemed to care so little for his feelings. "What do you plan to do if I agree, spend your whole life pretending we are happily married when you would much rather be another man's wife?"

His question was a valid one, and knowing it deserved a truthful answer, Erica chose her words carefully. "I know I would not be unhappy with you, Mark. You are a fine man. We could make a life together, if only you would agree to set Viper free. Won't you please do it?"

"Kiss me," Mark dared her suddenly. "I want to see just how good an actress you are before I take you to bed."

While she was stunned by that taunt, Erica swallowed her pride and leaned toward him. She raised her hands to his shoulders, then slipped her fingers through the curls at his nape as she had done so many times in the past. In a futile attempt to shut out all thought of the man she adored, she kissed Mark with what she hoped would be a close enough imitation of the way she had once felt about him to make him regard her as a very fine actress indeed.

His heart overflowing with desire as her lips touched his, Mark leaned forward, forcing Erica down into the grass. He deepened the kiss she had begun and languidly made it his own. While he knew he would never have his fill of her, he would not make her his wife at the cost of his pride. It did no good to tell himself that even if Viper's image never left her heart, he would be the one to share her bed and father the beautiful children she was sure to have. He could not allow Viper to go free when he wanted the man dead, forever beyond her reach. When at last he drew away, he shook his head, but the excuse he gave her was a long way from the truth. "I can't agree to your terms. The man's a killer, and I won't have the blood of his innocent victims on my hands, not even to make you my wife."

Strangely, Erica had expected Mark's answer, but that made his coolly worded rebuff no less humiliating to bear. Knowing how stubbornly he would cling to a decision once he had made it, she decided she would have to accept the sorry fact that he would never help her, and drop the subject of marriage. Despite Viper's angry insistence that he did not want nor need her help, Erica was still determined to provide it. If not before they reached Camp Release, then she would find a way to do it after they arrived.

Viper was seated and eating between two troopers who were barely out of their teens. Their rifles were carelessly balanced across their laps as they gave their full concentration to chewing the long strips of highly spiced jerky they had been given for lunch. Despite their inattention, the brave was not tempted to disarm either of the young men, for Sergeant Maguire was standing nearby with his rifle trained at his head. The Indian was paying no attention to the threat posed by the sergeant, however. He was far too busy watching the conversation taking place between Mark and his wife. While he could not overhear their words, he could tell by the intensity of her expression that the topic was an important one to her.

When the captain leaned across Erica, forcing her to lie down in the tall grass as he kissed her, Viper tossed his uneaten jerky aside. Seething with jealousy, which swiftly erupted into a furious rage, he forced himself to breathe deeply and wait until the man had left Erica alone in the shade and started toward the seated circle of soldiers. When Mark got within five feet of him, Viper leaped to his feet, exploding in a screaming fit of anger as he lunged for Mark's throat.

"She is my wife!" he proclaimed loudly, so no one would misunderstand why he had jumped the officer.

While he had foolishly allowed Viper to catch him off guard, Mark tossed his Colt aside and waved Maguire off, unwilling to allow the sergeant to end the fight before he had had a chance to show he could handle the brave himself. He knew the Indian had every reason to hate him, but he despised the brave as well and was eager to fight him. They were near equals in size, although he was slightly taller, but Mark realized too late that Viper was far stronger. The grip of the wily Indian's hands was like hot bands of iron around his throat, choking him so badly that his knees buckled and he pulled Viper down with him as he fell to the ground.

Scrambling astride Mark, Viper released his stranglehold upon Mark's throat and began to slam his fists into the officer with a series of blows so punishing that he quickly turned his once handsome face into a blood-red mask. Mark could do little but throw up his arms to defend himself as he struggled simply to refill his lungs with air. He had not been in a fistfight since childhood, and it was now pathetically obvious to him that Viper knew how to fight every way but fair.

Erica watched in horror as the soldiers got to their feet to surround the men struggling in the dirt. They were shouting rude words of encouragement and whooping with glee. None appeared to notice that their commanding officer was getting a terrible beating, as the fight was proving to be so wonderfully entertaining. Certain the fools would allow Viper to beat Mark to death and then feel justified in shooting the brave for murder, she dodged past them. Leaping upon Viper's back, she grabbed two handfuls of his gleaming black hair and pulled with all her might. Not only did that frantic tactic fail to dislodge him, he seemed not even to notice her presence and continued to pummel Mark with vicious blows.

Not about to give up her efforts to separate the two men, Erica let go of Viper's hair, slipped her right arm around his throat, and used her left to apply pressure. That barely slowed the Indian, but at least he did notice she had climbed on his back and he made a futile effort to pull her off with his left hand while he continued to beat Mark senseless with his right. He swore at her, but in his own tongue, so she understood only the outrage of his mood, not the meaning of his words. She wrapped both arms around his face then, succeeding in blinding him momentarily, and Maguire came to his senses long enough to fire into the air.

"That's enough, chief," the sergeant shouted in the calm that followed the loud report of his rifle. "Back off. I reckon the captain will admit you won the fight if you give him the chance to speak up."

Erica moved out of the way quickly, but when Viper turned toward her, his features were still contorted with fury. "You should have stayed out of it!" he scolded harshly. "He did not deserve your help."

"I was trying to help *you!*" Erica shouted right back at the infuriated brave. "Did you think you could kill Mark in front of a dozen witnesses and live to tell about it?"

267

The blackness of Viper's stare did not lighten, for he had not stopped to consider the consequences of his actions before he had taken them. "No man is going to kiss you in front of me and live to tell about it, either!" he screamed right back at her.

Erica turned her back on the belligerent Indian, only to find the soldiers were enjoying their argument every bit as much as they had enjoyed the fistfight. "What are you staring at?" she snapped. When they began to chuckle amongst themselves, she finally remembered Mark, and looked down to find him staring up at her, too. There was a cut above his left eye, which was sending blood streaming down the side of his face. His nose was bleeding profusely, and there was blood trickling from the corner of his mouth.

"You look like hell," she informed him peevishly, and disgusted with him, too, she walked over to the river and bent down to wash her face and hands. When Mark knelt at her side she ignored him, since she was thoroughly ashamed to have offered herself to him to help an obstinate Indian who suddenly seemed to regard her as a possession rather than as the one true love of his life. He was too proud for his own good, and she feared all his pride would buy him was a grave.

Mark's whole body was wracked with pain, and he felt himself a great fool for ever having been so stupid as to have gotten into a fight with Viper in the first place. At least he had not lost any teeth, although a couple felt loose. He splashed water on his face but succeeded only in transferring a shower of blood to his hands. "The man fights like a demon," he moaned through badly swollen lips. "How does he make love?"

Erica's first impulse was to tell Mark it was none of his damn business, but she was too hurt and angry for such a show of restraint or tact. Instead, she lowered her voice to a honey-smooth whisper. "Like a god, Mark, like Eros himself. He could give you lessons in that, too!" With that insulting reply, she gave him a savage shove that sent him toppling into the river, where the blood from his battered face was completely washed away before he could find the strength to pull himself out on dry ground.

# Chapter Eighteen

## October, 1862

When they stopped to make camp that afternoon, Erica knelt beside the river and scrubbed the dirt from her blue dress. She hoped it would last another few days, even if the fabric of the once elegant gown had worn so thin it now resembled lace. She had had such a pretty wardrobe when she had come to Minnesota, but all her clothes had been lost in the fires that had consumed so many of the homes in New Ulm.

At the memory of the unfortunate reunion with her relatives, the distraught girl's eyes filled with tears, for she knew the Ludwigs had suffered terribly, and she could not fault them for not understanding how she could have fallen in love with an Indian brave in the midst of an uprising that had cost them so dearly. Depressed by the fact that she would be unlikely ever to find anyone who would understand her love for Viper, or even be sympathetic to her feelings, she continued to sit by the river long after she had finished her laundry, hugging her knees and trying to ignore Bill Harding, the young trooper who, at Mark's insistence, had been closer than her shadow all afternoon. A talkative soul, he had kept up a steady stream of conversation as he rode along beside her. Now that they had stopped for the night, he still seemed to think it his duty to keep her company.

Erica tried to be kind, telling herself the young man probably had had few opportunities to talk to young women of late. She had had no idea the men of the Third Minnesota Regiment had so recently been prisoners of the Confederacy until he told her so, but that they had returned to their home state only to find a war raging there had naturally inspired them to fight all the harder to prove their worth. From Bill's casual comments about Mark, however, Erica correctly surmised that these men had not fully accepted him as a substitute for the fine group of officers still being held by the South as prisoners of war.

"Are you hungry, ma'am?" Bill asked politely. "The fish must be done by now."

Erica glanced over at the good-natured corporal, wondering if his enthusiastic outlook on life ever faltered. His attention was eagerly focused upon the fire the men had built to roast their catch, and he looked ravenously hungry even if she still had no appetite. "Please go ahead and get yourself something, but nothing for me. I'm not hungry," she replied listlessly.

"It'll just take me a minute, ma'am." Bill excused himself and hurried over to the fire to make certain he was not forgotten when the men began dividing up the fish.

Mark had spent the most miserable afternoon of his life trying to ride without weeping over the sharp pains that encircled his chest. With each step his mount took his torment had grown more acute, until he had had to call a halt to the march a good hour before he had planned to. When he saw Bill taking only one plate, he relieved him of the task of guarding Erica and carried her supper over to her with his own.

"You'll have to eat something," he directed firmly. "this is the third day we've spent together, and you've eaten so little I'm afraid you'll soon fall ill." He handed her a plate heaped with flaky bits of fish and two of the thick corn cakes one of the men had baked over the coals. "At least you know this is fresh, and it's got to taste a lot better than jerky or salt pork."

Erica winced as she glanced up at Mark, for his left eye was swollen shut and the rest of his face was so badly cut and bruised she would not have recognized him had she not known it was he. "How are you going to ride into Camp Release looking like that?" she asked, hoping to divert his attention from the supper she doubted she would have the energy to eat.

"I'll be badly embarrassed, but I'll make it." Mark tried sitting crosslegged, but when that proved too painful he stretched out on his left side. "Forgive me, I think that Indian of yours cracked a couple of my ribs, if he didn't shatter them outright."

That Mark was in even worse shape than he had at first appeared appalled Erica, but she still thought it was his own fault. "Viper is as jealous of you as you seem to be of him. What did you expect him to do when he saw you kissing me, look the other way?"

Mark attempted a smile, but his expression more closely resembled a grimace. "Frankly, I forgot all about him while we were kissing. That's a mistake I won't make again, ever."

When Mark split open a corn cake and stuffed pieces of fish inside to make a sandwich, Erica followed his example. She took a couple of bites, but whether it was lack of appetite or her companion's gruesome appearance that made the food so unappealing, she didn't know. She set her plate aside and waited for Mark to finish eating. "If you'd like more, please take mine," she offered generously.

"That's all you're going to eat?" Mark didn't wait for her reply before he replaced his empty tin plate with her full one. He had to eat slowly, but he was hungry despite the tortures that plagued his body. "What do you think of Corporal Harding? Would you like him to accompany you again tomorrow, or should I choose someone else?"

Erica didn't have to give that question any thought before she replied, "Harding has tried his best to keep me amused, but I'd much rather have my husband's company than anyone else's. Can that be arranged?"

Since Mark had been hoping she would ask to ride with him again, that answer left him bitterly disappointed. "No, it can't," he refused immediately.

Knowing full well how little good it would do to argue with him, Erica made no attempt to change Mark's mind. Instead, she scanned the campsite looking for Viper, but when she found him, he was watching her with so threatening a stare that she had to turn away. He was clearly furious again, or still. He had usually been so charming a man that it had never occurred to her that he

271

would react with such brutal hostility to the other men she knew. Of course, Mark was not simply another man, he was the man she had promised to marry. Perhaps it was only natural for Viper and Mark to despise each other, but being caught in the center of the fierce waves of hatred that flowed between them was horribly unpleasant for her. In her opinion, her behavior was above reproach. Viper had no grounds to be jealous, and Mark no longer had any right to be.

"I want to go for a walk," she announced suddenly.

Mark moaned. "Christ almighty, Erica, I can barely move, let alone walk."

"Fine, then you stay here." Erica rose, and without giving him the chance to accompany her, she started off in the direction they would go the next morning. It was almost dusk, and cool, and after two days of the steady company of a dozen men she wanted only to avoid, she was eager to spend some time by herself. Unfortunately, she had not gone far before she heard Corporal Harding calling her name. Exasperated, she waited for him to catch up with her.

"I planned to walk by the water, Corporal, so it's impossible for me to become lost. You needn't come with me."

Flustered by that greeting, since Mark's orders that he accompany her had been explicit, Bill shrugged his shoulders helplessly. "You shouldn't be out walking by yourself, ma'am. No telling who or what might be lurking around here."

"I'll take my chances," she responded with a defiant toss of her long curls. She continued her walk then, and when Bill followed at a discreet distance, she simply pretended he wasn't there until she was ready to return to the camp. "I'm going back now," she called as she walked past him, quickening her stride so that he would have to hurry, too. When she arrived back at the camp, nothing had changed. Mark was still lying on his side where she had left him, his scowl every bit as dark. Viper's glance was no less accusing, and Erica felt no more relaxed or refreshed for having gotten some exercise.

"Is there an extra bedroll for me?" she asked the battered captain.

272

"Of course," Mark assured her. "Bring Miss Hanson her bedroll, Corporal."

"Yes, sir." Bill dashed off to get it, hoping the troublesome blonde was going to sleep so he would have a chance to play cards that night with his friends.

When Bill returned with the blankets, Mark quickly dismissed him and saw to Erica's needs himself. "I'm sorry I can't offer you something better than this. I hate to have you sleep on the ground."

"It won't be the first time," Erica confided flippantly.

Mark knew he had made a serious mistake in the way he had tried to handle their situation, but he'd be damned if he would apologize. He struggled to his feet, and made an effort to help the obviously agitated Erica straighten out her makeshift bed. Not wanting to continue what had become a running verbal battle, he waited until she had fallen asleep before he brought his bedroll over and placed it beside hers. He ached in too many places to get comfortable, but having her close made the few hours he did sleep almost pleasant.

Even after another day of Corporal Harding's lively company, Erica was filled with dread when they reached Camp Release late the next afternoon. She was sick with a terrible apprehension, which far outweighed mere foreboding, and also dismayed to find the army had no more than tents and wagons at the site. A nearby rise was covered with the tepees of the Indian camp, but she doubted she could find the one she had shared with Viper. Knowing even if she had managed such a feat that Flowers of Spring would not be pleased to see her, Erica did not ask Mark if she could stay in the Indian encampment rather than the army's. When he showed her to a tent with two cots, she did not bother to ask who would be occupying the other before she chose one, lay down, and fell sound asleep. Mark was feeling so much better, he just laughed at her fatigue, but he was greatly relieved she had not refused to share the tent, as he had been certain she would have had he announced he was its owner.

It was nearly noon when Erica awakened the next morning. She pushed her tangled hair out of her eyes, but her wide yawn ended abruptly when she saw Mark seated upon the cot opposite hers. He was polishing his boots, so

273

at home in the small canvas structure that she realized instantly it must be his. "Why didn't you tell me this was your tent? You must have known I'd ask to sleep elsewhere."

The swelling in Mark's face had gone down sufficiently for his expressions to be recognizable. His smile was taunting as he replied, "Since you didn't mind sharing a farmhouse with an Indian, I saw no reason why you would refuse to share a tent with me."

"Well, you were dead wrong!" Erica scrambled off the cot, then, feeling dizzy from the meager diet she had consumed on the journey, she had to sit down again. Her blue dress was badly wrinkled and she knew she must look a fright, yet the state of her appearance was a small problem that day. "I want to take a bath and get dressed. Then I want to meet with whoever is in charge of the trials. The sooner I can convince him to let Viper go, the sooner we can leave and continue our lives."

Mark set aside the rag he had been using to buff the sheen on his boots to a high gloss and pulled them on, taking his time before he replied. "I'll take you over to the tent the women are using for bathing, but I can't promise Coloney Sibley will have the time to see you today. He's in charge of Camp Release, even if he isn't sitting on the commission himself."

"If he isn't running the commission, then what's the point of wasting my time and his?" Erica argued. "I need to speak with the officer who has the power to let Viper go. Your jealousy kept you from seeing reason, but that man ought to be more objective about my husband."

"Erica," Mark began with unconcealed impatience, "you can't walk around this camp calling that brave your husband. After what happened with your aunt and uncle, can't you understand that? The captives who have stayed here plan to testify against the Indians who murdered their husbands and children. They will not take kindly to your calling Viper your husband. You had sense enough to keep still at Fort Ridgely, and you'll just have to do the same here."

"Don't patronize me!" Erica shouted, then, not wanting their argument to be overheard, she lowered her voice to a threatening whisper. "Just what do you suggest I do, simply sit idly by and allow the commission to sentence Viper to death for the crime of being a Sioux? How can you ask such an impossible thing from me? I love the man, and I plan for our marriage to last a lifetime, not just a few short weeks."

"That might be all the time he has left," Mark pointed out darkly. "Since I know you are not going to keep still, I will ask Sibley to keep what you tell him in the strictest of confidence. If he feels Viper is innocent, then he can influence the commission on his behalf."

"Will he do it?" Erica asked excitedly, eagerly seizing that hope.

Mark shrugged. "He is a reasonable man, so I know he will listen to you if you can remember your manners and not insult him constantly the way you do me. There's also the matter of evidence, or testimony of witnesses who might have seen Viper during the uprising. Despite your obvious passion for the man, you can't know much about him, or what he was up to prior to the time he kidnapped you."

"Rescued," Erica corrected sharply. "It was a rescue, not an abduction." Or at least she would swear that was the truth, even though that had not been her opinion at the time. She took care to rise from the cot more slowly as she stood. "Please speak to Sibley about an appointment. Now about that bath?"

"Of course." Mark carried Erica's clean clothing and provided her with an escort to the bathing tent, then waited outside for her. Now that the uprising was over he had little to do and wanted to leave for Delaware as soon as he could possibly arrange for a transfer back to the Army of the Potomac. He would not leave Minnesota without Erica, however.

Pacing back and forth with a restless stride, Mark mentally played out a variety of schemes, hoping to discover a means to convince Erica to be discreet when it came to describing her relationship with Viper. It was not simply the fact that he did not care to be the laughingstock of the entire camp for having a fiancée who preferred to describe herself as an Indian's wife. That so-called marriage was over as far as he was concerned, and he planned to focus his attention squarely upon the future.

275

He knew he was right in believing he could more readily win back Erica's love if he were considerate of her feelings, rather than simply his own. In his view, Viper's fate was already sealed, so he had only to bide his time and appear to be a sympathetic friend to Erica while he did it. When she reappeared in her new pink gown, still shaking out her damp curls, he quickly took her hand and led her to a quiet spot where they could discuss her situation again before he sought out Sibley.

"I've had an idea. I think it is a good one, and all I ask is that you hear me out before you make any decisions," he requested as he gave her fingers an affectionate squeeze.

Knowing his feelings, Erica was naturally suspicious of his motives and withdrew her hand from his as she replied. "I won't promise a thing."

Mark chuckled to himself, thinking the willful young woman would never change. "It occurred to me that Sibley might become as upset as your aunt and uncle if you introduce yourself as Viper's wife."

Instantly on the defensive, Erica held up her hands. "You might as well stop now, Mark. I don't like the sound of this."

"No, just listen until I finish. Why couldn't you tell just part of the story? Say that you knew Viper before the uprising, and while you were with him he treated you very well, but like an older brother, or an uncle. Naturally you would not want to see him come to any harm. If you put it that way, it makes your interest in the savage sound more charitable than passionate. It also spares your reputation, and it will actually help Viper, in that it won't make anyone despise the man for seducing a white woman."

"I was not seduced!" the feisty girl swiftly contradicted, but she had to admit Mark's suggestion had some merit. She could not fault his reasoning, for she knew full well that the fact she had willingly taken an Indian as her husband could be counted upon to provoke the worst of responses in someone prejudiced against the Sioux, as every army officer in the state of Minnesota could be assumed to be. She chewed her lower lip nervously, unable to look at Mark as she replied. "I don't mean to sound conceited, but I'm far too pretty for that tale to be believed. Won't Colonel Sibley take one look at me and know Viper and I must have been doing more than carrying on polite conversations?"

"Wear your hair down loose as you have been. Then you will look younger than your seventeen years. The pink gown is a bit too sophisticated for this ploy, but since it is all you have, it will have to do. I think the innocence of your attitude will be what sways him. You are so obviously a lady it will not occur to him that you are stretching the truth well beyond its limit."

Erica considered his advice thoughtfully, horribly discouraged that the truth seemed to have so little value, but she knew no matter how many people were outraged by her love for Viper, she would love him still. "I'd much rather tell the truth, Mark. I've never been the conniving sort, you know that."

She looked so pretty and sweet, her damp curls caressing her cheeks as his kisses once had, and for a second or two Mark found it difficult to recall what they were discussing. Then he cleared his throat and continued his argument, "No, you have always been extremely direct for a woman, but in this instance, I am positive discretion will serve you better. Let's find something to eat, then I'll see if Sibley can make time for you this afternoon."

Obviously reluctant to agree, Erica finally gave in. "Yes, let's get this over with before I lose my nerve."

"I'll be there to back you up. Don't worry so." Mark's arm encircled her shoulders tenderly as he helped her to her feet. He then gave her a comforting hug. "You know you can depend on me to help you all I can."

While she was so preoccupied with worry she was barely listening, Erica thanked him for his kindness. "I would do the same for you, Mark. I want to see you are happy, too."

Mark's smile grew wide at that remark, for he was confident he could continue to appear to have Erica's best interests at heart when all the while he would be hoping that Viper was one of the first braves to be executed.

Henry Sibley had a spacious tent set up to serve as his headquarters. He was a congenial individual who was immediately impressed by both Erica's delicate beauty and the resources of inner strength her conversation soon revealed. She had the fine manners of a young woman who had grown up with all the advantages a wealthy home

277

could provide, but he soon discovered she had the same toughness of spirit the other female survivors of the uprising seemed to share. He listened to her story with complete and utter fascination, thinking her voice one of the most delightful he had ever heard. What she said, however, made no sense at all, in his view.

The colonel frowned slightly, then shifted in his chair. "This brave treated you as a sister or daughter, is that what you wish me to believe?"

"I was very well treated," Erica responded hesitantly, her heart sinking with the realization he suspected something was amiss. "Viper is a fine man, and I don't want to see him punished when he does not deserve it."

Sibley looked over at Mark then, astonished by his part in what struck him as a blatant attempt to influence him with an outright lie. "The soldiers here at Camp Release thrive on gossip, Captain Randall. Did you really think I would buy Miss Hanson's fanciful tale when within five minutes of your arrival here yesterday everyone had heard how you lost your fiancée to an Indian brave? It is fortunate for you that it would be difficult to prove that you used your command to abuse the man you brought in as a prisoner, since you clearly got the worst of whatever confrontations you had."

"Colonel," Erica interrupted, certain now the lie Mark had convinced her to tell had only made Viper's situation all the worse. She also thought he should have had sense enough to order the troopers with whom they had been traveling to keep what they had seen and heard to themselves. That oversight incensed her as much as her own stupidity in agreeing to lie. "Forgive me for not being completely truthful, Colonel Sibley. It is only that I want so desperately to see my husband is cleared of all charges. He can't be accused of kidnapping me as long as I swear it didn't happen, and it didn't," she insisted dramatically.

"The man isn't charged with kidnapping, Miss Hanson," Sibley responded impatiently. "His part in the uprising has yet to be assessed, but his trial will be a fair one."

Erica moved to the edge of her seat as she glanced over at Mark's sullen frown. He looked like a little boy who had been caught red-handed stealing from his mother's purse.

He had tried to help her. Unfortunately, his idea had been a poor one to which she should never have agreed, but she had already apologized for that.

"Colonel Sibley, I fail to see why any of the Sioux are being put on trial," she stated proudly, determined to seize the initiative and to defend her husband in every way possible. "The uprising was an act of war against the United States. A war precipitated by years of the most contemptuous treatment imaginable on the part of the government and its representatives. The Sioux's actions were no different than the South's decision to secede from the Union. They should be treated with the respect due prisoners of war, not put on trial as though they were common criminals."

As shocked by the audacity of that opinion as he had been by her lies, Henry Sibley decided he had heard quite enough for one day. "Now just a minute, young lady. First you come in here with some outlandish tale about a kindly Indian who rescued you from the horrors of the uprising a great many other people failed to escape. Now you think you can lecture me on how the Sioux ought to be treated? The uprising was no act of war involving opposing armies. The Sioux carried out a murderous rampage against innocent settlers who had caused no trouble and did not even have arms to defend themselves! Now get out of my sight and do not ever try to speak with me again. Good day."

Erica was already out of the tent before Mark rose from his chair. "I'm very sorry, sir," he offered contritely, for while he had hoped his plan would not succeed, he had never imagined it would backfire so badly. "Erica has clearly been influenced unduly by the Sioux she knows, but she is a sensible young woman and should soon realize how foolish she was to offend you."

"You're dismissed, Captain." Sibley returned Mark's salute, then offered another piece of advice. "I suggest you stay out of my way, too, until your release from my command can be arranged. Men who have nothing better to do than fight over women aren't wanted or needed here."

Stung by what he considered a totally undeserved rebuke, Mark turned on his heel and left. He was an

279

architect, not a soldier for Christ's sake, but he wasn't accustomed to being criticized for lacking character. He easily overtook Erica, but when they reached his tent, they found half a dozen women, some with small children by the hand, waiting for them.

A painfully thin woman who could have been anywhere from twenty-five to forty-five years of age spoke out as they approached. "Her kind ain't welcome here! We come to help her pack."

When Erica looked up at Mark, her eyes misty with unshed tears, he knew she was wondering what else could possibly go wrong. He took her hand firmly in his and pulled her to his side. "By her 'kind,' I assume you mean a lady, and I will agree with you. Ladies are extremely scarce here."

"She ain't no lady," a heavy-set woman in a faded print dress lashed out spitefully. "She's just some Indian's whore. She belongs over in the tepees, and if she don't have the sense to get over there on her own, then we'll take her."

"I am going to forgive you for those unfounded insults, since I know how much all of you have suffered of late," Mark replied with a disarming smile. "I suggest, however, that you start minding your own business and allow Miss Hanson to mind hers." To emphasize his point, he drew his Colt and used it to gesture. "Move along. If you insist upon making trouble here, I will end it here and now."

Aghast that he'd use a pistol to accompany that threat, the hostile group dispersed, but they continued to mumble insults, which could be clearly overheard until they had separated to return to their own tents. Mark then replaced his forty-five in his holster and again took Erica's arm. "That's just another example of what the good people of Minnesota think of your love affair, I'm afraid."

Erica was in no mood to discuss opinions that she considered insufferably ignorant, and hurried on into his tent. "If you have anything of value in here, I think you better move it," she suggested wisely. "The next time we are away they will probably burn your tent to the ground."

"You are the only thing of value here," the earnest captain replied quite sincerely. When Erica sat down on the cot where she had slept, he sat down opposite her on his own. "I think it might be a good idea for me to take you

280

back to New Ulm to stay until I can get orders to return to Delaware."

"No, that's impossible. I would be no happier there than they would be to have me. If I've got to leave here, then I will go on over to the Indian camp. I've met one of Viper's relatives, and there must be others who would take me in."

"I'll not have you living in a tepee!" Mark refused instantly. "Absolutely not."

"It's no different from a tent, Mark," Erica pointed out with a weary sigh. "At least among Indians, no one will call me a whore for being married to one."

"You're not married to that man, and you damn well know it," Mark insisted through clenched teeth. He saw the fiery light of defiance begin to glow brightly in Erica's eyes and was reminded he had promised himself he would share her burdens rather than add to them. "I'm sorry. I shouldn't have said that when I know how much the man means to you. We'll do the best we can here until his trial, but you'll stay right here with me. I am closer to family than any of the Sioux can possibly be."

Since she knew that to be true, Erica had to agree. "Can you find me a book or two to read or some mending that needs to be done? I will be content to stay out of sight as much as I can, but I do need something useful to do."

Mark reached out to take her hand lightly in his. "If there's a book within five miles worth reading I'll find it. Why don't you try and rest. I doubt those busybodies will have the nerve to come back to bother you today."

"I certainly hope not." Erica left her hand in Mark's just a moment, then had to remove it to cover a yawn. "Do you think I could attend the trials?"

Mark rose to his feet as he shook his head. "Not a chance. You'd never be able to keep still, and you would only make matters worse for the braves on trial."

"I suppose you're right, but you could go, couldn't you, and tell me what's happening?"

"Yes, I could go," Mark agreed hesitantly.

"Well, will you go?" Erica asked more insistently.

"Would it please you?"

"Yes, very much. I will die of curiosity if I don't find out what's happening soon."

281

"I'll go right now, then," Mark agreed with a good-natured chuckle, and before Erica could object, he leaned down and kissed her good-bye.

It did not take Viper long to discover that none of his close friends were among those being held to stand trial. To a man, they had fled for the Dakotas with Little Crow, and he was glad they had escaped what he knew would be far closer to a farce than to justice. He thought it significant that the first prisoner to be tried for the crime of participating in the uprising had not been a Sioux. Instead, it had been Joseph Godfrey, also known as Otakle, the mulatto son of a French-Canadian father and a black mother who had married a Sioux woman and lived at the Lower Agency. Godfrey had been condemned to death for murder, but his sentence had been commuted to a prison term after he had volunteered to provide evidence against the Sioux who had long regarded him as a brother. With his many years of schooling by missionaries, Viper was reminded immediately of Judas when he heard that story, for surely Joseph Godfrey would betray them all to the same gruesome fate that had awaited Jesus.

One face Viper did recognize among the prisoners was one he would rather not have seen: Claw of the Badger. Badger had his own life to worry about now, however, and did no more than raise an eyebrow when their glances met. Old grudges seemed unimportant to him now, since he had been one of the first sentenced to hang.

"Where's that pretty little wife of yours now, Viper?" he called out in a lazy drawl, but when Viper walked away without answering, he did not pursue him to find out. He did no more than shrug, and continued to worry about his own rapidly dimming prospects for the future.

The problem was, Viper could not stop thinking of Erica. Every minute of the day her lovely image filled his mind the way her slender body had once filled his arms. He missed her more terribly than he had thought possible. His whole body ached with a need for her that grew more intense by the hour, and he gave little thought to his own predicament when he wanted so badly to be with her.

How was she spending her time? Did her heart cry out

for him as his did for her? Did she feel as lost and alone as he did? While it provided a momentary bit of comfort to envision her weeping for him, Viper could not bear to think of Erica suffering the same torments as he because of their separation. They had been parted too rudely, torn from each other's arms, and he could see no way they could ever recapture the joy they had lost.

His emotions in a constant state of turmoil, Viper resigned himself to a long wait for a trial he doubted would last more than five minutes. He planned to say nothing in his own defense. He would not beg men he despised for the gift of his life. How could he deny he had fought in the uprising when he had done his best to kill every man dressed in an army uniform he could find? It was unfortunate that one of them had not been Mark Randall, for he knew the officer would be spending his every spare moment with Erica, trying to win back her love. A hatred so consuming it tore at his soul came over him at that thought. The man didn't really love Erica, he couldn't, or he would have told her good-bye when he found her living so happily with the Indian whom destiny had chosen as her husband.

It was the stunning power of that thought that gave Viper strength. He knew fate had made Erica and him not only lovers but mates, and so compelling a force could not have been wasted on a man with no future to live. He had a future, he was positive he did. Yet when he tried to imagine what it would be, he found only a void past which his thoughts would not go. But he stubbornly refused to believe that what he saw in his mind's eye was the face of his own death.

# Chapter Nineteen

## October, 1862

Mark had expected the trials of the Sioux warriors to be a tedious ordeal he would have to force himself to attend occasionally to provide reports for Erica and then forget, but he soon found himself so fascinated by the proceedings that he went as often as time allowed. The fact that Joseph Godfrey had bargained for his own life by implicating others in actions which would result in death sentences revolted him completely, but the man's testimony was highly regarded by the members of the commission. While there were instances in which the pitifully few survivors of once thriving farms positively identified the braves who had murdered their loved ones, all too often Mark heard men condemned to death on evidence he considered too flimsy to merit mentioning. The fact that Little Crow and his staunchest supporters were not on trial struck the officer as a travesty also, for it seemed obvious to him that it should be the ringleaders of the uprising who ought to be on trial for their lives, not the braves who had followed them.

Unexpectedly, there were moments of humor during the trials, for some braves, while admitting they had taken part in battles against the army, swore their aim was too poor to cause any casualties. Others provided equally unintentionally amusing excuses for not having taken part in the fighting, ranging from poor health to outright cowardice. It was clear to Mark throughout, however, that the Indians had little conception of the importance of the trials, and any who naively admitted to having anything whatsoever to do with the uprising were sentenced to hang with unseemly haste.

In spite of his original opinion on the Sioux's guilt, the manner in which the trials were conducted and the haste of the verdicts ate away at Mark's conscience, leaving him deeply troubled. Before long, he began to believe as Erica did that the braves should be regarded as prisoners of war, unless it could be proven beyond any doubt that they had wantonly slaughtered innocent settlers. The members of the military commission obviously did not agree, however, and since theirs was not a court of law, and Mark was not an attorney who knew how to argue effectively even if it had been, he did not know what he could do to change things. Finally he decided the one thing he could do was to see Viper and offer what little advice he could about the trials.

When summoned to the tent the guards used as their command post, Viper regarded it as a welcome distraction from a day filled to overflowing with boredom, until he saw it was Mark Randall who had asked to see him. He turned away in disgust then, having no interest in speaking with the man, but Mark wouldn't allow him to refuse his visit.

"I'll hold a gun to your head if I must, but you're going to listen to what I have to say, if not for your own sake, then for Erica's," the captain called out loudly.

Viper halted in midstride, then turned back to face Mark, but his expression was still the hostile one the officer had looked upon so frequently. "Send her to me then, and I will talk with her."

Mark crossed the distance between them in two long strides, then took the precaution of lowering his voice to a persuasive whisper. "Can't you stop acting like a jackass long enough to realize I've come here to help you?"

Viper laughed derisively at that remark. "Why would you want to help me?"

"I'm damned if I know," Mark admitted quite frankly. "I just don't like the way the commission is running the trials. From what Erica tells me, you fought only against the army and never attacked any farms. Of course, you were at New Ulm, but from what she says that was only to get her. Is that right, or did you deliberately mislead her?"

Viper motioned for Mark to follow him as he moved farther away from the guards' tent so their remarks would not be overheard. He saw no reason to admit anything to the officer and said so. "Perhaps this is a trick. If I say that I did this or that, then the commission may say I have admitted my guilt."

Mark took off his hat and slapped it against his thigh. "Christ, if you aren't the most difficult man to get along with I've ever met! The commission did not send me to see you. Erica doesn't know I'm here, either. Hell, I don't even know why I'm trying to help you myself, but from what I've seen, you've no chance at all to get a fair shake, and that's just not right."

Viper studied Mark's expression closely, wondering if anything he said could possibly be true. Then he realized he could trust Erica's judgment and that she would never have agreed to marry a man who was not trustworthy. Still, Mark's motive sounded absurd to him, and he called him on it. "You think if I am dead, Erica will marry you. Isn't that what you really want, rather than a fair trial for me?"

Mark eyed the handsome brave with an appreciative glance, again impressed by his intelligence. He had never spoken with another Indian brave, but he was nevertheless convinced Viper was unique. He had certainly never met a white man who had the insight this Sioux continually displayed. "I want Erica to marry me, but not by default. If I had allowed you to escape on the way here, she would already be my wife. That was a bargain she tried to make with me several times. I refused."

"That's a lie!" Viper responded instantly, disgusted to think he had been tempted, however briefly, to trust a white man.

"No, it's the honest to God truth," Mark stated calmly. "She begged me time and again to exchange your freedom for her promise of marriage. I said no, but that was when I thought you'd deserve whatever punishment the commission would mete out. I thought if they hanged you, so much the better. But now—"

"Now your conscience is bothering you," Viper interrupted with another bitter laugh. "It is a shame it is too late to do me any good."

"Maybe it isn't. Just don't admit anything when the commission holds your trial. I'll say you surrendered without a fight, and Erica will swear you were with her from August twenty-third on."

"No," Viper declared emphatically. "I do not want Erica there."

Mark flopped his hat back on his head. He was the one to break out in laughter this time. "Did you ever succeed in changing that woman's mind when she had it set on something?"

"Yes," Viper insisted, although he could not recall exactly when it had been. "Tell her that I forbid it. I do not want her there."

Unable to promise anything, Mark merely shrugged. "I'll do what I can. Now as I said before, if you weren't on any of the raids that attacked farms, there will be no one who can identify you as being a murderer."

"Did you ever kill a Confederate soldier?" Viper asked suddenly.

"Yes, but what has that got to do with anything?" Mark asked with a befuddled frown.

"Then you are as much a murderer as I am," the brave remarked slyly.

"That is neither here nor there!" Mark cried out in frustration.

Viper shook his head sadly. "You are forgetting Joseph Godfrey. It will be his testimony that hangs me. It will not matter what you or Erica say. He knows where I fought, and he will surely say so."

"Godfrey will present a problem, I admit that but—"

Viper stepped close as he pointed out the truth Mark still hadn't seen. "The government of the United States wants to be rid of the Sioux for good. Since the army failed to kill us, the commission will. They may call their hearings trials, but it is still a war, only this time we have no weapons. Nothing will change for us until each white man has a conscience that troubles him as badly as yours does." Having no more to say, Viper walked away, but Mark stood for a long while staring after him, wondering if he could find the man's calm resolve if a death sentence were hanging over *his* head.

Before returning to his tent that afternoon, Mark made it a point to find Song of the Wren. He handed over a leather pouch containing the gold coins he had promised her, but she was in tears as she grabbed it and ran away. When Erica greeted him with a pretty smile as he returned to his tent, he felt so guilty about his meeting with the Indian girl that he found it impossible to look her in the eye.

Mark looked so badly depressed, Erica grew frightened. "What's wrong? What's happened?"

Unable to face her, Mark tossed his hat aside, unbuttoned his jacket, then stretched out on his bunk. He placed his hands behind his head before he replied, but he was still far from comfortable. "We've got to get out of here, Erica. As soon as my orders arrive, we've got to go. Viper doesn't want our help at his trial. He's refused it, in fact."

"You've seen him?" Erica gasped in delighted surprise. "How does he look? May I go and see him, too?"

The love he heard so clearly in the excitement of her tone only made his already aching conscience hurt all the more. He could have saved her lover's life and married her. His pride had kept him from making what would have been the best bargain for them all. Now it was too late. "Yes, I've seen him. He looks as mean as ever, and no, you may not visit him."

"Is he all right?" Erica asked softly, depressed that her brief hope to see her husband had been dashed.

"He's bitter, and I'd say deservedly so. He's no more guilty than most of the others, but with his attitude they'll hang him for sure."

"There has to be something we can do, Mark. There just has to be." Yet as her eyes filled with tears, she feared all she would be able to do was weep. Kneeling beside Mark's cot, she laid her arm across his waist and rested her head lightly upon his chest. "Thank you for going to see him. Even if he won't let us help him, I appreciate the fact you made the effort. I know it was for me, rather than him."

Mark lowered his left hand to her hair, combing the glossy curls through his fingers as he thought how little pleasure he had gotten from his ploy to win her affection by appearing to be sympathetic to Viper's plight. Somehow, he had gotten caught in his own snare, and he felt thoroughly wretched for having tried to trick the woman who was so dear to him.

"When Viper is tried, I'll be there," he assured her. "He may have refused to allow you to attend, but he can't keep me from reading your sworn statement. If he was with you from August twenty-third on, then—"

Erica rose up so she could look at Mark directly. "There were a couple of days in September when we were in Little Crow's camp. I know he rode with the others then, but he said they weren't involved in any fighting. Will that matter?"

Mark pursed his lips thoughtfully. "It doesn't sound good. I know we got into an awful mess the last time we tried to stretch the truth, but I don't think you ought to mention the fact that he went back to Little Crow's band, even if it was only briefly."

"All right, I won't. He was adamant about fighting only against the army," Erica recalled suddenly. "Won't that tell the commission something about his character?"

"I doubt they believe the Sioux even have such a thing as 'character,' angel. Besides, any time a brave has admitted firing at anyone, the result has been the same: a death sentence. It won't help to say Viper chose his targets with care. If he admits killing even one white, he'll hang."

"Well, I thought it might be worth a try." Erica rose to her feet, her resolve strengthened, if not her hopes. "Do you have some paper I could use? I'd like to get started making notes."

Mark sat up and swung his legs over the side of the cot. "I wish I'd made that bargain with you, Erica. Viper would be in the Dakotas by now, and you and I would be back home. We could have forgotten this whole ugly nightmare, as though it never happened."

Erica opened her mouth to argue, for while the trials were indeed a nightmare, she would never, ever forget Viper. Realizing that was not what Mark would like to hear, she leaned down to kiss his cheek lightly. "You always do what you think is right. Since you're not responsible for this horrible mess, you mustn't blame yourself for what's happening to Viper."

"Well, perhaps not, but—"

Erica silenced his protest with a light caress of her fingertips. "No, none of this is your fault. Now find a pen, ink, and paper for me, so I can get to work on a statement that would make a stone weep."

Mark had to smile at that image, but from what he had seen of the commission's decisions, their hearts were made of something far harder than stone.

*　　*　　*

289

When Colonel Sibley had learned Erica was sharing Mark's tent rather than one with another woman, he had immediately called the captain to task, threatening to court martial him for flaunting an affair so openly. Mark had denied that charge vehemently in an attempt to convince his commanding officer that Erica was the most chaste of women and that she still considered herself Viper's wife, though she had not stated it publicly. They had been forced to share his quarters, he insisted, because of the hostility the other women had shown her. While Sibley found Mark's claim that their friendship was no more than a platonic one difficult to believe, he had no doubts about how the former captives viewed Erica, since he had heard more than one complain quite openly about the stunning blonde's lack of morals. Finally admitting Mark's fears for her safety might be well founded, he relented and did not insist she move into separate quarters of her own, but he continued to believe their scandalous living arrangements were cause for censure.

That a brave's exceedingly attractive white wife was occupying an officer's tent was only one of Sibley's many problems. When the army had arrived to receive the captives from the friendly Sioux, they had taken twelve hundred Indians into custody. Since that day, others had continued to surrender until their numbers had grown to nearly two thousand. He had sent the Indians out under guard to gather corn and potatoes left in the fields at the Upper Agency, but each day the problem of feeding his Sioux charges was becoming more acute. Finally he had no choice but to move his troops and prisoners south to the Lower Agency.

Pressing for retribution for the uprising, General Pope insisted the trials were to be completed promptly, and they were continued on October 25 in François La Bathe's log house, which had been one of the few not burned to the ground during the attack at the Lower Agency on August 18. As before, the commission's concept of justice was swift, with as many as forty cases being heard in one day. While Mark had no hope that he could change the verdict in Viper's case, he informed Lieutenant Rollin C. Ollin, the commission's judge advocate, or prosecutor, that he intended to offer evidence on the brave's behalf.

It was plain to Viper from the astonished gasps from the

spectators crowded into the small house that he was the only one an army officer had volunteered to defend. A mixed blood, Antoine D. Frenière, and the Reverend Riggs were acting as interpreters, but they were told that Viper did not require their services. Viper had no intention of offering comments in any language, however. In his view the trial was a farce, and he would not dignify it by participating.

As soon as Viper's name had been called, Mark had leaped to his feet. He wanted to speak before any charges had been read, and since he had informed Lieutenant Ollin of his intentions, he was recognized and allowed to do so. Wanting to make the best impression he could for what he considered an entirely hopeless cause, he walked over to the Indian and stood by his side as he addressed the commission.

"I would like to read a statement prepared in Viper's defense by Miss Erica Hanson, a young woman who became acquainted with him in July of this year." Erica had worked on this message with the care a scholar would give his doctoral thesis, and Mark knew it by heart. While Viper stared at him with a malevolent frown, he read Erica's words in so sincere a manner that he knew the stoic brave would be moved, even if no one else was. In phrases she had taken great care to give an almost childlike innocence and beauty, Erica described a friendship that had deepened into love, prompting Viper to come for her when the Sioux attacked New Ulm. She stated that she had been his constant and willing companion from that day until he was arrested on October 6 and brought to Camp Release to stand trial, an action she tactfully described in her conclusion as totally unwarranted and unjust.

Mark tapped Erica's neatly penned statement against his fingertips as he added a few comments of his own. "Since it has long been the government's intention to encourage the Sioux to take up farming, I wish to point out that this brave was living quite peacefully on property abandoned near New Ulm at the time I found him. He offered no resistance to my demand that he accompany me to Camp Release for what I mistakenly assumed would be a fair trial. Since it has now become obvious to me that such a prospect is doubtful, I would like to join Miss Hanson in requesting whatever charges there might be against him be dropped immediately, since punishing such a fine individual would serve no useful purpose whatsoever. Thank you."

Mark did not move to return to his seat, but remained beside Viper as the men on the commission broke their astonished silence to whisper excitedly amongst themselves. The people waiting to appear as witnesses against other braves made no secret of their opinion of Mark's comments, however, and had to be ordered to stop shouting obscenities or leave.

Colonel William Crooks finally succeeded in restoring order among the members of the commission and the audience, as well, but he had been as infuriated by Mark Randall's speech as everyone else. Quickly reviewing the lengthy list of charges against Viper, he scoffed at Mark's claim that he had taken up farming at the height of the uprising.

"Captain, quite frankly your interest in this brave simply amazes me. It matters not at all what he did after August twenty-third, when he was so active a participant in the uprising prior to that date." He continued by quoting the charges against Viper to make his point. "We have an eyewitness who places him in the midst of the slaughter that took place here at the Lower Agency on the morning of the eighteenth. He was also involved in the ambush of Captain John Marsh's troops that afternoon at the Redwood Ferry. He has been identified as having been among Little Crow's force while Fort Ridgely was under siege. That he went to New Ulm to find Miss Hanson is doubtful, since our witness states he was responsible for torching at least half of the town! Clearly, taking a wife was merely an afterthought.

"This is no peace-loving farmer who has taken a white bride, but a brutal and cunning murderer responsible for the deaths of countless innocent civilians, and a good many soldiers, to say nothing of the destruction of a great deal of valuable property. That you would speak up for him sickens us all. If you have anything to say for yourself, Viper, say it now, as I think we have devoted quite enough time to your case and are ready to pronounce your sentence."

Viper simply stared at the colonel, his gaze colder than ice as he remained silent, but the fury of his contemptuous glance was far more insulting than any words could have been. Knowing the commission could do little to him for befriending the brave, Mark made one last comment. "I will never believe the word of a man who has bought his own life by betraying his former friends. That you would accept the testimony of such a pitiful witness makes you every bit as guilty of murder as any Sioux you've condemned."

Mark was forcibly removed from the log house at that point, with an escort to Colonel Sibley's headquarters, but as he was shoved out the door he heard Crooks sentence Viper to hang, followed by the raucous cheers of the white audience who heartily agreed with him that justice had again been served.

After learning what had happened at the trial, Henry Sibley was so totally exasperated with Mark Randall's behavior that he could take no more. "There is a steamboat scheduled to arrive at the Lower Agency tomorrow around noon. Both you and Miss Hanson will be on board when it leaves, or you'll find yourself facing a court martial on charges of misconduct you will find impossible to refute."

Knowing the mood of the officers who would sit on any such disciplinary board, Mark knew he had no choice but to leave. "We'll be on board," he assured Sibley without argument.

"You will have to report to General Pope in Saint Paul, but I'm certain that will merely be a formality. Since he believes, as I do, that the Sioux should be executed for their crimes rather than provided with excuses for them, I'm certain he will see to it that you are provided with orders for an immediate return to duty with your former unit."

Undoubtedly with the provision he be placed in the front lines, Mark thought to himself. Strangely, that possibility didn't bother him in the least, and with a surprising calm, the still confident captain told Sibley he had enjoyed serving under his command and was instantly dismissed.

Upon his return to their tent, Erica needed only a brief glance at the furious expression on Mark's face to know how Viper's trial had gone. They had both known beforehand what the verdict would be, but still, she was devastated to think Viper would hang, and she clung to

Mark for comfort, thinking him the one true friend she had left in the world. When she had calmed down sufficiently for him to tell her they had to leave for home the very next day, she knew she should never have allowed him to become so deeply involved in her efforts to save her husband's life.

"I never meant to ruin your career, Mark. I never meant to do that," she apologized in a voice hoarse with anguish.

Mark brushed away the last of Erica's tears with his fingertips, then pulled her down beside him on his cot. "I'm an architect, not a soldier, and once the war is over it won't matter what sort of military record I had. I knew speaking up for Viper wouldn't make me popular, but I did it anyway. Besides, it will be much better for you to leave now rather than, well, rather than to wait until—" he faltered then, unable to speak Viper's fate out loud.

"Until they begin the executions, you mean?" Thoroughly sickened by that thought, Erica had to swallow hard before she continued. "How can I go, Mark? I don't want Viper to think I've abandoned him."

Mark pulled her into his arms again, patting her back gently as he tried to think of some way to convince her she had no choice but to leave when he did. Then the perfect solution occurred to him. "Viper didn't want you at the trial, sweetheart. He'd never want you standing beside the gallows. I think seeing you there would hurt him worse than having to die. He's too proud. You can't want to make him suffer any more than he already has. You can't do that to him."

Reluctantly admitting he was right, Erica closed her eyes to force back a fresh flood of tears. "I want to tell him good-bye, Mark. Won't they please let me do that?"

Mark took a deep breath and let it out slowly. "There's no point in my going to Sibley with that request, but I know enough of the men on guard duty that I might be able to arrange something. Don't get your hopes up, but let me see what I can do. Now why don't you try and rest? If I can work this out, it will have to be after midnight, and I know you'll want to be wide awake."

Intrigued, Erica quickly agreed. "All right, I'll rest, but the minute you have a plan, please wake me up and tell me about it. Will you promise to do that?"

"Yes," Mark agreed, determined to give the woman he

loved so dearly a few last minutes of happiness with the brave she adored. Hell, he didn't care if they did court-martial him for it, it would be worth it to see Erica smile again, even if it were for another man.

When Mark arrived at the compound where the condemned Sioux were being held, Viper was surprised, for he could not imagine why the officer had come to see him when there could be nothing left for him to say. He supposed he should offer some sort of thanks for the help the officer had tried to give him, but he found words of gratitude impossible to speak.

"Erica and I are leaving tomorrow. We've been ordered to go, actually," Mark admitted with a rueful smile. "Naturally, she wants to see you one last time." When Viper began to shake his head, Mark reached out to take his arm in a friendly grasp, but the brave smacked his hand away. Ignoring that insult, Mark continued, "Can't you do this for her? She's heartbroken. Although I will never understand why, she loves you. Now after the guards change at midnight I think I can sneak her in here for a few minutes and—"

"No!" Viper insisted dramatically. "This is no place for a woman or good-byes." Scowling deeply, he thought a moment, then offered another plan of his own. "Is the house where they hold the trials empty at night?"

"What?" Mark was simply dumbfounded by that question, but he managed to gather his wits to respond. "There's no way I'll help you escape. I'm sorry for what's happened to you, but I'll be damned if I'll spend the next ten years in prison for helping you escape, and believe me, that's exactly where Sibley would see I went."

Viper swept that objection aside with an impatient wave. "I will not try to escape. I want only to see Erica alone. We will not run away. I will not turn her into a fugitive again. She deserves more. Now can you do it? Can you arrange for us to meet at La Bathe's house or not?"

Mark shook his head. "It's too dangerous."

"Not for me," Viper joked with a ready laugh, then thinking of a way to inspire Mark to arrange the meeting, he grew serious once more. "If you do this for me, then I will tell Erica I want her to marry you. I do not want her to grieve for me all the days of her life, but she will if I do not set her free to marry you. I will do that tonight, but only if I can see her at La Bathe's house, and we must be left alone. I do not want you with us."

Mark was too bright not to immediately understand why. It was one thing to allow Erica and the wily brave to exchange a few fevered farewell kisses, but to arrange the privacy they would need to make love, that was another thing entirely. "You are asking too much of me."

"Why do you always think of yourself first rather than of Erica?" Viper asked perceptively. "Her happiness should mean more to you than your own."

"Don't lecture me!" Mark replied angrily. "I don't have to take that from you."

"No, you want to take only my wife," Viper reminded him sarcastically. "I do not think she will ever marry you without my blessing. Of course, if I do not see her tonight, alone, I cannot give it."

"You're a real bastard, you know that, don't you?" Mark was seething with anger now, for he was sorely afraid what the brave said was true, and that Erica might well remain a grieving widow forever.

"Yes," Viper replied proudly. "You have a choice. Give me Erica tonight, and you may have her for a thousand tomorrows. You would be a fool to refuse such a bargain."

Just as he had been a fool to refuse the last one he had been offered, Mark reminded himself. It was the bitter irony of that thought that helped him make his decision. "All right, I will do it, but I want to hear you tell Erica she is to marry me just as soon as it can be arranged. Is that clear?"

"You do not trust me?" Viper asked with a mocking grin.

"No, I don't."

"Good, because I do not trust you, either. I will be at the guard's tent at midnight. Come for me then."

How the brave could have taken command of the situation Mark didn't know, but as Viper walked away the arrogance he had always displayed tore through the officer's soul like a white-hot blade. "I'm making a bargain with the devil himself," he swore under his breath, but he was convinced that if he wanted to marry Erica anytime soon, he had no choice but to do it.

# Chapter Twenty

## October, 1862

Erica was already waiting inside François La Bathe's house when Mark arrived with Viper. She had not dared to bring a lantern, but she instantly recognized the silhouette of the Indian's powerful physique as he stepped through the door. She had promised herself she wouldn't shed a single tear, and with a small cry of joy she threw herself into his arms and covered his face with enthusiastic kisses.

"I have missed you," the brave whispered between the deeply passionate kisses he gave her in return. She had worn the buckskin dress he had given her, and its softness welcomed his touch, but he wanted much more and hurriedly untied the laces at her shoulders.

"We have until dawn," Erica pointed out sweetly, as though she saw no need for such haste.

"I know, but I do not intend to waste a minute," Viper confessed, and as the buckskin garment slipped to the floor he was delighted to find Erica standing nude in his arms. That she had not bothered to wear any lingerie made him laugh. "I see you did not want to waste any time, either."

"No, I didn't," Erica responded before giving him another warm hug and an ecstatic kiss. She had missed him so terribly, and she was delighted to find him teasing her happily rather than behaving like the hostile stranger who had given her so many black looks on the trail to Camp Release. Nibbling his earlobe, she whispered a seductive, "I love you," as she ran her fingers through his long, flowing hair while the tips of her breasts brushed his broad chest lightly. "I will never love anyone but you," she vowed softly. Her lips again found his, while her hands strayed to his belt buckle to free him of his clothes.

Viper sighed deeply, his voice a low moan in the back of his throat as her fingertips moved over him, peeling away his buckskins at the same time she began a smooth erotic massage. He had taught her well. Her touch was knowing, fluid, spreading over him with the warm sweetness of honey. Her hands were at his shoulders one moment, then caressing the flatness of his stomach or the curve of his hips the next. He leaned against her, wrapping his arms around her waist and pressing her hips so close to his their bodies seemed to melt together into one.

All afternoon he had planned to take her swiftly, to bury himself in her velvet heat, to allow his passion for her to rage without constraint until he had not only satisfied himself, but enveloped her in the perfect peace that had eluded him while they had been apart. That had been his plan until he had felt her first breathless kiss brush his cheek, and now he knew he wanted to savor each second of their time together rather than merely consume it in reckless haste.

"You are always so warm," Erica whispered against the muscular contours of his bare chest. "Your kiss, your touch, your whole body is always filled with so appealing a warmth I can't resist you." She rubbed her cheek against the flat bud of one nipple, then traced it lightly with the tip of her tongue before slowly sinking to her knees before him. Her lips brushed over his belly and her tongue tickled the indentation at his navel while her hands slid down his sides. Finding him fully aroused, she drew the tip of his manhood into her mouth for another, and even more deeply pleasurable, kiss.

Viper's fingertips played across Erica's temples lightly before moving through her cascading curls to press her face close as the gentle motions of her lips and tongue sent tremors of immense pleasure pulsating through his loins. Bathed in the light of her love, the small, darkened cabin took on the glowing beauty of paradise, but this was not how he wished to surrender to the magical spell of her love, and, exerting the last of his self-control, he gently pushed her away. Calling her name softly, he drew her to her feet.

"Have you a blanket, or something soft to spread upon the floor?" he asked as he again wrapped her in his arms.

"Yes, it is here right beside me." Erica slipped from his embrace to reach for the blanket she had taken from her cot. "The army's blankets are not very soft, but—"

"It is fine." Viper hushed her apology with another lingering kiss. He helped her to spread the coarsely woven blanket at their feet, then pulled her down upon it. "We have made love many times, but I will remember tonight as being the best of all."

Erica was grateful for the darkness then, for her eyes flooded with tears at the devastating thought that they would soon be parted forever. "We have had so little of love," she sighed regretfully.

"No, we have had it all," Viper argued convincingly. "There is no more than this." As his words were muffled by her kiss, his hands strayed to the lush fullness of her breasts. His thumb circled the petal-soft crests until his hunger for their delectable taste overwhelmed him with desire. His lips left hers then to begin a slow, adoring appraisal of her flavorful curves. When he at last moved away, he continued his glorious quest to explore each delightful nuance of her lissome figure, until he was convinced no man would ever know her divinely shaped body as intimately as he.

That the wooden floor beneath her was far harder than a feather bed escaped Erica's notice entirely, she was so blissfully happy to be with Viper again. His hair fell about her hips like a dark cloud, making her shiver with anticipation as he paused for a moment to bury his face in the soft flesh of her stomach. Savoring their closeness, she felt his fingertips part the golden curls between her thighs, and using her body's own fragrant essence, he prepared a delicious welcoming path for his eager kiss. It was impossible for Erica to think beyond that point, for his tender affections flooded her senses with an ecstasy so profound that she was lost in the loving he gave with such masterful ease.

Viper created within Erica's slender body a yearning for fulfillment so intense that she soon called his name in a breathless sob, begging him to take quickly what was rightfully his. "Now, Viper, now!" she urged, and in a futile attempt to escape the exquisite torture that threatened to consume her soul with desire, her nails drew bloody trails across the bronze skin of his broad shoulders.

Jolted from the pursuit of his own pleasure by that searing pain, Viper positioned himself above Erica, but despite her fevered cries of encouragement, he entered her slowly, using shallow thrusts, delaying their journey to rapture's shore by moving with a gentle rhythm until his own need for release equaled hers. He could not control the impulse to thrust more deeply then, finally infusing both their hearts and bodies with the stunning force of love's most precious gift. His senses flooded with that glorious sensation, he did not withdraw, but continued to hold Erica captive in his embrace until he could at last think clearly enough to say what he knew had to be said.

Viper rose up on his elbows, then leaned down to kiss Erica's cheeks and eyelashes sweetly before giving her another lingering kiss, which was still filled with a promise of passion. His eyes were accustomed to the darkness now, but he still could not make out her face clearly. Finally deciding that was a blessing, he made his request.

"There is something I want you to do for me," he began.

Misunderstanding his mood, Erica responded with a throaty giggle. "Why Viper, what is there left to do?"

The handsome brave had to laugh, too, then. "Perhaps nothing new, but we can do everything again. But first, I want you to listen to me carefully. I was not talking about making love."

He had grown so serious, Erica was frightened. She did not want him to talk of death, for that would be too sad to bear. "Oh please, don't—"

"Just listen," Viper commanded firmly. "I love you with all my heart and soul. I want only what is best for you. I want you to have a happy life, the life you would have had had we never met."

Erica could see Viper's face no more clearly than he could see hers, but she knew his expression would be as serious as his tone. "Without you, I will never be happy," she replied sadly. Tears welled up in her eyes and spilled over her lashes, but she made no move to brush them away.

Viper leaned down to kiss her, his affection flavored with the salty taste of her tears. "I will be with you always, Erica," he whispered as fervently as a prayer. "I will be in the warmth of the sun, the beauty of the stars, the gentle whisper of the wind. You will see my love painted across the sky in the bright colors of each sunrise and sunset. After each rain, I will put a rainbow in the sky to make you smile. I will teach birds to sing my love songs, and each spring I will cover the earth with a fragrant blanket of wildflowers so you will know I have not forsaken you. Keep me alive in your heart, my beloved, and we will be together always."

He felt her chest heave as she drew in a deep breath, but before she could give in to the torrent of tears he was certain his bittersweet words of farewell had inspired, he lowered his mouth to hers. As his tongue slid between her trembling lips, he began to move his hips with a fierce rhythm, bringing her swiftly to the brink of rapture this time. He took full advantage of the passion that flowed between them, eagerly lifting her spirit aloft with his knowing that the warm afterglow of this far more violent loving would restore a blissful calm to her soul. When she again lay relaxed in his arms, he explained the last part of his request.

"I want you to marry Mark, today, if it can be arranged."

"What?" Erica could not believe her ears. "How could you ask such an impossible thing of me?"

"Are you refusing to grant my last request?" Viper asked with a touch of his usual teasing attitude.

"Yes! I won't do it. How could you possibly expect me to marry him when I am so in love with you?"

Viper rolled over slowly with Erica still cradled in his arms, bringing her up on top of him where she could lie comfortably upon his chest as they discussed her future. His hands moved up and down her spine in a soothing motion he hoped would prove relaxing. "I will not pretend that I like or admire him, because I do not, but he will make a good husband for you. I want you to have a family and be happy. I told you that. I do not want you to spend the rest of your life all alone."

"I would never be truly alone," Erica reminded him

softly. "You promised to be with me always."

"Yes, and I will. Mark knows you love me, and it does not matter to him. When he makes love to you, he will know you are thinking of me. He will expect that and forgive it. No other man ever will."

Erica gave his request the careful thought she knew it deserved, but still couldn't grant it. "I don't want to make love with another man, nor do I want another husband. No. I won't do it."

"You are only seventeen years old," Viper pointed out wisely, "and very pretty, too. You may not think you will ever want another husband, but one day you will. I should be the one to choose him for you."

Erica did not reply. She could feel the steady beat of his heart and did not want to talk of spending the rest of her life with another man when she loved him so dearly. "I wish," she began slowly.

"No," Viper cautioned as he clasped her more tightly. "We can change nothing. Now you are to obey me in this, Erica. Mark would not have let me have you tonight, had I not promised to give you to him at dawn. I will not go back on my word, and you cannot either."

That Mark had made such a despicable bargain revolted Erica completely. "How can you ask me to marry a man who would force you to make such a heartbreaking trade?"

Viper chuckled to himself, then decided to admit the truth. "I was the one who forced him to make the bargain, not the other way around. This was my idea, not his, but I would have traded away my soul to have spent tonight with you. And it would have been worth it."

Erica wound her arms around his neck to press close as she kissed him. "I will love you forever, Viper. I will."

"You will marry Mark," the determined brave insisted before her delicious kiss sent all coherent thought from his mind. "It has already been decided, but for the rest of the night, you are still mine." That he returned her abundant love in full measure was apparent in his every caress and kiss. He made love to her again, this time with a playful sweetness, and as always, the pleasure they shared was rich and deep. He could not see the joy in her expression until the sky began to lighten in the east and filled the small house with a dreamlike aura. Then he knew their tragically brief marriage was at its end.

"It is time to go," Viper stated simply, a world of sorrow deepening the usually mellow tone of his voice. While it was the most difficult thing she had ever had to do, Erica left his arms and pulled the simple buckskin dress over her head. She fluffed out her hair with her fingers, but she had kicked off her moccasins and had to hunt a moment for them. When she turned back toward Viper, he was already standing by the door, fully dressed and holding the neatly folded blanket. Before she reached his side they heard Mark's insistent knock. Viper whispered a reply, then held out his hand.

As the lovely girl's fingers touched his, the Indian could no longer pretend a composure he did not feel. With a forceful grasp he pulled her into his arms, then, turning swiftly, forced her back against the door. Before Erica could utter more than an astonished gasp, Viper's mouth covered hers in a savage kiss, his whole body shuddering with a wild rejection of the terrible blow fate had dealt them. Casting the blanket aside, he pushed Erica's dress above her hips, freed himself from his buckskins, and took her with an all-consuming passion that proclaimed his anguish at their parting more eloquently than words ever could. She clung to him, eagerly accepting the depth of the sorrow he would never express with tears, until the life force of his last act of love had finally been spent within her. When he released her and hastily pulled her dress back into place, Erica drew him back into her arms for one last lingering kiss of farewell.

Viper did not apologize for being so impulsive, since he saw no need to ask Erica's forgiveness for the desperate emotion that had prompted their final union. He adjusted his clothing, grabbed up the blanket, again took her hand, and then opened the door. With an anxious glance he made certain Mark was still alone, then he slipped through the door and drew Erica out beside him.

Viper handed Erica the blanket that had proven to be so useful, then offered Mark his hand. After an awkward hesitation, the officer took it. He had been standing right outside the little house and could imagine only one activity that could have made the wooden door rattle with such a steady rhythm. While he was disgusted that the brave would treat Erica so disgracefully, he was too eager to return the man to the Indians' compound to tell him so.

"I am giving Erica to you," Viper stated solemnly as he shook Mark's hand. "She is the only woman I have ever loved. She is a great prize, and you must treat her well."

"I always have," Mark replied, and, insulted that the brave thought such a demand necessary, he ended their handshake abruptly. "We must hurry. You've been away too long as it is."

Viper did not turn back to look at Erica as he left the house, and she covered her mouth with her hands to keep from crying out as he and Mark walked away. As he passed into the shadows she saw the angry red welts where her fingernails had raked his shoulders and wondered how he would explain those telltale marks to others. That was the first time passion had so swept away her reason that she had left her mark on him, and it broke what was left of her heart to think it would also be the last.

When Mark returned to his tent, he was disappointed to find Erica sound asleep. She had tossed the buckskin dress over the end of her cot, and from the glimpse he had of one bare shoulder, he was certain she was sleeping in the nude. He had expected her to be awake so they could make their plans, but he knew she had slept no more than he had that night. While he was tired, he doubted he would be able to sleep, but the moment he stretched out on his cot, his mind slipped readily into the world of dreams.

It was nearly eleven when Mark awakened Erica. He had already spoken with the Reverend Riggs, and the veteran missionary had agreed to perform their wedding ceremony during the noon recess of the trials. "I'm sorry to wake you, but we're to be married in an hour, and I want you to have time to bathe and dress."

Erica raised her blanket to cover her breasts as she sat up. Far from refreshed, she felt completely drained, as though she had spent the night weeping uncontrollably rather than making love. "You want to be married today?" she asked hesitantly.

Mark tried to control his temper, but failed. "I had the word of that damn Indian that he would convince you to become my wife, so I'll not debate the issue with you. You must hurry, as we've no time to waste. The steamboat has

304

already docked. The provisions will be unloaded within a few hours, and we must be on board when it leaves. Since it will simplify our travel arrangements, I want to make you my wife as quickly as possible. If your fanny is filled with splinters, then I'll dig them out now, but you are going to marry me today."

At first Erica had no idea why Mark would make such a ridiculous remark about splinters. Then she recalled that he had been standing on the opposite side of the door while Viper had made love to her the last time. She blushed deeply at that memory, but managed to respond demurely. "I'm sure I don't have any splinters."

"That's good, although I'm surprised. Eros, my foot! That brave is more satyr than god. It makes me sick to think I agreed to his bargain, but I expect you to keep his promise about marrying me, although I doubt he would have."

"Viper's word is good," Erica insisted proudly. "He is a passionate man, and I'm sorry if we shocked you, but it is not every day that someone so proud as he is forced to give away the wife he loves dearly."

"I doubt the savage is even capable of love, but that is neither here nor there. Keep the dress he gave you, his bow and rifle, too, but I do not want his name ever mentioned again. As far as anyone will ever know, I am the only husband you have had. You need never discuss the details of the uprising other than to describe them as unpleasant. This whole affair will be forgotten soon, and I want it to remain forgotten. Is that understood?"

"Yes," Erica agreed reluctantly, but she knew she would never forget Viper nor how desperately she loved him. "I am to be your wife, you needn't worry that I will disgrace you by talking about my love for an Indian brave in front of others."

"Thank you. I told you I considered this whole regrettable incident my fault, since I insisted upon postponing our wedding last spring, and I will do my best to put everything right now. We'll make a home for ourselves in Wilmington, and I will get leaves as often as I possibly can to be with you. When the war is over, I'm sure there will be a rush to rebuild everything that's been destroyed, and I should do very well. I'll give you a happy life, Erica. I promised you that when we became engaged, and I'll make it happen."

He was so earnest in his promise, Erica tried to smile. "Yes, I know you will. I'll do my best to make you happy, too." Mark left her then to allow her the privacy to dress, but Erica found it difficult to leave her cot. The fragrance that clung to her every pore was Viper's heady masculine scent rather than her own, and she didn't want to wash it away, although she knew she would have to. "I will be with you always," she whispered softly to herself, and hoping she could be as brave as he, she got up and began to prepare for her wedding day.

Erica had only the pink gown to wear as her wedding dress, and after bathing she put it on. She combed her hair in the elaborate style she knew Mark admired and gave no further thought to her appearance. Had they been wed in Wilmington in the spring, she would have had an extravagant gown and a lavish wedding attended by more than a hundred family friends, but that this ceremony would be but a simple one did not make her feel slighted. When Mark came to fetch her, she was the vision of loveliness he had hoped to find. She had scrubbed herself so clean her fair skin glowed with the pink blush of health, while her hair had dried in the sun with a glorious golden luster. If anything, the tears she had shed during the night had made the remarkable dark blue of her eyes all the more deep, and she looked as pretty as he had ever seen her.

"I have never told you how handsome you are in your uniform," Erica replied to his effusive compliments on her appearance. He was tall and handsome, and the well-tailored dark blue uniform showed off his unusual coloring to every advantage. Few men had such light hair and dark eyes, and she had always thought it an attractive combination. She laid her hand upon his sleeve as they left his tent. "Where is the wedding to take place?"

"In the tent serving as the chapel. I haven't invited more than the two men we'll need to serve as witnesses. I hope you don't mind."

"No, not at all. I've no friends here but you."

Stephen Riggs had come to the Minnesota Territory in 1837 to minister to the Sioux. His Hazelwood mission had been located above the Upper Agency, so he had not known Viper. When Mark had asked him after the battle of Wood Lake to perform a wedding ceremony as soon as he could free his fiancée, he had quite naturally agreed, not realizing the young captain's romance would become such a complicated one. Like everyone else connected with the trials he had heard the gossip about Erica Hanson, but he had cautioned the women who came to him with tales to be more charitable, and he was trying to follow that example himself. That her Indian husband had been condemned to death only the previous day had both shocked and saddened him, but the minister had found Mark Randall so insistent upon their marriage as the best alternative for the young woman's future that he had agreed to perform the ceremony without delay.

To his delighted surprise, Reverend Riggs found Erica even more charming than she had been rumored to be. She had so elegant an appearance and refined a manner that he could not imagine her eloping with an Indian brave. Since the Sioux did not regard marriage as a sacrament as Christians did, he considered her free to marry and pushed aside his thoughts on the possible impropriety of performing the ceremony. He gave Mark a questioning glance when no more than the two witnesses arrived to attend, but the captain replied that there would be no guests and asked that he begin.

As the kindly gray-haired missionary began the service, Erica felt a curious sense of detachment rather than the delicious excitement she thought a bride should experience. Her heart still belonged to the virile brave who had stolen it, and she felt as though she were merely acting a part in a play rather than exchanging wedding vows. She knew Mark deserved far more than the reserved affection she would be able to give him, but more to ease Viper's mind than her own, she took him for her husband. Her voice echoed with a hollow sound in the near empty tent, but Mark seemed satisfied that her promises were sincere and gave her an enthusiastic kiss when the Reverend Riggs pronounced them man and wife.

They accepted the congratulations offered by the two witnesses graciously, then returned to their tent to pack. Erica listened with scant interest as Mark arranged for their few belongings to be carried down to the steamboat, for she still felt somewhat dazed. "Do you suppose the ship will stop in New Ulm?" she asked. "I would make the effort to see my aunt and uncle again, if I thought they would receive me."

"I suppose the ship might stop there to pick up cargo or passengers. Would you like me to ask the captain what his plans are?" Mark would be proud to introduce his bride to anyone. If the Ludwigs' store was not out of their way, then he would escort her there quite happily.

As they made their way to the river, Erica did not look back, for she wanted no memories of the Lower Agency. She didn't want to see the tepees on the hill, nor the neat rows of army tents. She wanted to remember only the beauty of the love she had found in Minnesota, not the tragic way it had come to an end. She heard the sound of quick footsteps behind them but paid no attention, thinking only that someone else was in a hurry to reach the steamboat. When she heard a shrill female voice call Mark's name, her heart fell. Thinking one of the hostile women she had done her best to avoid must have heard they were leaving and come to cause another embarrassing scene, she looked up at her new husband with a fearful glance. In that instant she saw the bright flash of a steel blade gleaming in the sun, and without a thought of her own safety, she shoved Mark aside.

Song of the Wren began to scream hysterically then. She had planned to plunge her knife clear to the hilt in Mark's chest, but deprived of that target she turned the full fury of her murderous rage on Erica. "I will kill you both!" she shrieked as she swung her knife in a wide arc, redirecting her aim for the pale flesh of Erica's slender throat.

Erica threw up her hands to fight off the attack, and as Mark regained his balance he joined in the fray. Wren fought like a wild beast, lunging repeatedly for Erica at the same time she tried to fight off Mark's determined attempts to subdue her. Soon all three were in the dirt, blood splattering their clothes as they rolled in a tangled heap. Their combined screams and shouts swiftly brought a crowd, but it took the efforts of three men to finally wrench the knife from Wren's hand and pull her away.

The Indian maiden was so consumed with hatred that she continued to scream the vilest of curses. "You lying

308

bastard! Viper will die because of you and that whore! You promised to bring him back for trial, not to his death!" She lapsed into her own tongue then, to call Erica every hideous name she knew. They could still hear her shrieking insults as the men who held her half carried, half dragged her away.

There was a long slash across Mark's left cheek, but it was a slight wound compared to the ones Erica had suffered. The right sleeve of her gown had been ripped from the bodice and blood was seeping from a gash in her shoulder. Wren's first wild lunge had pierced the palm of her right hand, and Erica sat holding it tightly as she wept, but she was shaking too badly to apply enough pressure to stop the bleeding, and drops of bright red blood were dripping all down the front of her gown. She looked up at Mark, her eyes still filled with fright as her tears splashed down upon her bloody hands.

"Someone bring a doctor to the ship!" Mark called to the crowd of bystanders, and scooping up his badly injured bride in his arms, he carried her on board the steamboat where the horrified captain quickly directed them to a cabin. He had been told he would have passengers, but he had not anticipated an emergency so dire as this.

Sitting primly on the edge of the bunk, Erica did not protest as Mark peeled away her tattered gown. He tore strips of clean fabric from the skirt and bound her profusely bleeding hand quickly, then pressed his handkerchief against the bloody wound in her shoulder.

"If Viper sent that bitch after us I'll kill him with my bare hands. I swear I will!" Mark vowed through clenched teeth. He had been so worried about Erica, he had not noticed the cut in his face until blood began to drip off his chin. He brushed it away with an impatient swipe without pausing in his string of threats. "She'd do whatever he asked, but if what he planned was murder, I'll see he's the one who ends up dead."

Everywhere she looked Erica saw blood. She felt sick to her stomach and faint with fright, but she knew Viper would never have made so many sweet promises had he wanted either her or Mark dead. "No, he wouldn't do this. He wouldn't. Wren despises me, but I don't understand why she hates you."

"You know her?" Mark asked incredulously.

As Erica nodded the small cabin began to spin. "I feel faint, Mark. I'm—" she went limp then, slumping forward in his arms as she lost consciousness.

Mark sat down and pulled Erica across his lap. He hugged her tightly, not realizing the blood from the cut in his face was dripping into her hair. He prayed a physician would come quickly, and in a few minutes a young army doctor newly assigned to Minnesota was there. "Some crazy Sioux bitch stabbed my wife," Mark explained in an excited rush. "She's fainted."

"I can see that," the young man replied with a smile so warm he instantly inspired confidence. He lifted the handkerchief to look at Erica's shoulder, and thinking it not too bad he unwrapped the makeshift bandage on her hand. "Looks like she's lost quite a bit of blood, but neither of these wounds will prove fatal. A few stitches is all she requires." He looked up then to get a better look at Mark. "I'll just bandage your face. That cut's not deep and it won't leave too bad a scar."

"Just take care of my wife," Mark implored him.

"I will. Let's place her on the bed, and if luck is with us, I'll have those cuts sewn up before she awakens. I'll give you some laudanum to help her sleep, as she's sure to be in pain for several days. Hands are very sensitive, you know." The friendly doctor kept up a steady stream of informative conversation as he worked, more in an attempt to distract Mark from the horror he had witnessed than out of a need for company. By the time he had dressed both Erica's and Mark's wounds, the steamboat's whistle had already been blown, announcing they were ready to depart.

"Damn it all," Mark swore. "There's someone I have to see before we get under way."

As the doctor packed his instruments back into his bag, he offered some advice. "From what I heard, they have the girl responsible for the attack in custody. Isn't it more important that you remain here with your wife? She's a delicate woman, and I imagine she'll not be feeling well when she awakens. I certainly wouldn't leave my wife alone at such a trying time."

"Of course, you're right. I'll stay here with her." Mark

310

was disappointed to have no other choice, but he consoled himself with the thought that even if he saw Wren, she would be unlikely to tell him the truth, and even if she did, Viper would only deny it. At any rate, the man had already been given a death sentence, so what more could he do to him? "Thank you for your help."

"You should have another physician examine your wife in St. Paul. I don't think any tendons were severed in her hand, but the wound is a bad one and could cause her problems if it doesn't receive proper care."

"Yes, I'll see she receives the finest in medical attention. Her father is a physician. I'm sure he will be of help to us, too."

"She is in good hands, then." The young doctor bid Mark a hasty good-bye, then hurried off the ship. He had been treating so many horrible wounds caused by war, it had been a pleasure for him to have a female patient for a change, but he was sorry he had had no opportunity to talk with her.

Mark pulled the cabin's one chair over beside the bed to wait for Erica to wake. "Dear God," he whispered, "what a horrible way to begin a honeymoon." As he sat by his sleeping bride's side, he prayed it was not an evil omen of what he could expect from their marriage.

# Chapter Twenty-One

## October, 1862

Erica awoke with a start. The steamboat was moving downstream at a brisk clip and the motion of the vessel compounded the queasy sensation she had felt prior to fainting. But that was a small complaint compared to the painful throb that radiated through her right arm from shoulder to fingertip. As she looked down at her hand she was amazed to find it now so generously swathed in clean white bandages that only the tips of her nails were visible. The sight of her left hand was equally disconcerting, however, for the plain gold wedding band Mark had brought with him from Delaware was a taunting reminder of a marriage she suddenly had grave doubts she should have begun.

"You're awake," Mark exclaimed with obvious relief. "How do you feel?" He had been pacing the small cabin, but returned to the chair at her bedside and moved close, his expression filled with both concern and hope as he awaited her report.

Erica licked her lips nervously. Her only thought was that their wedding night must be rapidly approaching, and she had never felt less like making love. Surely Mark would not insist upon consummating their marriage after what she had been through. At least she hoped not, and she quickly offered a silent prayer that he would be far more patient with her than that. "I feel sort of seasick, I guess," she began hesitantly, "and my whole arm hurts rather badly."

Mark nodded. "I was afraid of that. The doctor who treated you was a cheerful sort, but he said you'd have quite a bit of pain. Do you want to try and eat something, some soup perhaps? I'd hate to give you laudanum and put you right back to sleep when I've missed you so much."

He was on the edge of his seat, patting her knee lightly as he talked, but Erica was more frightened than encouraged by the warmth of his mood. "Have I been asleep long?"

"A few hours is all."

"We've passed New Ulm, then?" Erica frowned slightly, for a moment not recalling why she had wanted to stop there.

"Yes, and we didn't stop. I guess they've nothing left to ship. I know you wanted to see your relatives, but we can write to them from St. Paul and let them know you've married me and that we're returning home. That ought to put them in a sufficiently forgiving frame of mind to respond."

"What is there to forgive?" Erica murmured softly, confused by his comment.

Mark was astonished by that question. "If it isn't obvious to you, I won't upset you by explaining. Now how about that soup? You've got to eat. The doctor said you would need plenty of rest and good food."

"Yes, soup would be nice. Maybe some bread and butter, if they have some. And hot tea?" she added as an afterthought.

Mark leaned over to brush her lips lightly before leaving to see to her requests. "I hope you'll be comfortable resting in your camisole. Your dress was ruined, but I'm sure we can find you some nice things to wear in St. Paul. When we get back home I want you to order as many gowns as you like. You know price is no object. I always loved seeing you in all your pretty clothes, and I want you to replace everything you've lost."

That he would be such a generous husband made Erica feel all the more guilty at being a fraud as his wife. "I had too much," she apologized in a breathless rush. "I won't need nearly so many gowns now."

313

"Why not? You'll still want to do things like visit friends and entertain. Even though I'll be away, I want you to enjoy yourself. Now let me go see what I can find to eat. I'm hungry, too, now that I think about it."

The minute he was gone, Erica closed her eyes and tried to imagine how she was going to keep the promises she had made to him at noon. That she had once loved Mark only made her mental anguish all the more deep, for what she felt for him now was so different from what her feelings had once been. Had she not truly loved him last spring? Was that why her love had faded so quickly once they were apart? Would the same thing happen now that she would never see Viper again? Would the love that now made her heart ache with loneliness not last more than a few brief weeks? Only time would bring the answer to those painful questions, but while Erica had not expected life without Viper to be easy, she had not thought pretending to be happy with Mark would be so terribly hard.

Mark watched Erica attempt to eat with her left hand and could not help but notice what a difficult time she was having. "I should have had the cook put your soup in a cup."

"No, this is fine," Erica insisted, even though most of the clear broth sloshed over the edge of her spoon each time she raised it to her lips. Mark had buttered her bread for her, and setting her spoon aside, she took a few bites of it. "Maybe I was just hungry. I'm beginning to feel better."

"Well, that's certainly good news," Mark replied with a ready grin.

Erica looked away quickly, not up to replying with teasing banter, but the cause for the delight in his expression had been unmistakable. "Mark," she began hesitantly, reluctant to bring up the subject of their sleeping arrangements, and yet too nervous about them to let the matter slide. "Where are you going to sleep?" she finally gathered the courage to ask.

"Are you serious?" he responded with a puzzled frown.

"Yes, I am. This cabin is very small, and this bunk awfully narrow."

Upon awakening the pretty blonde had looked quite pale, but her cheeks suddenly held not even a slight trace of color. Not understanding her comment, or the fact that she seemed to be growing more frail rather than stronger, Mark was offended, but for the wrong reason. "This is a cargo ship, not a luxury vessel," he pointed out crossly. "I'm sorry if the accommodations don't please you, but you'll have to remember I'm not the one who booked our passage. Besides, this cabin is no smaller than the tent we've been sharing."

To cover her embarrassment, Erica managed to take a sip of tea without dribbling too much down her chin, but she then gave up the effort to eat and pushed her tray away. "I was thinking only of your comfort. I wasn't being critical."

Having finished his supper, Mark set his plate at his feet. "Married couples frequently share the same bed, Erica. I can't believe you didn't know that. It's unfortunate that we have just the one bunk, since you're not well, but it will have to do. I've no intention of asking the captain if he has other quarters available so I can spend our wedding night alone."

When Erica's expression mirrored her hurt and dismay, Mark grabbed her tray and his plate and returned them to the galley. He stood on deck to watch the sunset, then tarried there, lost in his own thoughts, until it grew dark. When he returned to their cabin, he felt like a fool for not realizing Erica would not have been able to light the lamp on her own. She was sitting in the dark, exactly where he had left her, but her eyes were filled with such incredible sorrow he was ashamed he had been so sarcastic and impatient with her.

"I'm sorry. I thought perhaps you'd like to be alone for a while, but I didn't mean to leave you sitting in the dark like this. That was very thoughtless of me."

"It didn't matter," Erica lied through trembling lips, for while he had been gone her misgivings about the wisdom of their marriage had increased to nearly intolerable proportions. Her fears had finally reached the point where she was certain Mark would demand she make love to him the instant he returned. She was also positive she would go into hysterics the moment he touched her. Making things all the worse, she feared once she began to scream, the heartrending pain of leaving Viper would overwhelm

315

her and she would never be able to stop. She would undoubtedly end up chained to a wall in an insane asylum where not even her father would come to see her. Her grip upon reality tenuous at best, she looked down at her injured hand as Mark lit the lamp.

Having no idea of his wife's secret terrors, Mark thought the light imparted a warm glow to the small cabin that was quite romantic. He then turned the wick low to enhance the intimate mood he hoped to create.

"Do you want some laudanum?" he remembered to offer. "It would help you sleep."

"What about your face? Doesn't that cut hurt?" Erica asked as she forced herself to look up him.

Mark shook his head as he began to unbutton his shirt. "It's just a scratch."

To her absolute horror, Erica found herself unable to look away as Mark proceeded to undress with what she considered a casual disregard for her feelings. He had a handsome body, one she would have admired had she not known another man's first. He sat down on the edge of bunk to pull off his boots, but as he reached for his belt buckle, she made a valiant attempt to begin a conversation she hoped would last several hours. "You didn't tell me how you happened to meet Song of the Wren."

Since that was the last subject he wished to discuss, Mark dismissed it with a convenient lie. "She overheard me saying I was looking for you, and we exchanged a few words about Viper. Obviously she blames me for his death sentence. I told you I didn't want to talk about him ever again, though, so let's just drop the subject."

Erica understood the reasons for that request well enough, but that did not relieve her terrible anxiety about how Mark might wish to spend the evening. When he rose to remove his pants, she hurriedly spoke up in another attempt to distract him. "Yes, I do want some laudanum. I'm sure I will never be able to rest without it. You said the doctor told you I needed my sleep to get well."

While surprised by her sudden enthusiastic request for the solution of opium in alcohol, Mark poured a small amount into a glass and held it out to her. "Is this enough?"

"No, I'm sure I need at least twice that much," Erica

316

insisted with what she hoped would sound like an authoritative tone, but she was now shaking so badly she doubted she would be able to hold the glass no matter how much or little it contained.

Mark shrugged. "I'm sure you know more about medicines than I do." He added more of the deep brownish-red liquid to the glass and handed it to her. When Erica grabbed it in a frantic clutch and gulped it down in one reckless swallow, he couldn't help but laugh. "Hey, I don't think you're supposed to toss that down like whiskey."

Erica handed him the empty glass, then moved over as far as she could, but there was still only a narrow strip of the bunk left for him. "I didn't think I'd be able to swallow it if I sipped it. You needn't leave the lamp on, I'm not afraid of the dark." Only of your desires, she added silently in her mind.

Mark had his own reasons for wanting the cabin lit. "Neither am I, but it's always a good idea to have a light when sleeping in strange surroundings. I don't want you to wake up in the middle of the night and become frightened."

Erica suspected she had taken so much laudanum she might not awaken for several days, so she didn't argue. "Yes, I suppose it's always wise to be cautious." She snuggled down into the pillow and closed her eyes tightly rather than watch him strip off the last of his clothes, but she held her breath as she felt the mattress sag as he climbed into the bunk beside her.

A slow smile played across Mark's lips as he looked down at Erica. She had never been so shy or nervous with him as she was acting tonight, and he found it strangely amusing. After all, he knew for a fact she was no longer a virgin, so why was she behaving more like one now than she ever had in the past? He called her name as he placed his fingers beneath her chin, "Erica, look at me."

Her heart was pounding so wildly in her chest that Erica was afraid the sound would drown out her voice as she whispered a plaintive, "Yes?" Her long lashes nearly swept her brows as she looked up at him with a glance that more closely bordered stark terror than polite interest.

"If we are lucky, we'll be married for fifty or sixty years,"

317

Mark confided with a smile. "I want the first time we make love to be perfect. I'd certainly not force myself upon you when you're in so much pain you need a drug to sleep. What kind of a monster do you think I am?"

"I'm sorry," Erica mumbled softly, ashamed her fears had overpowered her reason to the point where she had forgotten how sweetly he had always treated her. "I'm sorry," she repeated in a voice choked with the torrent of tears she dared not release.

Settling down beside her, Mark eased Erica into his arms. "Please don't cry. This is nice just like this. Now stop worrying and go to sleep. I'll be here if you need me."

The bunk was so narrow that Erica had no choice but to lay her head upon Mark's shoulder and her bandaged hand upon his heavily furred chest, but it was a long while before she grew calm enough to actually rest. While his embrace was pleasant, he was not Viper, and had she not taken so much laudanum, she would never have fallen asleep. As it was, her opium-induced dreams were vivid, forming a kaleidoscope of haunting images. Memories of her dashing Sioux husband flooded her mind with equal parts of joy and pain. She saw Viper riding the black stallion, his ebony hair blowing in the wind, his face streaked with the bright red war paint he had worn the day the Sioux had attacked New Ulm. The claws he had worn around his neck became those of the cougar she had shot, then ripped across the canvas of her dreams leaving the same bloody trails her nails had left upon his shoulders.

She felt his warm breath as his lips again caressed her breasts, and she pressed against him, eagerly enfolding him in her arms as she whispered the words of love she thought she would never again have a chance to speak. She wound her fingers in his hair, forcing his mouth to hers where the hunger in her kiss inflamed his own until his need for her became too fierce to contain. His sleek body covered hers then, and with one swift thrust he plunged to the white-hot core of her being and lay still, his breathing a wild roar in her ears as he allowed the passion that had driven him to the limits of sanity to subside to where he could again control it.

Fighting wildly against his cool restraint, she wrapped her legs around his waist, her nails leaving long trails across his back as she clung to him. Inspired by her

318

unbridled desire, he began to move with a forceful rhythm that soon reached a fevered staccato pitch. He felt her muscles contract in glorious spasms of delight and flung himself upon those wild waves of rapture, riding them until their passion for each other reached a shattering peak and engulfed them in a shimmering ecstasy as blinding in its beauty as their love.

The fiery impact of that erotic dream haunted Erica all day, for it had seemed far too vivid to have been triggered merely by memory. It was not until Mark again undressed for bed and she saw that the smooth skin of his back was unmarred that she finally drew a sigh of relief. It had been a dream, after all, she told herself. Then, looking down at her injured hand, she realized she should have known she could not have scratched him with her nails, even if she had tried. She looked up at Mark, her eyes mirroring the sorrow she feared would have no end. He was a kind man and a good one, but how could he ever hope to break the bonds of love she and Viper had forged? No, their brief marriage could not simply be put aside, for the memory of Viper's love permeated not only each of her waking hours, but flooded her dreams with rapture, as well.

"Mark," Erica called softly, her anguish clear in her breathless tone.

Mistakenly believing her pain was physical rather than emotional, Mark poured a generous amount of laudanum into a glass and saw she drank it all. He then joined her in the narrow bunk and held her until she fell asleep, content merely to enfold her in his arms for the time being.


Just as Mark had expected, he had been given orders in St. Paul to return to his former unit immediately. When he and Erica arrived in Wilmington she begged to go to her own home rather than the one he had shared with his sister, and since she had not fully recovered from the stab wounds, he granted her request without argument. He was disappointed that they had been unable to begin their honeymoon. They had yet to share the delicious nights he had hoped to fill with romance, but he took comfort in the fact that Erica had willingly become his wife and had not once complained about that situation. He hoped by the time he could arrange a leave that she would be completely well and he could then make all his dreams for a happy marriage come true. He left her at her father's house in Mrs. Ferguson's capable hands, then stopped for a brief visit with his sister on his way out of town.

Sarah Randall was remarkably pretty. She shared Mark's unusual coloring, although she used liberal amounts of lemon juice to enhance the blond highlights in her honey-brown hair. Her brown eyes were usually alert with mischief, for she was a flirtatious young woman who loved fun. At twenty-five, she was a year younger than her brother, but unconcerned by the fact that she was still single. She had always had many beaux, and the fact that most had drifted away to wed her friends did not depress her. She had always had a way with men and been so popular that she was certain when the war was over she would be deluged with impassioned proposals.

"Mark! Why didn't you send word you were coming home? What if I'd missed you?" Sarah exclaimed excitedly as she threw herself into his arms with an ecstatic squeal of delighted surprise.

Mark readily returned her enthusiastic hug, for they had always been close. Their parents had died within a year of each other while Sarah was in her late teens, and he had kept a watchful eye on her ever since. "Aren't you going to ask me about Erica?" he teased. The two were acquainted, but were not good friends, which he thought was his sister's fault, since she was the elder of the two and should have made the first effort to be friendly.

A twinge of jealousy tugged at her emotions, but for her brother's sake, Sarah forced it aside. "I wanted to say hello to you first, but of course I want to hear about everything that happened. I can tell from the width of your smile that you found your precious Erica. Did you marry her as planned?"

"Yes, I did," Mark admitted proudly, although nothing had gone as he had planned. "I have to report for duty this very day, so I've no time to relate the whole tale, but I do want you to know the most important part." Mark had given considerable thought to how much of Erica's recent past he wished to share. "You must keep what I am about to tell you to yourself, Sarah, but when you go to visit Erica, which I want you to do often, I know you'll notice a difference in her manner, and I want you to understand why. It must be our secret, though. You are not to spread a word of this to your friends, who spend more time gossiping than any lady should. Now give me your word you'll not breathe a word of this to anyone. Ever."

"Of course, I'll keep what you say in confidence," the brown-eyed beauty agreed. By asking for such a promise Mark had won her rapt attention, but the story he told was so difficult for Sarah to accept that when he completed it and rose to leave, she simply stared up at him with her mouth agape.

"You don't mean it! Erica ran off with an Indian brave? Erica actually did that?"

Mark reached for his sister's hands and pulled her to her feet. "Come walk me to the door. Don't judge anything Erica did, or ask her to explain it. I am so happy to be her husband, I am not troubled by the fact that I am not her first. I don't want you to be troubled by it, either."

"I don't know what to say," Sarah replied with a befuddled frown.

"You will say absolutely nothing to Erica or anyone else. I have your promise on that, and I expect you to keep it," Mark admonished her sternly. "Now give me a kiss and wish me continued good luck. I'll try and come home soon."

Sarah's eyes filled with tears as she bid him good-bye, for she loved her only brother dearly. "Be careful, I couldn't bear it if something happened to you."

Mark laughed as he waved good-bye. "Nothing can happen to me now!" he boasted confidently.

As Sarah closed the front door behind him she thought him very cruel for telling her such a fascinating story and then insisting she keep her promise not to share it with her friends. Such a demand would have been impossible coming from anyone else, but for Mark, she would keep her word, although she knew it would be the most difficult thing she had ever done. "An Indian brave!" she giggled to herself, wondering what had possessed Erica to do such an outrageous thing. Inspired by the hope of learning more from his bride than Mark had revealed, Sarah decided right then to become the best friend Erica had ever had.

*　　*　　*

Henry Sibley had no idea how to go about punishing Song of the Wren. Since Mark and Erica were gone, there was no one to press charges against her, so he could not put her on trial for assault. Finally he released her to the friendly chiefs who thought the jealous young woman's hatred for whites not unusual and did nothing at all. At the end of the trials, she and her family were among the seventeen hundred Sioux who were transferred to Fort Snelling where the army could more readily feed them. Although there were no charges against this group, they spent a wretched winter in a fenced camp on the Minnesota River, while their future was being debated in Washington.

On November 5, 1862, the military commission completed their work. They had tried 392 braves, handed down 307 death sentences, 16 long prison terms, and 69 acquittals. Colonel Sibley approved their findings in all but the case of John Other Day's brother, whose death sentence he commuted to a prison term because of lack of evidence and Other Day's persuasive appeal.

General Pope and Colonel Sibley both wished to execute the condemned Indians at the conclusion of the trials, but fearing that would be overstepping their authority, they asked President Lincoln to decide that question in October. When, after another review, the final list of condemned was set at 303, Pope telegraphed their names to the president. With the exorbitant cost of the war placing an enormous burden upon the federal treasury, Lincoln was not pleased with that four-hundred-dollar expense and replied with the request that Pope send the complete record of the convictions by mail. A man possessed of remarkable wisdom, Lincoln, when the papers arrived, appointed two men to study them thoroughly, so that the Sioux braves accused of rape and wanton murder could be separated from those who had done no more than fight in battles.

On November 9, the condemned prisoners were transferred from the Lower Agency to Camp Lincoln in South Bend. As their wagons passed through New Ulm, the citizens eagerly seized the opportunity to vent their hatred on the braves who were securely bound and could do little to escape injury other than attempt to dodge the barrage of rocks hurled their way.

Viper was as badly abused as the rest of his companions. He saw Erica's uncle and returned his hate-filled stare until the young man at his side threw a stone that tore a jagged cut in his forehead and blood began to drip into his eyes. He reminded himself these were people who had lost family members they held dear, but it amused him to realize the violence of the whites' behavior was far more savage than his own had ever been. It was not until the troops providing their escort charged the crowd with bayonets that the battered prisoners were allowed to continue their journey unmolested.

On December 4, a group from Mankato bent on taking the matter of the Sioux's executions into their own hands was stopped on the road to Camp Lincoln. Fearing for his prisoners' safety, Colonel Sibley then moved the condemned men to a log structure in Mankato where they could be guarded more effectively. Here again, the braves had nothing to occupy their time but their own dreary thoughts. Crowded and miserable, their tempers were short, but Viper kept to himself, and when fools like Claw of the Badger taunted him about losing his wife, he ignored them, for in his mind and heart, he knew Erica would never be lost to him.

As the holidays neared, Erica spent each morning poring over the newspapers. With a morbid fascination, she searched out each mention of the Sioux. Governor Ramsey of Minnesota, General Pope, and countless others called daily for the immediate execution of the condemned braves. With the notable exception of the Episcopal Bishop, Henry B. Whipple, who had been to see President Lincoln to plead for the braves' lives, and the Reverend Riggs and Dr. Williamson, who wrote letters on the Indians' behalf, the whole world seemed to be clamoring for their deaths with a ghoulish frenzy.

To add to Erica's worries, it had been nearly six weeks since she had spent the predawn hours wishing Viper a passionate farewell, and with each new day she grew more certain she had become pregnant as a result. While the hope that she would have his baby was a wonderfully comforting one, the fact that Mark might not wish to raise an Indian's child was deeply troubling. Were the baby to be a blond girl he might possibly accept her, but Erica thought it far more likely she would present him with a black-haired boy he could never love as his own. Just the prospect of telling him she thought she was pregnant filled her with such a horrible sense of dread that she became physically ill.

Actually, since returning home she had never felt completely well. Whether it was due to morning sickness or to the lingering effects of Wren's brutal assault she didn't know, but she was often too ill to eat and had little energy. Sarah Randall had insisted upon supervising the selection of her new wardrobe, and she had simply lacked the strength to refuse her help, although she had managed to refuse each invitation the persistent young woman had offered in an effort to encourage her to get out and see her friends again. Social obligations were simply too great a strain in Erica's frame of mind, but to the people of Wilmington, who regarded her as a new bride who should welcome their invitations, she seemed unaccountably aloof.

In November, Major-General Ambrose E. Burnside had been placed in command of the Army of the Potomac, a position he had twice refused to accept, stating he felt unequal to the task. He was an 1847 graduate of West Point who had left the army to manufacture firearms. At the outset of the war he had become a colonel in the Rhode Island volunteers, was soon made brigadier-general of volunteers, then major-general. In early December he was preparing an assault upon Fredericksburg, Virginia. Erica tried to keep abreast of the news regarding the war, too, but she was confident Mark could take care of himself, while she knew Viper was in no position to do so.

On December 6, 1862, President Lincoln approved death sentences for only 39 of the 303 condemned Sioux. In his own hand he wrote out the names of those to be executed on December 19, and sent the order to Colonel Sibley to carry out. This was the day Erica had been dreading, and her hands shook so badly as she read the headline in the newspaper that she could scarcely make out the print.

"Only thirty-nine?" she whispered as her heart swelled with hope. Hurriedly she scanned the list of names for the one of the man she adored. When she realized the miracle she had not dared expect had happened and his life had been spared, she was too dazed to either laugh or weep. She sank down on the settee in the parlor and tried simply to comprehend what this totally unexpected piece of good fortune meant.

"Viper isn't going to die," she whispered as she broke into an angelic smile. That was so marvelous a relief it was difficult to grasp. The president had had the wisdom the members of the military commission had sorely lacked. He understood that there was a difference between men who fought for their beliefs and those who would use war as an excuse to murder and rape. Tears of joy began to trickle down her cheeks.

Viper was going to have a future, and she wanted to spend it with him. Her hands went to her stomach, which as yet showed no trace of her pregnancy, and she whispered, "You'll know your daddy after all, my darling, and I know you'll think him as wonderful a man as I do."

Erica spent the next week in a blissful fog. There were still problems ahead: apparently Viper might have to serve some time in prison, but she regarded that as a small inconvenience when compared with the fate he had so recently faced. She planned to return to Minnesota as soon as she had the opportunity to tell Mark of her decision. There was a good chance he would be given a leave at Christmas, and while she knew he would be heartbroken, she hoped he would love her enough to let her go.


Before dawn on December 11, a Union force numbering a hundred thirteen thousand men under Major-General Ambrose Burnside's command attacked General Lee's Confederate stronghold at Fredericksburg. With a desperate series of frontal attacks he tried, without success, to break through the South's defenses. The Confederates repelled each of his poorly timed assaults, and after suffering staggering losses, Burnside withdrew. Twelve hundred of his troops had been killed in the battle. Another ninety-six hundred had been wounded, and Captain Mark Randall was one of those casualties.

# Chapter Twenty-Two

## December, 1862

Lars Hanson looked out at the long line of ambulance wagons drawing up outside the hospital and heaved a weary sigh. "God help us," he prayed under his breath, wondering where he would find the strength to see even one more injured man, let alone the hundreds he knew would soon be flooding the wards. All too often, soldiers had suffered such horrible wounds before they could reach a hospital that they had already expired. With that dismal thought in mind, Lars went down the steps to the wagon currently being unloaded by two burly orderlies to make certain no dead were carried inside.

"Evenin', doc," the driver of the vehicle called out cheerfully. "Where you want these boys?"

"They're men," Lars corrected him firmly. Many of the wounded were teenagers, but as far as he was concerned, any of them who had chosen to serve their country as soldiers ought to be considered grown men. He waited as the wounded were placed on stretchers, then greeted those who were conscious. He smiled as he offered the same words of encouragement he always did, ignoring the men's powder-blackened faces and torn uniforms as he quickly assessed the extent of their injuries and their chances for survival. In his opinion, this group was exceedingly lucky. They had all reached the hospital alive and in each the odds were at least fifty-fifty or better they would recover from their wounds. Encouraged by that optimistic thought, he quickly commanded the orderlies to begin taking their charges inside and moved on down the line of wagons hoping his next group of patients would be as fortunate as the last.

The driver of the second ambulance apologized as he greeted Lars. "I'm 'fraid I lost one on the way, doc. At least he don't seem to be breathing to me. He's an officer, too, and I sure hate to lose one of them on the road."

So as not to alarm his other passengers with that gruesome news, Lars climbed into the back of the ambulance to help the driver ease the wounded out onto stretchers. The two leather-covered benches that ran along each side of the wagon were sticky with blood, but he was used to that now. This group didn't look nearly so good as the last, but in the dim interior of the wagon Lars could see that one fellow did seem worse off than the rest. His head had been heavily bandaged, and Lars wondered why a surgeon in the field had wasted precious space in an ambulance on so severely injured a man when it was far kinder not to make them suffer the perils of a long journey and simply allow them to die where they had fallen.

He saw the captain's bars on the man's coat as he reached for his wrist to try and detect a pulse and thought perhaps his rank was the reason he had been accorded preferential treatment. When he found a faint but steady beat, Lars wasn't encouraged, for there was little he could do to treat men who had suffered head wounds. Still, he gripped the young man's hand firmly and whispered, "Don't worry, son, I'll do all I can for you."

It wasn't until he had moved the unconscious captain out of the wagon onto a stretcher that he could see his face clearly enough to recognize him as Mark Randall. "Oh no," he moaned. Overcome with despair, he turned away to grab hold of the side of the ambulance to steady himself. Mark had sent a wire when Erica had been found, then another telling of their marriage. He had stopped by the hospital to provide Lars with the details he had not trusted to a wire, but Lars had been so stunned by his new son-in-law's tale that he had said little in response. Now Mark was back, more dead than alive, and Lars feared he could do nothing at all to repay him for the loving forgiveness he had shown his daughter.

Puzzled, the driver started at Lars's back for a moment, then found his voice. "You knew him?"

"I know him," Lars replied as he turned around, steeling himself for the long, weary hours that lay ahead. "You were wrong. The captain is still among the living." He signaled to a pair of orderlies and saw that Mark was the first of that ambulance's passengers to be carried inside, but he was already searching his mind for the words he might need to tell Erica she was no longer a new bride, but sadly, a widow.


The very minute she finished reading the disastrous news of the battle of Fredericksburg, Sarah Randall rushed over to see her brother's wife. When she reached Erica's home she ran up the steps and pounded with so frantic a rhythm that Mrs. Ferguson feared she would shatter the beveled glass in the heavy oak door before she could swing it open. As soon as the gray-haired housekeeper greeted her, Sarah pushed her way inside.

"Where's Erica?" she asked breathlessly as she glanced into the parlor and found it empty.

A woman of impeccable taste and fine manners, Anna Ferguson could see no possible reason for Sarah to call at so early an hour or with such unseemly haste. "Mrs. Randall has yet to rise from her bed, Miss Randall. Perhaps you would like to return this afternoon when—" She was interrupted in midsentence as Sarah waved her aside and dashed up the stairs. With a disapproving frown Anna closed the door, turned the key in the lock, and returned to the kitchen, thinking young women had no manners at all any more. At least Miss Erica did, she thought proudly. Since she had come to work in the Hanson home shortly before Erica was born, she knew she could rightly claim part of that credit herself.

Caring not at all what a housekeeper thought of her, Sarah called out Erica's name loudly as she made her way down the hall. When she reached her bedroom, she threw open the door in the same instant she knocked upon it. "Have you seen this?" she cried out, waving the latest edition of the paper.

Erica had heard Sarah's approach, as indeed she

thought half the neighborhood must have. Since she knew it had to be obvious she had just awakened, she thought the young woman's question ridiculous. "I have just this minute opened my eyes, Sarah. What's wrong?" Her first thought was of Viper, but she had never mentioned his name to Mark's sister, although she suspected from the curious way Sarah regarded her at times that she knew all about him.

Having no idea she might not be as welcome in Erica's bedroom as she believed herself to be, Sarah assumed a comfortable perch on the foot of the four-poster bed. "The casualty lists from Fredericksburg go on for pages and pages, but there's no mention of Mark's company, and I am so dreadfully worried about him. We are very close, and I have this horrible feeling that he's been hurt. You've not heard anything from him, have you?"

"Not this week," Erica admitted, but Mark had written to her quite faithfully since his return to the war, so she expected to hear from him again soon. She could see Sarah was upset, but she wasn't in the least bit apprehensive herself. Since she didn't know what to say to ease her caller's mind, she chose instead to try and distract her. "You know it always takes several days, if not weeks, for the casualty lists to be complete, but it's highly unlikely anything happened to Mark. Why don't you stay and have breakfast with me? Mrs. Ferguson always has something special for me, and it would be a treat to have your company to share it."

Exasperated that Erica seemed so unconcerned about her brother's welfare, rather than accept her invitation, Sarah lashed out at her angrily, "What you really mean is that you don't care! There's no point in your pretending with me another minute. Mark told me about your Indian. He's off the hook now, isn't he? I'll bet you're hoping something does happen to Mark so you can run off with that savage again!"

Stunned by that insulting accusation, since she did indeed have every intention of returning to Viper, Erica simply stared at her uninvited guest for a long moment before she found the words to respond. "I would never, ever, want to see Mark hurt. How can you possibly even imagine such an awful thing, let alone accuse me of it?"

Erica's manner and expression were so undeniably sincere that Sarah knew instantly her fears for her brother had influenced her to speak unwisely, and she burst into tears. "I am so frightened, Erica. I just know something awful has happened to Mark. I just know it."

Erica pushed her covers aside and reached for her pink silk dressing gown before going to the distraught young woman's side. She put her arm around Sarah's shoulders as she offered her what comfort she could. "You mustn't carry on so, Sarah. I'm sure Mark would laugh if he knew you were crying when you've no reason to believe he's been hurt. If you'll give me just a moment to dress, I'll join you in the breakfast room. You're always telling me I should get out more often. Why don't we plan to do something together today? We could go shopping, or perhaps pay a few calls. Whatever you'd like to do would be fine with me."

Listening to Erica's calm reassurances, Sarah became even more embarrassed that she had gone to pieces with fear for her brother when she had only unconfirmed suspicions rather than evidence that he had come to harm. Determined to take firmer control of her emotions, she brushed away her tears. With a carefully projected nonchalance she picked up the now wrinkled newspaper and moved again off the bed. She had as exquisite a wardrobe as Erica again possessed, and she shook out the billowing skirt of a flattering gown of rich autumn gold and slowly crossed to the door. "I could use a cup of tea, I suppose," she admitted rather shyly. "I'm sorry for what I said about the Indian. Mark made me swear I'd never breathe a word of that story to anyone, least of all you. Will you forgive me?"

"There is nothing to forgive," Erica insisted warmly, the optimism of her mood undiminished by their brief confrontation. Since Viper's life had been spared, she couldn't believe Mark would come to any harm. "I'll be with you in just a few minutes."

"Take your time. I'll read the rest of the paper while I'm waiting." Sarah slipped out the door, and with a few loud sniffles, was on her way downstairs.

Erica dressed hurriedly in a gown of slate gray elaborately trimmed with black velvet braid, then tried to be pleasant as she sipped her tea. She nibbled upon the flaky apple pastries Mrs. Ferguson had baked that morning, but as usual she had little appetite so early in the day. Now that Sarah had actually been bold enough to mention Viper, the Indian's presence in her life seemed impossible to ignore, and yet Erica remained discreet and was not even tempted to refer to him. It made conversation difficult, since Sarah was extremely curious about him, and Erica was equally reluctant to divulge any of her secrets. Despite the stilted nature of their discussion, they had just decided to visit the shops when Mrs. Ferguson returned from answering a knock at the front door carrying a telegram for Erica upon a small silver tray.

"Oh my God!" Sarah shrieked, her face going deathly pale. "It's about Mark, isn't it? Well, isn't it?"

While Erica was as greatly alarmed as her guest, she took care not to rip the envelope as she slit it open and withdrew the brief message. While the wound in her right palm had healed without leaving too horrible a scar, her hand was often sore and stiff in the mornings. Trembling as badly as she was now, it made grasping the paper tightly almost impossible. She read the wire through twice before glancing up at Sarah.

"It's from my father." Badly shaken, she hid her anxiety for Sarah's sake. "He says Mark is at the hospital where he's assigned and we should come right away. Is your carriage outside?"

Her most terrifying suspicions confirmed, Sarah leaped to her feet. "Of course, but it's more than one hundred miles to Washington!"

"Yes, I know that, and the sooner we leave the sooner we'll be there. I'll go upstairs and gather a few things, then we'll stop by your house so you can pack. With any luck, we'll be able to bring Mark back with us. He can recuperate here as well as he can in any hospital."

"Recuperate?" Sarah whispered hoarsely, her brown eyes wide with fear.

"Yes," Erica insisted, refusing to believe the worst as Sarah obviously did. "We can make plans on the way."

When she reached her room, Erica hastily folded three of her new gowns, and placed them in a leather satchel. She added a nightgown, a change of lingerie, tossed in her toilet articles, and after adding a substantial amount of cash, considered herself ready to depart. Returning to the first floor, she asked Anna Ferguson to send her father a wire so he would be expecting them, then kissed her goodbye. She grabbed her cloak, took Sarah by the hand, and was out of the house within twenty minutes of having received her father's wire. At the Randall home, she rushed Sarah with her packing and enlisted the service of not only their driver, but also a young groom. While she doubted two women would be molested on the highway when the war had created so much traffic, Erica thought having an extra man along would prove useful if Mark needed help to walk.

They traveled only as far as Elkton, Maryland their first night, but the next day they were up before dawn and covered half the distance to Baltimore. The third night they stopped at an inn outside that bustling town on the Chesapeake. In another day and a half they reached Washington, D.C. Despite the fact that she was eight years younger than Sarah, as they entered the hospital Erica was still very much in charge of their mission, as indeed she had been of the whole trip. She walked up to the nurse at the front desk in a businesslike tone asked where a doctor by the name of Lars Hanson might be found.

The nurse needed only one glance at the remarkable blue of Erica's eyes to correctly guess she must be Lars's daughter. She quickly sent for him and he appeared at the desk almost immediately. He was embarrassed that he had not been home or written since Erica's return from Minnesota, but he had simply not known what to say to her. She had always been far more headstrong than her dear mother, but that she had chosen to live openly with an Indian brave was not something he could excuse as easily as Mark had. It seemed to him to have been a totally immoral and unprincipled thing for her to do, but the instant he saw his daughter his shame at her scandalous behavior was instantly forgotten. He swept her off her feet in a boisterous hug, then noticing she was not alone, he set her down gently and smiled as he greeted Sarah.

"Miss Randall, isn't it?" he asked in his most charming manner. He thought she resembled Mark slightly, but her features were far more delicate than her brother's, making her a very attractive young woman.

Sarah stared up at Lars a moment too long, then blushed deeply, but she had never met Erica's father and had had no idea he was such a young and handsome man. That she would notice such attributes at so inappropriate a time horrified her, however. "How do you do, Dr. Hanson. May we see Mark now?" she asked primly, hoping he had not noticed how boldly she had been staring at him.

"In just a minute." Lars stepped between the two women, and taking each by the arm, he escorted them outside to the garden where the afternoon air, while cool, was not bone-chilling. "Mark has been here nearly a week. While his chances for survival grow better each day, he has been severely injured, and I don't want you to have unrealistic hopes for his recovery when there is no way it can be guaranteed."

Erica had frequently heard her father use similar words with relatives of his patients when he wished to soften the impact of his prognosis if the outlook wasn't good. She took a deep breath, then insisted he tell them the truth. "Nothing you can possibly say can be worse than what we imagined on the way. It's been such a long and tiring trip, but if we can see Mark for a few minutes it will be well worth our trouble. Just warn us what to expect."

Lars nodded, thinking his daughter wise to make that request. "I think you better sit down first." He indicated the bench where he and Mark had once stopped to talk. He admired his daughter's courage, but he could tell by the way Sarah was shaking with dread and clutching Erica's hand that she was almost totally lacking in that quality herself.

Clearing his throat, he began to describe Mark's condition. "I think an artillery shell must have exploded almost in his face. He suffered a severe head wound as a result. There's no way I can remove all the fragments of the shell from his brain but—" Lars stopped in midsentence as Sarah gave a small cry of alarm and fainted in a graceful heap across Erica's lap. "What did I say?" he asked with a helpless shrug.

"Oh Daddy," Erica scolded. "Sarah has been so upset she would have fainted no matter what you said, but you might have been a little more diplomatic. Is there a place she can lie down for a few minutes?"

"Every bed we've got already has someone in it, sweetheart." Moving to her side, he plucked Sarah from the bench and started back toward the hospital with her in his arms. "We'll be lucky to find a vacant chair," he called back over his shoulder.

Erica ran along behind him, if possible more frightened than Sarah because she knew what the wound her father had been describing meant. "Has Mark been conscious at all?" she asked apprehensively.

They entered the back door of the hospital and Lars turned down a dark hallway, which led to the small room he used as his office. He placed Sarah in the chair at the desk and began to rub her wrists. "A few times, yes, but very briefly. He was coherent, though, and that's a good sign."

"Did he ask for me?" Erica whispered with deepening dread.

"Yes, he did." Leaving Sarah to rest quietly for a moment, Lars turned to face his daughter. He pulled her into his arms for another warm embrace, then began to apologize. "I've done all I can for him, baby, and it's precious little, I'm afraid. A head wound this severe might affect not only his memory, but his ability to think, as well. His hearing may be impaired, and while it makes me sick to tell you this, I'm almost certain he'll be blind."

Erica felt worse than sick at that announcement, but still grasped for any hope he could offer. "But you're not positive?"

"Well no, I'm not absolutely positive about anything as yet. Right now, I'm just trying to keep him alive. There are four days until Christmas. If he's still with us then, I think the worst will be over, but there's a good chance he'll never be really well again."

Erica sighed sadly as she rested in her father's arms. She had had time on the journey to Washington to become resigned to the fact that her own plans would have to be postponed indefinitely. At nearly two months her pregnancy didn't show at all, but she knew it would only be a matter of weeks before it did. If Mark were still seriously ill then, she feared it would be extremely difficult for him to

334

accept the news that she was carrying Viper's child. For the time being, however, she knew that wasn't going to be her main concern.

"Can I stay with him? I'm certain I know more than any of the nurses here do." Erica took her father's hands as she stepped out of his arms. "Sarah has a close friend at whose home she can stay, but I want to be here when Mark wakes."

"Dorothea Dix has recruited the nurses for the army," Lars confided with an easy grin. "She refuses to accept women who are either pretty or young, so I know your presence will be appreciated by all the men here. Since Mark's condition is so grave, I will see you're given special permission to live in the nurses' quarters and tend him; as for Sarah—" he looked down at her then and was relieved to see she had begun to stir. Dropping his daughter's hands, he knelt down by her side.

"Are you feeling better, Miss Randall? I didn't mean to give you such a scare. If you're feeling up to it, I'll take you to see Mark. I know he'll be glad you're here."

Lars Hanson's deep blue eyes were level with hers, and again Sarah found herself thinking his looks and charm wonderfully appealing. Again appalled by a rush of emotion she considered highly inappropriate, she struggled to sit up. "I'm sorry to be so silly. It's just that my brother is very dear to me, and I can't bear to think how horribly he must be injured." She attempted to focus her gaze upon the seams in her kid gloves rather than the handsome blond doctor, but that effort proved totally unsuccessful and she again found her gaze drawn to the comforting warmth of his smile.

"You'll find him no less handsome," Lars assured her. Rising to his feet, he offered his hand. "He'll probably be sleeping, but I'll let you see him for a few minutes. Then I want you to get settled wherever it is you are staying. Tomorrow, when you're more rested, I'll arrange for a longer visit."

"You are very kind," Sarah whispered shyly. She had never felt so inadequate with a man, but she feared a physician must think very little of a woman who would faint at such slight provocation. "I know Mark is in very good hands."

"Thank you, but unfortunately—" Lars gasped then as Erica jabbed him in the ribs with her elbow. Realizing his daughter was warning him to keep still, he gave her an embarrassed smile and gestured for her to precede them as they left his office. "It's the second ward to the right. I put Mark next to the widow, since it's the most cheerful spot in the room."

Sarah gave Lars another shy smile, and gathering all her courage, she managed to walk to her brother's bedside without allowing the heartbreaking sight of the heavily bandaged young men occupying the ward's other beds to unnerve her. As Lars had predicted, Mark was asleep, but other than the thick bandage that covered his crown and dipped down over his left eye, he appeared uninjured, and her heart swelled with hope. "He looks very good, doesn't he, Erica?" She leaned down to kiss Mark's cheek lightly, then gave his fingers a loving squeeze. Smiling happily, she turned to look up at Lars. "He's going to be all right, isn't he?"

The fact that Sarah desperately wanted to hear him say yes was not lost on Lars, but he never lied to a patient's family, and he would not begin with her. "I have done all I can, Miss Randall. Mark's recovery is in God's hands now."

While Sarah seemed reassured by that noncommittal response, Erica wasn't fooled. She walked around to the other side of the bed. As her hand covered Mark's she felt for his pulse and silently counted its rhythm. He was young and strong, and those were invaluable assets in overcoming the effects of any injury. He was also an architect, with wonderful dreams for the future. If he were to recover his health, but not his sight, would he have a future he would think worth living? Fate had dealt her another cruel blow, but Erica clutched Mark's hand tightly, knowing that for as long as he needed her, she would have to stay. She had once promised to love Mark, no matter what awful thing happened to him during the war, and that was not a vow she would break now.

When news of President Lincoln's decision to spare all but thirty-nine of the condemned men reached the Sioux,

Viper could scarcely contain his joy. His first thought was that Erica would again be his and that at that very moment she must surely be on her way back to him. Like the other braves, the executions that finally took place on December 26 affected him deeply, but even the profound sorrow of that day did not dim the bright flame of hope that burned in his heart.

He spent the winter with his fellow prisoners in Mankato, each day expecting to receive a letter or to be told Erica had arrived to see him, but neither a letter nor Erica herself appeared to lighten the grim tedium of his days. Through Stephen Riggs's efforts the prison served as a school, and Viper found himself recruited to help the missionary teach those who could not do so how to read and write in their own language. To his surprise he discovered he had some talents as a teacher, and was soon drawn into the prayer meetings Riggs and Dr. Williamson held. His only thought being to please the woman he still considered his wife, when more than three hundred prisoners were baptized he was among them. He had fought all his life against accepting the religion of the white man, but after having escaped the hangman's noose by so narrow a margin, he felt too great a kinship to Christ to continue to deny the truth of his teachings. While Erica had never once asked him to accept her religion, he hoped that his having done so would please her. The fact that he had still not heard from her both puzzled and pained him, however.

At the height of the uprising, Governor Ramsey had demanded that the Sioux be driven beyond the state borders. That cry was enthusiastically taken up by the citizens of Minnesota and continued when the hostilities were over. The settlers wanted to be rid not only of the Sioux, but also of the peace-loving Winnebago, who had taken no part in the uprising, but who occupied prime farm lands. In December, Minnesota Senator Morton S. Wilkinson and Congressman William Windom introduced bills in Congress designed to relocate the Indians to agricultural lands beyond the border of any state. On February 21, 1863, the Winnebago Act became law, followed by the Sioux Act on March 3. It was decided both tribes would be relocated on land bordering the Missouri

River, in the Dakota Territory.

When navigation resumed upon the Mississippi River in the spring of 1863, the prisoners at Mankato were selected as the first group to be escorted from the state of Minnesota. On April 22, they were chained in pairs, and under heavy guard to discourage reprisals from irate citizens, they were taken aboard the steamboat *Favorite*, bound for Camp McClellan near Davenport, Iowa. There was a brief stop at Fort Snelling where the forty-eight men acquitted of all charges were put ashore along with the nearly two dozen women who had served as cooks for the prisoners. They were to join the seventeen hundred Sioux, predominantly women and children, who had spent the winter there to await relocation with them.

As the *Favorite* pulled away from the docks, Viper caught sight of Song of the Wren. With an anxious glance she was searching the faces of the prisoners standing on deck, and when she saw him she began to smile and wave excitedly, but he turned his back on her. She was a pretty girl; perhaps one of the newly freed men would claim her, but Viper would not waste even so little as a wave of his hand on her himself. By some quirk of fate, he had been chained to Claw of the Badger, who easily recognized Wren and began to tease him.

"There is one of your women, and you will not even look her way?" He waved then, but Wren seemed unimpressed and did not return the gesture.

Viper did not respond to the heavy-set man's question. Granted reprieves, their uneasy truce had held, but neither had any love for the other. It had been six months since Viper had said good-bye to Erica, and his only interest was in being with her again. Since she had not come to him, he was determined to go to her. Escape had been impossible in Mankato, but as he watched their guards stroll the decks of the *Favorite*, he began to devise a plan. Unfortunately, it would have to be a plan to which Badger would have to agree. Knowing the brave to be a scoundrel, however, he thought it very likely he would.

Viper chose dusk as the time for the escape. He waited until the *Favorite* was rounding the wide curve of the Mississippi above Camp McClellan, then whispered the last of his directions to his partner. Badger nodded, understanding the importance of waiting until the guards had walked past them to jump. They had taken a place at the port rail, carefully judged the distance to the water, and adopted the same expressions of bored nonchalance they had worn for months. Knowing each could rely on the other to show the courage needed to follow through on an attempted escape, on the count of ten they scrambled over the rail and plunged headlong into the river.

Badger's heavier weight pulled Viper down deeper than he had expected to go, but he did not struggle to swim to the surface until the steamboat had passed overhead. Then he matched his strokes to Badger's and swam up and toward the shore at an angle. When their heads appeared at the surface, shadows caused by the rapidly approaching night hid them both from the soldiers' view. They could hear men shouting to each other, and one trooper fired, but having no target in view, his shot did not come anywhere near them. Treading water until the steamboat was far in the distance, the two prisoners swam awkwardly to shore and pulled themselves out laughing heartily at finally having outwitted the army.

His wagon parked by the river for the night, a flamboyant peddler by the name of Percival McBridge had witnessed the braves' escape. Picking up his rifle, he trained it on them as he walked their way. "Don't come any closer until we come to an understanding," he called out in a voice too cheerful to sound like a warning.

Their ankles chained together, Viper and Claw of the Badger were on their hands and knees. Water poured off them forming little rivulets in the mud that surrounded them, but despite their bedraggled appearance, neither looked defeated. They looked dangerous still, and while Percy admired their daring, he didn't get too close.

"Best wife I ever had was one of your people. She got disgusted with me, though, took our babies and went back home, but I've never forgotten her, and I always try to give a Sioux a helping hand whenever I can." He was in his late forties, and while the incident to which he referred had taken place some twenty years earlier, it was still one of his most vivid memories. He had had an inordinate fondness for the Sioux ever since.

Viper glanced toward Badger and saw in the evil light in

the man's eyes that he was thinking the same thing he was: they could rush the man, overpower him, and shoot him to death with his own rifle. Viper was smart enough to realize that would only set more people on their trail than there already were, and he discarded the idea immediately and sent Badger so threatening a glance that he discarded it, too. Sitting back on his heels, he raised his hands. "If you are a friend, you will be one of the few white men who is. Let us go. We mean you no harm."

While he was inclined to help them, Percy was curious about their plans. "Looks like you must be part of the braves the army is sending down to Camp McClellan. I can understand why you don't want to go to prison, but what are you gonna do now? You can't go tramping around chained together like that. Hell, anyone who sees an Indian is likely to shoot him. I'd say you are in bigger trouble than you were on that boat."

Badger tried to stand up, but Viper yanked him back down beside him. "We can get these chains off tonight. He is going his way, and I am going mine. All we ask is that you stand out of the way."

That was no request, however, but stated in so calm a tone that it carried the weight of an order. Impressed by the brave's show of confidence, Percy lowered his rifle, stepped forward, and offered Viper his hand to help him rise. "I think I've got a saw in my wagon that will take care of that chain. Spent some time in jail myself, and I don't mind helping you get away. Where are you headed?"

Viper did not reply. He and Badger followed the man, who was of a slender build and dressed in one of the fancy suits of clothes he had found enhanced his trade. Still keeping a watchful eye on the two braves, Percy searched his gear for a hack saw, and handed it to Viper. "I'll let you do the work." Badger put his foot against the wagon, and with a half dozen furious strokes, Viper cut through the lock that held his end of the chain.

Now free of his ties to his companion, Badger immediately began to back away. "You'll never find that white wife of yours. Come with me to the Dakotas instead. Little Crow will welcome us both."

While Viper had never told Badger his plans, he wasn't surprised the brave had guessed them. "I wish you good luck, but I will not go with you."

"Hey wait!" Percy again reached into his wagon and this time pulled out a knife. "You'll need one weapon, at least. Take this. It's a gift."

When the peddler tossed him the knife, Badger regarded him with a befuddled frown. "Why are you helping me?"

"Told you. Can't forget that Sioux woman of mine. Now get going before the army comes looking for you."

As Badger took off at a run, going north where he would again cross the river, Viper bent down to use the saw to free himself from the chain. When he had removed it, he carried both ruined locks and the length of chain back to the river and hurled them so far out into the water they would never be used on any man ever again. He then walked back to Percy's wagon and handed him the saw. "Thank you. Can you tell me how to reach Delaware?"

"Delaware? Jesus Christ, man, that is a hell of a long way from here. That where your wife is?" When Viper nodded, Percy whistled softly. "That will be some trip. With the war and all, it's been a while since I went back East. Tell you what, I'll get you headed in the right direction, at least. First thing we've got to do is cut your hair, then I'm sure I've got some clothes here that will fit you. Like I said, people won't be willing to help an Indian, but with those light eyes of yours, you just might be able to walk right by without being noticed. Did you ever think of that?"

With a slow smile, Viper admitted he had. "Yes, that is exactly what I planned to do." With Percy's help, by the time it had grown dark the Indian brave had been transformed into a charming young Frenchman who could travel where he wished without drawing any glances save admiring ones. At dawn he and the friendly peddler set out for Delaware and the long-awaited reunion with his wife.

# Chapter Twenty-Three

## March, 1863

With Lars's constant attention and Erica's devoted care, Mark made slow but steady progress, but he did not recover sufficient strength to return home to Wilmington until late March. Erica had hidden her pregnancy by wearing long aprons at the hospital, but at five months, the additional inches at her waistline were becoming increasingly difficult to disguise. She had tried to find the courage to confide the truth of her situation to her father, but each time they were alone her resolve had swiftly deserted her, leaving her feeling all the more lost and alone. Now that she was ready to go home, however, she knew she would have to confront the matter no matter how dreadful she feared his reaction would be.

She waited until Sarah had gone to summon the carriage, then lured her father to his office on the pretext of discussing Mark's condition one last time. Misreading the cause of her troubled expression, Lars reached out to take her hand. "I know this is a terrible burden for you, baby. I only wish that I could make the trip home with you, but it's simply impossible for me to get away now."

"I understand," Erica replied softly, then, knowing she could expect only a few minutes of his time since he had so many desperately ill patients to attend, she simply blurted out her news. "I'm pregnant, Daddy. The baby's due toward the end of July."

Dumbstruck by that astonishing announcement, Lars stared at his daughter a long moment before breaking into a delighted grin. "That's wonderful news! Why didn't you tell me before now? Does Mark know? He's certainly done as fine a job as you of keeping your secret, if he does."

Erica was equally amazed, for she had expected her father to regard her pregnancy as the worst of tragedies rather than as an event to be welcomed. Realizing he still didn't understand the truth, she swallowed hard, and tried to explain what the problem truly was. "No, I haven't told Mark. You see—"

Thrilled by the prospect of having a grandchild, Lars brushed aside what he mistook as the beginnings of a hesitant apology. "I understand. He was too weak for such excitement before this, but I think he can tolerate it now. Once you get home, you'll have both Mrs. Ferguson and Sarah to help you, but you'll have to be careful you don't become overtired caring for Mark. Let's go tell him about the baby right now. His attitude is remarkably good after what he's suffered, but the prospect of having his first child this summer will lift his spirits tremendously. I'm convinced attitude has been the deciding factor in a number of cases I've seen where two men have had similar injuries but only one has recovered his health. Hope does wonders for a wounded man, sweetheart, and Mark needs every bit of hope we can give him."

It hadn't once occurred to Erica that her father would think her child was Mark's but since she had married him the very day she had conceived the babe, the timing would lead anyone to assume her husband was the father. Anyone but Mark, that was. As her father continued to stress what a wonderful boost news of a child would be for her husband's morale, Erica tried to imagine what Mark's response would be. He was often confused, and terribly forgetful. He had headaches, which were at time so severe he could recall little of what had happened that day. Was it possible his memories of the first days of their marriage were so dim he would not know the child she carried could not possibly be his?

Torn by the agonizing question of whether to lie for Mark's sake, or to tell the truth for her own, Erica allowed her father's arguments to sway her. She would tell Mark only that she was pregnant; if he assumed himself to be the father of her child then she would let him believe he was. By the time the baby was born in July, he would surely be far more healthy than he was now and all the more able to cope with the truth if she had to reveal it. If, on the other

343

hand, he knew damn well that he wasn't the baby's father, she knew he loved her too much to blame her or to treat her badly for having become pregnant with Viper's child.

"I'd rather wait to tell him when we can be alone, Daddy," Erica decided at last. "There are so many people here, such confusion. I think I should be alone with him when I give him the news."

While Lars was disappointed that he would not be able to see Mark's reaction, he understood his daughter's point of view. "Yes, confusion is a good term to describe this place, and Mark doesn't need any more of that. I keep hoping that when he gets home and gets settled in a comfortable routine, he won't have so many problems."

Erica tried to smile, but she knew while he didn't that Mark's problems might only be beginning. Sarah found them then, and with the shyness she had never completely overcome with the physician, she thanked Lars Hanson for all he had done for her brother and bid him a fond farewell.

When they stopped at an inn that night, Mark was greeted cordially by the proprietor. He'd lost so much weight that his once handsomely tailored captain's uniform now hung on him like a scarecrow's baggy old clothes, but since he had obviously been wounded in the service of his country, he was accorded a hero's respect. He tired easily, and after the long carriage ride Erica considerately ordered supper to be served in their room. Equally exhausted, Sarah also asked to have her meal in her room, and they parted for the night at the desk.

Once she had guided Mark up the stairs and into their room, Erica led him over to the bed. "Sit down and I'll take off your boots," she offered helpfully.

Mark sat down as ordered, but once Erica had removed his boots he reached out to grab hold of her. "Come here," he ordered playfully. All during the carriage ride, he had clung to her hand tightly, but now that they were alone he wanted closeness of another sort. "This is the first time we've been alone in months, and I want to enjoy it." Pulling her between his legs, he wrapped his arms around her waist, laid his head upon her bosom, and hugged her tightly.

Not having expected Mark to have such romantic thoughts, Erica hesitated a moment before encircling his neck with her arms. She brushed the top of his tawny curls with her lips and tried to find the words to tell him the secret she had kept so well hidden. They would share a bed that night, and she knew if she didn't tell him now, he would undoubtedly discover it for himself later that evening. "Mark, there's something I must tell you," she began nervously, unconsciously clinging to him all the harder.

"Hmm, this is nice," Mark interrupted with a delighted hum. "I can hear your heart beating, thump, thump, thump."

Erica bit her lip to force back her tears. When Mark had grown well enough to talk, conversation had often proven difficult, for he could not pursue a subject from beginning to end without changing it often. "Mark, listen to me," she tried again, hoping to gain his full attention. "I'm going to have a baby. This summer, by the end of July, I think. Do you understand what I mean?"

"A baby?" Mark asked in an incredulous whisper. "We're going to have a baby?" He lightened his hold upon her momentarily, then hugged her with a fierce devotion. "I want a little girl, one who looks just like you. You'll tell me how pretty she is, won't you?"

Erica ran her fingers through his hair as she agreed. "Of course, Mark. I'll tell you all about the baby. Boy or girl, you'll be able to hold and cuddle it. You'll be able to tell what a sweet child it is for yourself." When he did not release her, she relaxed her pose and stood in his arms until a light knock at the door signaled the arrival of their supper. But as they shared the tasty meal, she grew increasingly depressed. Mark had been very anxious to leave the hospital. He tried so hard to care for himself, to be independent, but he was a mere shadow of the fine young man he had once been. While her love was no longer tinged with passion, it was no less deep, and it was all she could do not to weep each time she looked at him. To let him think her child was his for even a minute seemed like a terrible sin, and yet she could not deny how delighted he had been to think they would soon become parents. Yet wouldn't the joy he felt now make his disappointment all the more devastating when she finally had to admit the truth?

Unable to find the answer to her dilemma that satisfied both her desire to comfort Mark and her need to have a clear conscience, the troubled young woman ceased to torment herself with impossible questions. After supper she helped her husband prepare for bed, hoping he would fall asleep before she joined him, but he reached for her the minute she climbed into the bed beside him. "Can you feel the baby move?" he asked in an excited whisper.

"Yes, he's an active little tyke." Erica put his hand on her abdomen. "Wait just a minute, he's sure to give you a kick or two." Just as she had predicted, the baby soon began to stir, and with a satisfied laugh, Mark snuggled even closer.

"Now I can hold both of you," he murmured softly against her curls.

Erica held her breath, hoping he would have neither the stamina nor the inclination to want to make love. She knew she couldn't refuse him, but she remembered Viper's words too clearly: he would be the man in her arms, not Mark. How could she betray either of the men in her life so cruelly as that?

"I love you," Mark whispered sleepily.

"I love you, too," Erica replied sweetly. She put her hands over his, but she didn't begin to relax until she realized he would be content to fall asleep with her in his arms. Tears began to roll down her cheeks, leaving wet trails that tickled her ears. She did love Mark, and it hurt terribly to think how dependent upon her he had become. She was not yet eighteen years old, but she thanked God she had the financial resources to allow her to care for an invalid husband, and the beautiful memories of love for a remarkable Indian brave who would be with her always.

Percy McBride found Viper's dashing good looks melted housewives' hearts faster than his line of sweet talk ever had. He made twice the sales he usually did on their swing through Illinois, and his luck held as they crossed Indiana. With so many men gone to fight in the war, many a lonely woman invited them in for a meal, but the Indian quickly excused himself if their hostess's intentions turned romantic, and Percy was doubly grateful for that. When they reached the Ohio-Pennsylvania border, the peddler gave Viper a fair share of his profits and saw he had stylish clothes and a sound horse to ride for the rest of his journey. They were coming too close to the war for Percy's liking, but he wished the young man good luck in his quest, and there were actually tears in his eyes when they parted.

It was a Wednesday in early June when Viper finally arrived at Lars Hanson's home. That Erica had grown up in so imposing a structure impressed him deeply, for the gracious brick house was both large and well kept. Built to reflect an appreciation of the classical architecture of ancient Greece—a popular style after the Revolution nearly a century before—the Hanson family home was as elegant as any ever built in Wilmington. The white shutters and decorative trim had been newly painted, and the flowerbeds were overflowing with bright blossoms, giving the correct impression that the owners took great pride in their residence.

He had half a dozen stories prepared to enable him to gain news of Erica's whereabouts, but when she answered his knock herself, Viper was speechless. She was so lovely he was overwhelmed, but as his eyes traveled from her glorious blond hair and enchanting smile to her swollen figure, his delight abruptly turned to stunned dismay. Her pale pink gown was flattering, the delicate lace at the neckline and sleeves exquisite, but that she was so obviously pregnant was so great a surprise he could do no more than gape.

With Mrs. Ferguson out to do the marketing, Erica had had no choice but to go to the door herself. With the bright sunlight at Viper's back, at first glance she could not make out his features clearly enough to recognize him. She stood aside to allow him to enter as she supplied the same greeting she had given several others that week. "Won't you come in? I'm Mrs. Randall, and if you don't mind, I'd like to ask a few questions about your qualifications for the job we've advertised." She closed the door and then turned to face the man she had just welcomed into her home. Since he was the very last person she had expected to see that day, his identity escaped her until her curious glance reached his eyes.

"Oh, dear God," Erica gasped, and feeling faint, she leaned back against the door for support. "What are you doing here?" she asked in a frantic whisper.

"I came to find you," Viper replied, as astonished as she.

347

His shock at her condition swiftly turned his mood of elation to one closely bordering rage. "Why the hell else would I be here?"

"Hush!" Erica warned him. "You must leave," she insisted. "We can't talk here."

Since he had planned, once he had found Erica, to do a great deal more than merely talk, Viper found it difficult to lift his eyes from the soft folds of finely woven pink cotton that covered her well-rounded belly. "All these months, you had not even five minutes to write to me and tell me what had happened?"

"Oh please, you must go!" Erica pleaded, but she felt too weak to move away from the door. "I'm sorry. I'm so sorry for everything, but I simply can't talk with you now!"

Fearing his surprise at her condition had made him behave rudely, Viper apologized for upsetting her. "You needn't be frightened, I'll not hit you." He had not meant to unnerve her so completely as he obviously had. All winter he had thought of her as his wife; that she might have become pregnant had not even occurred to him. This was a complication he had not foreseen, but damn it all, she had been his wife before she had become Mark's! When he heard Mark calling her name, he wheeled around to face him. He had not expected him to be there at the Hanson home any more than he had thought Erica would be.

"Has someone else come about the job?" Mark called out from the entrance to the parlor. "You know I want to speak with any man who does."

Viper stared at the pale, thin figure in the doorway. Mark was looking right at him, but clearly he saw absolutely nothing. When the brave turned back to Erica with a questioning glance, he found her eyes were rapidly filling with tears and she had raised her hand to her mouth to stifle the sounds of the sobs he was certain she was crying inside. With heartbreaking clarity he suddenly understood the reason she had abandoned him. Turning back toward Mark, he swiftly crossed the entrance hall and took his hand in a firm grip.

"Bonjour, Monsieur Randall," he began with the thickest French accent he could affect. Since both Erica and Mark had mentioned something about a job, he decided no matter what it entailed, he was anxious to apply. "Allow me to introduce myself, I am Etienne Bouchard. I am Canadian." With a hearty chuckle, he told the first story that came to his mind. "I came to your country to marry, but alas, the young woman proved so fickle she would not have me. Now I must earn the money to go back home, where, I am happy to say, I have always found the women far easier to please."

"Finally, a man with a sense of humor." Delighted, Mark grinned happily as he replied to Viper's greeting. "As you must have noticed, my charming bride is expecting our first child soon, and she cannot care for me and a tiny baby, too. Do you think you would like to work for us?"

Viper glanced over his shoulder at Erica who was shaking her head emphatically. Disregarding her clear objection to his accepting that offer of employment, Viper slyly arranged to speak with Mark alone. "It is a beautiful morning. Is there a place where we might talk outside? A garden perhaps, or a porch?"

"Yes, there is a nice garden at the rear of the house. Follow me and I'll take you there." Mark put his hand upon the wall to guide his way. "I can't see a blasted thing, but luckily I can find my way around the house."

"That is indeed lucky." Viper turned again to find Erica now glaring at him with a malevolent stare. He caught the word "bastard" upon her lips and blew her a kiss to let her know he was so happy to see her again he didn't care what she called him. When they reached the french doors in the dining room, he helped Mark unlock them and flung them open.

"Ah yes, the garden is lovely. Be careful of the steps." Viper reached out to take Mark's arm, but held back when he realized the man knew his way. He followed him along the stone walk until they came to a wooden bench placed beneath a fragrant peach tree. When they had both been seated, he leaned back to get comfortable and encouraged Mark to talk about the job he had to offer.

"Tell me what it is you need, monsieur, and I will tell you if I can do it."

"My wife is very pretty, isn't she?" Mark asked with another engaging grin.

"She is a great beauty," Viper responded quite sincerely, but he soon discovered as he tried to find out just what it was he would be expected to do if he came to work for the Randalls that that seemed to be the last subject Mark wished to discuss. Mark asked if the gardener were keeping the garden well, then he promised that Mrs. Ferguson's meals were superb. He asked if Viper liked to fish and seemed pleased when he replied that he did. At the end of their rambling conversation, the Indian was convinced that Mark did need someone to look after him, just as a small child did.

"Am I to make my home here with you, or come and go each day?" Viper inquired when Mark suddenly fell silent, hoping his preference was not too obvious from the way he had phrased that question.

"Our housekeeper has her own family, as do the maids who come in to clean, so you would live here in the servants' quarters." Mark started to rise then. "Would you like to see them?"

"You needn't show me. I am sure they are very nice."

"I couldn't say," Mark admitted readily as he resumed his seat. "I didn't live here when I could see. This is my father-in-law's house, not mine. My wife brought me here when I left the hospital, and I didn't argue with her. She is very good to me, and I'd do anything to please her. I'm glad you think she's pretty, too. Did you tell me if you wanted to work for us? Forgive me if you did. I forget two things for each one I remember. Erica is very patient, though. She never gets angry with me when I ask her the same question a dozen times."

To realize the man he had once taken such delight in beating half to death could have changed so completely left Viper badly shaken. While he had lost a great deal of weight, Mark had also lost a good deal of himself as well, and Viper considered that a worse tragedy than the loss of his sight. "Yes, I would like very much to work for you, monsieur. I do not know if your wife will approve, however."

Mark frowned at that remark. "But why not? If I like you, why shouldn't she? Oh yes, I forgot to ask if you can read. She will ask that for sure, as she reads to me each day. If you don't know how, say yes anyway, and we can just sit and talk and she will never know the difference." He laughed then, as though that were a very amusing thought.

"I know how to read," Viper assured him. He had come

to Delaware to fetch his wife, not to become a blind man's companion, but from the way Erica had greeted him, he was certain the only way he would be able to see her was if he became a member of her household. Getting to his feet, he reached down to help Mark rise. "Shall we go talk with your wife? As I said, I am in need of work, and if she will agree, I can begin today."

"Good. I have talked with a half-dozen men this week, but liked none of them. One talked to me as though I were a child, another shouted as though I were deaf rather than blind. The others, oh I don't even remember them now. I just didn't like them. I think you will be a friend to me. That's what I want." As they started for the house, Mark suddenly remembered something else. "My sister, Sarah, comes to see me each day. She can be a difficult person, but you'll be working for me, not her. Don't let her bother you."

Viper was glad to have that warning, for he had not counted on the presence of anyone other than the hired help Mark had already mentioned. A sister, a housekeeper, maids, a gardener, how many people would he have to fool? With a determined frown he decided if he had to convince the whole town of Wilmington he was a Frenchman from Canada, he would do it.

Erica was seated in the parlor, crocheting the trim on a tiny garment obviously meant for her unborn child when they joined her. When Mark said he had hired Viper, she regarded the Indian with a triumphant smile, thinking she had outsmarted him. "Just one moment, dear. Mr. Bouchard, was it?" she asked with what sounded like innocence. She had no idea what sort of a stunt Viper was trying to pull, but she heartily disapproved of it. "There is the matter of references. Since you will be living here in our home, I must insist upon at least three references attesting to your fine character before you begin working for us."

Viper had never heard of references before, and he didn't even know three people in Wilmington, let alone three who would swear he was an honest man. "As I said, madam, I am Canadian," he announced with an imploring look to the woman he adored. "Those who know me are a long way away, but I can assure you you will be pleased with my work."

Mark sighed dejectedly, clearly unhappy with Erica's request. "I want him to stay, Erica. If he proves to be a thief, or fails to be helpful, then I will let him go. We agreed I was to be the one to choose the man, and I want Etienne. If I like him, then you must, too."

Erica cursed Viper silently for tricking her husband so cruelly, but she could not ignore Mark's woebegone frown, and not wanting to upset him, she let him have his way. "Of course, Mark. If references are not important to you, then I will not insist upon having them."

Grinning happily, as he relaxed his wary stance, Viper excused himself. "All my belongings are outside on my horse. If you will permit me a few minutes to see to the animal's comfort, I will bring my things inside and be ready to do whatever it is you require."

"Take your time, Mr. Bouchard. We will have dinner soon, and then my husband rests during the early afternoon. We won't need your services before three." Erica found it exceedingly difficult to sound sweet at the same time she was giving Viper furious looks, but she knew it would become easier with practice.

Viper went to her then, and with a courtly bow bent forward to bestow a light kiss upon the back of her hand. When she looked up at him with a hate-filled glance, he turned her hand over to place another far more lavish kiss upon her palm. "As you wish, madam. If there is anything I might do for you while your husband is resting, please let me know. I will be happy to perform any service for you." He winked as he straightened up, his suggestive gesture saying far more than his words, but Erica shook her head emphatically.

"Thank you, Mr. Bouchard, but my needs are few."

"Please call me Etienne, madam." Then turning to Mark, Viper again excused himself and left to attend to his horse.

"I like him," Mark quickly restated, pleading for her approval. "Please let him stay, Erica, please."

"The matter has already been decided, my darling. Unless Mr. Bouchard, Etienne, proves to be a scoundrel, he may stay."

Mark went to her side then, and with only slight clumsiness managed to kiss her cheek. "Thank you. I do not want to be a burden to you, Erica, and I know that I am."

Taking his face between her hands, Erica kissed his lips tenderly. "No, my love, you are no burden, no burden at all." But she was grateful he could not see the tears that filled her eyes as she told that loving lie.

Regarding that Wednesday as one of the most wretched days of her life, Erica could not wait for it to draw to a close. When Viper went with Mark to his room to help him prepare for bed, she paced angrily in hers. She had waited all day for the opportunity to talk with the Indian alone, but from the adjoining room she could hear the two men talking and laughing together long after the hour Mark was usually asleep. Exasperated, she finally climbed upon her bed to rest, but she didn't dare disrobe and don a nightgown. When finally Viper came through her door, as she had known he would, she could barely contain the fury of her temper.

"Have you lost your mind?" she asked accusingly. "How dare you play so horrible a trick on Mark? How dare you do that to him, and to me?"

He had already discarded his coat, and as he sat down upon the edge of her bed, Viper began to unbutton his shirt. The frills that adorned the front of the white cotton garment provided a sharp contrast to the deep bronze of his chest. He was a handsome man and knew it, but Erica reached out to stop him before he could remove his shirt.

"You can't sleep here!" she insisted in an anguished whisper. "My God, did you think I would invite you to share my bed?"

"I am your husband. I do not need an invitation," Viper responded as he leaned forward to brush her lips softly with his. "Mark told me he sleeps by himself out of regard for your comfort. I would prefer to make you comfortable in my own way."

His words were not spoken as a threat, but Erica took them as such. "No! Can't you understand what I have been trying to make you see all day? I can't have you here. I won't betray Mark's trust. Can't you tell how much he has suffered? Today was one of his good days. There are times when he has headaches so severe he can't rise from his bed without getting dizzy and sick to his stomach. He's not well and—"

Viper slipped his hand around Erica's throat and drew her lips to his for a soft, lingering kiss he did not end until he felt the tension behind her resentment completely melt away. She had never been able to resist his affection, and he was glad to see that at least in that respect she hadn't changed. "Do you really think I have suffered any less?" he finally whispered as his lips brushed her temple. "Or you? Can you swear to me you are happy?"

When she could not reply, he enfolded her in his arms. Still torn between her duty to Mark and her love for Viper, Erica did not attempt to draw away but rested her head lightly upon his shoulder seeking to enjoy his comforting warmth as she tried to reason rather than argue with him. "Mark was hurt just after I found out you weren't going to hang. I was so happy that you were going to live that I knew I could stand whatever I might have to face here. I thought I'd never see you again." She leaned back then, looking up at him with the openly loving gaze he had longed to see all day. "I loved your hair." She caressed the deep wave that fell down over his brow, then ran the back of her fingers along his cheek. "You're very handsome with it worn short, but still, it was absolutely magnificent long."

Overcome with despair at that memory, Erica raised her hands to cover her face as she began to cry. "Oh please, you must leave," she begged between heart-rending sobs. "It is so difficult for me to always be cheerful for Mark. I have tried so hard to be the wife he deserves, but it will be impossible with you here."

As Viper pressed her face against his chest, he pulled the pins from her hair to spill the perfume-scented curls about her shoulders. When finally her sorrow seemed spent, he spoke. "I love you too much to leave, Erica. Don't you know that? If you must stay here and care for Mark, then I will stay and help you. He likes me. If I keep him occupied, then you will not find being his wife so difficult."

Determined to make him understand her plight, Erica struggled to dry her tears. "I want you to go," she insisted once again. "Stay a week or two and then tell Mark you've been called home to Canada. You seem to be full of imaginative stories, so I know you'll be convincing. Who is Etienne Bouchard, anyway?"

She was attempting to dismiss him as though he really were a servant, but Viper ignored that insult, since his mind was already made up. "It was my grandfather's name, and I knew he would not mind if I borrowed it for a while. Had I known I had any hope to live, I would never have given you to Mark. I came to take you back, and I mean to do it. Stop asking me to leave, because I will not leave here without taking you with me."

Erica had not forgotten what a fiercely determined individual Viper could be, but she had hoped he would see the depth of her emotional turmoil and understand why she had asked him to go. "This is wrong, Viper, don't you see that? This is wrong. We can't constantly lie to Mark and expect to find happiness with each other."

"You must remember to call me Etienne," Viper reminded her before lowering his mouth to hers for a gentle yet loving kiss, which proved to him her fears were completely unfounded. "You see," he whispered as he drew away. "We will always be happy together." When she simply stared at him, her deep blue eyes filled with a glistening mixture of awe and sorrow, he stood up and peeled off his shirt.

"I will stay with you tonight and every other night I am in this house. We can make love without harming your child. I can make it nice for you. You know that I can."

It was the way he had said "your child" that gave Erica the strength to refuse his offer. He didn't realize the babe was his! She had thought he would sense the truth, if not see it in her eyes, but he didn't. Clasping her hands tightly in her lap, she replied in the most forceful manner she could. "I asked you to marry me in a church, Viper."

"Etienne," he interrupted.

"Whatever you wish to call yourself." Erica was getting angry again, and that reinforced her resolve to continue. "I wanted God's blessing, but you didn't care anything about my beliefs. I consider my marriage vows to Mark sacred. I will not break them. Adultery is a mortal sin. You can't ask that of me, you simply can't."

"Do you really think God would send so pretty a woman as you to hell?" Viper asked with a teasing smile, but he was deeply disturbed that she appeared actually to believe she would be damned for loving him.

"Being pretty has nothing to do with having high

morals." Erica kept her eyes focused upon her trembling hands rather than Viper's half-clothed body. She wanted him still, and desperately, but Mark loved her with a childlike trust she knew she ought not to betray. She was already living one lie, and she could not bring herself to begin another when it could have such disastrous consequences should Mark ever learn of it. Should he discover she was unfaithful, it would simply destroy him, and that was far too terrible a price to pay.

Viper looked down at Erica, loving her more dearly than he had thought possible. "To me you are still beautiful, do you think you are not?" he asked softly.

"I know how I look," she replied with a bitter laugh. "And it certainly isn't seductive."

"To me you still are. I have never wanted another woman as I want you."

Hating herself for having to resort to threats, in desperation Erica used one anyway. "If you so much as touch me I'll tell Mark who you really are and he'll make you leave," she swore in so serious a tone her sincerity could not be doubted. "I'll do it. If you won't leave on your own, I will see you're thrown out."

Incensed by that vow, since he considered it absurd, Viper leaned down to grab a handful of her hair and forced her gaze up to his. "You will say nothing!" he hissed. "If you do not want me in your bed I will sleep in my own, but by God, I am staying in this house. Do you understand me?"

His eyes were smoldering with a silver fury, and Erica swallowed hard as she tried to nod, but she found his hold upon her hair far too tight for that. "Yes," she whispered breathlessly instead.

"Good." Viper released her then, picked up his shirt, and stormed out of her bedroom. Erica stumbled as she got down off the bed, but managed to catch herself and cross the spacious room to lock the door. She was not locking him out, however, but rather locking herself in before the passions of her heart overruled the sensible thoughts of her head and she ran after him to beg him to come back and share her bed.

# Chapter Twenty-Four

## June, 1863

Sarah gestured dramatically with a yellow silk fan whose exquisite color and embroidery exactly matched her stylish gown, as she confided her opinion to Erica. "Please, do not misunderstand me. I think Etienne's presence has been an enormous asset. Don't you think Mark looks better? They spend so much time out of doors he's gained some healthy color.

"Sitting with them in the garden just now, I was every bit as amused as they were by their efforts to play chess while Etienne is just learning the game and Mark is unable to see the board." She paused a moment, and smiling happily, continued, "I guess that's what I like best about Etienne. He keeps Mark not only occupied, but happy. On the other hand, it still disturbs me that we know so little about the man. I must have spoken with him half a dozen times, and I still don't know where he is from or what he did there. Doesn't it strike you as rather strange that he would be so reticent about himself? He is well mannered, so he must have come from a respectable family, and yet he never mentions them. That worries me, too. Most bothersome of all, isn't it remarkable that so handsome and intelligent a man would be content to accept work here as a servant?"

Erica scarcely knew how to respond, since the man Sarah and Mark knew as Etienne Bouchard was merely a charming façade Viper seemed to be able to adopt at will.

"He is an unusual man in many respects, I'll agree, but he is the only Canadian I know, and perhaps they are all such private people. I am so thankful for the happiness he gives Mark, however, that I think his past is really quite unimportant." Truly, Erica had been amazed when Viper had taken his duties so seriously. He wasn't simply lurking about the house keeping an eye on her as she had feared he would do, he had instead become the perfect companion for Mark. He was both attentive to her husband's needs, and resourceful in satisfying them, for which she was extremely grateful.

Sarah perched upon the edge of the rosewood chair opposite the settee where Erica had been seated reading before she had joined her. Choosing her words with care, she broached another subject that troubled her. "Have you heard from your father? Is he still planning to arrive this weekend?"

"As far as I know, he is. I think he would have sent a wire if he'd been unable to get away." It was difficult for Erica to smile as she responded, since Viper's presence was giving her strong misgivings about the outcome of her father's visit.

"It will be interesting to hear what he has to say about Etienne," Sarah mused thoughtfully.

"Well, I certainly hope that he likes him, too," Erica wished aloud, but she was deeply concerned about what her father would think of the "Canadian" who had joined their household. Sarah was perceptive enough to realize something about Viper's story rang false, but would her father take one look at the deep bronze of his skin and the jet black of his hair and know he had more Indian blood than French? It would then be a simple step to guess just which Indian he was. Both she and Viper had gone out of their way to avoid each other since their confrontation in her bedroom. But wouldn't the strained aloofness of their relationship make her father suspicious? While she was still looking forward to her father's visit, her fears were running high that it might end in disaster.

Sarah folded her fan and tapped it lightly against her knee as she tried to appear merely considerate of Lars rather than fascinated by him. "I think it will be very nice for your father to get away from the hospital for a few days' rest."

"Yes, and that rest is long overdue. He works much too hard, but that's his choice, I'm afraid."

Sarah nodded agreeably, but her curiosity was still not satisfied, and she continued to try and draw Erica out about her father. "I think his reasons for wanting to occupy his time are understandable. He must have been very deeply in love with your mother and miss her terribly."

That was one thing about her father Erica knew for certain. "Yes, I'm sure he does. They were a very close and loving couple."

Sarah studied Erica's pensive frown, thinking her thoughts must be of her mother. Still, Lars had been a widower for more than three years, and the pain of his loss must surely have begun to subside. "You said he's just turned forty, didn't you?"

"What?" Erica asked, then realizing Sarah was still talking about her father, she relaxed slightly. "Yes, in May, our birthdays are just two days apart."

While she had done her very best to catch his eye, Sarah had had absolutely no success in gaining Lars Hanson's notice during the winter months she had spent in Washington. He had treated her with courtesy and respect, but never as though she were a young woman he might grow to love. That he had no romantic interest in her had both infuriated and saddened her, but she had not known what to do about it. Now that she had finally summoned the courage to discuss Lars with his daughter, desperation made her bold. "Do you think he'll remain a widower forever, or is there a chance he might remarry someday?"

There had been an occasion or two when Erica had suspected Sarah's regard for her father might have been more than merely gratitude for what he had done for her brother. She had always had far too much on her mind to inquire whether that were truly the case, as indeed she did still, but since Sarah had finally asked a question that could be interpreted as expressing interest, she decided to encourage her. After all, the more distractions her father had, the less likely he would be to realize who Etienne Bouchard really was.

"I think my father is too devoted to his profession at

present to have any thoughts of women. It's unfortunate, too, as I would hate to see him spend the rest of his life alone."

"You'd not object then, if he did become interested in someone?" Sarah held her breath, hoping Erica didn't realize how desperately she wanted to be that particular someone.

Erica knew she and Sarah had not grown nearly as close as they should have considering the vast amount of time they had spent together. She also felt she had to accept the blame for that herself, since from the first day she had returned to Wilmington she had been so anxious about her own problems she had had little interest in cultivating Sarah's friendship. First there had been the matter of her marriage to Viper to create tension between them, then the pain of Mark's long convalescence, coupled with the burden of a pregnancy she had kept hidden until the last possible moment. Now, hoping to make up for her lack of attentiveness in the past, Erica offered what she thought would be helpful advice.

"If you are sincerely interested in my father, I think you should simply tell him that you find him an attractive man and would like to know him in other than a professional capacity. You have always seemed so terribly shy around him, I doubt he realizes you have any feelings for him one way or the other."

Sarah's large brown eyes widened in surprise, for she simply couldn't believe her ears. She knew how to attract a man's notice and flatter his vanity with innocent flirting, but then it was up to him to respond. With a man like Lars Hanson, who had completely failed to notice her desperate attempts to impress him, she didn't know what more to do. To speak of her feelings seemed not only forward, but foolish. What if he were merely embarrassed, or worse yet, laughed at what would surely be a halting declaration of love?

"Oh no, I couldn't say something like that to him. I simply couldn't," she insisted with a bashful blush. "Since I was a young girl, men have always liked me. I've never had to chase them. It would be much too awkward a situation for me to endure, and I think your father would be as embarrassed as I would be if I tried to encourage his

360

attentions in such a fashion. No, I just can't do it."

Although exasperated with the young woman's unwillingness to take matters into her own hands, Erica knew her father needed love and affection as much as anyone did. Since Sarah was the only woman she knew who was interested in him, she wanted to help her. "Would you like for me to discuss the matter with him? You'll join us for dinner while he's here, won't you? If I suggest he might enjoy getting to know you better, would you object?"

Sarah opened and closed her fan quickly, the nervousness of her gesture accurately reflecting her mood. Finally she took a deep breath and agreed. "Will you promise to be discreet? I wouldn't want Lars to think I was behind whatever comments you make. If he laughs, or says he doesn't care to know me any better, or however he responds, will you tell me? I'd rather know where I stand than go on like this just hoping he might one day notice me."

"I'm certain he has already noticed you, Sarah. Don't be silly. I will be extremely discreet, and I'll let you know what he says, too, but I think it will be complimentary. After all, you are a very attractive woman, and your company is always enjoyable."

Sarah looked at Erica a long moment, then realized she was serious. "Why, thank you, that's a very sweet thing for you to say."

"I mean it, too." Erica's smile was quite genuine then, but by the time Sarah had left, she had realized she should take her own advice and be more direct herself. After dinner when Mark went upstairs to rest, she told Viper she needed to speak with him in the parlor. While she knew it wouldn't be easy to talk with him, it was something she couldn't delay. Like Sarah, he chose the chair opposite the settee, but then moved it so close their knees were nearly touching.

"You could have come to my room any night," Viper whispered softly. "My door has always been open."

"Please, I didn't ask to speak with you to plan a midnight rendezvous," Erica admonished him in a voice as low as his. But the teasing light in his eyes didn't waver, and she doubted he believed her. "My father should arrive here Saturday. He plans to stay several days, and I'd like for you to make up one of your fanciful excuses and spend your time elsewhere while he's here. He's far too clever a man to be so easily fooled as Mark or his sister, and if he recognizes you, there will be hell to pay."

Viper frowned slightly as he considered her request, but he promptly refused it. "There are many Frenchmen who marry Indian women. He might guess I have mixed blood, but why should that upset him? If he knows anything about me, then he will think I am in prison at Camp McClellan. He won't expect to find me here."

"I read that some braves were acquitted of all charges, but their names weren't listed in our paper. Weren't you one of them?" Erica had assumed he must have been.

A slow smile played across Viper's lips as he shook his head. "Tell me what happened to your hand, and I will tell you how I left Minnesota."

Erica looked down at her hand. She had been using her left hand to cover the scar upon her right for so many months that it had become an unconscious habit. Viper had obviously noticed the scar, despite her attempts to conceal it. "No, you tell me your story first," she insisted, embarrassed that for the rest of her life her hand would bear a reminder of Wren's attack.

Viper laughed at her shyness, but gave in. "All right. I will go first." He needed a few minutes to describe his escape and the help he had received from Percy McBride. He gave Percy full credit for teaching him enough about behaving like a gentleman to allow his ruse to succeed, but he had failed to anticipate Erica's astonished reaction.

"If you escaped, then surely the army must be looking for you, and it's only a matter of time before they come here," she exclaimed excitedly. "Oh Viper, this is awful."

The handsome brave dismissed her fears with a careless shrug. "The army has better things to do than look for me, Erica. No one will come here to arrest me. Now tell me what happened to your hand. That was the bargain we made."

Erica was too upset by his tale to phrase her own story well. "I cut myself," she finally lied.

Viper reached out to take her hand in his and turned it over. "Do you remember the first day I came here? When I kissed your hand I saw the new scar and discovered it also crossed your palm. I did not have a chance to ask you about it that night, but I have been very curious. Would you rather I asked Mark what happened to his lovely bride's hand?''

At the mention of her husband's name, Erica yanked her hand from him. "No, you mustn't bother Mark with such silly questions."

"Then you must tell me the truth yourself." Viper's sly grin was an insult in itself. "You are very good at fooling everyone else here, but with me you must speak the truth."

"How dare you accuse me of fooling people when you tell nothing but lies?" Erica found it difficult to make her point in a whisper, but she hoped that she had.

Again Viper shrugged nonchalantly, unconcerned by the hostile nature of that query. "I have no other choice."

"And you think I do?" Erica gave him no opportunity to reply before she continued in a breathless rush. "Well, I don't!" Disgusted that he took such delight in turning everything she said against her, she angrily admitted the truth. "Wren tried to kill Mark and me. Obviously she didn't succeed."

"What?" Viper reached for Erica's wrists, holding her fast so she could not escape him, forgetting that the advanced stage of her pregnancy would have made a hasty exit impossible to affect. "Why didn't you tell me?"

Erica shook her head. "What good would it do? It's over and done. The army had her in custody when we left."

"Well, the army must have let her go," Viper explained angrily. "I saw her at Fort Snelling. She was dancing along the dock, waving to us when our boat stopped there."

While she was disappointed to hear that, Erica was more disappointed that she had allowed Viper to lead their conversation so far from its original purpose. "You won't even consider leaving here for a few days? I just don't want any more grief than I already have, and from my father."

"Is that all I am to you now?" Viper asked as he released his hold upon her. "A cause for grief?"

"I told you when you came here that I wanted you to go," Erica reminded him crossly, hoping he would not notice she had not answered his question. To have him so near and yet out of reach was not merely grief, it was agony.

Her averted gaze told Viper more than Erica wished him to know, but after first looking over his shoulder to make certain they were not being observed, he leaned forward to kiss her with a passion so unmistakable that he laughed at her shocked glance when he drew away. "If that is your idea of grief, you are very wrong. All I taste in your kiss is love." With a wicked grin and a jaunty stride he left the parlor, but a long while passed before Erica found the strength to leave her place.

When Lars reached Wilmington, he stopped first at the cemetery at Old Swedes' Church to spend some time with his wife before going home. Missing Eva every bit as much as he had the day of her funeral, he stood at the foot of her grave and thought about all the things he wished he could tell her. He was accustomed to sharing his problems with her and doubted he would ever get used to the fact that it was no longer possible. There were several doctors at the hospital with whom he had become friends, but talking with them just wasn't the same.

Eva had been an extraordinarily devoted wife, and Lars had adored her. She had been so proud of the fact that in 1638 one of her ancestors had sailed with the first Swedish expedition to the Delaware River. Since his relatives had not arrived for another fifty years, she had often teased him that her family had played a far more important part in Wilmington's history than his had. It was a point he was willing to concede now that she shared the same hallowed ground so many of the early settlers occupied.

What would Eva think of the way he had raised their daughter? he wondered silently. Indeed, he was afraid he would have to admit to his wife that Erica had raised herself. That Eva would never see their grandchild broke his heart anew, and brushing the tears from his eyes, he bid his dear wife good-bye and promised to return to see her again soon.

By noon on Saturday, Erica was nearly beside herself with worry. Since Viper had stubbornly refused to leave, she held to the slim hope that he would be able to fool her father as effectively as he had everyone else. When she heard Lars come through the front door, she remained in the parlor and called out to him. When he appeared at the door, he seemed to think her condition a sufficient excuse that she had not gone running to meet him.

First and foremost a physician, as soon as Lars sat down with his daughter he immediately inquired about her health. "Are you feeling well? Not getting too tired?" he asked as his glance swept her delicate features and noted the clear signs of stress.

"I am very tired of being pregnant. I would have the baby this very afternoon if I had my way." Erica tried to laugh and sound as though she were joking, but she wasn't. She wanted the babe born, hoping it would be easier to face whatever consequences the child brought than to continue worrying about them. "Could you arrange to deliver the child while you're here?"

Lars refused graciously. "No, I'm afraid children choose their own time to be born, and usually a most inconvenient one. You've spoken with the midwife, haven't you?"

"Yes, Mrs. Denenberg promises to arrive within ten minutes from the time I send for her."

"Don't send for her too early, sweetheart. Unfortunately, first babies are usually born after a lengthy labor. I hope you'll be lucky, however, and have as easy a time as your mother did. She produced you with such little effort, it is a shame all women do not give birth so easily." He turned then as he heard Mark's voice out in the hall. "How is Mark doing?" he asked as he rose to his feet.

"He is better," Erica assured him, but then had to be honest, "but still not himself, and I fear he never will be."

Mark entered the parlor then, Viper at his side and a small striped kitten in his hands. "Look what we found, Erica!" he exclaimed happily. She always chose the same place to sit so he would have no difficulty finding her and could always sit by her side.

The instant Erica saw the kitten she sent Viper a questioning glance, for the tiny animal had the exact same coloring as the tomcat they had left behind at the farmhouse, complete to the white rings around its eyes and the bright orange nose. She quickly caught herself, however and spoke to her husband rather than the Indian. "What an adorable kitten. Where did you find him, or is it a her?"

"Etienne says it is a tom," Mark responded as he held the kitten out to her. "We were walking down by Brandywine Creek and heard him meowing. He was either lost or abandoned, and we thought we should bring him home."

"Hello, Mark," Lars greeted his son-in-law warmly, then turned to Viper. "I am Lars Hanson, Erica's father."

"How do you do, sir." Viper shook Lars's hand, then looked down at Erica with a triumphant grin when after a casual glance the man turned his attentions back to Mark. He stepped aside and at his first opportunity volunteered to go find a basket to serve as the kitten's bed.

"Ask Mrs. Ferguson for some scraps of flannel or other soft fabric," Erica called out as he went toward the door.

"I will do that, madam," Viper replied politely, but again his glance was a defiant one.

Erica held her breath, waiting for her father to inquire about Etienne, but he did not. Instead, he sat down and talked at length with Mark, or at least he attempted to make some sense of the rambling conversation that ensued, since Mark was more interested in playing with the kitten than in talking. Then Sarah arrived and the kitten was banished to the pantry while they had dinner.

Not tasting a single bite, the distraught Erica kept expecting her father to leap from his chair and at the very least challenge Viper to a duel, but again the conscientious physician paid her husband's companion scant attention. When Mark went upstairs to rest, and Viper went out to the stable to tend his horse, she announced that she also intended to take a nap, and with an encouraging smile to Sarah, she left her alone with Lars.

While he was as surprised as Sarah to suddenly find himself alone with her, Lars delighted the young woman by suggesting they go for a stroll in the garden. They took the kitten out with them, and laughed as he ran about on wobbly legs chasing butterflies.

"I am pleased to find your brother looking so well," Lars commented as they reached the bench near the peach tree. "Would you like to sit down for a while?"

"Yes, thank you." Sarah had worn a beige gown that day, hoping the pale color would make her hair appear more blond. Now she wondered if perhaps that hadn't been a mistake, since from what she recalled of Eva, she had been as fair as Erica. Everything she did seemed to be wrong where Lars was concerned, and she prayed she would not make a total fool of herself while they talked. "Yes, he does look well, but that's because Etienne has him spending so much time out of doors. That's good for him, isn't it?"

"Fresh air and exercise are good for everyone," Lars replied. "It will certainly be beneficial for Mark." Fearing that had sounded rather pompous, he called to the kitten, hoping the little fellow would provide the basis for some sort of a distraction, since now that he was seated with Sarah he couldn't think of a damn thing to say to her. Unfortunately, the tiny tomcat continued to cavort about the grass and paid him no mind.

Sitting back, he looked around the yard, hoping an inspiration would strike him. "It's a beautiful day, isn't it?"

"Yes, our weather has been very pleasant. How is it in Washington?" Sarah replied, feeling every bit as awkward as he. She could not help but note that Lars seemed ill at ease and was certain something she had done, or had failed to do, was the cause.

"Humid, as it is every summer," Lars admitted with a nervous smile.

"Your patients must be quite miserable, then," Sarah observed thoughtfully.

"Well yes, they certainly are, poor devils." Lars sat forward then, tempted to say more about the wounded men in his care, but then he caught himself. "I'm sure you don't want to hear about them."

Disappointed that they were having such a difficult time holding a simple conversation, Sarah assured him that wasn't the case. "I spent nearly three months visiting at the hospital while Mark was there. While I'm certain most of the men who were patients then must have recovered sufficiently to go home, I'm still interested in how those who remain and the new arrivals are doing. Won't you please tell me something about them?"

Surprised to find her interest genuine, Lars at last began to relax and talked at length about his patients and his continuing belief in the benefits of having a positive attitude. "Unfortunately, we see so many men we have little chance to get to know them as individuals, but I do my best to match the names with the faces and let them all know I care about them, just as I did with Mark."

While Sarah had enjoyed hearing his comments, now that their discussion had returned to her brother, she asked the question she had never dared mention to Erica. "I was so thrilled just to have Mark survive his injuries and come home, but shouldn't he be more like his old self by now?"

Lars looked away for a moment, wondering what had happened to the kitten. Then he saw him beneath a rosebush, snuggled in a tight ball sound asleep. "There is a vast difference between having a positive lookout and having totally unrealistic expectations, Sarah." He looked back toward her then, thinking her brown eyes wonderfully expressive, and hating to think how swiftly they would fill with pain. "Mark is as well as he will ever be. He'll have to have someone like Etienne to accompany him wherever he goes. He'll never be able to earn a living to support my daughter and their child. It's a blessing that won't create a financial burden for either your family or ours. I'm truly sorry, but while I managed to save your brother's life, there was nothing I could do about the injuries to his brain. Just love him for who he is, but don't expect any more from him than he is able to provide now."

While Sarah had suspected that might be the case, she had kept hoping and praying that Mark would gradually continue to improve, so that even if he were always blind, he would one day be as bright and fun-filled as she remembered him to be. Her eyes filling with tears, she drew a lace-trimmed linen handkerchief from her sleeve and brought it to her eyes.

"Forgive me for being so foolish. I have known all along that miracles don't really happen, and I shouldn't have kept waiting for one. Would you excuse me, please? I really must be getting home."

"Of course." Lars rose and offered his hand to help her to her feet. "It's Saturday, and I know despite the war there must be parties and dances tonight."

Still dabbing away her tears, Sarah hesitated upon the path before gathering all her courage and replying in a breathless rush. "As a matter of fact, I am going to a party tonight. It's at the Bergstroms' home. I'm certain if they knew you were in town they would be happy to include you, too. I could come by for you with my carriage, if you'd like to go."

That she would want to invite him to go with her surprised Lars so greatly that it took him several seconds to think of a reason to refuse. "That's very nice of you, but no. I came here to see my daughter, and obviously she's not up to going to parties now."

Sarah nodded, grateful he had used Erica's pregnancy as an excuse rather than saying he had no interest in spending the evening with her. Her hopes dashed for both her brother and herself, she bid him farewell and left, but she cried all the way home and considered sending an excuse to the Bergstroms' rather than attending their party alone.

Erica had not even tried to sleep, and when she heard Sarah's carriage leave she knew there was no longer any need to pretend to be resting. When she found her father still outdoors, she joined him. She loved the fragrant serenity of the garden, but she seldom spent time there, since Viper and Mark preferred it to the house and she avoided the brave's company whenever possible.

Lars greeted his daughter with kisses upon both cheeks and kept her hand clasped in his as they strolled along the winding path. "Sweetheart, you know how much I love you, but there's something I feel I must say."

Fearing the worst, Erica braced herself. "What is it, Daddy?"

"You're only eighteen, baby, and well, I know Mark isn't the man you married. After your baby is born, I'm afraid you'll have two children to care for rather than one." Lars feared he was stating what he wished to say poorly, but knowing it was important, he forced himself to press on. "Well, what I mean is, it isn't easy to be married to an invalid, especially for a woman as beautiful and young as you, and you're bound to be tempted to form alliances with other men."

That warning was so unexpected that Erica started to giggle and couldn't stop. "Allilances, Daddy? Isn't what you're really talking about affairs?"

"Damn it all, Erica, this isn't a bit funny!" Lars scolded.

"Oh yes, it is!" Erica couldn't help herself. She had been so worried her father would guess Viper's identity that it was a tremendous relief to discover he was worried about something else entirely. Overcome with laughter, she made her way to the bench and sat down. When finally she was able to regain her composure, she apologized.

"I'm sorry, but just look at me. Do you honestly think I could drive any man wild with passion now?" she asked with an impish smile.

"I said after the baby comes. That's what I'm talking about, but believe me, there are plenty of men who find pregnant women attractive. I never could leave your mother alone, but that's neither here nor there. What I'm trying to say is that while some women in your circumstances might be prone to having affairs, it is something you must avoid. I don't mean for you to stay shut up here in the house all the time. You ought to go to church, join ladies' circles and clubs, but as long as Mark is alive, don't let a breath of scandal touch your name. You owe that to your dear mother's memory, if not to Mark and me."

Now alarmed, Erica interrupted what she considered a totally unnecessary lecture. "What do you mean, 'as long as Mark is alive'? Is there something you haven't told me?"

Lars sighed, fearing he was upsetting everyone that day. Joining his daughter on the bench, he tried to be more tactful. "I told you I couldn't remove all the shell fragments from his brain. Does he still have headaches?"

"Yes, occasionally he does, but you told us that was to be expected."

"Well, I think it is, but I don't know enough about his type of injury to say whether or not he'll have worse problems in the future. We'll just have to hope that he doesn't, but at the same time be prepared that he might."

Puzzled now, as well as worried, Erica did appreciate his honesty. "I understand," she whispered softly, all traces of humor gone from her expression. "We'll just continue to do the best that we can for him."

"Yes, that's all we can do." Lars wasn't certain he had made his original point, however, and returned to it. "Look, I have no idea what could have possessed you to run off with an Indian, but since your behavior has been, to say the least, wild in the past, I don't think it is presumptuous of me to caution you to be more circumspect in the way you live your life now. As an example, I don't think it's a good idea having Etienne living in the house. His behavior appears to be respectful toward you, but who is to say he won't someday try to take advantage of you? He is a nice-looking young man, and you're bound to be lonely. You could find yourself beginning something with him you might swiftly regret but find impossible to end. It could happen. I've seen how good he is with Mark, but for your own sake, I think you should dismiss him and find an older man. Someone who won't provide an ounce of temptation for you."

It was the reference to her "wild" behavior that had snapped the thin hold Erica had on her emotions, and when he paused to take a breath she immediately defended her actions. "It was love that prompted me 'to run off with an Indian,' as you put it, and I don't consider what I did wild at all. As for Etienne, his friendship means far too much to Mark for me to dismiss him simply because you think I might someday have an affair with the man. That's an absurd request, and I'll not even consider it.

"Since you are so free with your advice, I have some for you, as well," Erica continued in the same hostile tone. "Sarah thinks you're the most wonderful man she's ever met. God knows why. You are handsome, but so oblivious to her charms it's a wonder she will even speak to you. I know how much you loved Mother, but you're a young man still, and you can't go on grieving for her forever." Erica realized she hadn't been in the least discreet as she had promised Sarah she would, but damn it all, her father had made her mad.

Lars was so astonished by Erica's revelations about Sarah that he could scarcely believe she was serious. "Isn't Sarah about your age?" he asked incredulously. "Why would she be interested in me?"

"Sarah will be twenty-six soon, so she's certainly old enough to know her own mind. You have intelligence, looks, charm upon occasion, so why wouldn't she be attracted to you?"

"I had absolutely no idea," Lars replied in dismay. He slumped back against the bench, certain he must have unintentionally hurt Sarah's feelings by refusing her invitation for the evening. "She's an attractive woman, and very sweet, but, baby, it would be wrong of me to encourage her affection when I've none to give in return."

"It was Mother who died, Daddy, not you," Erica reminded him gently.

Unconvinced, Lars continued to frown. "She asked me to be her escort for a party at the Bergstroms' tonight. At least I think now that was what she was trying to do."

"Then you're going with her?" Erica asked in delighted surprise.

"No, I said I had come home to see you, not the Bergstroms," Lars admitted sheepishly.

"Oh Daddy, you're hopeless." The kitten had awakened, and after stretching languidly it bounded over to Erica and rubbed against her ankles. She scooped him up in her hands and gave him an affectionate squeeze. "I think you better go over to Sarah's this very minute and apologize for being such a dolt. If she still thinks she can tolerate your company, ask to take her to the party. After all, you and Nils Bergstrom used to be good friends."

"Yes, we were." Lars reached over to scratch the kitten's ears. "You'd not mind if I went to the party?"

"Of course not. Go and have a wonderful time. You can tell me all about it tomorrow." With her father's assistance, Erica managed to rise from the bench without too much difficulty, but it wasn't until he had left for Sarah's house that she drew a deep breath. He could imagine she might be tempted to have affairs if he liked. She didn't care what he thought, actually, as long as he didn't guess the truth.

# Chapter Twenty-Five

## June, 1863

Viper was reading aloud to Mark from a worn copy of *The Last of the Mohicans*, but when he looked up, he found the young man sound asleep. He was lying on his stomach, his right arm dangling over the side of the bed, his hand curled around the sleeping kitten who had made himself at home in an old wicker basket Viper had found in the carriage house. A happy smile graced Mark's lips, and Viper marked his place and closed the book slowly to avoid waking him.

The brave had seen few novels in Minnesota, but that Mark had wanted to hear an adventurous tale concerning an Indian's love for a white woman had struck him as a peculiar coincidence. Mark never mentioned the time he had spent in Minnesota, and Viper couldn't help but wonder if he even remembered being there now. It was highly probable that he didn't, since all his memories tended to be hazy.

Mark had remembered kittens, though. The minute he had seen the playful little animal Viper had wanted to take it home for Erica, but it was clear that Mark considered the kitten his. With all their other problems, that mix-up was a slight disappointment, however. Erica would soon have a baby to take up all her time, while Mark would be content with the kitten.

Certain his charge would sleep until the morning, Viper left the book on his chair, snuffed out the lamp, and started for the door. Then he hesitated. He was certain Erica kept her door locked now, but she was so devoted to Mark that she would surely not lock him out of her room. Making his way carefully in the dark, Viper went to the connecting door between Erica's and Mark's room and slowly turned the handle.

Erica was seated at her dressing table. Too restless and uncomfortable to sleep, she was brushing her hair with long, even strokes when she saw Viper's reflection in her mirror. She first raised her finger to her lips to beg for silence, then motioned for him to come in.

Viper stepped through the door, then turned to close it with the same care he had given to opening it. Crossing the room to Erica's side, he bent down to brush her cheek with a light kiss. "How are you this evening, my darling?" he whispered in the thick French accent he conjured up whenever he became Etienne.

Waving him away with her hairbrush, Erica scolded him crossly. "My father actually believes you are who you're pretending to be. He also told me you are far too handsome and suggested I hire an older man instead, so I'd never be tempted to have an affair with you."

Viper couldn't help but laugh at Lars's advice. "Fire me, if you must. I will be back tomorrow with a white wig and a cane and you can hire me all over again. Of course, I will still have no references," he added with a mocking grin.

Erica stared up at him, disgusted that he would tease her when she had been so frightened of what her father might discover about him. Obviously he didn't care how greatly she had suffered because of him. "You'd do it too, wouldn't you?" she asked with a haughty toss of her curls.

"I would come back disguised as a woman if I had to, but I am not leaving you alone here, my beloved." Clasping his hands behind his back, Viper let his glance wander over Erica's delicate features and the slender curve of her throat, which was so attractively displayed by the layers of lace that trimmed the neckline of her nightgown. As always, she looked stunning. Her room was painted in a soft shade of rose, and in the evenings the dim light provided by the lamps gave the walls the warm glow of early sunset. That subtle color set off her fair beauty to perfection. "You are more beautiful each time I see you," he whispered reverently.

While blushing deeply at that praise, Erica was tempted to hurl her brush at him to make him stop the flattery she was certain was undeserved. "I look wretched, and you know it. Save your lies for others."

Viper stepped forward, and placing his hands upon her shoulders, he turned Erica toward her mirror. "Look for yourself. You are a very beautiful woman. Don't say that you are not."

Still embarrassed, Erica refused to study her image and looked away. "You must go. Goodnight."

Disappointed that she would give him so little of her time, and nothing of her love, Viper made no move to leave. "Where did your father go tonight?" he asked as he lifted his hands from her shoulders and began to caress her fair curls. He wound the ends around his fingers as he had once loved to do with the lock of hair he had taken without her permission. "I saw him as he left the house. Do you think he looks more impressive in his uniform than I did in buckskins, war paint, and feathers?"

The sly curve of Viper's lips told Erica he was teasing her again, and she almost laughed at the comparison he had made, then reminded herself she had to be as stern with him as she was with herself. "He looks as handsome in his uniform as you do in your buckskins, Viper. Stop fishing for compliments and tell me goodnight."

"Not until you tell me where he's gone," Viper insisted.

Knowing how stubborn the man was and wanting him gone, Erica immediately gave in. "He's taking Sarah to a party. She likes him very much, but unfortunately, he hasn't been interested in any woman since my mother's death."

"Sarah and your father?" Viper considered them as a couple for a moment, then nodded approvingly. "Yes, they should get along together almost as well as you and I do."

"Viper!" Erica had to force herself not to scream. "Please go!"

"Etienne," the wily brave reminded her.

"Well, whoever you are, get out of my room!"

"Or what?" Viper asked in a challenging tone. "Your father is gone, and Mark is asleep. There's nothing you can do if I refuse to go."

Using the edge of the dressing table for balance, Erica rose to her feet. "Don't you dare threaten me."

Viper was delighted she had stood up, since that made her all the more easy to kiss. He leaned forward and did just that. "I love you. In my mind you will always be my wife. Don't ask me to go, not tonight or ever."

Suddenly feeling dizzy, Erica raised her hand to her brow. "I'm sorry. I don't feel well enough to argue with you."

"Is it the baby?" Viper quickly stepped to her side, slipped his arm around her shoulders, and helped her over to the bed. "Well, is it? Tell me where your father has gone and I'll go for him right away."

"No, it's not the baby," she assured him shakily. "You just upset me and I stood up too fast. I'll be fine in the morning." When he turned down the covers, she didn't need his help to climb into the bed. "Thank you, now goodnight."

Viper, however, was in no mood to be dismissed so casually. He was too worried about her to leave her alone and promptly decided to stay. To avoid another argument, he snuffed out the lamp at her bedside and went back to take care of the one on her dressing table. Rather than leave her room, though, he moved to the foot of the bed to remove his clothes.

"What are you doing now?" Erica called out, since the room was too dark for her to see him clearly.

In less than a minute, Viper had disrobed and crawled into the other side of the bed. "I want to stay with you," he declared as he drew her into his arms. Instantly Erica put her hands upon his bare chest to push him away, but he easily brushed aside that objection to his company. "You needn't fight me. Just go to sleep. I will sleep beside you like I did the first night we spent together. Do you remember that?" His mouth brushed her ears, then her eyelids before lightly caressing her trembling lips. "I want to stay with you so you will understand you are still pretty and still loved."

Enveloped in the loving warmth of his embrace, Erica had difficulty fighting back her tears. Finally she could no longer deny the depth of her true feelings. "Oh Viper, I don't want to be mean to you. I love you so, but—"

"Hush. Think only of our love. Nothing else matters."

As his mouth covered hers Erica found that command impossible to obey, for she was lying to him as well as Mark, and he was bound to find out when the baby came. Her life was in such horrible confusion that not even the sweetness of Viper's affection could erase the pain that filled her heart and tormented her soul. She ended the kiss before her senses overpowered her reason and she begged for more. Sensitive to her distress, although he misread its cause, Viper pulled her against his side, and true to his word, simply held her cradled in his arms until she fell asleep. When she awoke the next morning, he was gone, but all of her perplexing dilemmas remained to taunt her.

Still astounded that Sarah Randall had a romantic interest in him, Lars did his best to be an attentive escort, but the delicious excitement he had always felt in Eva's presence was sadly lacking when he was with her. Perhaps he had treated her in a fatherly fashion too long for the pleasant nature of her company ever to provide a thrill. Whatever the reason, while he enjoyed seeing many of his old friends at the Bergstroms', he was grateful when it came time for the guests to depart. As they rode home in her carriage, Lars held Sarah's hand, quite awkwardly, he thought, and hoped she would never make the mistake of inviting him to be her escort again.

Without realizing it, Lars projected his desperation so vividly that Sarah had no doubt what he had thought of the evening. Clearly it had been a complete and utter disaster for him. Lars had always been confident, so relaxed in his manner at the hospital, and she had expected him to display that same easy charm that night, but sadly, he had spent more time glancing at his watch than looking at her. Clearly, she bored him to death, and heartbroken to think she would be unlikely ever to spend another evening with him, she forced herself to put on a brave front to save what was left of her pride.

"Everyone was delighted to see you tonight. You must have noticed that. Now that you have taken the first step to re-enter Wilmington society, I'm certain you will be deluged with invitations whenever you are in town. A handsome widower never lacks for feminine companionship. You will be very popular with the ladies, I assure you."

That she would discuss his popularity with women in so flippant a fashion startled Lars, for Sarah had always seemed so demure he couldn't imagine what had possessed her to make such a bold remark. "I really don't care whether I am popular or not, actually," he admitted quite frankly.

Now fearing she had insulted as well as bored him, Sarah didn't know what to do and fell silent. She had been drawn to Lars not only because of his pleasing appearance, but because he possessed a depth of character young men her own age often lacked. But apparently he had revealed all of himself that he ever would. Crushed to think the only man she had ever really wanted to impress cared nothing at all for her, she had all she could do not to weep openly in front of him.

Lars felt every bit as inadequate as Sarah. He opened his mouth, then shut it quickly when he could not think of any way to ask her forgiveness that didn't involve mentioning Eva, and he knew that was the very last thing he should do. It would only hurt the dear young woman all the more to think he was comparing her to his late wife. But he knew that was exactly what he had been doing all evening. She would never be Eva, and he didn't even want her to try and take the dead woman's place. No one could ever do that.

When they reached her home, Sarah graciously offered him the use of her carriage. "I'm glad you could go with me tonight. I'll ask Roger to drive you home."

Not waiting for the driver to climb down from his perch, Lars opened the door and stepped out. "Thank you, I'm glad you had an enjoyable time. I'll see you to your door, but then I'll walk home. I don't need to ride."

"As you wish," Sarah dismissed her driver, and as the carriage continued on toward the rear of the house she realized she would probably never be alone with Lars again. Unfortunately, that dismal prospect did not inspire any uniquely fascinating way to say goodnight that would instantly change Lars's opinion of her. As they reached her front door, she turned toward him, her expression more forlorn than grateful. "I really did enjoy being with you tonight, but I know it was a difficult evening for you. I'm sorry for that. Well, goodnight and thank you again."

When she offered her hand, Lars took it in a tender grasp, but again he had no idea what to say and did the only thing that seemed appropriate. He drew her close, meaning to give her the briefest of goodnight kisses, but her lips were surprisingly soft, and instead of releasing her quickly as he had planned, he slipped his left hand around her waist to pull her closer still.

That Lars would want to kiss her shocked Sarah, but she was delighted and returned his affectionate gesture with all the love that filled her heart apparent in her kiss. The kiss then took on a far more passionate flavor, endless, warm, sweet, then lingering and deep. When at last Lars released her, Sarah was as breathless as he. Since nothing she said to him seemed right, she decided to do no more than smile sweetly as she slipped through the door, but her heart was pounding so wildly she had to stop and lean back against it before going up to her room to bed. Was it possible Lars Hanson had some feelings for her after all? she wondered, hardly daring to hope that he might. She had been kissed perhaps more often than a respectable young woman should be, but never had she found another man's kiss so stirring. Thrilled clear to her toes, she took the stairs two at a time, so eager to see him again that she didn't think she could possibly wait until the next day.

Equally surprised by the ardor he had displayed, Lars jammed his hands in his pockets and scowled deeply as he strode home. He feared he had made it painfully obvious that he was a very lonely widower. Whatever would Sarah think of him now? She was a far more passionate young woman than he had suspected, but still, he felt the fault was his that their kiss had gotten so out of hand. He had let an innocent goodnight kiss turn into a near seduction, and he would not make that mistake again when the consequences could prove disastrous for them both. He was forty years old! he berated himself. He ought to have more sense than he had shown. Still, Sarah's lips had had such an inviting rose tint that when she had smiled so shyly as she said goodnight, the emotions he had kept suppressed for so long had swiftly betrayed him. It was something he would not allow to happen again, however. He told himself that again and again as he walked home, the words becoming a chant in his mind. "No, definitely not," he said aloud. "Never again."

On Sunday, when Sarah came to the Hanson home to visit her brother, she found Lars had gone to have dinner with William Dexter, the physician who had taken over most of his practice, and wasn't expected home before dark. Certain that he must think her wanton and that he had absented himself on purpose, Sarah stayed only long enough to chat briefly with Mark, then left without staying for dinner as she usually did on Sunday. On Monday she remained home all day, thinking if Lars wanted to see her, he would come to call. He did not. Too proud to turn up at his house each day, even though she knew her brother looked forward to her visits, Sarah stayed home two more days, and when she went to see Mark and Erica on Thursday, she discovered to her dismay that Lars had already left for Washington. Convinced that her memories of their kiss must have been far different from his, she refused to discuss the elusive physician with his daughter, and kept her sorrow that their brief encounter had led nowhere to herself.

Erica still read the newspaper each day and followed the news from Minnesota with avid interest. When she read that there had been more killings in the Big Woods and in Kandiyohi County where the uprising had begun, she found it difficult to believe that Little Crow would have left the safety of the Dakotas to again prey upon the settlers of Minnesota. Then, on July 3, the chief was shot and killed while picking berries with his sixteen-year-old son near Hutchinson on the border of the Big Woods. He had been slain by Nathan Lamson, who had been out hunting with his son, Chauncey. The Lamsons had not recognized Little Crow, but had shot him simply because feelings against the Sioux were running high because of the recent rash of murders.

At noon, Erica passed the newspaper to Viper. He read the account of Little Crow's death, then looked up at her with an expression of such unbearable sorrow that she had to look away. She knew exactly what he was thinking:

380

would the Sioux and white man never be able to live in peace? Since the answer to that question was too obvious to merit comment, she kept still, but the way the chief had died troubled her greatly. He had been shot not because he was a wanted man, not because his guilt in the latest murders had been proven, but because he was an Indian. The unfairness of that was no easier for her to bear than for Viper, for not only was the man she loved a Sioux, but her child would be half-Sioux, as well. That they might one day be shot, not for their crimes but for what they were, only added to the fears that daily threatened to suffocate her with dread.

As July wore on, Erica found no escape from her inner turmoil. It was not the ordeal of childbirth that terrified her, but the certainty that the identity of the babe's father would be unmistakable. The baby was going to be the image of Viper, she knew that beyond the slightest doubt. She had had many friends come to call when she had returned home, and they would all come to visit the moment they heard of the birth. There she would be with a fair-skinned, light-haired husband and a dark-skinned, black-haired child, and there would be a far worse scandal than her father had warned her to avoid. She had lied to everyone, not only to Mark, Sarah, and her father, but to Viper as well and she knew they would all soon hate her with a virulent intensity she felt she deserved.

To make matters worse, Erica decided she had been a fool not to run away as soon as she had learned she was pregnant. She wasn't well enough to flee now, and she couldn't leave Mark in so sorry a state even if she were. Despite her pleas that he stay away, Viper continued to come to her room each night. While they did not make love, she clung to him until, finally exhausted by her fears, she fell asleep, knowing even those brief hours of peace would soon come to an end.

While Viper had tried in every way he knew to set Erica's mind at rest with reassurances of his love, nothing he said seemed to have the slightest effect upon the nervousness of her mood. Thinking she was overwrought from the strain of her pregnancy, he tried to be patient, but he was as unhappy as she. The wife he adored would not admit they were wed, but he still considered their marriage a valid one. As for Mark, his headaches had become more frequent, and often he had to give him laudanum to help him sleep, but he kept that practice a secret from Erica, thinking she was already overburdened with the worries he feared he could never understand or relieve.

As fate would have it, Erica's contractions began in the early hours before dawn. At first they were so gentle she did not even feel them, but when they became more intense they jolted her awake. She found the room very dark, and Viper's arm draped over her swollen waist. At first she refused to believe her time had come and lay very still expecting the pains to stop, as she had heard they sometimes did. When the contractions not only contin- ued, but came between shorter intervals and grew increas- ingly sharp, she finally accepted the fact that her child in- tended to be born that day. The next pain sliced through her with the tearing agony of Wren's knife, and she could not keep from crying out.

Awakened as rudely as Erica had been, Viper sat up and shoved the hair out of his eyes. "What's the matter?" he inquired in a hushed whisper, then, recalling he had given Mark laudanum again, he ceased to worry about waking him and spoke in his normal voice. "Are you all right?"

"No, I'm not," Erica admitted with a terrified gasp. She reached for his hand and held on as the pain of the next contraction swelled to a nearly unbearable level. "My father told me to expect a long labor, but I think he was wrong."

When the pain subsided and she released her grip upon his hand, Viper scrambled out of bed and fumbled around through his scattered clothes for his pants. After yanking them on, he lit the lamp on the dressing table, but when he reached for the one on the nightstand Erica stopped him. "No, leave the lamp unlit."

Thinking she was objecting to the lamp's glaring brightness rather than to what it would soon reveal, Viper did as she asked. "You told me the midwife lives just a few blocks away. In the big white house at the corner of Walnut and Eighth, wasn't that it?"

"That's right." Erica had no time to say more before the next contraction caught her in its paralyzing grip. Viper reached for her hand of his own accord this time, but when she could again draw a breath, she forbade him to go. "No, you can't leave me all alone now. It's too late."

"How can it be too late?" Viper asked as he surveyed what he could see of her anguished expression in the dim light provided by the lamp on the opposite side of the room. "Have you been lying there all night suffering like this without waking me?"

"No, but—"

Viper could almost feel the pain himself now as it again swept through the fragile young woman. It seemed to him the contractions were coming very close together, and while he knew absolutely nothing about bringing children into the world, he thought that was a sign that this one would be coming soon. Sioux warriors did not serve as midwives, but he knew Erica would not be reassured if he offered that excuse out loud. "Look, I will go to the closest house and awaken their servants. One of them can go get the midwife. I will only be gone a few minutes."

"No!" Erica screamed the word this time, and Viper discarded that plan as too great a risk in her agitated state. While dreading the birth, Erica had prepared for it. There was a stack of towels on the corner of the dresser, scissors, and string. He had noted the collection of useful items, never suspecting he would be the one to use them.

Sitting down on the edge of her bed, Viper gripped Erica's hand more tightly. "All right, I will stay. Can you tell me what to do to help you?"

Erica shook her head. Midwives usually delivered infants, not physicians, so she had never witnessed a birth. From the gossip she had heard, this babe was far too impatient to be born, but she had no idea how to help him do it. She had never expected the pain to be so excruciating, and she tensed as it came again in an agonizing wave. She looked toward the windows, but the sky had not begun to lighten. Mrs. Ferguson wouldn't be there for hours, and Mark would be no help. She and Viper were all alone, and as helpless as children. For the first time, Erica realized she could die, from the severity of the pain alone, if not from the trauma of the birth itself.

"You must forgive me," she begged hoarsely. "Please forgive me."

Viper had no idea what Erica was talking about, but he quickly agreed. "I will forgive you anything, my love." He laid his left hand upon her belly and felt the muscles tighten as the next contraction began. "It can't be much longer," he assured her. "Try to hold on to me and think how pretty your child will be."

While Erica continued to cling to his hand, thoughts of how handsome her child would surely be were anything but reassuring. She grabbed up her pillow and shoved the corner into her mouth to muffle the scream she couldn't contain.

Since anything would be better than listening to his wife scream, Viper got up to fetch the stack of towels and carried them back to the bed. "I think we should take off your gown."

"No." Erica wasn't about to show off her swollen figure nude. "We can just push it up out of the way."

While that seemed silly, Viper did not argue. He picked her up to carefully move her aside while he draped the towels across the bed, then he placed her upon them. When in the next minute her water broke, he laughed. "You see what a good midwife I am? I know enough to protect your bed."

Erica didn't care if he set the damn bed on fire. She was drenched with perspiration, worn out from the pain that wracked her whole body, and terrified that if giving birth to Viper's child didn't kill her, he soon would. How did any woman keep her sanity if giving birth was always so hard as this? her tormented mind asked herself. "Your things are in my closet," she whispered, her thoughts still of him. "Your knife, bow, all your things."

"You kept them?" Viper was surprised Mark had allowed it.

Erica nodded, as engulfed in pain she could no longer find her voice, except to scream. The sound echoed in her mind with an eerie howl, like the wind blowing off the sea, and she felt herself slipping ever closer to the brink of an endless void in the most horrifying premonition of death imaginable. Terrified, she couldn't catch her breath as every muscle in her body seemed to be straining to force the babe from her body. The pain tore through her in blinding waves, pressing her down upon the bed with the enormous weight of the secrets she had kept for so many months. The water surrounding the babe had been warm, but what she felt now was the stickiness of blood. In her mind she saw a horrifying vision of her body being ripped apart by the claws of a thousand demons, and when her son gave his first frail cry she feared it was her own dying gasp, and able to stand no more, she fainted.

Not even the horror of facing execution had been as hard on Viper as having to watch Erica suffer so badly when he had neither the medicines nor the skills to ease her pain. He now understood why men did not tend their women during childbirth, for what man would ever put his wife through this agony twice? He had seen newborn infants only after they had been bathed and made ready to be presented to their relatives. He had had no idea they were born all slippery with their mother's blood. It was all he could do not to vomit as the child slid into his hands, but he laid the boy on Erica's now hollow stomach and ran to get the string and scissors to cut the umbilical cord. He then wrapped the baby, who had still not ceased crying, in one towel, and the placenta in another, but Erica was still bleeding, and he feared if he couldn't stop it, she might soon bleed to death.

That the baby seemed angry that his birth had been so arduous convinced Viper the child could be left with his unconscious mother long enough for him to call at the neighbor's house for help. He left the noisy little tyke snuggled in Erica's arms, pulled on the rest of his clothes, then dashed down the back stairs to summon aid. He had done all he could, but he would not allow Erica to die just because he did not know how to do more. He awoke the housekeeper of the closest home and implored her to send someone for the midwife, then raced all the way back to Erica's room.

Nothing had changed in the minutes he had been gone, and feeling as sorry for the whimpering infant as he did for his wife, he brought a pan of water to rinse him clean. He wanted Erica to be proud of her son when she saw him for the first time, and supporting the lad upon his left arm he splashed the water on him with his right hand. It was not until he had washed the boy's head thoroughly that he realized his hair wasn't simply dark with blood, but as black as his own. For a newborn, he had a thick thatch of hair, and it was as black as pitch. Wrapping the babe in a clean towel, Viper carried him back to the bed, but this time he held him in his arms rather than lay him beside Erica. Content to rest in his father's arms for the moment, the baby finally stopped crying and opened his bright gray eyes for his first look at the world.

When Erica had begged his forgiveness, Viper had never imagined she could have been burdened with the guilt of a deception so monstrous as this must have caused. The sympathy he had felt for her suffering now vanished in a furious fit of temper. She had repeatedly tried to send him away. Had he gone, he knew without a doubt she would never have told him he had a son. Was so vile a lie her idea of love?

Before Viper could confront Erica with her lies, the midwife arrived. Accompanied by two of her daughters, the buxom woman quickly banished him from Erica's bedroom, but he wouldn't let her touch his child. He took his son outside to the garden and sat down upon the grass with him cradled comfortably in his lap. Awaiting the coming dawn, Viper's handsome features were set in a dark scowl, for he could not wait to shake the truth out of the lying bitch he had once stupidly believed he would love for all eternity. She had made a mockery of his love, and that was a sin he would never forgive.

# Chapter Twenty-Six

## July, 1863

It was Mark who came outside to find Viper. He had gotten dressed by himself and looked it. The buttons on his shirt were misaligned, the cuffs undone, his hair uncombed, his face unshaven, and he was barefoot. He was also crying as though his heart were broken.

Shifting the sleeping child in his arms, the Indian brave rose to his feet and called out to the blind man as he approached him. He had intended to end his masquerade that very morning, but seeing that Mark certainly wasn't up to learning who he really was, he continued using the French accent everyone expected to hear when he spoke. "I am coming, monsieur. What has happened to put you in such a state?"

Mark continued to sob as he tried to explain. "Erica had the baby and I wasn't with her. I wanted to be with her. Now the midwife says she's worried about her, and she's sent for Dexter. What are we going to do if Erica dies, Etienne? Whatever will we do?" Mark tried to wipe his eyes on his shirtsleeves, but succeeded only in getting the garment sopping wet rather than drying his torrent of tears.

"Who is Dexter?" Viper asked quickly.

"A physician. He's a friend of Lars," Mark mumbled between loud gulps and sniffs.

"Of course, I recall the name now." Once the midwife had arrived, Viper had ceased to worry over Erica,

387

believing she was in capable hands. While he was not frightened to the point of tears, since he doubted Mark fully understood the situation, he was greatly disturbed to learn the delicate young woman wasn't making as normal a recovery from her ordeal as he had assumed she must be.

"Let's go inside, monsieur. I have the baby right here with me. Find a place to sit down, and you may hold him. He's sleeping, so you must be quiet."

"The baby? Oh no, I had forgotten all about him." Mark turned and hurried back through the french doors and took the first chair he came to in the dining room. Patting his knees, he held out his arms. "Give him to me. I wanted to name a girl for our mothers, to call her Eva Elizabeth, but I don't think we ever decided upon a name for a son. Does he look like me?"

As Viper placed the small bundle containing the sleeping child in Mark's arms, the young man's face lit up with such radiant joy that the Indian could not bring himself to tell the truth. "It is difficult to say who a babe resembles when he is so small, monsieur, but yes, I think he does favor you."

Afraid he might drop him, Mark held the baby boy very tightly. "Does he have all his fingers and toes? Is he perfect?" he asked excitedly.

"He is a fine son," Viper assured him. "He will need a fine name."

"Maybe Erica has thought of one." Then, recalling his wife was not doing well, Mark hugged the babe even more tightly, then asked Viper to take him again. "I must go back upstairs to Erica. If she calls for me I want to be there this time. Will you watch my son?"

"I will do my best." Viper scooped the babe from Mark's arms, then stood aside to let him pass on his way upstairs. He had no idea what to do himself, since whether or not Erica called for him, he wasn't ready to see her. When William Dexter arrived, Viper opened the front door to let him in, but turned away so the man could get no glimpse of the black-haired child. Dexter was a tall man, quite thin, with dark curly hair. After mumbling a hasty "Good morning," he tossed his hat aside, and, eager to see his patient, he nearly sprinted up the stairs. Margaret, the younger of the midwife's daughters, had gone to fetch

Dr. Dexter, and as soon as she stepped through the front door, she came to Viper's side.

"I think I should take the babe up to his mother now. If she wakes, even for a moment, she will want to see him."

"No, he will only be in the doctor's way. He will stay with me," Viper responded in so stern a tone that he knew she would not question his decision.

Astonished that the man wanted the responsibility for the infant, Margaret realized she had no idea who he was. "Are you a relative, sir?"

In spite of himself, Viper had to laugh at that question, but he did not reveal that he was related to the baby, if to no one else in the house. "I am Mr. Randall's manservant, mademoiselle, and he has placed the child in my care. Now don't you think you should go up and see if the doctor needs you?"

Flattered that he would call her mademoiselle, as though she were a lady rather than no more than a servant like himself, Margaret blushed as she turned toward the stairs. "I will come for the baby later, then."

"Yes, of course." Viper flashed a wide grin, as though he would readily relinquish the infant should she reappear. That was a trick he had learned from Percy: people were quick to trust a man who wore a smile. Viper knew as long as the boy slept they would get along fine together, but he did not know what he would do if the child awakened screaming in hunger. If Erica were too weak to nurse the infant, he supposed they would have to find another woman to feed his son, but he did not know how to go about looking for such a person or whether he should start.

Anna Ferguson came through the back door a short while later. She put her things away, put on her apron, and lit the fire in the stove to heat some water for tea, thinking the day was no different from any other. When Viper strolled into the kitchen with his son in his arms, she squealed with glee.

"Miss Erica has had the baby?" She liked Etienne, for he never complained when she asked him to run errands for her while Mark slept in the afternoons. She rushed to his side, and before he could object, she plucked the child from his arms. "Let me see the little angel," she exclaimed happily as she slid into a chair at the kitchen table. She placed the baby upon the table and unwrapped the towel that covered him.

"Mrs. Ferguson—" Viper began, but before he could offer any explanation for the babe's coloring, she looked up at him with a gaze of such astonished disbelief that he knew he would have to tell the truth, and he would not insult her by using a phony accent while he did it. "Erica was my wife before she became Mark's," he stated simply. "The child is mine, but since Erica and I haven't decided what to do yet, please don't tell Mark the boy looks like me. He thinks the babe is his son."

Anna had no idea what to say to such unexpected news, and rather than respond in any manner, she focused her attentions upon the naked tot in front of her. "We've made plenty of clothes for this child, and he ought to be wearing some, Mr. Bouchard." She wrapped the baby up again in the towel and held him pressed close to her bosom as she rose to her feet. "I will see to getting him dressed, and you needn't worry. I won't say a word to Mr. Randall until Miss Erica tells me her side of your preposterous story herself."

"You don't believe me?" Viper inquired, hurt that she had gone so quickly from joyful to distant in her manner.

"I have only to look at the babe to see you are telling the truth about being his father. It's how you could ever have been married to Miss Erica or what you're doing in this house that I don't understand. Poor Mr. Randall," she whispered softly, as an afterthought. "After all he's been through, and now this."

While Viper would not argue that Mark had indeed been through a lot, so had he, and he thought he deserved as much sympathy as the blind man, if not more. Clearly he was not going to get it from Anna Ferguson, however. "Dr. Dexter is with Erica now. You ought to look in on them. She isn't doing well."

"What? Why didn't you tell me that in the first place?" Still holding his son, the housekeeper rushed up the back stairs and hurried to Erica's room.

When the tea kettle began to whistle, Viper pulled it off the fire, but he was in no mood to sip tea. He sat down at the kitchen table and put his head in his hands. He was still furious with Erica, but he didn't want her dead. He knew if she died, though, that he would have to take his baby and go before anyone realized that was what he was bound to do and stopped him. He had enough experience with white men to know Lars would think his claim to his grandchild far outweighed an Indian's claim to his son.

When Sarah arrived for her daily visit and found the Hanson home in a state of turmoil, she was upset that no one had had sense enough to send for her earlier that morning. Her brother was still beside himself with worry, and she did her best to comfort him, but he couldn't seem to accept Dr. Dexter's opinion that Erica was merely suffering from exhaustion and would recover her strength after a few days of rest.

"Mark, listen to me," Sarah ordered sharply. "Erica is just tired. She'll sleep all day today and probably most of tomorrow, but she's not going to die. Please don't carry on so. Why don't we go into your room and get you dressed. Where is Etienne? Why didn't he help you dress this morning?"

Horribly depressed about his wife's condition, Mark shook his head dejectedly. "Sarah, it doesn't matter how I look."

"It most certainly does! I'll not have you looking so neglected. I will shave you myself if Etienne can't be found to do it, but I'll not have you looking anything but your best on your son's birthday."

That thought brought a wide grin to Mark's tear-streaked face. "Etienne says he looks just like me."

"Wonderful! He'll be very handsome, then." Sarah gave her brother another enthusiastic hug and propelled him toward his room. "I can't wait to see him, but I insist we get you cleaned up before we begin admiring the baby, since that might take all afternoon."

"Am I still handsome, Sarah?" Mark asked rather plaintively. "Even now?"

His question brought a painful lump to her throat and tears to her eyes, but Sarah managed to respond. "Even though you are my brother, in my opinion there's not another man in Wilmington who is better looking than you are. Granted you are a mite too thin, but you are every bit as handsome as you ever were. You just sit down. I won't bother to look for Etienne. I used to shave Daddy when he was ill, so I know how to do it."

"Wasn't that a long time ago?" Mark asked apprehensively. He raised his right hand to feel the stubble that covered his chin. "Maybe I should grow a beard."

"Nonsense, you are far too handsome to hide that splendid face of yours behind a beard. Now don't worry, I won't nick you even once, I promise."

When he heard her lathering up the shaving brush, Mark tried one last time to change her mind. "I think we better find Etienne."

"Hush," Sarah scolded. She sharpened his razor with a few quick strokes upon the leather strop, and true to her word, gave him an expert shave. When she had Mark cleaned up and dressed as fashionably as he was usually attired, she took his arm. "Now where is the baby? Is the cradle in Erica's room?"

His smile becoming a befuddled frown, Mark shrugged. "I don't kow if he's in the cradle or not. Mrs. Ferguson had him a while ago."

"Well, he can't have gotten lost." Sarah peeked into Erica's bedroom where Margaret remained to watch over the new mother after her own mother, sister, and Dr. Dexter had left. The room was very quiet, and while the cherrywood cradle both she and her brother had used had been placed beside the bed, it was empty. "Where's the baby?" she whispered.

"With the housekeeper, I think," Margaret replied softly.

"Thank you." Sarah closed the door and led the way to the main staircase at the front of the house. "It is a terrible shame Erica is so worn out, but I'm certain she'll be her old self with a few days' rest."

"I hope so," Mark agreed, but he was still not convinced Erica would recover her health that rapidly. "I couldn't go on living without her, Sarah, I just couldn't."

"Mark, really, she'll be fine," Sarah assured him once again. "Now stop thinking such sad thoughts. What is your son's name? Did you and Erica choose one?"

"I don't think so." Mark was certain he would have

remembered something so important as a name for a son if they had selected one. "Do you have any suggestions?"

"Not yet, but perhaps I will when I see the babe." Sarah had been delighted to learn her brother had a healthy and attractive child. Since she quite naturally expected the baby to be fair, she was no more prepared than Anna Ferguson had been when she saw him for the first time. The little tyke was in the kitchen, dressed in one of the white linen gowns Erica had made for him, and he was again snuggled in Viper's arms. He was wide awake, sucking on his fist, and when Sarah leaned down to get a better look at him he looked up at her, his eyes as filled with curiosity as hers.

Sarah looked from the gray-eyed babe to the man holding him, stunned at the realization that the striking resemblance between them could not possibly be a coincidence. She looked over to the housekeeper for help, but the woman merely shook her head, clearly as appalled as she was, and provided no help. Shocked clear to the marrow, Sarah had to reach for the back of one of the kitchen chairs to steady herself before she spoke. "The baby is adorable, Mark, just as I knew he would be. Do you want to sit down and hold him a while? I need to speak with Etienne privately for a moment."

Mark was too excited about having a son to care about what his sister wished to discuss with his friend. "I'll be right here." Groping for a chair, he sat down and waited for Etienne to put the baby in his arms. "I wish I could see him," he murmured wistfully.

"He is every bit as handsome as you imagine him to be, Mark." Sarah leaned down to kiss her brother's cheek, then turned, and with a furious glare gestured for Viper to follow her into the suite of rooms at the front of the house that had served as Lars's office. All her life she had had others to look after her: first her parents, then her brother. She had been more than willing to allow Erica to assume that same role when Mark had been injured, but this was a matter she knew she would have to handle herself whether or not she had any experience in being independent. She closed the door, and certain they would not be overheard, she demanded an explanation for her nephew's astonishing appearance.

"I can think of only one possible reason why that baby resembles you so closely, but if you have an opinion, I'd certainly like to hear it." Etienne had to be the Indian Mark had told her about, but even knowing that, Sarah found it impossible to believe a savage could have tricked them so thoroughly as this man had.

The lavish charm Viper had displayed whenever he had spoken with Sarah prior to that day was completely absent from his manner as he stepped close to the irate young woman. Not bothering to use a French accent any longer, he replied in as heated a tone as she had used with him. "Erica was my wife before she became Mark's. That her son is also mine proves that she is my wife still."

"You lying bastard." Sarah did her best to convey a shriek in a discreet whisper. "I want you out of this house before the sun sets. You might have fooled us all before about who you are, but there's no way you can get away with that any longer."

"This is not your house, so you've no right to tell me to leave," Viper pointed out with a defiant sneer.

Alarmed by how close he was standing, as well as by his height and obvious strength, which until that moment had never seemed menacing, Sarah stepped back quickly to put more space between them. A charming Canadian was one thing, a murdering Sioux quite another, and she didn't want to remain in the same room with him a second longer than necessary.

"I have every right !" she countered. "My brother is in no condition to look out for himself, but if he were, you know you'd not dare show your face here. That you have been living here with Erica is disgusting, and I will not allow it to continue another night."

Unconcerned, Viper continued to regard her with a belligerent stare. "Whether I stay or go is a matter for Erica and me to decide. Stay out of this. It is no business of yours."

"It most certainly is my business!" Sarah protested. "Do you think just because my brother is blind I'll allow you to make a cuckold of him? You savages may have no morals, but my brother and I most certainly do! Before Erica met you, she had high standards, too," she added as a further insult.

Since he had no idea what a cuckold was, Viper did not

respond to that accusation, but instead turned his back on Sarah and walked to the door. "You can tell your brother who I am if you must, but I doubt he will remember me. The only thing he cares about now is that baby. Do you really want to tell him the boy isn't his?"

Sarah clenched her fists at her sides, unable to think of any name worse than the one she had already called him. Knowing Erica was a reasonable person, even if her arrogant Indian lover wasn't, she decided to wait and speak to her before she did anything more about sending him away. First of all, she would use Erica's weakened state as an excuse to move into the house. Then she would see to the matter of a wet nurse for her child. Perhaps it was a bit late, but now that she knew what the true situation was in the Hanson home, she would do her best to see it improved drastically, and soon.

"Don't try and make me think you care about Mark's feelings, because it's more than plain you don't," she admonished. "I'll wait until Erica is again well, and then the three of us will straighten out this horrid mess. Until that time, I suggest you stay out of my way, and I will make it a point to avoid you."

"That will be a pleasure," Viper replied as he left the room. He was as anxious to talk with Erica now as Sarah was, but unfortunately the young woman was too weak to speak with anyone for the time being.

Erica wanted to sleep forever. Each time she was awakened the aroma of food upset her stomach, making eating impossible, and after taking only a few sips of water she would return to her dreams. Dr. Dexter came to see her each morning and night, and while he had no more success than Mrs. Ferguson in tempting Erica with food, he was certain if she craved sleep so badly then that was all she needed.

Viper waited until their son was four days old before he went to Erica's bedroom. Mark had begun spending most of his time there seated at his wife's bedside patiently waiting for her to awaken and ask for him. He was in his own room for his afternoon rest, though, and with the whole house quiet, Viper decided it was the perfect time to pay Erica a call.

After he had calmed down sufficiently to think more clearly, it had occurred to him that it was just possible Erica had not known who had fathered her child. That she had gone so suddenly from being his wife to Mark's had not been her choice, he reminded himself, but his. He decided if she had merely been uncertain about the babe's father, there was nothing to forgive. If, on the other hand, she had deliberately failed to tell him the baby was his, he had no idea what he would do. The very thought of that deception made his ruse to conceal his identity seem a child's prank by comparison.

Viper had not been in Erica's room since the morning he had delivered their child. To dispel the atmosphere of a sickroom, Mrs. Ferguson had flung the windows wide open to let in the breeze, and the bright summer sunlight made the soft rose color of the room as pretty as a young girl's blush. Sarah had picked several colorful bouquets from the garden, and the blossoms lent a delightful fragrance to the air. The brave had come to demand answers from his wife, but the tranquillity that engulfed him as he entered her room made the idea of starting any conflict seem ill-advised.

Erica had been bathed each day and clothed in a clean nightgown, but Viper was shocked to find her skin as pale as the white lace garment she wore. The linens on the four-poster bed were also so dazzling white that her blond hair shone like silver where it fell upon her pillow. As he sat down on the side of the bed, he thought more than ever that she was as lovely as a princess, but he doubted her heart was as pure as her sparkling appearance made it seem.

Shaking her shoulder lightly, Viper called her name, "Erica, wake up. You've slept long enough." When that effort failed to wake her, he took her right hand and brought it to his lips. Her skin was cool and soft. Even sound asleep, the sight of her stirred his blood. Refusing to allow her beauty to affect him, Viper gathered his resolve and grew increasingly insistent, until at last Erica's eyes fluttered open, and their vibrant blue provided a distraction too compelling to ignore.

At first Erica saw only the man she loved and a pretty smile brightened the pale contours of her face. Then she noticed the stern set of his features and knew she had no reason to smile. She tried to pull her hand from his but lacked the strength to do so.

"We have only a few minutes," Viper cautioned, ignoring her attempts to escape his touch. "We must make the most of them. Did you truly think the child was Mark's? Is that why you did not tell me he was mine?" When Erica's eyes instantly flooded with huge tears, Viper had his answer without needing to hear it in words. "Why? Why did you want to keep such a secret from me? If you love me as you say you do, why did you treat me that way?"

Although Viper was furious with her, Erica saw only his pain, and felt it as deeply as her own. "I knew if I told you," she began hesitantly, "you'd make me leave with you, and I can't abandon Mark when he's as helpless as a child. I told you that before. I'm married to him, so it makes no difference what I feel for you. I can't leave him."

"Do you even want to?" Viper asked pointedly, still torn between wringing her neck and kissing her until she finally understood she belonged to him. When she did no more than stare up at him with a tear-blurred gaze, he started to rise.

"No, please don't go," Erica begged softly.

Before Viper could respond, Sarah peeked into the room. Seeing him there, she came in and locked the door behind her so they would not be disturbed. "If you're up to speaking with him, Erica, then you can't refuse to talk with me."

When Erica turned to Viper with a questioning glance, he moved over slightly to make himself appear even more at home on her bed. "As you can see, Sarah is anxious to talk with us. Have you seen the baby?"

"Well, no, not yet, but—"

"You needn't apologize," Viper assured her, more for Sarah's benefit than Erica's. "You've given me a fine son, but now that everyone knows who I am, Sarah thinks I am no longer welcome here."

Erica had been so certain the child would be a boy, she wasn't at all surprised to hear that news. She vaguely recalled people coming in and out of her room, disturbing her rest, but none of their conversation. Maybe others had tried to tell her the child was a boy, but she didn't remember. My memory is getting as bad as Mark's, she thought to herself, but she still felt so tired she found it

397

difficult to think, and she decided it was no wonder her memories weren't clear.

"The boy looks like you?" she managed to ask Viper.

"The baby looks more like him than he does," Sarah replied before Viper could. "I've told everyone you're not up to having visitors, which is true, but I can't keep our friends away forever. Then there's the matter of the christening. What are you going to call the child? My brother is your husband. The babe's name will be Randall, but he certainly doesn't look like one of us, and when words of that gets around, the gossip will never cease."

As Erica listened to Sarah's complaints, she didn't hear anything she hadn't thought of herself. "I'm sorry," was all she could think to say.

"You're not half as sorry as I am," Sarah replied. "Thank God, Mark doesn't suspect anything is wrong, but we'll have to be careful some fool doesn't ask him why his son looks nothing like either of you. Maybe we can say the child is sickly, then send him away to school. As for Etienne, I told him he would have to go, but he refuses to listen to me, so you'll have to be the one to send him away. The sooner you do it, the better off we'll all be."

While Erica could understand Sarah's anger, since she had had plenty of time to anticipate it, she couldn't agree to her demands. "I don't know what to do, Sarah. I want to do what's best for Mark, but that's so awfully hard on the rest of us."

Viper couldn't abide being left out of the conversation as though he weren't even there, and he gave his own opinion then. "If I am the only one who cares more about my son than Mark, then I will take the babe and go. I will not have to apologize for him. I am very proud of him."

More relieved than she cared to admit, Sarah immediately agreed. "That's the perfect solution. I don't know why I didn't think of it myself. Give him the child, Erica. Tell him to take him home to Minnesota or wherever he wants to go. Many couples lose their first baby, and we'll just say the boy didn't survive. You and Mark are bound to have more children."

Erica was so appalled by that ghastly suggestion that she clung to Viper's arm and pulled herself up into a sitting position. "Get out of my room!" she screamed at

Sarah. "I'll not send my baby away just to please you. How could you even suggest such an awful thing? Children can't be replaced, and when Mark is like a child himself, how can you imagine I would want to have a child with him?"

Sarah realized instantly she had said too much, but quickly tried to smooth things over. "I am not the one who suggested Etienne take the child, he did. If you insist upon raising the boy, maybe we can tell people you adopted him. We can decide what to do about the baby later. Right now I want you to tell Etienne to go. That's something you simply can't delay."

Erica was still shaking with anger, but she wouldn't give in to Sarah's badgering. "No," she cried again and again. "No! No!" She felt the same sense of hopeless rage she had felt when Viper had been condemned to death, and she only knew that she would not send him away.

Realizing the fragile beauty was now hysterical and knowing that couldn't possibly be good for her, Viper wrapped his arms around her and hugged her tightly. He then looked up at Sarah with a malevolent gaze. "I think you're the one who ought to get out; now go. We'll get along here fine without you."

Sarah opened her mouth to argue, then thought better of it. There was no point in warning the Indian about what she intended to do. Even if she had failed to make Erica do the right thing, she knew Lars would. She would leave for Washington that very day, and she was certain once Lars knew his daughter planned to continue living with her Indian lover in his house, he would come straight home and put an immediate stop to it.

"All right, I'll go. In fact, I'll be happy to leave, but you've not heard the last of this, Indian. You can be certain of that."

Viper didn't think Sarah's threat serious enough to merit a reply. After she had stormed out of the room he remained seated on the bed, rocking Erica gently in his arms until she again fell into an exhausted sleep. How had she managed to bewitch him again? he asked himself in amazement, but he was so happy she had refused to send him away that he vowed no one would ever part them again.

# Chapter Twenty-Seven

## August, 1863

In early July, the Union Army finally handed the Confederates a crushing defeat at Gettysburg. When the Southerners began their retreat, their wagon train, filled with more than twenty thousand wounded men, had extended for seventeen miles. At the same time, Union forces under General Grant had won control of Mississippi, after reducing the city of Vicksburg to ruins and the population to near starvation with a six-week siege. On July 8, General Banks captured Port Hudson, Louisiana, which lay to the south and had served as a vital source of food and supplies for the Confederacy. After those impressive victories, the mood in Washington was one of elation. As before, the hospitals were flooded with casualties, but men wounded when the tide of the war was turning their way had far higher morale than those who had taken not only a physical beating, but a psychological battering, as well, when things had been going poorly for the Union.

Encouraged by the northern army's victories, Lars hoped the war would soon end. He wanted nothing more than to see peace arrive, rather than ambulances bearing young men with badly mangled bodies. He thought often of how wonderful it would be to return home and practice medicine again in a tranquil community where gruesome injuries would be a rare exception, rather than the rule.

Much to his dismay, he also found his thoughts frequently filled with memories of his brief encounter with Sarah Randall. He knew he had behaved like a frightened schoolboy in leaving Wilmington without making the effort to see her again. He was not only embarrassed but ashamed of his conduct, where she was concerned. He feared once he returned home that she would go out of her way to avoid him. He wouldn't blame her if she did, but the fact that his daughter was married to her brother would make that effort damn awkward for them all. She was a sweet and sympathetic young woman, but he had simply not known how to respond to her affection. So he had behaved like a jackass and undoubtedly hurt her feelings badly, which was something no gentleman would have done, and he could not forgive himself for it and doubted she ever would.

Feeling as he did, he was quite naturally taken aback when he saw Sarah enter the hospital one afternoon during the first week of August. In sharp contrast to the stark hospital decor, she was beautifully dressed in a fashionable summer gown woven of threads of yellow and pink cotton, which created the shade of a rose-tinged sunset, and a straw hat adorned with silk daisies. He was so certain the attractive young woman had come to visit a patient that he dared not approach her until he heard her speak his name at the desk. Trying to appear far more confident than he felt, he quickly went to her side, but he couldn't keep himself from grinning like a fool, he was so happy to have a chance to make up for the abysmal way he had treated her.

"Miss Randall, how lovely you look. It's so nice to see you again. What news can you give me of my daughter and grandson? Dexter's wire told me little other than that I was a grandfather. What about Mark, is he still getting along well?"

Now that she was there, Sarah found it difficult to look at Lars without recalling how they had parted. She had been so excited by his kiss that she had not dreamed he would return to Washington without wanting another. She had not forgotten that hurt, but the pain she had suffered then was a very private one, and not nearly so acute as that caused by her distress over Erica's continued affair with her Indian.

"They are all fine," she responded evasively, "but there is something we must discuss, privately, if we may." She glanced toward the woman behind the desk, who was listening attentively to their conversation, and hoped Lars would understand that she did not wish to talk with him there where they could be overheard.

Disappointed that Sarah had not seemed nearly so glad to see him as he was to see her, Lars decided her cool aloofness was what he deserved. Assuming a far more professional manner, he took her arm. "I'm afraid my office is even more cluttered than when you last saw it, but it is private." He escorted her there, offered her a chair, then took the one at his desk for himself and swung it around to face her. "I can't promise we won't be interrupted, but I'll give you all the time I can," he offered generously.

"Thank you, I appreciate that. I know how busy you are, and I wouldn't have come here if I had had anywhere else to turn, but I thought you'd want to know what's been happening at home."

Lars frowned apprehensively. "Is it Mark? Are you concerned about him?"

Sarah shook her head. Concentrating upon the ivory fan clasped tightly in her hands rather than the deep blue of Lars's eyes, she began to pour out her story in so emotional a fashion that she was swiftly reduced to tears. She got through it, though, every shocking, shameful, scandalous bit of it, then slumped back in her chair. "So you see, you really must come home and make Etienne leave before he and Erica disgrace us any further."

Lars was so stunned by Sarah's tale that it took him a full minute to gather his wits to reply, but his reaction was not the explosive one she had expected. In the years following her mother's death, he had neglected his daughter shamefully, and he knew the overwhelming sense of betrayal he felt now was a direct result of the fact that he and Erica were no longer as close as they had once been. He could not help but think that if anyone were to blame for the heartache Sarah had just confided in him, it was he.

"I'm sorry this has upset you so badly," he began

sympathetically, "but I really don't know what to say, other than that I'm every bit as shocked and hurt as you must have been when you learned who Etienne is. That Erica would lie to us about so important a matter as his identity is inexcusable, but from what you say, she has no intention of apologizing for deceiving us.

"In my mind, I can see her face so clearly when she told me about the baby. I think she was actually trying to tell me the truth then, and I'm afraid I just didn't give her the chance. Then when I came to see her a few weeks ago, I could see how unhappy she was, but I had no idea she had even more reason for her sorrow than I expected. Perhaps if I had been less critical of her she might have confided in me then, but she didn't."

Lars leaned back in his chair, his expression still registering disbelief, for he found the complexity of the situation Sarah had described almost impossible to comprehend. "I can see why you're so upset, Sarah, but will you give me a chance to think about the news you've given me for a while before I give you my opinion on what ought to be done?"

Since, in her view, what ought to be done was painfully clear, Sarah was disappointed that Lars hadn't immediately seen where his duty lay. "Of course," she responded rather stiffly. "I had hoped to begin my return trip home tomorrow, but if—"

"Tomorrow?" Lars inquired regretfully, then citing the complicated nature of their dilemma rather than his desire to put things right between them, he continued. "I want to consider all the ramifications of this situation, Sarah. There might even be legal problems involved, I don't know. I don't think either of us should make hasty judgments on so delicate an issue as this. Please plan to stay here several days. Are you again staying with your friends, the Fletchers?"

"Yes, but I don't want to impose upon Louise's hospitality," Sarah replied primly.

His visitor was behaving in so cold and distant a manner that Lars feared he had ruined all possibility of a friendship, let alone a romance, between them. That pained him almost as much as the news she had brought him.

"I wonder what Etienne's name really is. Do you know? When Mark told me about him, he didn't call him by name," Lars wondered aloud.

"I've no idea. Does it really matter?" Sarah replied in as near sarcastic a tone as she dared use with him.

"No, not really. I was just thinking of how kind he was to your brother, the way he would peel a piece of fruit for him without being asked, or take his arm to guide his way without being overprotective. His regard for Mark appeared to be completely genuine. Was that merely an act for my benefit, or has he always been so considerate as he was when I was there?"

Sarah licked her lips thoughtfully before she answered as honestly as she could. "No, you didn't see anything out of the ordinary, but everything the man did was an act, and he was remarkably consistent. From the first time I saw them together it seemed as though he and Mark were old friends. Now, of course, I can understand why. They did know each other, but they can't possibly have been friends."

Before Lars could comment on that, there was a loud knock at his door. "I was afraid we'd be interrupted," he apologized as he got up to answer it.

When the orderly saw the beautifully dressed young woman seated in Lars's office, he grew flustered. "I'm sorry to bother you, sir, but Harris is hemorrhaging again, and we need you."

Lars turned to Sarah. "It's an emergency and I've got to go. I took Erica to Louise's house several times, so I remember where it is. Will you be at home this evening?"

"Why yes, I think so," Sarah responded as she rose and moved toward the door.

"Good, I'll come and talk with you tonight."

As Lars dashed off down the hall with the orderly at his heels, Sarah remained by his door for a moment, not certain she actually wanted to see him later, since his first impulse had not been to grab a shotgun and return to Wilmington with her. "Damn!" she whispered under her breath, and finally deciding she would talk to him until midnight if she had to inspire him to take some prompt action, she left the hospital and returned to her friend's home.

By the time Lars reached Louise Fletcher's house it was quite late. He had left the hospital meaning to go straight there, but had ended up wandering the azalea-lined streets for more than two hours before turning up the walk of the brick townhouse where Sarah was staying. An elderly servant showed him to the parlor where he found the young woman seated by herself. She had not been reading, nor doing handwork, but merely sitting there looking very lost and alone, and he instantly regretted his tardiness and apologized.

"I'm sorry it's so late. Would you rather I came back tomorrow? I did my best to keep Harris from bleeding to death, but unfortunately, I failed. I knew I'd not be good company, but I should have come right over here and said so instead of hoping exercise would improve my mood."

The man looked as miserable as she felt, and Sarah immediately patted the place beside her on the striped satin settee. "I'm so sorry you lost your patient. Please come and sit down and rest a while before you go. Can I have Hugo bring you some brandy?"

Grateful she wasn't as upset by the lateness of the hour as he had thought she would be, Lars sat down with her, but he refused the brandy. "I don't drink anymore. Would it be too much trouble to have coffee or tea instead?"

"It's no trouble at all." Sarah asked Hugo to bring coffee, then had another thought. "Do you like peach cobbler? Louise's cook makes the best I have ever tasted. Would you like some of that, too?"

That was too tempting a dish to refuse. "I would love it." When Hugo had left, Lars shook his head sadly. "I'm going to feel as guilty as sin eating that when I've got men in the hospital right now suffering not from wounds, but from malnutrition. We even had cases of scurvy during the winter. There's good food purchased for the hospitals, but we have the devil of a time having it cleared for our use and delivered. The men in the field have such a poor diet it is a wonder more aren't too ill to fight."

Sarah had hoped she would be able to control the restless sense of longing she felt whenever she was with Lars, but tonight it was more intense than ever. The night was warm and humid. She had worn a sheer muslin gown in a pale mint shade to keep cool, but she needed the refreshing breeze created by her fan rather often to keep from appearing wilted. Despite her disappointment that Lars had failed to take some action immediately upon hearing her complaints, she still found much to admire about the man.

"I think your patients are very lucky to have a physician who cares so deeply about their welfare," she complimented him sincerely.

Lars sighed wearily. "I used to think I was as competent as any doctor I knew, and a damn sight better than most. That was what prompted me to enlist. I thought, with the desperate need for physicians, that I could put my skills to good use. Now after more than a year, I know the contribution I've made to the army is slight. I've seen wounded men packed in cattle cars that weren't even cleaned out before they were used to send the injured from the battlefield here to a permanent hospital. With treatment like that, it is amazing any survive the trip. Then when we lose one who didn't succumb on the journey here, it is doubly troubling. Maybe if I had done something else, something more. Oh, I don't know. I am just sick to death of seeing boys in their teens with their arms and legs blown off."

"I'm sorry," he apologized suddenly. "You can't want to hear things like that."

While that was certainly true, Sarah was still sympathetic. "My discomfort at hearing about it can scarcely compare to yours, when every day you have to view such horror," she hastened to assure him.

Hugo arrived then, and as soon as he placed the silver tray upon the table in front of the settee, Sarah picked up the silver pitcher filled with cream. "The cobbler is delicious, as I said, but it is ever so much better with cream. Would you like some?"

"Oh God, you aren't going to give my conscience any peace tonight, are you?" But Lars laughed, his downcast mood having already improved considerably at the arrival of the scrumptious refreshments.

"I think you deserve luscious treats like peach cobbler. You're far too modest. I'm certain you are the best doctor in Washington."

Lars laughed out loud at that lavish praise, since he felt

it was completely undeserved. "Please, Miss Randall, I'm conceited enough already."

"Please call me Sarah," the shy young woman asked with a charming smile, pleased to find the evening was not going to be a total loss after all. She poured a generous amount of cream on his bowl of cobbler, then served him a cup of coffee.

Lars watched the grace of her motions, knowing she had undoubtedly been tutored from childhood in the arts that would make her the perfect hostess she was. He found her so charming he hoped their friendship would continue to develop as smoothly as it was going that night. "I would like you to call me Lars, if it doesn't sound too strange to you."

"Why should it sound strange?" Sarah inquired between bites of the tasty cobbler. "Lars is a nice name."

With his mouth full, Lars had to wait a moment to reply. He had found the cobbler better than good: it was exquisite. The peaches were sweet and the golden-brown crust so flaky it melted the second it reached his lips. Anna Ferguson's pastries were good, but not so delicious as this. It took him a moment to focus his attention upon his companion rather than on the delectable dessert. "It wasn't the name I thought you might object to, Sarah. It's just the fact I am a good deal older than you and—"

"Hardly a 'good deal older,' Lars. I'm almost ten years older than Erica. You aren't old enough to be my father, if that's what's worrying you."

Lars had not expected their conversation to become so informal when Sarah had seemed to be under such an awful strain only that afternoon. Thinking it fortunate she was now more relaxed, he hoped nothing he planned to say would spoil the evening. "I am not particularly worried," he replied with a teasing wink. She laughed then, and so did he, for he could not recall the last time he had felt like flirting with a young woman, let alone done anything about it.

When they had finished eating the luscious dessert, Lars knew it was growing late and that he could no longer avoid dealing with the matter at hand. "I gave the problem you described a great deal of thought on the way here tonight. I know what you want me to do, but let's think about our options for a moment."

Sarah patted her lips lightly, and after setting her napkin aside again picked up her fan so she would have something to do with her hands other than wringing them pathetically. "I'm afraid I really don't understand what those options might be other than the obvious one: to throw Etienne out of the house immediately. What else is there to consider?"

Lars reached over to take her hand in the comforting clasp he often used with his patients' womenfolk. "Have you ever been in love, Sarah? I don't mean the infatuations everyone has growing up. What I mean is, have you ever really loved someone so dearly their happiness meant more to you than your own?"

Sarah hoped that question was not an accusation that she was such a great failure as a woman that she must be a stranger to love. She knew the difference between the sweet excitement of a girlish crush and the anguish of unrequited love quite well. That was a difficult thing to admit, however, since if she had ever been in love, why wasn't she married to the man?

Lars watched the blush rise in Sarah's fair cheeks and cursed his own insensitivity. "I'm sorry. That's really none of my business, is it?"

Sarah shook her head. "I'm not too embarrassed to answer. Yes, I've been in love, but unfortunately it was completely one-sided."

"Well, the man was a stupid fool, then, if he didn't consider your love precious," Lars assured her, not realizing how ironic his remark truly was.

Sarah didn't understand how their conversation had gone from playful to serious even so quickly, but she was horribly embarrassed, even though she had denied it. "I don't think he suspected what my feelings were, Lars, but that's really unimportant now. What are we going to do about Erica and Etienne?"

"That's what I'm trying to discuss," Lars reminded her with a puzzled frown, not comprehending why she didn't understand where he was trying to lead their conversation. "I love my daughter dearly, and while I haven't been much of a father to her in the last few years, I'm going to try and do what's best for her now. She spoke with great fervor when she told me she loved her Indian, and I think she loves him still. If I told her I'd not permit her to have her lover living in the same house with her invalid husband, she would be forced to choose between them. While it's plain Erica has great affection for Mark, and gives him wonderfully attentive care, I don't think he would be her choice."

"But she is married to him!" Sarah protested a bit too loudly.

"According to whatever customs the Sioux have, she was married to Etienne first. I think she is closer to being a bigamist than an adultress, but I don't want to hear her called either."

Sarah's brown eyes grew wide at that thought. "Is that what you meant about legal problems? Could Erica be sent to prison for bigamy?"

"I doubt it." Lars brushed that possibility aside quickly. "Look, I didn't mean to frighten you. What I'm trying to say is that the question of who Erica's husband really is might be an extremely complex one. As long as she and Etienne are discreet, and Mark is content, then I'm inclined to let their situation, as unconventional as it is, continue a while longer. I know that's easy for me to say, since I'm living here where what they do doesn't affect me, but will you give the idea some thought before you refuse to consider it?"

Stunned that the man actually seemed to approve of a bizarre living arrangement she found not only immoral but totally abhorrent, Sarah sat back and remained silent a long while. Finally when she spoke, it was out of her love for her brother. "Mark adores Erica, Lars, he just adores her. He was terrified she was going to die when her child was born. This is all so unfair to him. It's so terribly unfair."

Lars moved closer and put his hands on Sarah's shoulders to turn her toward him. "I didn't expect Mark to live. I have no idea how long he will live, either, Sarah. It might be years, it might be only a few more weeks. If Erica and Etienne are misleading him, they certainly aren't being malicious about it. Frankly, I have to admire them for it. I don't know that I would choose to live a lie rather than break a blind man's heart."

Sarah considered the full import of Lars's words before she replied. "That is the choice, isn't it?" she asked dejectedly. "If I insist Mark be told the truth about Etienne and the baby, then Erica will leave him, and he'll be heartbroken. He'd probably also blame me then for sending Erica away."

"Yes, I think that's a likely possibility," Lars agreed. He let his hands slide down her arms to her wrists, then brought her hands to his lips and kissed her fingertips tenderly. "Please stay here a few more days so we can keep talking about this. Maybe another alternative will occur to us."

At that request, Sarah revealed her thoughts out loud. "I suppose it would be different if Mark weren't so confused about everything. Still, it hurts me to see the people he loves and trusts lying to him."

Lars released her hands then and rose to his feet. "Are they really lying to him, Sarah? Or are they making what might be Mark's last summer a wonderfully happy one?"

"Oh, please don't say that, please don't." Sarah burst into tears then, unable to discuss her brother's death in so detached a manner as Lars.

The physician waited a moment, then, fearing she might cry the whole night through if he left her in such a state, he sat down again by her side and pulled her into his arms. "You need a rest as badly as I do. I'm sorry if you thought I could untangle this impossible mess with a quick trip home. I'd go back home with you if I could, but I'll not interfere in my daughter's life, when from what I've seen, she's doing the very best that she can to make an impossible situation bearable."

As Sarah relaxed in Lars's arms, she recalled the last time he had held her in so fond an embrace and how badly that had ended. Not wanting a repetition of that night, she sat up, brushed away the last of her tears, and tried to say goodnight. "I'm sorry. I hope I didn't get your uniform wet."

"It will dry," Lars assured her, startled by her sudden change of mood. "I'm more concerned about you. If you're not careful, worrying about your brother will become an impossible burden, and you'll end up resenting him, rather than loving him as you do now. Don't let that

410

happen, Sarah, for both your sakes."

While Lars was being considerate of her feelings, Sarah could not help but feel cheated that he did not want to give her more than sympathy. "So you think I should just go home, and pretend everything is as it should be?" she whispered skeptically, still not convinced she could do as he asked.

"No, I want you to stay here in Washington for a while, so we can get to know each other better. You see, I'm not nearly the fool that other man was. If you were ever to fall in love with me, I'd not only be flattered, I'd make you feel loved in return. I think every gift of love should be repaid."

Sarah was so thrilled by that unexpected vow that she was tempted to confess that he was the man she loved. She quickly discarded that idea, preferring to let him think he was providing wise advice to letting him know he was too stupid to realize she had been speaking of him. "I would like very much to get to know you better," she said rather bashfully. "I had hoped that when you were home—"

Lars interrupted her there. "Please, I am dreadfully out of practice when it comes to courting pretty young ladies, and I was simply too ashamed to admit that to you."

Sarah thought that excuse a feeble one. "You kissed me, Lars, so I'll never believe you need practice."

Lars tried to look disappointed then. "Oh really? I was hoping that you would think I needed a great deal of practice."

For an instant, Sarah didn't understand his joke, but when she got it, she laughed and threw her arms around his neck. "I must have been thinking of someone else. Now that I recall that night more fully, you're right. You could do with a bit of practice."

Lars found the taste of her kiss delicious, flavored with peaches and cream and delightfully soft and sweet. When he returned to the hospital after midnight that night, he fell asleep without realizing he had enjoyed himself thoroughly without once being tempted to compare the dark-eyed Sarah to the lovely wife he had lost.

When Sarah returned home two weeks later, she brought a letter from Lars to his daughter. Wanting her to have it immediately, she went to her home as soon as she had unpacked. When Anna Ferguson showed her out to the garden she found her brother lying in the grass beneath the peach tree. His head was cradled comfortably in Erica's lap, while he talked with Etienne who was seated beside him holding the baby. The four comprised a most unusual family, but it was clear in the width of her brother's smile as she called to him that it provided Mark with perfect contentment.

Mark sat up when he heard his sister's voice. "Sarah, is that you?" he called out excitedly.

"Of course, it's me." Sarah knelt by his side to give him a warm and lengthy hug. "I had such a good time with Louise I stayed in Washington longer than I expected, but now I shall be able to come see you every day if you like."

"Yes, I'd like that very much." Mark clutched her tightly in his arms, his greeting enthusiastic. "I missed you terribly. Please don't go away ever again."

When he finally relaxed his hold upon her, Sarah kept his hand in hers as she sat down by his side, but she did not promise she would not make another trip to Washington, and soon. "I have a letter here from your father, Erica. He said if you still had not chosen a name for his grandson, he would be happy to have you name him after him."

Erica found Sarah's pleasant smile and friendly manner a most welcome surprise after the wretched scene they had had when they parted. She looked over at Viper, wondering what he thought of the miraculous change in Sarah's attitude, but he seemed more interested in the contents of her father's letter and urged her to open it.

"I will stay here with the babe and your husband if you wish to read your letter in private, madam," he offered in the polite tone Etienne always used.

"You saw Lars?" Mark asked. "We should have sent him another wire. We already named the baby for Etienne and me," he revealed proudly.

"You did what?" Sarah replied, dismayed by that announcement.

Viper couldn't help but laugh at Sarah's bewildered expression, since he was certain people seldom named their sons after their servants. "The boy's name is Stephen Mark Randall. Etienne is the French form of the name

412

Stephen. It is a good name, is it not, Miss Randall?" That question was spoken as a clear challenge, but Sarah ignored it.

"Why yes, I think Stephen is a good choice. I don't believe we've had a Stephen in the Randall family, so he will be the first." She smiled at Viper then, giving him the clear message that she would not fight with him in front of her brother.

"Well, little Stephen is sleeping so peacefully I'll not disturb him by carrying him inside. If you'll all excuse me for a moment, I would like to take my father's letter up to my room to read," Erica said then.

"You're excused," Mark responded happily. "I want Sarah to tell me everything she did in Washington."

Slender once again, Erica rose to her feet with her former grace, then ruffled Mark's curls as she moved behind him. "I won't be long, but I'll stop and see what Mrs. Ferguson is preparing for dinner. You'll stay and eat with us, won't you, Sarah?"

"Yes, thank you, I'd like that." Sarah gave her brother's hand an affectionate squeeze. "I've missed you, too, Mark. You must tell me what you've been doing, too."

Erica blew Viper a kiss Sarah didn't see, then turned toward the house. She waited until she had reached her room to slit open her father's envelope. She dreaded reading his letter. She remembered another letter then: the one she had gotten from Mark when she had first reached New Ulm. It had said everything but what she had wanted to hear. Fearing this would be another such disappointing note, she withdrew the three sheets of stationery slowly, wondering what her father could possibly have to say that would require so much paper. Since he seldom had the time to write, he was usually quite brief.

To her delighted surprise, what Erica found was a quaintly worded request that she accept his growing affection for Sarah rather than considering his interest in the young woman disrespectful to her mother's memory. He had not proposed to Sarah as yet, he confided, but he enjoyed her company so much that he thought, if their friendship continued to flourish as it had during her recent visit to Washington, that by the holidays he might be ready to ask her to become his wife.

It was such a dear letter it brought tears to Erica's eyes, for she had never wanted her father to spend the rest of his life alone, and she knew it was not a sacrifice her mother would have demanded, either. It was not until she reached the last paragraph that he directed his remarks to her, and again he surprised her. He apologized for not being more attentive to her needs in the past, but promised to be far more considerate in the future. He said he admired her for bringing the happiness to Mark's life that he knew would be lacking in her own without Etienne's being there to help her.

Erica read those words several times to make certain she understood exactly what he meant, and she was soon convinced that she did. That he understood her plight, and did not condemn her for the manner in which she had chosen to solve it, was so loving a gesture that she could not wait to share it with Viper, for it explained the change in Sarah's behavior, as well. She went to her window and looked out over the garden. Sarah and Mark were still talking together, the sunlight dancing off their tawny curls while Viper and the baby seemed to be lost in a world of their own. When the Indian looked up at her she waved and blew him another kiss, overjoyed to think it was a world to which she also belonged.

As Erica turned away from the window, she hoped the illusion of harmony she and Viper had taken such care to create for Mark would not soon become an impossible burden. They had carried on what could be called an innocent pretense before Stephen was born, but now their son was more than a month old. Erica knew their deception would become increasingly difficult to continue, for while she would willingly devote her days to Mark, she wanted ever so desperately to again fill her nights with the beauty of Viper's love. Now, with her father's tacit approval, she couldn't believe that giving in to her desires would be wrong.

# Chapter Twenty-Eight

## August, 1863

Viper lay stretched out on his bed, his head propped on his hands and a pensive frown marring his handsome features as he recalled the strange twists the path of his life had taken during the year since the uprising had begun. He had taken a wife, then lost her, come close to death, then been granted a reprieve. Now he had a son he shared with the same man with whom he had been forced to share his wife. He could scarcely imagine what the next twelve months would bring when the last year had been filled with such an abundance of soul-searing events.

He had had no chance to speak alone with Erica and so had been left wondering what her father had said in his letter. Since her mood was such a good one, he knew Sarah must have failed to convince the man to help her carry out her threats. Then again, Sarah did not seem upset, either, which puzzled him completely, since she had made no secret of what she thought of his being there.

While Sarah had been away, Erica had recovered her strength, dismissed the wet nurse, and spent her time lavishing attention and affection upon their son. Viper was certain she had been too busy to notice the subtle changes in Mark's behavior that he had observed. At first he had thought the young man merely wanted to stay close to Erica and the baby when he no longer had any interest in going fishing or out for rides or walks. Then Mark had begun taking longer naps each afternoon and falling asleep earlier at night, and Viper knew it was not simply the baby that kept him so close to home. The injured man clearly had less energy than he had had only a few weeks earlier.

Concerned about the state of Mark's health, Viper had begun keeping track of how often he complained of severe headaches. When he had first come to the Hanson home, the man he had been hired to tend had suffered from that pain perhaps one day in five. For a while Mark had seemed better, eager to get out and enjoy the summer weather, but often at night he had felt unwell and needed laudanum to sleep. That had worried Viper, for he did not want to be blamed for making Mark ill. Rather than continue suggesting activities to keep him busy, he had begun to wait for Mark to say he wanted to do something, and then he would arrange it. The headaches had still come, though. He glanced at the calendar on the small table beside his bed. There were three x's marked for the previous week. He was certain Erica knew about only one of those headaches. The others Mark had managed to hide from her with his extended naps and early bedtimes.

That Mark would try and deceive her touched Viper deeply. Mark might not be the same man he had known in Minnesota, but they had been rivals for Erica's love then, and now that they shared it, they were friends. When he had come there, Viper had promised to stay and help the woman he loved care for her invalid husband. Now it saddened him immeasurably to think that task might not last much longer. Mark had never been truly well, but now what health he had enjoyed was failing. Viper could not help but think the once vital young man would have been better off being killed on the battlefield than dying slowly at home. Then he thought of how dearly Mark loved the son he thought was his own, and knew he would have been cheated of far more than his life had he missed having the joy of knowing the little boy.

A light knock at his door put an end to his sad reverie, and Viper leaped off his bed and rushed to answer it. When he found Erica clad in a flowing nightgown whose sheer folds were sweetly scented with lavender, he gaped in surprise. Her bright curls framed the faint blush in her cheeks, and since she had never come to his room before, his first thought was of her husband, and her charming prettiness escaped his notice completely. "Does Mark need me?" he asked anxiously.

Mystified by that greeting, Erica wondered if Viper would be disappointed to learn the truth. "No," she replied petulantly. "I do." She ducked under his arm, quickly surveyed his neatly kept quarters, then turned around to face him. "You've not come to my room since Stephen was born. Not once. I thought curiosity about my father's letter might lure you back to me tonight, but I got tired of waiting."

Viper carefully closed the door rather than slam it as her high-handed attitude inspired him to do. He then leaned back against it and crossed his arms over his bare chest while he studied her defiantly tilted chin with the coolest glance he could affect. He was wearing only a pair of gray pants Mark had given him, but he considered himself well enough dressed to entertain her.

While she had made it clear how desperately she wanted him to stay with her, he had not thought she would be any more eager to make love now than she had been before their child was born. Not wanting to force the issue he had stayed away, hoping one day she would come to him. He had never expected she would be so angry when that day came, however. Trying to avoid an argument, he gave so novel an excuse he hoped it would be believed. "Perhaps your customs are different from mine, but I did not think you would want me in your bed until after our son is weaned."

That was so preposterous a statement that Erica was flabbergasted by it. "You don't mean it!" she exclaimed, her expression clearly conveying the depth of her dismay as her hot temper was cooled by a chill wave of disbelief.

Viper was pleased he had succeeded in directing her anger away from himself for a change, but he frowned slightly, as though he were as confused as she. "Do white men sleep with their wives while they are nursing babies?" he asked cautiously.

"Well, of course they do," Erica assured him, still astonished to learn the Sioux did not. "I distinctly recall your telling me you followed few of the old customs. Is that one you plan to observe?"

"What if I did?" Viper asked slyly, unwilling to answer without knowing what difference his answer would make

417

to her.

Erica gestured helplessly, her mood now one of despair. "If only you had told me that before I dismissed the wet nurse, I would not have let her go. I won't nurse our son myself if it means we can't make love."

Not wanting this astonishing conversation to end poorly, Viper took Erica's hand and led her over to the bed to be seated, since the room had only one straight-backed chair which was none too comfortable. When she had settled herself upon the single bed in what he regarded as a delightfully distracting pose, since it was obviously unintentional, he continued. "While I did share your bed before Stephen was born, you were always too miserable to have any interest in making love, so I thought you would be happy if I allowed you to sleep alone now. Are you telling me all I've done is make you unhappy instead?" Now that she had not only Mark dependent upon her loving care, but a new baby as well, he had thought she would have little time to spend thinking about him. He was flattered to think he might have been wrong, but he suppressed the impulse to grin from ear to ear.

At that question, Erica suddenly felt as self-conscious as she knew Sarah had once felt around her father. She had expected him to fling open his door and welcome her enthusiastically. That he had not had left her both surprised and hurt. Now he claimed he had not been neglecting her at all, that her disappointment in him was the result of a misunderstanding. She looked down at her hands, silently cursing the scar as she spoke. "It's been a long while since we've had any time to talk. I know how difficult living here is for you, but it is difficult for me, as well."

Viper sat down by her side and began to slip his fingers through her gorgeous cascade of glossy curls. Her hair was so long it reached clear past her waist, and he loved the way the light of the lamp danced upon the soft waves. But not nearly so much as he loved her. "At first you were too sick to want company, Erica, and since I know how seriously you take your wedding vows, I did not think you would want me to spend my nights with you anymore. I can hardly keep my hands off you during the day, at night it would be impossible. I wish you had asked me to come to your room before now, if that's what you really wanted."

She had come to him craving the tumultuous love she had once known in his arms, but he was being so coolly logical she wished she had stayed in her room. "There are always so many people around," she complained sadly. "If we do not see each other at night, then when can we be together?" she asked rather shyly, afraid her company was not nearly as important to him as his was to her. "Do Indian men not bother to speak to their wives if they do not plan to make love to them? Are all of them so rude as that?"

"I am trying to do as you have asked again and again, to respect your marriage to Mark, and you call me rude?" Viper responded bluntly. "Will you make up your mind what it is you want, then tell me, so I will know, too?" Erica tried to move off the bed then, but he reached for her arm and kept her at his side. "I'm sorry. I do not want to fight with you. Now tell me what was in your father's letter. I have waited all day to hear."

Hoping she could save her pride by giving a brief report of the letter and then excusing herself, Erica attempted to do just that and concluded promptly. "So you see, he knows who you are, but he is being more sympathetic than I had any hope he would be. Perhaps that's what love has done to his outlook."

Viper suspected there was more to Lars's kindness than love for Sarah could explain, but he did not want to cite the physician's regard for Mark's fragile health as a possible reason. "I would like to read the letter," he said instead.

"You don't believe what I told you?" Erica asked, clearly offended.

Viper shook his head, sorry he had upset her needlessly when that was exactly what he was trying not to do. He rose to his feet and took her hand to help her up. "I believe you. Let me walk you back to your room. We can't hear the baby cry up here."

Crushed by the practicality of his rejection, Erica didn't argue. She had been so excited by her father's letter, and so tired of pretense, all she had wanted was to spend the night in Viper's arms. What he wanted her to do, apparently, was to tend his son. She loved the baby dearly, but she loved him too, and she didn't like being ignored, no matter how noble his excuse might have been for his extended absence from her room.

Determined not to cry in front of him, when they reached her room Erica wished the brave a soft goodnight, then slipped through her door. At night she left the lamp on the dressing table turned down low so she would not have to waste time lighting it should the baby need her attention. When Viper followed her into the dimly lit room she turned and regarded him with a curious glance. "Did you want to see the letter?" she asked, thinking that must be what he wanted.

Viper closed the door behind him and crossed the short distance between them in a single stride. "I have done my best to help you care for your husband and our son. If only I had known you wanted more of me, I would have given it gladly. After all, it has been longer since I made love than you," he confided with a teasing smile, hoping to make her laugh, but he did not succeed.

"What are you talking about?" Erica asked in a tense whisper. She didn't want to wake the sleeping babe, but she didn't want him to misunderstand her relationship with Mark, either.

Since what he had meant was so damn obvious to him, Viper felt like a fool having to explain. "Was Mark so poor a lover you have forgotten being with him already?"

The room was very still. The baby was sleeping soundly, and Erica was worried their voices might wake him. She turned away from Viper and went over to the windows, then waited until he followed her to reply. "Mark and I have never made love. Wren cut me up too badly, and then he had to report for duty. The last time I made love was with you."

Viper stared at the delicate woman, wondering if she could possibly be so incredibly stupid as she sounded. It was impossible for him to hold his temper in check now, and overwhelmed by it, he shouted at her, "Erica, if you never slept with Mark, then you are not his wife! Did you think you had to do no more than repeat pretty promises to be married?"

Erica raised her hand to his lips in a frantic attempt to silence him, but it was too late. Baby Stephen had been startled as badly as she, and he began to cry in a pitiful wail. Without replying to Viper's astounding accusation, she went to the cradle to pick up her son. When changing his diaper and a few minutes of cuddling would not stop his tears, she carried him to the rocking chair and sat down. She had fed him before going up to the third floor to see Viper, but knowing of no other way to get him back to sleep, she loosened the ribbon at the neckline of her gown so he could nurse again. Since she had no idea how to answer Viper, she hoped he would have the sense to leave. When she looked up a few minutes later, she was surprised to find he had not.

This was not the first time he had watched Erica nurse their child, but as always, the sight of them together filled him with an embarrassing combination of pride and desire. How could she have come to him to complain he had not visited her room when it had taken every bit of self-control he had to stay away? He walked over to the rocking chair and knelt down by her side.

"I did not mean to wake him," he apologized as he patted the little boy's back lightly. It had not been half an hour since he had thought to himself that his life could not get any more complicated, but Erica had just turned his world upside down again, and he was more shaken than he would admit. He waited patiently for his son to drift off to sleep again, and as soon as Erica placed him in his crib he took her hand and led her back to the windows. This time he sat down on the cushioned window seat and pulled her down across his lap so even if he whispered very softly she could hear him.

"Hell can have no tortures worse than what you and I have suffered this last year. I promise not to yell at you again, but how could you not have known your marriage to Mark was not a legal one?"

As flustered as he, Erica slipped her arms around Viper's neck. "I never even thought about it. He and I were married by a minister, and you and I weren't. I thought Mark and I were married, I really did. Are you certain that we aren't?"

"Positive," Viper swore with a wicked grin. He had never allowed himself to dwell on thoughts of Mark making love to her, but to learn that the man had never had that pleasure pleased him enormously.

"Viper," Erica began to plead very softly. "I don't think Mark is as strong as he was. Have you noticed how content he is to spend all his time with me now? Please don't ask me to tell him we aren't married. I couldn't explain why we aren't without telling him Stephen isn't his, and I don't think he could survive so terrible a shock as that. Please don't ask me to do that to him."

That she had noticed the changes in Mark was a relief, for while he had been willing, Viper had not wanted to carry the burden of that knowledge alone. "The answer to your first question is yes. I have noticed Mark isn't as well as he was. When you answer your father's letter, please tell him what you have noticed, so he will know, too. As for your second question, to tell Mark he has neither a wife nor a child would be unspeakably cruel, and I would never ask you to do that to him. I care about him, too. I think we can find our happiness without costing him his."

"Are you really certain I am not married to him?" Erica asked once again, still unconvinced that what he said was true, since her commitment to Mark had always been such a sincere one.

"Ask an attorney if you do not believe me." Viper had a hard time stifling a laugh at that thought, but he decided the best way to do it was with a kiss. With an agile move, he pulled her down beside him on the window seat, which fortunately was not only comfortably padded but also wide enough to accommodate them both. "I love you," he whispered hungrily, his mood now the openly passionate one she had hoped to find earlier. He covered her face with light kisses before he allowed his lips to stray to the enticing sweetness of her mouth.

Erica's hands moved over Viper's broad shoulders as she drew him near. "I've been such an awful fool," she confessed breathlessly between kisses. "I should have written to you last winter. I should have told you everything once you were here. I was afraid you would hate me, or try and make me leave Mark, or—"

"Hush," Viper scolded. "How could you have so many fears when I promised to be with you always? How could you have forgotten that?"

"I didn't forget. I remembered it all, and I did see you everywhere. I really did. In the colors of dawn and sunset, in—"

Viper interrupted her with another kiss, which he did not end until he felt the last of the tension that had filled her for so many months begin to melt away. They were together again, bathed in the light of the stars, and while he had not thought it possible, he knew they were even more deeply in love than when they had had to part in the fall. How the worst year of his life could also have been the best he could not explain, but he knew it was true.

"Let's go outside to the garden," he suggested suddenly. "With your windows open, we can hear if Stephen starts to cry. Come with me."

When he stood and offered his hand, Erica could not refuse. This was exactly what she had wanted: the same wild abandon he had always brought to their loving. She stood and grabbed the coverlet from off her bed as they left her room. They ran down the stairs, trying not to giggle like children as they rushed from the house and danced down the stone path to the grass.

"I love you!" Erica whispered as she let her nightgown slip off her shoulders, exposing her newly slender figure to his view. Her pale skin glowed with the reflected light of the stars, while her hair, catching each beam of moon-light, shimmered like the finest silver.

Viper had taken the white coverlet and unfurled it upon the grass with a quick toss rather than wasting a second of the night in arranging it neatly. He then discarded what few clothes he wore with the same haste. When he pulled Erica down upon the light quilt he found it held the same enchanting fragrance of lavender as her skin. Surrounded by the sweet scent of that perfume and the lingering essence of the lush garden's many blossoms, he remembered the nights they had spent under the stars and thought this would be the best of all.

His hands traced the velvet-smooth swell of her breasts as his lips caressed hers in nearly endless kisses, which, while filled with the magical sweetness of her love, left him hungry for still more. He leaned back for a moment, and when she smiled he thought the soft radiance of the moonlight made her look more like an angel than ever. "There must be no more secrets between us. Will you promise me that?"

423

Having learned what a terrible burden a secret could be, no matter what the reason for keeping it, Erica readily agreed. "I promise," she replied, then sealed that vow with another lingering kiss. Her fingers slid through his hair, still wishing it were the glorious mane of silken ebony it had once been. He was holding her in a tender embrace, but she didn't feel in the least bit fragile. She merely felt alive, for the first time in months, and she moved against him to draw him closer still. "You won't hurt me," she encouraged playfully. "We can make love any way you like."

"I like all the ways," Viper confided with a deep chuckle. Still, he regarded her as even more precious than he had before now that she had given him a child. "You are not afraid of having more children?"

"Most women do not conceive when they are nursing, Viper, so we needn't worry about that tonight."

"Most women, but not all?"

"No, not all," Erica had to admit, "but since we both like babies, I would be happy to have another. Wouldn't you?"

"Yes." Since he would welcome all the children she gave him, Viper decided not to remind her of what an ordeal Stephen's birth had been if she had forgotten. They would both know more with their second child, and he was confident the birth would be far easier than her first. He kissed her again, wanting to savor every delectable inch of her lovely body but too hungry for her kisses to begin an adoring appraisal of her figure until the slow circular motion of his fingertips drew drops of creamy white liquid from her nipples. He leaned down then to lick the moist tips of her breasts and found the taste of her milk too delicious to move away. When she moaned softly, he looked up. "Shall I stop?"

"No, that feels wonderful," Erica purred as she ruffled his hair. "Nursing Stephen feels very much like making love. Why do you think he is so well fed?" she asked with a seductive giggle.

Viper laughed, too, glad to know feeding their son was so pleasurable for her. While he was certain he would never tire of nuzzling her breasts as his son did, he did not want to steal the infant's breakfast, and he spread his kisses over the smooth flatness of her stomach instead. "You are so pretty," he whispered as he pressed his lips against her lavender-scented flesh. "You have always been beautiful to me."

Knowing he had viewed her pregnant figure through a bright haze of love, Erica did not argue, but she was confident she was far more attractive now that she was again as slim as she had been when they had first met. She was glad they had come outside, for it was easy to pretend they were again lying beside the Cottonwood River where he had first taught her how fulfilling making love could be. She adored him still, and she welcomed each of his lavish kisses and tender caresses until she was so lost in the rapture of his loving that nothing mattered but sharing that beauty with him.

Despite Erica's reassurances of her health, Viper treated her as though she were made of porcelain rather than flesh and blood. His adoring kisses were light as his lips traced the beauty of her graceful limbs from fingertip to throat, then toe to hip. The last time they had made love, his heart had been filled with the anguish of their parting, but now he knew they would have a lifetime to share their love. This night was only the first of many he planned to fill with passion rather than the lonely dreams of the last months, and when he moved over her, now poised to bring them together as one, he paused to whisper words of love he hoped she would never tire of hearing. "I will love you always, until the moon and stars no longer shine, until the sun no longer rises and sets."

Cushioned by his loving embrace, Erica felt as though she were floating in Viper's arms. His first thrusts were shallow, slow, and gentle, until the eagerness of her response convinced him he need hold nothing back. She clung to him as she felt his mood change from cautious to wild, but there was nothing he could ask of her that she would not willingly give. She loved his strength as well as his tenderness, the fire of his Indian soul as well as the warmth of his love. Their agile bodies entwined in a variety of graceful poses, their hearts pounding with a primitive beat, they passed the hours until dawn so eager for the splendor each gave the other that it seemed as though they had made love only once rather than a dozen times. Their loving promises were slurred and their kisses accented with laughter, but when they parted company at Erica's door, each hoped the day would pass quickly so they could again fill the night with love.

When Sarah arrived to see Mark that day, she found him in a serious mood. He wanted to have Stephen christened, and thinking they could put a lace cap on the child to hide his dark hair, she saw no reason to object. "I'm sure Lars won't mind if you have Stephen's christening without him. After all, if we don't do it soon, that beautiful christening dress Mother made for you will be too small for him, and it would be a shame not to use it."

Mark looked puzzled. "What does it look like? Is it all tucks and lace and that sort of thing?"

"Yes, I'm certain you must have looked adorable in it, although I wasn't there." Sarah gave her brother's hand a squeeze, then leaned over to kiss his cheek. They were outside in the garden where they usually spent their mornings with Erica, Viper, and the baby. "Have you asked anyone to be godparents?"

Erica had been surprised when Mark had mentioned the christening, since she had completely forgotten about it herself, but she didn't know what to say when he responded to his sister's question.

"We want you, of course, and Etienne. You'll do it won't you, Etienne?" he asked with a nervous smile. "I guess I should have asked you about it before now."

With Sarah and Erica eyeing him with skeptical glances, each waiting to see how he would refuse Mark's request gracefully, Viper waited a long moment before satisfying their curiosity. "I would be honored, monsieur. Do you want to have the ceremony here, or at the church?"

"Here," Erica announced before Mark could respond. Then realizing she had spoken too quickly, she explained her reasons. "I would prefer a private ceremony, and it would be ever so much nicer to do it out here in the garden. Don't you think that's a nice idea, Mark?"

"Yes, I guess so." Mark was holding the tomcat who seldom left his side. The animal slept on his bed at night and followed him wherever he went during the day. He scratched the striped animal's ears as he made another request. "Can you go down to the church today, Etienne? I want the christening tomorrow or the next day. We should have done it before this. Why didn't you plan it, Erica?"

Since Mark had not spoken a single critical word to her since he had been injured, Erica was dismayed by his tone, but she managed to reply sweetly. "You're right, I should have made the arrangements as soon as I felt up to it. Since I didn't, I'm so happy you remembered. Let's make a party of it, shall we? You could wear your uniform, and let's hire a photographer so Stephen can see how cute he looked when he was a baby. Would you like to do that?"

"I think that's a charming idea," Sarah agreed, but she was still amazed that Etienne had accepted Mark's request to be Stephen's godfather. "It would be the perfect time for a family portrait. I can stop by the church on the way home. That way I'll know when the priest can come, and I'll tell the photographer to be here, too."

Erica glanced at Viper, only to find him trying not to laugh. She leaned over to give him a poke in the ribs. "Do you know what a godfather is supposed to do, Etienne?"

"But of course, madam. When a child is baptized, his godfather promises to see that he will be taught about God. I will be happy to teach your son all I know."

Unable to imagine what his beliefs might be, Sarah shook her head and excused herself. "If I'm going to arrange this by tomorrow, I'll have to hurry. I'll send you a note if I can do it."

"Thank you!" Mark called out as his sister walked away. When Erica left them a short while later to take Stephen indoors, he continued playing with the cat, not responding with any enthusiasm to Viper's attempts at conversation. Finally he suggested a topic of his own. "I made out a will leaving everything to Erica when I joined the army," he began. "Money will never be a problem to her. I hope we can baptize the baby this week, then what more should I do? Can you think of something?"

At the mention of a will, Viper grew alarmed. "For what are you preparing, monsieur?"

Mark shrugged, as though their topic were a light one. "My head hurts nearly all the time now. I don't want to be a burden to Erica. If I get too sick to get out of bed. . . ." he

427

paused then, apparently unable to focus his thoughts for a moment. "I won't be a worse burden than I am now. I would rather be dead. How much laudanum do you think that would take?"

His question was asked with near childlike innocence, and, astonished, Viper needed a moment to come up with what he considered the perfect reply. "What you are suggesting would break your wife's heart, monsieur. You would not save her pain, but cause her the worst sort of grief."

"How would she know? Would you tell her?"

"No, of course not, but—"

"Would you want to live if you were sick more often than well?" Mark asked, thinking he could predict his friend's answer.

"If Erica were my wife, yes," Viper swore dramatically. "I would cling to life like ivy to a wall."

Mark laughed at that thought, and as his heart lightened, he grew more optimistic. "Maybe I will get better."

"I hope so, for your sake as well as your wife's." Viper reached out to give Mark an encouraging pat on the back. "Try and think happy thoughts rather than such sad ones."

"I will try," Mark agreed, "but you must promise me something."

"If I can," Viper replied cautiously, for he would not help Mark take his own life. It was not simply out of fear that he would be accused of murder, either. It was simply a secret he did not want to have to keep from Erica.

"I want you to look after Erica, as well as the baby. Will you do that? I had other friends, but they are in the army still. They could not be here when she needed them."

"I will be happy to help your wife in any way I can. Now I think we should go see if dinner is ready." Viper got to his feet, then gave Mark a hand. "Let us take each day as it comes and not worry so about tomorrow."

"I'm sorry, Etienne. I don't want to be a burden to you, too."

Viper grabbed Mark in a boisterous hug. "You are no burden, you are my best friend."

"Yes, we are best friends, aren't we?" Mark slipped his

arm around Viper's waist as they walked toward the house. "I'm a very lucky man, aren't I? I have a beautiful wife, a fine son, and a best friend."

"Yes," Viper agreed. "We are both very lucky men."

As Erica watched the two men approach the house, she could not help but wonder at the cause of their high spirits. At least Mark seemed to be feeling well that day, but she was still quite worried about him. During dinner they continued to plan for the christening, and the next day it went as beautifully as she had hoped it would. Mark's christening gown fit Stephen perfectly, while the matching lace cap concealed his dark hair so the priest offered no comment on his coloring. The babe looked like a cherub and giggled happily through the brief ceremony. The photographer Sarah had found took photographs of them all in every possible combination, and, certain they would never forget so marvelous a day, Erica again looked forward to spending the night in Viper's arms.

By the time Viper turned the page of his calendar to September, an x marked nearly every day. Mark had never again spoken of death, and the brave hoped he had forgotten their conversation had ever taken place. It was not a subject he and Erica ever discussed, either, although he could sense it was on her mind as well as his, and yet when one afternoon Mark failed to awaken from his nap, Viper could not believe death had taken the young man so soon.

Knowing he would have to break the sad news to Erica, the Indian got as far as the stairs, but overcome with sorrow, he sat down on the top step, put his head in his hands, and wept, for truly he had lost one of the best friends he had ever had. When she found him still seated there crying, Erica did not have to ask what had happened. She put her arms around Viper and held him tight, loving him all the more for having loved Mark, too.

# Chapter Twenty-Nine

## September, 1863

Lars arrived at the church just as the funeral service began. He had not expected so many people to attend, but the old stone building was filled with his family's friends, as well as Mark's. That pleased him enormously, for he had hoped the young man had not been forgotten during his lengthy convalescence. He knew where Erica would be seated, and hurried down the aisle, anxious to join her. When he found Viper already seated by his daughter's side, he slid into their pew beside Sarah and took her hand as he tried to offer a comforting smile.

Although he knew the truth about Erica and the Indian, Lars had not expected the man to flaunt their relationship in public. Knowing this was neither the time nor the place to air such feelings, he put them aside as the service began and thought instead only of Mark, and of what a fine man he had been. When the Indian joined him as a pall bearer, he recognized the dove-gray suit he wore as having been one of Mark's favorites, and he looked away quickly, wondering what more he had helped himself to now that Mark was no longer alive to object.

The day was warm and sunny, the weather perfect for a last picnic before the fall arrived, but most of those gathered at the graveside were too filled with sorrow to think the lovely day wasted in mourning as Mark was laid to rest in a grave beside his parents. One by one his friends said their own good-byes, departed, and met again at the

Hanson home, where they offered what comfort they could to the grieving family.

Margaret Denenberg had been hired to care for the baby, as Erica had not wanted to subject a child barely two months old to such a crush of people. She went upstairs often to check on Stephen and proudly displayed the photographs from the christening to all who asked about the babe. Mark was holding Stephen in each of the portraits, his smile wide as he cuddled his son, and that was the way she wished to remember him. It had been Viper who had insisted upon preparing Mark's body for burial, and when he had wanted to bury his friend in his captain's uniform she had readily agreed, since he had looked so very handsome in it. It was a strange sensation to bury one husband with the help of another, but Erica found Viper's generous sympathy a source of great comfort and strength.

Each person who came to the Hanson home arrived with baked goods or other food, and with refreshments so plentiful, the visits grew lengthy. It was nearly midnight when the last of their friends finally said goodnight. After closing the front door behind them, Lars returned to the parlor and offered to escort Sarah home.

"Thank you, but Erica suggested I stay here tonight, and I've accepted her invitation, since I'm really too tired to go home." She smiled as she gestured invitingly. "Please come and sit down with us. I haven't had a chance to talk with you all day." She hoped the fact that she had felt neglected wasn't too obvious. When Lars had sat down next to her at the church, she had hoped he would remain with her all day, but he had been so attentive a host to all their guests that he had given her little more than an occasional smile. That wasn't nearly enough to please her.

Lars had been prepared for anything from screaming accusations that he should have been able to save Mark's life to hysterical tears that the young man had died needlessly in a senseless war, but Sarah had displayed an admirable calm all day. That she had accepted her brother's death without casting blame on him or anyone else was a tremendous relief to him. Happy for an excuse to sit down, he quickly took the chair beside hers, then picked up the photograph that had been left on the end table nearby. "I think it's wonderful you had these photographs made." That the Indian was in most of them, again dressed in the gray suit, had startled him at first, but he had had sufficient time to get over that shock by now. "When do I get to see my grandson?"

Erica covered a wide yawn before she apologized, "I'm sorry. I didn't want to bring him downstairs, but I should have taken you up to my room. He's sleeping too soundly to disturb now, but he'll be up before you are in the morning, so you'll have plenty of time to spend with him tomorrow."

"I'll try and stay a few days, at least," Lars said regretfully. "I need to get back to Washington as quickly as I can, though."

Viper was standing by the fireplace, his pose relaxed even though his mood was not. He had waited all day for Lars to ask to speak with him alone, but other than sending him frequent glances, which he had interpreted as being disapproving, if not openly hostile, the man had avoided him. If an angry confrontation were unavoidable between them, he was anxious to get it over with that very night. When Lars continued to exclude him from his conversation with the two young women, Viper went over to the settee, sat down beside Erica, and taking her hand, laced her fingers with his.

"The last time you were here, you were far more polite to me than you have been today, Dr. Hanson. If you plan to ignore me on this trip, what will you do on the next?"

Surprised that the Indian would be so direct, when he knew him to prefer subterfuge, Lars stalled for time by putting the photograph aside before turning to face him. It was difficult to reconcile what he knew the young man to be with what he saw, but he had to admit the rogue played a gentleman very convincingly. Attempting to display the same level of gentlemanly conduct in a sincere manner, Lars leaned forward slightly, trying to make his comments sound like helpful suggestions rather than harsh demands.

"Please forgive me if I seemed rude. It was unintentional. I don't even know what to call you," he began with a disarming smile. "Since Etienne Bouchard isn't your real name, what would you rather I use?"

432

Viper recognized Lars's charming grin for the attempt to win his confidence it obviously was, but he wasn't fooled. White men smiled often, but their actions were anything but pleasant. Grateful Erica had kept still, he gave her fingers a loving squeeze before he responded to her father's question. "I have no choice but to use that name a while longer. Please call me Etienne."

Lars nodded, disappointed, but not surprised the Indian had not chosen to confide in him. "All right, Etienne it is, then. You were living here as Mark's companion. Now that those duties have sadly come to an end, you'll have to leave before anyone becomes suspicious of your relationship with my daughter."

"Daddy!" Erica was too tired to leap from her chair or she would have done so. "It was Mark's feelings we wished to protect, not my reputation. Etienne is my husband, and I'll not hide that fact a minute longer. When your letters were so wonderfully sympathetic to our plight, why have you had this sudden change of heart?"

Lars swept that compliment aside as no longer pertinent. "Erica, when you have so recently been widowed, you can scarcely introduce Etienne as your husband. Widows are expected to observe a year of mourning before they remarry. I can't believe you could have forgotten something so important as that."

Outraged by the absurdity of that comment, Erica did attempt to rise this time, but Viper refused to release her hand. Her new black dress was made of a crisp taffeta that rustled noisily as she was drawn back into her seat.

Viper responded before his wife could catch her breath to speak. "This conversation is pointless," he announced firmly. "Erica is no longer a daughter who must be obedient to her father's wishes. She is a wife and mother who can think for herself." He rose and with a graceful bow took Erica's hands and drew her to her feet. "We will be proud to show off our son in the morning. Until then, goodnight."

Erica was astonished that Viper had not said she was a wife who had to be obedient to her husband's wishes. Grateful for that generosity, she did not argue with his decision to bid Sarah and her father goodnight. She paused briefly to kiss her father's cheek and then Sarah's before leaving the parlor on her husband's arm. Anxious to talk, she hurried him up the stairs, for it seemed their lives were never going to run smoothly and she wanted to have a plan ready to present to her father in the morning.

Left alone with Lars, Sarah found herself in an extremely awkward position. She didn't want to speak her mind and jeopardize her chances to win Lars's love when he had given her reason to hope he might soon declare it. On the other hand, after all the compassion Erica and Etienne had shown her brother, she felt she owed them her loyalty.

Disgusted with himself for allowing Etienne to escort his daughter from the room and undoubtedly right into his bed, Lars frowned sullenly. He berated himself for not having foreseen how little the wily devil would care for his daughter's reputation. To make matters worse, it seemed clear Erica didn't care about it, either.

"Lars," Sarah began hesitantly, hoping to ease his mind.

Embarrassed by how easily the Indian had gotten the better of him, Lars apologized immediately, "I'm sorry, Sarah. This is my problem and I shouldn't have subjected you to it."

Swallowing hard to gather her courage, Sarah continued in a breathless rush. "When I was so worried about appearances, you convinced me they didn't matter nearly as much as Mark's happiness. Isn't that true still? Aren't Erica's and Etienne's feelings more important than the opinions of people who might be tempted to gossip about them?"

The expression in Sarah's luminous brown eyes was so serious that Lars knew his reply was important to her, and he chose his words with care. "Of course, I care more about my family than busybodies. I've already admitted that I handled the matter badly just now. I should have been smart enough to speak with Erica privately before I asked Etienne to leave. Etienne!" he exclaimed sarcastically. "Do you realize we don't even know the man's name?"

"That is disconcerting, I'll agree, but—"

"But what?" Lars interrupted abruptly. He was puzzled by her reluctance to lend her support to his cause. "I didn't forbid Erica to see Etienne. All I said was the man should live elsewhere. Since this is my home, I am well within my rights to make such a request."

Sarah was as conscious of offending Lars as he was of disappointing her, but she simply couldn't bring herself to agree with him. "Etienne is the father of Erica's child. Telling him to live somewhere else won't change that. Perhaps you should let them make their own decisions about where they wish to live."

While Sarah's gaze was now concentrated upon her tightly clasped hands rather than on him, Lars could see she was as upset as he. He didn't understand why, though. "I'd say I have had no choice but to allow them to make their own decisions all along. Etienne didn't come to me to ask for Erica's hand in marriage. He simply announced she was his wife! Perhaps it is a bit late to insist he follow our society's rules, but I think I should at least make that attempt. I would be a poor excuse for a father if I didn't."

Sarah was silent for a long moment, and when she returned to look at Lars, her manner was touchingly bashful. "I know only too well the heartache of loving a man I can seldom see. I would not wish that loneliness upon anyone. Won't you reconsider your decision to ask Erica and Etienne to live apart? When they love each other so, I think it would be very cruel to separate them."

Her inquistive gaze swept Lars's expression as she searched for a flicker of emotion that would betray the love she hoped he felt for her. She had waited patiently for his infrequent letters to become passionate pledges of love, but sadly, his brief messages had conveyed no more than a friendly warmth. This was the first time they had been alone all day, yet he had made no attempt to kiss her. Seated beside him, the excitement his presence always brought filled her with desire. The obvious fact that he no longer seemed to feel that same magical attraction brought tears to her eyes. Embarrassed, she brushed them away.

"Forgive me. I know you must think this none of my business, but Erica was married to my brother. You are the one who convinced me to be charitable toward her, and if I am not offended by her conduct, then surely no one else has the right to be."

Lars stared at his companion as she fumbled for her handkerchief before bringing it to her eyes. The fact that she would disagree with him about Etienne was not nearly so upsetting as her mention of loving a man she seldom saw. Thinking she must be referring to some young man away fighting the war, he slumped back in his chair, more hurt than he cared to admit. He liked everything about Sarah, for she had many endearing qualities, but he recalled how reluctant she had been when he had first asked her to remain in Washington so they could become better acquainted. He had thought her merely shy, but had she simply been interested in someone else? He thought she had enjoyed his company as much as he had enjoyed hers when she had extended her visit, but apparently his efforts to impress her had failed. He knew his letters had lacked any hint of poetry, but he *had* written, which had not been easy when he was always so pressed for time, and he had considered her friendly replies assurance enough that their friendship was moving toward something permanent. Apparently he had been mistaken, and her affections lay elsewhere. Now that she had admitted as much, he felt thoroughly betrayed and incredibly foolish. "I don't know what to say," he finally admitted aloud.

"About what?" Amazed that he was so badly disappointed that her opinion differed from his, Sarah thought she would be wise to bid him goodnight before things grew even more strained between them, but she was too curious as to why he seemed to be at a loss for words to do it just yet.

Lars shrugged unhappily. "Well, I simply had no idea there was someone else. You told me you had loved a man who was unaware of your feelings and did not return them, but still, I didn't suspect that you cared for another man now."

"I thought we were talking about Erica and Etienne. Do you want to talk about you and me instead?" Delighted by that prospect, Sarah couldn't suppress a delighted smile.

Confused by her sudden change in mood, since it seemed so highly inappropriate, Lars's frown deepened. "You just said there was someone else: a man you loved and seldom saw. If you say we can be no more than friends, I will try and accept your decision graciously, but I won't pretend that I like it, since I wanted far more. I won't say that you deliberately misled me, but I had hoped that

436

someday, well that someday—"

Sarah reached for his hand as she coaxed him to continue. "Someday what, Lars?"

Sarah had lovely hands. They were soft and white, with well manicured nails. He felt like a stupid fool as he watched her fingertips move over his with a light caress. "What does it matter now?" he asked as he withdrew his hand from hers. "If you are in love with another man, I am just wasting both my time and yours."

Realizing now that she had made a grave mistake in not telling Lars the truth when he had misunderstood the comments she had made about love in Washington, Sarah tried to correct that error. It was a difficult confession to make, but she could not allow him to continue to think he had lost out to nonexistent competition.

"Lars, I don't know why we have such a problem understanding each other, but when I mentioned loving a man who was unaware of my feelings, I was talking about you. It was you I meant just now, too. I have missed you terribly, and I wish we could see each other more often. I'm sorry I express myself so poorly that I have only confused you, but I wanted you to be the one to speak of love first, and I feared you never would."

Shocked that he could have been so dense, Lars's deep blue eyes widened in surprise. "You were talking about me?" Even though Erica had told him Sarah cared for him, Lars had never dreamed she cared that much. It made him feel all the worse. "You must think me absolutely heartless," he murmured apologetically.

"No, I thought only that you must have loved your wife very much and that there was little chance you would ever love me."

While Sarah's charm was undeniably different from Eva's, Lars thought that an asset rather than a fault. "Yes, I did love Eva," he admitted readily, "but I've discovered that doesn't mean I can't love you. I'll apologize for being so slow about realizing that possibility, but I didn't recognize it myself until nearly too late." Excited that their conversation had taken so positive a turn, he rose from his chair and with a quick tug drew her to her feet. "You were talking about me all along?" he asked with the widest grin he had ever seen from him.

437

Sarah nodded shyly. "Yes, I was completely shameless about admitting it, yet it meant nothing to you."

"No, that's not true," Lars argued. "I distinctly recall telling you that a gift of love should always be repaid."

Sarah raised her arms to encircle his neck. "Yes, you did say that, but you did little about it."

Lars had kissed her frequently in Washington, light, teasing kisses and slow, far more passionate kisses, too. Why had he not followed her home and allowed their budding romance to flower? He would not blame the war, nor the demands the hospital made upon him, when he knew he had to accept the blame himself. He had wanted Sarah, but not if it had meant losing his precious memories of Eva. It had taken him a long while to realize that Eva was a part of him that would never be forgotten, but that he was alive and desperately needed the love someone bright and vivacious like Sarah could give him.

"I do love you, Sarah," he murmured against her tawny curls. "It may have taken me far too long to realize it, but I know it now. Will you marry me?"

While she was thrilled by his proposal, Sarah couldn't help but push for another advantage now that things were going her way. "Mark was my only living relative, Lars. I know I will not be expected to mourn for him for an entire year, but how long must we wait to marry so that people will not criticize me for not showing my brother's memory the proper respect?"

Lars placed his hands upon Sarah's waist to push her an arm's length away. "Are you trying to use my own arguments against me, Sarah?"

He had already said that he loved her, and Sarah knew a man like Lars Hanson did not speak those words lightly. Very pleased with herself, she could not help but giggle. "What if I am?"

That she would admit to such underhanded tactic amused him enormously, and Lars threw back his head and laughed with her. That was what he loved about Sarah, she had taught him to laugh again. "It will take you several months to plan a wedding, won't it? Mark was a man who loved life, and I know he will not be offended if we wish to live it to the fullest. If he would never be critical of us, then why should we care if others are?"

"I believe I said something like that only tonight, didn't I?" Sarah asked as she moved back into his arms.

"Yes, you did. Whenever I behave like a pompous ass, will you promise to point it out to me? In private, though, please."

"Oh Lars, you are never pompous." Sarah kissed him to prove her point, for she loved his kisses. The love he had been reluctant to admit had always flavored his kisses and made them delicious. When at last she could bear to draw away, she stepped back only slightly. "You will not be too hard on Etienne and Erica, will you?"

Since that was a question he needed time to consider, Lars sat down again and pulled Sarah down across his lap. She was dressed in a flowing black gown, but its somber color did not dampen the ebullience of his mood. "We can talk about them tomorrow. Let's not waste the rest of tonight."

When his mouth again covered hers, Sarah relaxed in his arms. It would be unusual to have an Indian in the family, but since she had won the heart of the man she loved, she saw no reason to deny Erica that same privilege. "I love you," she whispered between fervent kisses, not admitting how impressed she had been with him when they had first met, since it had taken Lars so long to notice her. She sighed dreamily when he replied with the same three-word vow. What did it matter who had been the first to speak of love when each of them now loved the other so dearly?

At last Lars recalled the significance of the day, and he brought Sarah's right palm to his lips. "We all did our best for Mark. I'm so sorry it just wasn't enough."

Sarah nodded, then laid her head upon his shoulder. "I felt guilty about being part of a deception, until you pointed out nothing was more important than Mark's well-being. I will always be grateful to you for that. Because of your advice, Mark spent his last days surrounded by people who loved him. No one can ask for a greater blessing than that."

With her snuggled so comfortably in his arms, Lars had no reason to disagree. It was not only being loved he had missed, but having someone to love, as well. "I'm going to make you deliriously happy, Sarah. I give you my word on that."

"You already have, Lars," Sarah assured him. "I'll do my best to make you wonderfully happy, too." She thought of her brother as Lars kissed her again, and wished Mark could be at their wedding to give her away. He would have loved that. She made herself another promise then, that for the rest of her life, whenever her days overflowed with happiness, her brother would be with her. They had always been close, and she wanted that same loving closeness to remain in her heart forever. Somehow she knew without asking that that was the type of love Lars would heartily approve.

While Lars and Sarah were lost in the blissful contentment of newly found love, Erica paced her bedroom with an anxious stride, her mood as black as the gown she had worn that day. Stephen had been fed and lay sleeping soundly in his cradle, while Viper, clad only in the gray pants, lay stretched out across the foot of her bed. He seemed unconcerned by her father's ridiculous demand that he move out of their home, but she was deeply troubled by it.

"Will there never be any end to our problems? Are we going to be hounded until the end of our days, never allowed to live in peace or to be happy?"

"There has been no time for us to decide what it is we want to do. I mean your father no disrespect, but I do not give a damn what he wants. What you and I want is all that matters." As Erica swept by he reached out to grab hold of her nightgown, but missed. "Come to bed with me. I will take care of you as I always have. You needn't worry about the future."

"But I do worry!" Erica continued to pace, her gaze locked upon the design of the rug at her feet. "Where will we go? What will we do? We can't even use your name! What are we going to call ourselves? How are we going to raise our children to be proud of themselves when we cannot even speak your name?"

Seeing he would have no success coaxing the volatile beauty into bed, Viper slipped off the high mattress and moved to block her way. He pulled her into his arms and pressed her close to his bare chest as he wove his fingers in her free-flowing curls. "Mark was very generous, and I have saved every penny of my salary so I can take care of us for the winter. In the spring, I want to return to Minnesota. With the reservations gone, the government has more land to sell, and I will simply buy some.

"It doesn't matter what name we use, we will know who we are. Being a farmer is not such a bad life. There is plenty of time to hunt while the crops grow. A farm is a good place to raise children, too. At least, I think it could be. What do you think?"

As Erica looked up at her husband, her heart filled wtih dread. "Look what happened to Little Crow. How can you want to live where men shoot Indians as though they were no more than foxes? I want something far better for my son."

"He is our son," Viper reminded her proudly. "What is it you want to do, stay here?"

"Yes, why not? If you are going to continue to pose as a white man, you can do it here as easily as anywhere else. At least we would be safe here. No one would be hunting us for a bounty." Erica slipped her arms around his slim waist and held him close. "I nearly lost you once, Viper, and I can't go through that horror again. I just can't."

Viper stood very still as he stroked her hair lightly. He adored his wife, and he understood her fears, but he had no intention of giving in to them. "The Sioux have been scattered in so many directions the people of Minnesota will soon forget we ever existed. I won't forget, and I won't let our son forget either. It may only have been fate that gave me light eyes, but since they let me pass among white men like a brother, than I would be a fool not to do it. Perhaps the Sioux have lost their homeland, but I can claim at least a small part of it for our own. When I came here, I meant to take you home with me. Since I have waited for you so patiently, I think you should come with me without argument."

"But we can't leave until spring?" Erica asked perceptively, grasping for the ray of hope that brought her.

"No, there isn't time to buy land and build a house before the first snow falls," Viper explained.

"We are going to argue about this until spring. You

441

realize that, don't you?" Erica asked with a rueful shake of her head.

"We can argue as long as you like," Viper offered graciously, "but in the spring, we will still go back to Minnesota."

"And what if someone recognizes you?"

"No one will," Viper insisted calmly. "Etienne Bouchard has never been there before, so how can anyone know him?"

"But—" Viper's mouth covered hers before she could point out there were dozens of people who would recognize her, and therefore him, as well. As his tongue slid over hers, she recalled the first time he had kissed her, for his action had been a surprise then, too. So much had happened to them since then, but she wanted the future to be far happier than their past. When at last he drew away, she laid her head upon his chest and gave him a fierce hug. "It's hopeless, isn't it? No matter how much I object, you're going to go back to Minnesota, and you know I won't let you go alone."

Viper could not help but chuckle, since she was right. He bent down to lift her into his arms and carried her to the bed before he replied. "Since you know you will never change my mind, don't waste our time by arguing. Wouldn't you rather do this?" he asked as he slid his hand beneath her soft linen gown and began to caress the smooth flesh of her thigh.

Erica slipped her fingers through his hair, her touch as loving as his, although her mood was still far from complacent. "Yes, I would, but you have forgotten how many people I met while I worked in my uncle's store. In fact, my aunt and uncle were so upset that I had married you, they might betray you themselves. If the army didn't shoot you on sight, they would take you back to prison, wouldn't they?"

Viper rose up on his elbows, his glance no longer teasing, for he knew what Erica said was true. "I wanted to take you back to the Cottonwood River, but you are right. It would be too dangerous for us to be so close to New Ulm. The state is a large one, I will find land for us where no one can cause us trouble. I will not ask you to dye your hair and call yourself by another name so you will not be

442

recognized. It is too difficult to pretend I am something I am not. I will not ask the same of you."

"Is it truly difficult for you to be Etienne? You play that part so well, I had no idea it was a chore for you." His comment had amazed Erica, for he had so greatly enjoyed taunting her in his French accent that she thought he relished his role as the Canadian.

Viper sighed wearily as he stretched out upon his back. He had wanted to make love, but with Erica in so talkative a mood, he knew he would have to answer all her questions first. "I would rather be myself, but the life I knew and loved is gone. I want you to help me make a home where our children will be safe and happy. It may be impossible, but I want to try."

The sadness in his voice touched her deeply, and Erica leaned over him to brush his lips lightly with hers. "Nothing is impossible, Viper, and I want us all to be safe and happy, too. We will have to be careful is all, but I will go wherever it is you want to go. Maybe in time I will even become a good cook," she confided with a lilting laugh.

Viper groaned as he recalled the first of her meals. "You were learning. We'll not starve." When she leaned down to kiss him again, he wrapped his arms around her waist so she could not escape him. He soon realized she did not want to. "There is one other thing," he remembered suddenly.

Unable to imagine what more he could want, Erica stared down at him with rapt attention. "What else could there possibly be? I have promised to go with you, and even to learn to cook. What more can you want of a wife?"

"I want you to marry me. Tomorrow. I want your father to be there, so he cannot complain I have no morals. I want him to understand how precious you are to me. We can tell anyone who is curious that you were married to me in Minnesota. When you thought I had been killed in the uprising, you married Mark. Since I am obviously alive, you want to be married to me again. That makes sense, doesn't it?"

"I don't know if it makes any sense or not, but it is closer to the truth than any other story we might make up." Erica reached out to trace the line of his jaw with her fingertips, and he caught her hand and brought it to his lips. "There's bound to be gossip no matter when we marry, so I think tomorrow is as good a day as any. I know you are doing this for me, and that is so sweet of you, but I have always felt as though we were married even though we had no ceremony."

"I am not doing it for you," Viper protested vehemently. "I am doing it for myself. I don't want anyone to say you are not my wife ever again, most especially not you!" With an agile push, he succeeded in rolling over and pulling Erica beneath him where he nearly smothered her with enthusiastic kisses before a loud pounding at the door interrupted them. Viper swore angrily, then rolled off the bed and hurried to answer before the noise woke the baby. When he found Lars and Sarah standing outside in the hall, he greeted them coldly.

"You have chosen a most inconvenient time to call," he announced without a trace of a smile. Erica came to his side then and ducked under his arm.

"Yes, what is it?" she asked brightly, apparently not in the least bit disturbed that her father had found Viper in her bed.

Lars's glance swept over Viper's well-muscled torso before coming to rest on his daughter's smile. "Sarah made me realize how cruel it would be to try and separate you two. Rather than worry about gossip, I've chosen merely to be practical. Since you have a child, you two should be married, the sooner the better, I might add."

"Did you plan for us to be married tonight?" Viper asked skeptically.

"No, tomorrow or the next day will do." Lars broke into a wide grin then, thinking he had the upper hand now, for the Indian could not refuse to wed Erica and keep the young woman's respect.

"I do not know," Viper began hesitantly. "Among my people a widow does not remarry for several years."

"Oh Viper, stop it!" Erica wrapped her arms around his waist, but when she turned to look up at her father she found his expression one of horrified disbelief.

"Your name is Viper?" Lars asked with an incredulous gasp. "Have I just demanded my only daughter marry a man called Viper?"

Erica had done far more than give away his name, and

444

Viper held his breath as he waited for Lars to realize how much trouble he could cause him now. It would take one wire, perhaps two, to discover the army would be delighted to learn his whereabouts and return him to prison.

Erica felt Viper's tension and realized her mistake. "An Indian frequently has many colorful names," she explained with a warm smile. "That's only one of his. Since you have to return to Washington so soon, do you think we could arrange for a marriage ceremony tomorrow? I'm certain with the war, many couples are arranging hasty marriages."

"I didn't hear him agree," Lars turned toward Viper then as he waited for him to respond.

Viper was desperately sorry he had teased Erica rather than agreeing immediately to her father's demand. "I will be happy to marry Erica, tomorrow or any other day. Now goodnight." As he started to close the door, Erica slipped through it.

She threw her arms around her father's neck as she thanked him. "Everything will turn out beautifully, I just know it will." Before Lars could respond, they heard a plaintive meow and turned to find the tomcat at Mark's door. "Oh Sarah, will you take the cat to your room? He doesn't understand where Mark is, and he's used to sleeping on his bed."

"Of course. Come here, little fellow." Sarah scooped up the cat, and as she and Lars started off down the hall with him Erica returned to her room.

"I am so sorry," she apologized as she locked her door. "How I could have been so stupid I'll never know, but you needn't worry. My father won't give your name to the army."

Viper was standing in the shadows by the door, his frown as deep as his gloom. "How can you be so sure?"

Erica took his hand and led him back to her bed. "Because he loves me too much. He'd not harm you when Stephen and I would be the ones to suffer."

"He is that good a man?" Erica's hands were at his belt, but Viper was uneasy still.

"He is like you in many ways. I trust him, and you can, too. I'm the one you'll have to worry about. What if I can't

445

remember to call you Etienne?"

"Do you enjoy being a widow?" Viper asked pointedly.

"What an awful thing to ask. No, of course not."

"Then remember to call me Etienne, or better yet, simply call me beloved."

Erica remembered vividly the afternoon he had made that suggestion, and she began to laugh. As he slipped out of his clothes she tossed her nightgown aside and got into bed. "I like that idea. I will call you nothing but sweetheart or darling, or beloved, since you like that name best." When Viper joined her in the bed and drew her into his arms she pressed close, drinking in his warmth as though it were fine wine.

"You really are my beloved, and I know the life we make for ourselves and our children will be a wonderfully happy one," she promised him sweetly.

Viper smiled as he gazed into her sparkling blue eyes. In the room's dim light their deep color shimmered with a bright glow. The future would not be without danger and adventure, he knew that, but with so magnificent a wife, what a marvelous life it would be. He lowered his mouth to hers, his kiss now soft and sweet as he proved again that when she had chosen him for her husband, she had made a wise choice, indeed.

"I will love you forever," he whispered, before the passionate young beauty in his arms made all thought of words impossible. There was only the wondrous sensation of her love flooding his senses to overflowing with the beauty of her devotion, and he gave that splendor back again and again until, sated by pleasure, they fell asleep in each other's arms. A lingering smile graced Viper's lips at the thought that in a few hours he would again take Erica for his wife. He made a silent vow that he would fill her life with love, for as long as the sun rose and set, for always, and that each day he would give her a new reason to call him her beloved.

## Note to Readers

The Minnesota Sioux Uprising of 1862 was only one tragic episode in the lengthy warfare between the army and the Sioux that culminated in the bloody massacre at Wounded Knee in 1890. While Viper and Erica are fictitious characters, I have included the people actually involved in the events of the uprising whenever possible in this book. The name of Dr. William Mayo, who served briefly in New Ulm, is undoubtedly familiar. It was his sons who founded the renowned Mayo Clinic in Rochester, Minnesota.

In May 1863, the Sioux who had spent the winter at Fort Snelling were deported under horrendous conditions to a hastily chosen site in what is now the state of South Dakota. The Crow Creek Reservation proved to be such a poor location for agriculture that after three disastrous years the Indians were moved to the Santee Reservation near the Niobrara River, in present-day Nebraska.

The prisoners confined at Camp McClellan fared just as poorly as their relatives. Dr. Williamson was able to secure pardons for forty men in 1864. In April 1866, after 120 braves had died in prison, President Andrew Johnson pardoned the remaining 247. These men then joined their families in Nebraska.

By the end of the 1860s, the Sioux were returning in small numbers to their homelands in Minnesota. In 1869, twelve families left the reservation at Niobrara seeking to live as white men on land of their own choosing. They became successful farmers in Flandreau, South Dakota.

Little Crow's sixteen-year-old son, Wowinapa, who had

been with him when he was killed, was captured and sentenced to hang for his part in the uprising. He managed to escape that fate, however. Wowinapa became a Christian, and as Thomas Wakeman, is remembered for founding the YMCA among the Sioux.

For the shooting of Little Crow, Nathan Lamson received a $500 reward from the state of Minnesota. His son, Chauncey, whose shot had actually killed the chief, received a $75 bounty for his scalp. In 1971, Little Crow's remains were finally returned to his family, and he was buried in Flandreau, South Dakota.

The army continued to pursue the Sioux who had fled to the Dakota Territory in an attempt to discourage raids upon the Minnesota frontier. Forts were manned until 1866, and gradually the raiding stopped and the settlers who had fled the uprising began to return to their homes. Peace returned to the Minnesota River Valley, but at a terrible price to the Sioux.